OUR PICNICS IN THE SUN

OUR PICNICS
IN THE SUN

A NOVEL

MORAG JOSS

DELACORTE PRESS
NEW YORK

Copyright © 2013 by Morag Joss

Published in the United States by Delacorte Press,
an imprint of The Random House Publishing Group,
a division of Random House LLC, New York,
a Penguin Random House Company.

DELACORTE PRESS and the HOUSE colophon are registered
trademarks of Random House LLC.

Library of Congress Cataloging-in-Publication Data
Joss, Morag.
Our picnics in the sun: a novel/Morag Joss.
pages cm
ISBN 978-0-385-34276-6
eBook ISBN 978-0-345-53967-0
1. Married people—Fiction. 2. Bed and breakfast accommodations—Fiction. I. Title.
PR6060.O77O97 2013
823'.92—dc23
2013001417

Printed in the United States of America on acid-free paper

www.bantamdell.com

246897531

First Edition

Book design by Elizabeth A. D. Eno

In memory of my brother

GAVIN WALLACE

the champion and advocate of Scottish literature over
three decades, whose dedicated love of words and
loyalty to those who make them into books endears
him in perpetuity to writers throughout Scotland.

27 May 1959–4 February 2013

Nor ask what doubtful act allows
Our freedom in this English house,
Our picnics in the sun.

W. H. AUDEN,
from "A Summer Night"

Let us examine more closely the significance of this vague word, reality . . . We may regard it as embodied in the physical world, the world of land and sea, of sky and trees, of sunshine and of storm. The real therefore will be to us that which we can touch and see, smell and taste . . . and the testimony of the senses is the superior court of appeal in controverted questions. But the world of reality may be regarded from quite a different point of view, as the world of consciousness . . . the experiences of the inner self . . . It is a realm of ideas, of memory images, of fancy, of will, and of desire.

John Grier Hibben (1861–1933)
The Problems of Philosophy

Contents

OUR PICNICS IN THE SUN

Police and Social Services are appealing to the public to help identify a man alleged to have preyed on an isolated couple, one of whom was disabled. The man carried out a "sustained, callous and premeditated deception" over several months before disappearing, it is claimed. Describing him only as tall and aged around 30, police wish to question him in connection with charges including theft, cruelty, assault, and obtaining goods by deception. Attempts to trace the man have so far proved unsuccessful.

Claiming to be homeless and unemployed last year, the man talked his way into the home of the couple whom he "probably considered gullible," said the couple's only son, who lives abroad. Promising to help with their run-down small-holding, he manipulated his mother's affections and persuaded her to let him move in, the son alleges.

"There is no doubt he callously and systemically exploited their goodwill in order to obtain control over their lives. Had I not intervened there is no knowing how far he might have gone in pursuit of his own ends," he said.

Police declined to comment on the present condition of the couple. A neighbor who asked not to be named said they were known to be eccentric. "They kept themselves to themselves. We never saw them," he said. The couple's lifestyle may have been a contributory factor in their vulnerability to abuse, a police spokesman said. Superintendent Fred Davis of West Country Police said, "People who are in their retiring years are entitled to feel safe . . . the sad thing is that in their later years, it seems this couple had no one else to turn to."

The West Country Examiner

MAY 2008

Howard Morgan was on the floor of the old pig shed in transition from Cobra to Locust when a blood vessel burst in his head. As his brain began to leak, a sudden cloud shift high in the sky cleared a gap for the sun; bluish needles of light from several holes in the roof slanted through the amber underworld of the shed and landed in small, brilliant studs on the floor around him. He shook the hair from his eyes, lifted his chest, stretched his arms back, and wondered how he could have failed to notice them before: a myriad particles of stone and straw dust spinning in each slender column of light. He would be able to count every sparkling one, he thought, if he gazed long enough. Time slowed. Shining dust went on dancing in the air of the old pig shed. Howard gazed. Time stopped.

Was it happening? Was he poised at last in yogic bliss, on a bridge between the physical and divine worlds, reaching through the one toward the other? If only Deborah could see him now. Just then another cloud passed in front of the sun, the light beams vanished, and Howard's bliss (if it was that) vanished, too. Of course the proper place of bliss was in the striving for it, he knew that; it lay in the virtue of the attempt. Nonetheless he felt a little cheated. Should a glimpse of eternity (if it was that) leave him feeling so sad and emptied out? The big hand of his watch beside him on the floor moved to seven minutes to nine, and pain began to pound in the left side of his head.

Howard abandoned Locust, eased himself out of position and tried to sit cross-legged, but his body was slow, his limbs heavy and rigid. He tilted over and fell on his side, off the yoga mat. The next thing he noticed was that his cheek against the cool floor was strangely loose and squashed-up under one eye, and it was partly obscuring his view of the watch, which was now just a few inches away. Several dry wires from his beard were caught between his lips and he could not push out his tongue to lick them away. But he could hear a faraway snoring that was nonetheless coming from his own nostrils, and he could smell the stony, dank, animal scent of the ground where he lay. It was likely, he found himself thinking, that some time had passed since his face had landed there. He reached out his right hand and brought the watch up close. Through the tickling veil of his hair he saw that the numbers had gone and in their place was a circular tangle of unintelligible marks. The pins radiating from the center of the watch were familiar but he could not grasp what they meant, either. He lost his grip and let his arm drop to the ground. The watch rolled away.

There was always a reason for pain, Howard believed. It was a protest, some misalignment of mind, body, spirit, and cosmos, a disharmony for which the sufferer had to be, in karmic terms, responsible. But this pain wouldn't let any such belief anywhere near it, never mind close enough to stick. *This* pain was simply itself. Howard couldn't tell if the method of his torture was burning or freezing—whether boiling water was being poured through his ear into his brain or his teeth held clamped on a mouthful of ice—but either way it was torment. And it was paradoxical, being both random and malicious: nothing to do with him, yet personal. Perhaps he'd feel this way about being struck by lightning—aggrieved at being singled out to suffer an extreme of some inescapable but natural cruelty that was as pointless, in the end, as any chatter in his head about higher meanings for it.

He couldn't go on lying there.

But when he tried to think about sitting up, he heard a thousand small voices firing disconcerting messages all around his body; back and forth they went through the circuitry of nerve and cartilage and muscle, checking, synchronizing, double-checking the effortful and blindingly complex work they were going to have to do to achieve the action of raising his torso from the floor. He lay listening to the clamor and for a while nothing moved. Then, babbling its interior commands, very slowly his body performed the task of getting him to sit upright, for which, though the exertion made him nauseous, he felt grateful. He wondered what to do next. Stand up, obviously. But with his head pounding, instead he looked at his hands moving inconclusively in his lap and could not summon any certainty that they were his hands, or even hands at all so much as a pair of waving, clawlike objects, no more and no less than two weird objects among all other objects that were, had been, or ever would be in the world, present, past, or future. They existed. That was that. His control or ownership of them was a notion he no longer understood. In a universe newly revealed as transparent, indifferent, and timeless, they, along with any claim to be called anything as arbitrary as *hands,* had lost all their Howardness, somehow.

Meanwhile, his head hurt. But as he went on staring Howard felt more of the boundaries between himself and the rest of the world dissolve, and soon he could not tell where the matter of his—or the—hands (or the wrists or arms or legs) ended, and the matter of the floor (or the roof, or the lately departed shafts of light shining through the holes in it) began. Even so, the part of Howard that couldn't tell any of this was aware that it couldn't, and was also aware that it seemed itself to be expanding and filling a space somewhere above the spot where the rest of him sat half off his yoga mat, unable to stand up and mesmerized by a pair of hands. It came to him again: everything in the universe, including himself, just *was.* Then he felt joy—ineffable, entire, surely the whole world's joy—surging into him and swamping him, not unlike (if he only knew it) the tides of blood that were simultaneously flooding the interstices of his brain. It was a splendid agony, enough to knock him off his feet had he been on them; instead it pulled all the breath out of him in one long, surprisingly distressed and high-pitched squeal that he'd intended more as a song of praise. No matter—he was drowning in joy and pain, and oh, where was Deborah, whom at this moment he loved utterly and who ought, no, *deserved* to be with him and drowning, too?

The detached and euphoric part of Howard floated on, observing

the other part of himself stupefied by pain and incapable of pinpoint-
ing the nature of his agony, but quite possibly in a dialogue between
himself and all Creation.

More time passed, probably. Howard drifted closer and closer
toward disembodiment, ageless, weightless, and free to roam where
nothing was required of him save his surrender. Then a practical,
hurrying voice no less his own would wrest him away, reminding
him that he had a biting pain in his head and it was necessary to go
somehow and announce this trouble to Deborah. That was when,
trying to get himself on all fours, he realized his left arm wasn't
working. As it folded under him he had time to register another new
idea: the possibility of damage. Levering and yanking his left leg this
way and that, he managed to drag his body across the floor to the
wall. His eyes weren't working properly, either. Using his good hand
and the side of his face, he scraped his way along to the open doorway.

In the morning light of the yard, he sensed that the world was
carrying on as usual. The day itself came back to him. It was a Monday and there was work to do; they were painting the outside of the
house. He remembered that things were not going well. They were
supposed to be getting the place in a fit state for the Bed and Breakfast season and were running late—Easter and the first May Bank
Holiday had already been and gone—and he was also trying to ap-
pease Digger, who'd been around the place waving the lease under
his nose and threatening court. The exterior painting was supposed
to be done by the tenant every six years and Howard had managed
it three times in twenty-seven, the last time eleven years ago, and
what did Howard think the district judge would make of that?

His vision cleared a little. Across the brick-cobbled yard two ladders led up to the familiar homemade scaffolding he'd fixed against
the wall. Two or three hens meandered underneath pecking in the
sodden leaves that had lain all winter around the base of the down
pipes. Up on the scaffolding, buckets sat along the plank that ran
under the upstairs windows, and that was where Deborah was standing with her back to him, ten feet off the ground, slapping whitewash
on the pebbledash. But as he opened his mouth to call out, it struck

him that the Deborah on the scaffolding was not the easy, open-hearted, adored Deborah who'd come to his mind in the pig shed. Somehow in the disorientation of his headache he'd forgotten that years had passed, and that that Deborah had gone with them. He recalled, in a way that made his heart shrivel with sadness, that the Deborah on the scaffolding was part of what was not going well. The fight they'd had first thing that morning came back to him, too, bursting with filmic exactness upon his frayed mind as another of the many for which, he also recalled, she was to blame. Through the deranging throb of the headache came an extra thud of annoyance, and he closed his mouth. His throat felt clogged; he had an idea his voice wouldn't work. She'd been in her overalls at the kitchen sink, gazing out of the window and complaining that the whitewash was too thin. She said it wouldn't last, it was another false economy. Then she'd gone on about the hens being all over the yard again so he'd have to fix the fencing properly this time or the fox would get them overnight. All he'd done was point out that her negativity was counterproductive and ask why couldn't she take things more in her stride.

"*My negativity? Counterproductive?* And you spending half the day on yoga, that's *productive?* I'm to take that in my stride as well, am I?"

"It's not half the day, it's an hour and a half," he'd said. "You're free to join me. It might calm you down."

She'd burst into tears. "Free? That's your idea of *free?*" she'd cried, and banged out of the kitchen.

She looked calmer now. Howard was exhausted by the journey from the yoga mat to the door of the shed, and for a few moments he did nothing except lie and watch the bending and rising of her back and the slow stroking of paint on the wall from the brush in her hand. Just as he'd been mesmerized by the swimming dust motes in the light beams and the fleshy, fringed appendages that were his hands, he felt an impersonal desire to go on watching forever. Woman. Brush. Paint. Wall. He didn't want to get up again. Please could he not just lie forever on the ground, emptied of all belief, emptied of the need for any? But as he watched, the notion of Deborah as *woman* detached itself and departed, and his mind filled with an even more restful contemplation of Deborah as organism, her body beneath the overalls animated by the same involuntary and more or less marvelous zoological impulses that compelled the hens beneath the scaffolding to dip at the dead leaves in the drains and the banded bodies of earthworms to wriggle in their beaks. He had never before felt so objective and curious about his wife, and so certain she had no meaning at all. Like everything else, she just *was*.

But he also needed Deborah, as wife, to come and put right the matter of this pain in his head. Concentrating hard, he instructed his lungs to produce the breath to speak. He managed to call out but the sound he made was not her name, nor a word at all. He tried again. His second attempt was no nearer to speech but it was louder. Deborah turned, saw him, and called back, but she was not speaking words either, as far as he could tell. She dropped the brush. Her feet were thumping along the plank, too fast, in the direction of the ladder. Howard summoned all his will to cry out to her to slow down, but all he could let loose were urgent, broken noises. At the sound of them Deborah turned too sharply from the top of the ladder. It shook, swung outward on one leg with the weight of her body, crashed back against the scaffolding, and began to slide. The hens scattered in a flurry of splayed wings. Howard closed his eyes and did not see Deborah fall, did not see how heavily she landed. But he heard and understood her fear and pain, even though she was using words he no longer knew.

JULY 2011

Long before the stroke something had been saying to me that we couldn't go on. I was accustomed to the way we had to live, of course, but even so I kept hearing a voice, fading but not quite drowned out, and seeing in my mind, like glimpses through a pinhole, pictures of an easier time.

Although not of a time I'd actually known, not of a time past. Our years at Stoneyridge wouldn't have withstood even sentimental retrospective scrutiny, at least not from me; Howard would probably have pasted a false glow on it, right up to the moment he was unable to speak. Howard and his cheap paint, Howard and his tardy reparations—Howard now wordless and purblind and for all I know still in search of riches of some sort: truth, enlightenment, love.

But I've never been nostalgic—it would help if I were. Long before I met Howard I knew the difference between how a thing was and how you could make it seem to yourself when you looked back on it, so it's not just Stoneyridge I don't get romantic over. My Scottish upbringing, for instance, that Howard liked to imagine as all that mists and mountains nonsense, I've always held inside myself as a memory of what it actually was, seventeen years in Auchenfoot, a featureless lowland town. Even in the summer of 1979, when the one thing I was sure of was that falling in love with Howard would set me free of it all, I still didn't recast in a softer light the childhood Sundays I spent in the chill of the tin-roofed church under the trickling of rain, whispering my prayers of dread and longing through aching, steel-braced teeth. I didn't forget that all other concerns about life had been marginal alongside my love for God and my minister father—a crushed and crushing love that amounted, really, to a powerlessness to tell them apart. Until, it turned out, the March of that year, when in the course of a four days' illness as sudden as the onset of the Spring, my father and God together faded and fell away from me, the one dying of peritonitis, the other disintegrating in the shadow of that death. I was inconsolable, not just for their loss but for the certainty their invisibility brought, that neither of them continued anywhere beyond life. Their going was absolute.

My mother made the transition from minister's wife to minister's widow within two months. She turned publicly serene, conducting the course of her grief like another bout of arthritis, from which she also suffered. By the wan quality of her smiles people knew she felt pain but that the pain would be borne; in answer to inquiries she would acknowledge a degree of affliction but burden no one with details. I think, looking back, she derived great satisfaction from fulfilling the congregation's expectation that she would cope. Mourning became her, by and large, and the drab, enclosing town, the rain, and the tin-roofed church wore her weeds along with her.

I, on the other hand, tried to turn invisible, in the manner of very small children who cover their eyes to convince the world around them that they've gone away. I stopped eating and stayed in my room. I wouldn't go to church and after Easter refused to go back to school. In June, my father's elder sister Auntie Joan was summoned. At the age of forty-six she had married a prosperous, older Edinburgh widower whose children (by then heading for university) she'd taught at the private school where she was Head of English. She lived her married life with a kind of brazen enjoyment that bordered on authority, acquiring a new wardrobe to match the widower's gifts of large rings and scarves of real French silk, and taking up bridge and golf to keep him company. Perhaps because she was so stylish and worldly, in our household her opinions, at least on children, were listened to. She whisked back the curtains in my bedroom and told me it was time I got a grip on myself. To my mother she said that unless she wanted a full-blown neurotic on her hands (neurosis in sheltered only children being a well-documented tendency) she'd better let me see something of the world beyond Auchenfoot and not to thank her, she was paying for me to spend the summer in London before I drove everybody round the bend.

I was enrolled with several other girls, mainly Americans, on a fairly frivolous course in Art History, and Howard was our long-haired, tall, theatrically handsome (and so *English*!) tutor. The girls snapped gum and flicked their hair and when one laughed they all did, with a strangely homogeneous nasal clanking like the striking of so many small, cracked gongs. I didn't do any of those things, but I found to my surprise that I wanted to smile a lot, and by then my teeth were straight. I was dazed, not by them or any one particular thing, but by the very fact of London, simply by being there, part of its compacted, energetic life, and so far from home. And far away as that felt, it was almost inconceivable to me how far the Americans had traveled. Maybe that was what made them giddy—all that distance they'd crossed, the sheer spaciousness of the world.

I was not like them; I was becalmed by the seething streets, the crowded trains and cafés. In the late afternoons I would loiter with them in the obligatory way around the buskers at Piccadilly Circus, numbed by the thought that I was just one among billions of human dots on the planet. The thrill of liberation came later, and gradually, in knowing myself for the first time unobserved and therefore powerful; from now on, under the cloak of my own insignificance, I could do what I wanted. I was being let off some sort of hook.

In need of a new hook, I found Howard, who seemed to have been waiting for me. I was dazed by him, too, by his knowledge of Art and Life but especially, as he began to expound it to me over a bottle of brackish wine on a warm, rainy night in his bedsit off Goodge Street, about the matter of my own—as he put it—beautiful spirit. He stroked my hair and told me that I, like him, was a questing soul. Fine Art, galleries, museums, they were all very well—he'd done two years of sculpture at art school before realizing how shallow it was—but what was important was the spirit. And fulfillment of the spirit. That was what fascinated him most about me, my potential for spiritual fulfillment. It was far more fascinating to him than my body, although he was sure that it had potential for physical fulfillment, too, as he further put it, beginning to remove clothes.

How could he be wrong about any of this? As well as being much older than I was, he was so handsome. I sneaked back into the hostel past the midnight curfew and climbed into my dorm bed still dressed—I could not bear yet to see or touch my body, now forever changed. A small, secret pain still blazed where his fingers had entered, but already I felt soothed as well as excited.

After that there were many nights when we lay in the glow of candles placed on the floor around the bed, while Howard talked about Art and Life and further explained me to myself. Once I'd filled in the basics, he made my saying much about Scotland or my father unnecessary, and anyway I preferred to listen to him mulling things over for me. It was comforting to have my overwrought teen-age self dismantled and reassembled, to be told not just who I was but who I was to become. It was good to have my grieving over-looked. At the end of three weeks, it was good when physical fulfill-ment was accomplished, again without too much being asked of me. That's the truth of it. Howard promised me heaven on earth and delivered me from my unhappiness, and I was desperate to be molded into any shape that pleased my new savior.

Our feelings stood up well enough against my criteria—assembled from chat with the benignly envious Americans, magazine articles with titles such as "How Do You Know If It's the Real Thing?" plus the vestiges of my abandoned God-fervor—to qualify as falling in love, and so I called it that. Enthralled, I wrote my mother a long letter all about him (except physical fulfillment, of course) and the miraculous change in my life, seven pages filled with love and praise.

And Howard? He became playful—almost daily I was taken aback by some small, impulsive kindness or other: my lunch apple polished on his sleeve to an absurd gloss, an old silver sixpence that turned up in my change pierced through and threaded on a leather bootlace for me to wear around my neck for good luck, when neither of us had a notion we'd ever need any. In the evenings we talked and read poetry aloud, holding hands; we laughed over the strange cheap meals we cooked together on the single gas ring, we brushed each other's long hair. At times I caught him looking at me with an expression on his face so unguarded and adoring I resolved to keep secret from him forever how ordinary I was.

He was delighted, I think, by my determination not to return home after the course finished, for although my role as follower to his leader was established by then, I did rather put my foot down about staying with him. But he was in love, too. As he told me one evening in the airless bedsit, what he realized now was that he'd been more or less permanently in love, meaning in the abstract, in search of an object for it, living all this time in a heightened state of being on a quest for meaning and ecstasy, and now he had me. He was completely sincere. I needed no more than that, but when he went on to inform me that we would get married (a proposal requiring my consent could not have been further from our minds), then truly my cup ran over.

My mother's arthritis prevented her from traveling down to reason with me and Auntie Joan thought that since I had no alternative plans for a career I might as well make a go of it. When I turned eighteen the following June, Howard and I got married in a registry office in Finchley. It wasn't a proper wedding, of course; we downplayed the whole thing as if some higher truth about marriage lay in a refusal to celebrate it with the usual trappings. I wore an Indian print dress in green and white, and a few beads in my hair, and afterward we picnicked on Hampstead Heath with some friends of Howard's who brought guitars and marijuana. We didn't invite anybody and my mother couldn't have attended anyway, but relieved we were no longer living in sin, she sent us her blessing.

Auntie Joan sent a check with instructions to spend it on learning something useful. I knew she meant shorthand and typing, but I enrolled in a course in textile crafts and spent the mornings spinning and weaving. I waitressed in the afternoons and evenings, while Howard got a job in a crammer tutoring people for exam re-sits. The following year his mother died and left him a little money, and still—or again—in search of meaning and ecstasy, he decided we had to get out of London. The idea of spiritual and creative renewal through self-sufficiency on an Exmoor smallholding he got from somebody else or from a magazine, I don't remember exactly, but he made it sound like his own, and of course I was happy to follow. It seemed to me that too many things of an almost unbearable nature had occurred in a short while, and I wanted a life where much less was going to happen.

That was almost thirty years ago, and for those thirty I have been loyal and resigned. I carried on as usual after Adam was born, as far as anyone could tell, and even after he left home. I didn't hold out any particular hope for a change in our circumstances, nor did I have greater gifts of imagination than those that most lonely women are surprised to find in themselves, eventually. I was just keeping hold of something, an obstinate splinter of knowledge, that it couldn't go on. It was a disaffection too quiet to be mutinous, it was more like a faith—if faith is what argues the case for invisible truths—that I would not always have to feel this sadness about living. I had a proven capacity for faith, after all.

That wasn't the same as knowing that the afternoon before the shearing was the first day of the end of it.

<adam.morgan@logisticsomnicorpsystems.com>

To: deborahstoneyridge@yahoo.com
Sent on sun 3 july 2011 at 01.52 EST

Hi mum

Loads going on here, hope your both ok You'll get this on wed as usual I suppose, assuming you'll get to Bridgecombe with dad as usual and logging on at library? He is still going to the stroke club isn't he? You said he didn't enjoy it or something. What you should ask him is would he rather be just sitting at home in front of the tv, I bet he can't honestly say he would. Also he has to understand you need to get out and do shopping and stuff and you can't unless he goes? You maybe need to be tougher with him on that, the trouble is he doesn't push himself.

So I was out on the latest monitoring round all last week and there's loads more coming up, everything's been changed so now we've got this crap new system whereby every location gets visited every other quarter and it's a rolling program so basically about twice the workload and still just five of us meant to cope with it, it's manic – we need at least two more people below my grade for admin and follow-up or basically it just won't get done. I'm giving way more pre-sentations in the next three months than I did the whole of last year and they're keeping me on the same grade at least till end of Q3 which I'm not too happy about. Anyway Sacha could tell I wasn't happy – I am SO not happy! – so she said she'd speak to HR and I'm seeing them tomorrow about an Additional Hours Uplift that would make it more worth my while, fingers crossed. Sacha's ok as a boss, but she hasn't been here a year yet and she might be getting trans-ferred ☹.

Better go, take care. Love to dad
A xxx

From: deborahstoneyridge@yahoo.com

To: <adam.morgan@logisticsomnicorpsystems.com>
Sent on wed 6 july 2011 at 11.57 GMT

Dear Adam Well here I amagain! The library's busy this morning, have had to wait to get to the keyboard! Dad went to stroke club without too much fuss, I can't say I blame him for not liking it, they are mostly a lot older. I think he finds it depressing. Especially as he's not finding talking any easier and walking is the usual strug-gle. He gets v tired and that depresses him too. It's not easy but we're fine, don't worry about us, we cope on the whole pretty well.

The weathers chopping and changing, hot one day then humid, then downpours, then hot again, typical English summer! Typical Ex-moor summer more like. Am doing what I can in garden. Still holding out for Digger to come and do the sheep. It's urgent now, the poor things must be so hot and when it rains they have a ton of weight to carry on their backs, I feel sorry for them! I'm waiting to hear from him, he said he'd do it but not when, I may have to nag. I go up twice a day just to see they're all right.

Oh dear I have to go – somebody else wants on here, they've been hovering.

So, darling and no I'm not nagging! But what about your birthday this year? It would be SO lovely to see you. Can you let me know? It would give D a lift not to mention me – now that really is NOT nagging just a fact. See what you can do, you've surely earned some time off!? More next week take care don't let them overwork you! Lots of love xxxxxx M

The shearing was overdue. Weeks had gone by when I should have put it in hand and didn't; I don't really know why. I'd had some Bed and Breakfast guests to attend to in June, but only an elderly couple for a weekend and a cyclist who rang on the day to book two nights but in the end stayed one, so that didn't explain it. I'd just gone past wanting to think about our wretched handful of sheep on the hill, I think that was it. There were only the nine old ewes left, more or less pets except I was no longer fond of them. I'd wanted to get rid of the lot after Howard's stroke but they were worthless—I couldn't have given them away—and there was the problem of our tenancy, which was protected only as long as we worked the land. Grazing a few sheep still counted as working the land, or so we would claim if it came to it. Anyway, I couldn't have afforded the vet or abbatoir fees to have them destroyed. So they hung on, grazing the far side of the moor ridge among the alders and gorse on the edges of the combe. They didn't need much looking after because I wasn't interested in them for wool or for meat.

I guess I'd also delayed the shearing because I was reluctant to ask the favor again of Digger, that's to say nervous of the ways he might find of calling in the favor. I hadn't seen him for weeks; I didn't mind acknowledging Kevin and Kyle at waving distance for the sake of their old childhood friendship with Adam, but I avoided going up on the moor when their father would be on his land, in case he started bullying me again about the outside painting or picked some other fight about the state of our place. A lot of it was bluff, but I didn't know how much. So when I got around to calling him to ask if he'd be good enough to do this year's shearing for me and could he once again accept the fleeces in lieu of payment, I must have come across as if I thought our sorry circumstances were his fault, not mine. I'd forgotten to sound humble, or so grateful in advance of whatever he replied that he wouldn't be able to refuse. He turned surly, wouldn't give me a proper answer, said he'd see to it by and by when he could spare the time, and only for the sake of the godforsaken beasts; it was them he'd have on his conscience, not us.

By the middle of July the sheep were heavy and itchy and I was still waiting. I thought they could hold on. I went out on the moor to check on them two and three times a day and I'd hauled up a couple of bits of old picket fencing and banged them in the ground as scratching posts, but one day, after a morning of torrential rain, I found one off her legs. I couldn't tell how long she'd been on her back but she'd worked herself into a split in the turf so she was in a state, struggling and panting and bleating, half-buried in a trough of broken bracken and bramble. At first I thought she'd just gone down under the sodden weight of her fleece.

It was much worse than that. Her back end was caked and filthy, of course, but I didn't need to get close enough to lift the dags— I couldn't get close enough, for the smell—to see that underneath she was dripping with maggots. They were heaving through her wool, burrowing into the sloughed skin, and dropping off bloated and squirming into the ground around her. I'd been checking the flock from too great a distance, just counting them and making sure none had fallen. I hadn't really looked at them properly. I hadn't seen this one maddened by flystrike, rubbing and biting herself as she must have been doing, shivering with pain and being eaten alive.

I stared at the repulsive, writhing havoc of it. I broke out in a sweat and retched and turned away. Even if I could have brought myself to touch her, I had no strength in my bad shoulder and couldn't have got her up on my own. I ran all the way back to the house and managed to get in and call Digger without waking Howard from his nap. There was no reply. All I could do was leave a message.

When I got back to the ewe over an hour later, she was dead. Flies were already clustered on her face, feasting on the tongue and spinning inside the nostrils. The crows had had her eyes. I covered her head and sat with her for a long time, and I wept for shame. And long after I couldn't cry any more, I went on sitting there, supposedly waiting for Digger, in truth just waiting. I wondered about Howard, who would be waking up dry-mouthed, trying to unfold his fingers, wanting tea, and I thought about his wrecked lips chewing on the words of complaint if, later, he were able to grasp that he'd been alone at the house all afternoon because I chose to stay on the hill with a dead sheep. Then I let myself remember Howard's mouth as I'd first seen it, forming all those mesmerizing words about essence and spirituality and going back to the land, how I would sometimes put a stop to the talking by placing a finger on his lips and kissing him deep with my tongue, a gesture unimaginably bold for me that never failed to delight him. It came to me again that so great a change in two people must be impossible, that the sadness of it could not be borne forever. Yet there it was. Another soft, dark wall of cloud was descending over the moor, and foolishly I still didn't move. I welcomed the soaking, rainy fog that would come soon, and went on waiting.

Then I saw that time does one of two things. Either it rushes by, collapsing the years between Howard as he was that first shearing season and what he has since become into no more than a space between two days. Or it stops altogether, making an eternity of a humid July day spent sitting alone in the moor grass, worn down by decades and listening to a voice whispering that it can't go on. The other sheep were swaying hock-deep in the heather. A thundery wind presaging the rain parted the wool on their backs and bent the tall grass and reeds around the dead ewe this way and that, surrounding her with faint clicking and shirring sounds like a kind of offhand funeral music. I knew I should move myself and return to the house, but I didn't want to. I lay back and closed my eyes.

When I next sat up and looked around, my eyes were still blurry from crying, and maybe from sleep. But in the far distance on the ridge of the moor I thought I saw a walking figure, hardly touching the ground, a shimmering, dreamy silhouette against the warm, watery air. It moved without resistance toward me, yet did not draw near. It could only be Digger, and yet it couldn't; Digger was the least spectral person I could imagine. There was nothing of Digger's short-legged trudge in the liquefaction of the figure's effortless, slow stride under the rain-laden sky.

As I watched, what little I remembered of Howard's stuff about land spirits and earth deities came to mind, the kind of stuff I'd gone along with once, a long way; how did it go? The ancient Greeks deified the soil. They worshipped the female earthbound by her fertility, they revered the cycle of birth to grave and to rebirth, and so they cast living sacrifices into pits in the ground. The time when I had watched Howard's mouth form the very words seemed hardly more recent. I hadn't objected, then, to the female's hapless servility in this scheme of things, I didn't even see it. But the Celts—or was it the Druids—worshipped the male, and built altars open to the sky and burned animals on them, offering flames and smoke upwards to aerial spirits, in pursuit of eternity. Well, so much for all of that. I didn't believe in Howard's spirits anymore and his phallistic theories just made me feel cranky. All his theories had tired me out, in the end; there had been too many of them as failures and afflictions accrued, requiring excuses.

Yet how else to describe this figure, as I watched it, other than as a spirit, or at least a presence, holy or otherwise? And whether sacrificially invoked or not by a sheep lying dead in a sunken chamber of earth, as I went on watching, this presence charged every breath I took with a mysterious gladness and yearning, a kind of pushing and pulling at my heart, as if both those feelings were part of the same emotion. I stared, willing him to cross the ground between us, longing for him to draw near and bring me fully inside the circle of his benediction. But he came no closer. I grew impatient; it was nothing but a bending of the light through cloud shadow, it was myopia. It was stupid. I shook my head to clear my mind of the absurdity of it.

But then the no less impossible idea came to me that the figure was Howard, straight and strong and tall again and coming toward me across the thirty years. At once that was followed by the thought that that, too, was ridiculous (the facts being what they were), and it could only be Adam, who was built so like his father and walked as Howard once had. That, of course, was also impossible. Adam wasn't here; he hardly ever came to Stoneyridge now. At that moment he'd most likely be on a flight to somewhere or at least in an airport; his emails were full of how they were always sending him places though he seldom said which places. I swear that the other impossibility, that it was Adam's twin somehow alive and grown like Adam to be a man of twenty-seven, did not cross my mind.

The clouds had descended and were low and gray over the moor, shifting horizontally like fire smoke. Large raindrops began to fall, and into the air rose the smell of dust and damp earth. From not so far away came the first groan of thunder. A sudden brushing noise started behind me, and two rabbits skeetered out of a hole; the startled sheep took off at a tottery run on their brittle, overloaded legs. I got up and went among them until they settled, and when I next looked back down the hill, I caught a movement close to the trees. It was Digger, after all, tramping along under the weight of ropes and a tarp sheet and carrying his gun, in case it was needed.

The afternoon turned ordinary and difficult again.

"Too late, am I?" he said. "Look at that. She's suffered, she has, lying there."

"I didn't know how to help her. I didn't know what to do," I said.

"Shot her, that's what you should've done. Kinder, a clean hole through the head."

He knew we didn't use guns; it was a way of saying he despised us for it. He checked the rest of the flock and told me he'd be back with his dog in the morning to drive the sheep down and we'd shear them in the evening when they'd dried off and their stomachs had settled. Then he hauled the carcass up, wrapped it in the tarp, and hoisted it on his shoulder. I followed him down off the moor.

On the day of the shearing, if she'd bothered to ask him how he'd slept, Howard would have tried to tell her very badly, because all night he'd been too hot and in the wrong pajamas. He'd tried to take them off but the left sleeve got stuck on his elbow and the trousers twisted themselves around his groin and squeezed his balls until they hurt. He hated wearing pajamas—any pajamas—and she knew it, so he was angry with her even before she hadn't bothered to ask.

He'd woken up in pajamas in the hospital. She said the nurses had told her he had to wear something and they'd sent her into Taunton to get some. After three weeks the pajamas went with him to Rehabilitation, for another four. When they were leaving there to return to Stoneyridge he'd watched her fold and pack the pajamas in the determined way she now went about everything she had to do for him. For their previous twenty-eight years together he'd slept naked but back at home she made him go on wearing them, even after he objected. It was more practical, easier on the sheets, she said. He'd been too embarrassed to go on objecting.

As the months passed, she made, avoiding any mention of them, other significant operational changes in his life: spoons for every meal, clothing without buttons or zips. She also avoided putting the word *your* in front of *stroke*. It was always *the* stroke. She disliked, perhaps, ascribing ownership of it to him alone when its ravages demanded from her a hundred daily, bitter sharings of his incapacity. When she did have to say them, she used the words with reluctance, as if it was wrong to allude matter-of-factly to an event so transformative and dreadful, in the same way that he, sitting day after day at

Stoneyridge surrounded by the dilapidated walls within which he'd been left to go on living, loathed the compulsion in himself to make trivial little pictures out of ominous cracks in the plaster.

Also without discussion, she decided on separate bedrooms. The stairs were too much for him, she said, in her changed, slightly hectic voice. She was going to divide the old back parlor off the kitchen to make a smaller sitting room and a bedroom. She'd applied to the council and got a grant; he'd even be getting his own little shower room. It would be easier for him on the ground floor: for the bathroom, the meals, the nurse's visits, the naps in the afternoons. She would continue to sleep upstairs.

Howard wasn't fooled. It would be easier for her, by keeping his useless bulk out of her bed at night, to spare herself the sight of him. He tried to say as much, and also that he didn't blame her, but by then she seemed to have tired of trying to understand him and even of pretending to try. Her attention would wander, and she was always doing something else anyway, while she affected to listen: thumping pillows, clearing a tray, counting out tablets. If ever she could find an excuse to leave the room, she did.

He knew that was why, also without consulting him, she'd got the television, a thing they'd done without on principle their entire lives. He had an idea it was Adam who'd paid for it, there being no money anywhere else for such a purchase, but Deborah had gone vague about that and told him just to be grateful. He could see why she was. With the television on, she could disappear more often and for longer because, to her mind, she was leaving him less alone. The trouble with his objection to that, both on the principle of its being there at all and her practice of abandoning him to its fatuous babblings, was that he loved the television. He bloody loved it. She was right; he was less alone. The old black-and-white films—his favorite viewing—filled the afternoons with companions, reconjuring his boyhood (more imagined than accurately recalled) and a world heroic, sentimental, and just. If, as often happened, he lost the thread of a film, there was always something else: horse racing or somebody making pancakes or people being arrested; the novelty of flicking channels and playing with the volume never quite wore off. The television was a friend with a hundred different moods, of which fatuousness was only one, and a hundred different stories that he could silence or interrupt at will, a friend in front of whom he could cry or fall asleep.

Rendered mute himself, Howard thought about speech a great deal: his earlier waste of it, the words he'd squandered talking about God knows what, and all the words of Deborah's he'd missed because he'd been so busy listening to himself. And saying what, exactly? He couldn't for the life of him articulate the reasons why, for example, he'd forbidden them a television. It was too late for amends, he knew, but now he tried as never before to hear Deborah, brooding over every nuance of timbre and vocabulary and striving to form a sound, even if sometimes only an echo, to send back to her. He recalled conversations from the past and yearned to conduct them again, to do them better. There were times when he caught her speaking softly not to him but to herself, or as if she were addressing another person present who was capable, as he was not, of answering. And then he grieved for her. In the silence of his head he composed long, phantom strings of oratory to her, *in apologia,* that he knew she would never hear.

There were worse days than those, when language disintegrated altogether before him, when he couldn't recall the sound of his own voice and couldn't understand Deborah's at all; on such days it was as though not words but random letters of the alphabet came swooping out of her mouth and crackled around him like incomprehensible swarms of black insects, and he had to squeeze his eyes shut and flap them away with his good hand. But on the morning of the shearing she was speaking in her habitual way, in statements and instructions. Her voice was too loud, as if she was talking over a disturbance from the room next door, or maybe just in the back of her own mind.

Adam will be here for his birthday this year.

There, take your toothbrush. Try, Howard.

Stand up, Howard. Here's your frame.

I know it's early but I've got to see to the sheep today.

It'll have to be toast and banana, I haven't time to do anything else.

Howard worked his jaws and jerked his limbs; his stomach churned. I shouldn't blame you, he wanted to say, but I do. He blamed her for thinking that he wanted her to pretend things were all right. Why did she want him to believe it wasn't important that she was struggling, that the place was falling down around them? That their son hardly ever visited? That he hadn't touched her for years?

Come on, you like toast and banana. Here, take it.

I have to go and get dressed. Digger will be here soon.

Howard, don't cry.

<adam.morgan@logisticsomnicorpsystems.com>

To: deborahstoneyridge@yahoo.com
Sent on sat 9 july 2011 at 16.45 EST

Hi

Mum I thought you were getting rid of the sheep anyway, you were saying you're going to? I'm amazed they're still there, they are a total waste of space! Honestly, do you really still need them at this point in your life??? Did you ever? ;-)

Sorry, you've heard all that before...but at least you don't have to worry about the fleeces any more, it's one less pressure if you're not trying to keep up with all the spinning and weaving stuff.

Sorry to sound negative but there is zero demand for all the hairy brown scarves etc etc no matter they're handmade and nice and unique, which they are. It's just not viable. I mean as a hobby fine if you enjoy it but it's never going to wash its face as a viable business. Yeah-yeah, I'm a cracked record, I know I know! I worry about you though.

Am at the conference here at HQ and staying over the w/end and after that will be at the new Europe office for a while, on and off. Thank god for air con, it's really hot! The presentation went well, glad to say – the guys here are bright, but demand-driven supply chain management is like breaking news to them. Inside I'm like, what century are you in? but I don't say that to them obviously. I think they took a lot of it in anyway. I'm going out to this place tonight with a couple of them, really nice guys, apparently the beer's amazing. Regards to dad, take care A x

PS forgot, re birthday – of course I'll try but see above, pretty busy.

The next day I tried to get Howard up and dressed early and in his chair for breakfast so I'd be ready to start as soon as Digger arrived. I hadn't told him about the dead ewe or that he was going to miss Stroke Club because the shearing happened to be falling on a Wednesday. He didn't care about the days of the week and didn't usually want to go to Stroke Club anyway, but he picked up on something and wouldn't be hurried. The rain and thunder of the day before hadn't cleared the air and his room was hot and stuffy; he'd woken badly with a greasy face and his eyes crusted and sore. He wouldn't take a piece of toast and banana in the good hand and try to eat, just locked his fingers into a claw and let both hands flop in his lap, as bad as each other. When I lifted the good hand and tried to push the toast inside his fist he turned his head and gazed past me with that milky look in his eyes I used to think he couldn't help. Then he moaned and dribbled a bit so I knew he wanted to speak, probably just to tell me he wanted cereal on the one day I didn't have time to spoon it into him. On any other day I'd have made a joke of it and brought him round, but this time I admit I got impatient. Then he began to cry.

I took the toast and wiped his hand clean. I stroked his head and said I was sorry. His shoulders shuddered for a while and after a time were rigid and still, and then they softened under my hands. His hair was still damp from the shower, and I finger-combed its thin snakes of white through the rest of it, still a lion's mane, abundant and long and backward-sweeping, though the dark gold color was faded. Oh, Howard's hair, and his bronze, curling beard—he was more than handsome, he inspired confidence. It didn't cross my mind that his flamboyant looks might not signify a character of far greater dimension and dynamism than mine. My conviction that he was infallible seemed established in those pale green eyes, set deep under his brow, so hawklike it was some time before I saw gentleness in the light they cast upon me.

"You need a trim," I said, pulling his hair out along his shoulders. I drew my fingers down through his beard. "You'll be a bit cooler after a trim. I'll do it for you later." I leaned over and kissed the top of his head, and he managed to lift and place his hand on my breast, round and loose under my dressing gown. He made his fingertips perform a fluttery, circular caress, and then he dropped the exhausted arm. He tipped his head and looked up at me, his lids half-closed. That day the veins in the whites of his eyes were a tracery of tiny pink tributaries under the gluey surface, and I knew he could barely see me. "I have to get dressed," I said, and moved gently away.

Just then Digger's pickup came into the yard, the dog barking in the back. There was no time to disappear upstairs. Digger jumped down and came straight into the kitchen with the dog at his heels, and even though it was early they brought more of the day's heat in with them, trapped in Digger's rank sweat and the yellow light on his skin, and in the baked, wiry hair and meaty tongue of his dog. They stood there, both restless; the dog's saliva dripped on the floor. It hung in the air unsaid that I was annoyed he hadn't left the dog outside, where all working dogs belonged, and that Digger knew it and couldn't care less. I was also furious that my dressing gown was so old. I bought from charity shops so everything I owned was old, even before it became mine.

Digger sat down and winked at Howard. "How-do," he said. "Lie-in, did we? Had a lie-in, then? All right for some!"

"He's just having his breakfast," I said.

Digger picked up the piece of toast and waggled it close to Howard's mouth. "Here you are, then," he said. "Here."

Howard glared and turned his head away. But he let Digger place the toast in his good hand, and he lifted it to his mouth and began to chew.

"He's fine," I said. "Aren't you, Howard? He can manage fine. I'll be back down in a minute. I have to get dressed."

"Shame. Looking good as you are," Digger said, winking again. "Eh, looking good, isn't she, eh?"

Howard thumped his good arm in his lap and reared back in his chair, coughing, and spat out his mouthful of toast. He hadn't the strength to send it far enough to hit Digger, and most of it got stuck in his beard. Digger yelped. "Oy, stop that now! Don't you give me none of your old cud!"

I got the sink cloth and wiped Howard's beard clean. He was rocking back and forth, his mouth bubbling with saliva and mashed toast, a varnish of tears over his eyes. "It's all right, Howard," I said. "It's all right. No need to fuss. He didn't mean any offense."

I turned to go, but Howard snarled again. "Digger's here to help," I told him. "He's here to do the shearing."

"Not before time, neither," Digger said. "In a right old state, they are, this weather. Should've got me sooner."

I didn't rise to that. I'd pestered him as much as I could and I didn't want him to say anything in front of Howard about the dead ewe.

"Adam's due back for a visit soon," I said. "That's probably why Howard's a bit restless. We're waiting to hear when he's arriving."

"That right? I'll tell Kevin and Kyle. They ain't seen 'im for a while. 'E don't keep in touch much."

"Oh, he keeps in touch with us, of course! His visits are always last minute. That's just the way it is, his office keeps him dangling," I said. "Never knows where they're sending him next. But he should know any day. Probably he'll be here for his birthday. The twenty-eighth."

Howard nodded and smiled, blinking his sore eyes, and I went to get dressed.

It was one of those warm, sparkling days that comes on Exmoor after a spell of rain; beautiful weather. Digger pulled some bales off the van and we carried them across the yard to the barn at the back.

We set up the two holding pens inside and spread the straw ready for the sheep. As we left the yard I turned to wave to Howard, who I knew would be sitting at the window. He probably wouldn't be able to see me, so far away and through glass, and even if he did he might not be able to tell it was me, but I waved anyway, in case he could detect the movement of my hand and interpret it as a sign he was not forgotten. But at that time of morning the light fell on the glass in such a way that I was gesturing at a mirror. I was blinded by the eclipse of my own body and its long shadow against the sun's reflection on the window, sheer and dark as steel, and I couldn't see Howard at all.

In silence Digger and I walked alongside the hedgebanks between the fields and on toward the flock on the moor, past pale, swaying weed stalks flickering with crickets and little enameled flying insects. It was a glorious day—I couldn't help saying so and Digger allowed himself to agree, smiling momentarily as if I'd complimented him on something that was his. The dog loped on ahead of us toward the ridge until I couldn't see him for the glimmering haze on the horizon. Away from the reedy, bright green patches where the bog seldom dried out, the moor was shriveled and dusty, and as we walked our feet sent up from the heather clouds of ragged brown moths like scraps of burnt paper. Once over the ridge, we wound separate ways among the rocks and clumps of gorse until we found and counted the lumbering, dowdy forms of the sheep, grazing in the shade of the combe.

"Eight. One less to bother us," Digger said, and called, "Come bye!" to the dog, sending him to the back of the flock for the drive off the hill. We got them down in a loose bleating gaggle, through the field gates and into the pen in the barn. Digger looked at his watch.

"Half-eleven. Six hours'll settle the gas in their stomachs," he said, above the bleating. "I'll be back at half-five."

He must have noticed the way I glanced over at the house. "Got the day to fill, have you?" he said.

"I'm always busy," I said. "There's plenty to do."

"And there's plenty needs doing," Digger said. "If it wasn't for your situation I'd have more to say, I don't mind telling you. State of the place."

"Howard needs a lot of help."

"Even so. Point is, the rent you're paying. I could get that ten times over as a holiday let, a place like this. You want to think about that. Lease comes up again Christmastime, don't it. You want to think about it."

"It's a protected tenancy, as you well know. We're entitled to stay as long as we're farming."

"Call that lot farming?" Digger said, snorting in the direction of the sheep. "That ain't farming. Want putting out of their misery. I'm telling you, clean hole through the head."

"I'll see you at half-past five," I said, and then I thanked him again for the favor and returned to the house.

From: deborahstoneyridge@yahoo.com

To: <adam.morgan@logisticsomnicorpsystems.com>
Sent on wed 20 july 2011 at 3.32 GMT

Hi darling

Hardly know how to keep up with you! They're always sending you
somewhere – you didn't say where. It would be good to know, just so
if I need to get hold of you on your mobile in between the Wednesday
emails I have an idea of the time difference. But I suppose by the
time you read this you won't be there any more anyway! I think you
said you can get emails on your phone, is that really true? I wish we
got a mobile signal at stoneyridge.

And yes I know that's not the same as the internet and I'm sure
we'll be able to get connected up with a computer and email pretty
soon. Everyone keeps saying it'd be useful for the B&B bookings but
I'm not sure I have time for much more B&B trade.

Anyway I hope you haven't been worried – this is way past my
usual time to email because I was busy with the sheep all morning.
No village trip or stroke club for Dad today as a result. I'm just managing to sneak a bit of time in Bridgecombe while he has his nap
after lunch, I needed to get some shopping etc as well as pop into
library to write this. Have promised him a hair and beard trim later but
may not get round to it today. My shoulder's playing up a bit (nothing
to worry about, just a bit of a bore), plus the shearing still to come

and that's pretty tiring too though Digger does the hard bit obviously. We got them all into the barn so you can imagine the racket! It goes on all day, do you remember? I don't know how they don't get hoarse – you just have to get used to it or go mad I suppose!

Your work sounds so busy, I'm glad you're being appreciated! How long do you have to keep doing these visits all over the place? And where to next? Adam, is there any firm news yet about spending a few days here? You were going to let me know how long you could have off. I hope there isn't a problem. I hope you have told them how much leave you're owed, it must be weeks and weeks now! Looking at the diary, what would work really well would be if you could come on the Thursday, that's the 25th August. You'd have plenty time to get over the jetlag before your birthday on Sunday 28th, which we are dying to celebrate!!! I was thinking, how long is it since we had a birthday picnic on the moor?!?

Weather permitting I thought between us if we could get Dad up there somehow, it'd do him such a lot of good. And after Sunday you stay as long as you like. Make it worthwhile coming all this way, make it a proper break and a rest in the country!

Of course if those dates don't work, come whenever you can manage.

Well, todays busy, which of course is good, so I must get back or Dad will be feeling neglected.

Take care. Let me know where you are! And dates please – and we are HOPING you'll be here for the big day.

Love, Mum xxxxxxxx

The sun beat down all day on the barn roof. When I went in at half-past five, the air was thick with the smell of warm hay and urine and vibrated with the cries of the ewes; I was sweating and feeling sick even before Digger arrived, late. He rigged up sacks for the fleeces and I unrolled the extension cable for the electric cutters across the yard to the socket in Howard's old pottery shed. Digger had brought blowfly treatment and said we should dose the rest of the flock. He told me to get some gloves and then showed me how to work the spray. He set planks on the floor where he would do the work and started the generator; we had to shout above its drone and the bleating. As I went into the first holding pen I reminded Digger that since I broke my shoulder I could only work from one side, and he nodded, either bored or skeptical. He didn't seem to remember it at all, my fall from the ladder, although at the time he'd been scathing about Howard letting his wife do a man's work. Together, taking a horn each, we hauled the nearest ewe away from the others, got her out of the pen, and dragged her on her skidding hooves across the floor. Digger tipped her off-balance and held her down on her back, between his legs. The clippers began to buzz. He wasn't an expert shearer—his father had stopped farming sheep when Digger was in his teens—and he struggled to keep her feet from kicking against the floor. By the time he had her done she was wild-eyed, and thick strings of spittle hung from her mouth. I already had the gloves on, and while he held her I sprayed her with the insecticide. She bucked at the feel of it on her newly exposed skin but I kept going until Digger, swearing and spitting, said it was enough. He swung her over and back on her feet; I got the gate of the second holding pen open and he shoved her in. She skittered around for a while as if startled to find herself suddenly skinny and white. It's not true that shorn sheep look like the lambs they once were. She looked impossibly small, but old.

I did my best to roll and tie the tattered cloak of her fleece, hiding my disgust, while Digger watched. My hands shook, and they were greasy and stinking with the lanolin off the wool. The air was sharp with insecticide. We brought out the next ewe from the others and went through the same procedure with her, and with the next two. After nearly an hour we were only half-way done, and I was drenched in sweat and my shoulder ached. I made Digger stop. I brought a jug of cold water from the house, and although he paused and drank, he made it clear he resented the delay. On the fifth sheep he found maggots. She was not nearly as badly infested as the sheep that died; it was nothing, he told me, that a good drenching wouldn't deal with. I watched the maggots writhe faster under the shower of insecticide. They dropped off dead on to his feet, and I was almost sick.

It was after seven-thirty before we'd finished and driven the sheep back on to the moor. Digger returned to the shed to pack up the generator and clippers and other bits of equipment while I went on into the house. When I stepped into the kitchen I heard faint drifting voices from the television and through the glass panel of the door to the sitting room I could see the top of Howard's head silhouetted against the screen. He didn't turn round.

I didn't want him to know I'd come in. The kitchen smelled almost pleasantly of summer damp, a sharp smell like milk curds or wet chalk, and my face and arms were prickling from the sudden coolness. My skin still crawled; I shivered, remembering the foamy jaws of the sheep and their jutting yellow teeth, the lousy fleeces. From the sitting room came the sound of a commercial break; jittery music gave way to an excited, high-pitched voice. Howard switched channels, slicing from the advert to fluttery studio laughter, and then he brought the volume down so that over it I could hear the kitchen clock tapping out the seconds in low, tinny pulses. The old freezer in the scullery across the passage at the back of the kitchen let out a tired, electrical grunt. It was the first time all day I'd had a moment to realize how close to tears I was, how completely I would give up and sob with self-pity if this patch of solitude were not so obviously finite, so frail against certain interruption. All I could do was guard it for as long as it lasted and use every moment of it to keep very still, the way a cat uses a square of sunlight on a stone floor. I stood motionless, my fingertips arched on the tabletop, and closed my eyes, afraid that my breathing would give away my whereabouts. I wondered if Adam had read my email yet. *I hope you have told them how much leave you're owed, it must be weeks and weeks now!* However desperate that sounded to him it was far, far less desperate than I felt.

I opened my eyes at the sound of Digger scraping his feet over the threshold. I glanced at the sitting room; Howard hadn't moved and was watching a cartoon now. Digger waited, chewing on a blister he'd got from the sheep clippers and watching me as I bent down to the fridge and brought out cans of beer. He drank one leaning against the sink, set it down empty, wiped his mouth, and said he'd be off. I didn't try to persuade him to have another. For every one of his unkind remarks there seemed to be another that he turned into a look of disdain instead of speaking aloud, and I couldn't bear his presence another moment. His contempt for us, the doomed, naïve, arrogant Londoners who thought they could make a go of it on Exmoor, he had once tried to hide; now that he believed he'd been proved right he extended to us—between threats about our tenancy—a kind of snide pity. After he left, all I wanted to do was get in a bath, wash off the whole filthy day, and sleep. Instead I loaded up a tray with Howard's supper and took it into the sitting room.

He wasn't watching the television at all. He was crying. His good hand, the fingers still crooked in the scissor handles, lay shaking in his lap, half-buried under drifts of his silky hair and darker curls from his beard. What was left of the hair on his head fell across his brow and stood up around his ears in chopped tufts, and the remains of his beard looked like torn patches of matting glued to his cheeks. He lifted his face, soaked in tears and sweat and now falling in folds to the papery-white, naked wattle under his chin. His weeping came

more from his mouth than his eyes; his newly exposed lips were pink
and quivering and the bottom one was cut and swollen. It struck me
that I had never properly seen his mouth—indeed his face—before.

"For God's sake, Howard, what have you done? What the hell
have you done?" I said. Above the television my voice was hard and
flat as if I were testing it for an echo against the walls of an empty
room. I turned and switched off the television. And as I often did, I
also flicked a switch in my mind. I began to imagine the amusing,
valiant email I would try to write to Adam about what was happening, reaching for phrases that would convince him, and thereby myself, that we were coping all right. It was one of the ways I kept
going, by summoning quite unreal and sudden surges of spirit and
energy so that later I could report to my son another of my plucky
little retaliations against circumstance.

"Really, Howard, what on earth did you think you were doing?
Don't cry. Never mind, it'll grow back. For God's sake, Howard,
please don't cry!"

He held out the scissors, mumbling something I didn't understand. As he did so, some skeins of hair in his lap slipped to the floor.
I picked them up in my hands and brought them to my face; his hair
was warm, the cut ends like tiny needle pricks against my cheeks. It
smelled of him.

But it was only hair. Howard stripped of nothing more important
than hair, but humiliated and transformed, not so much denuded as
defused—the charge dead, the power gone. The pity of it, the misery
and foolishness in his eyes. I reminded myself that beneath his dis-
guise of beard and hair, nothing had in fact altered for a very long
time. I took the scissors and finished the job.

The heat was unbearable. Already the day was unbearable. He should not have been left alone with Digger and yet she'd gone, disappeared upstairs. He glared at him but must have failed to convey anger, because Digger shook his head and murmured, "You poor old bugger," and wandered back outside.

And because the breakfast routine was upset, all that followed was upset. When she came back downstairs dressed she didn't help him to his usual chair in the sitting room. Hadn't time, she told him, and he was supposed to walk by himself with the frame as much as he could, that's what they said at Stroke Club. She forgot about his tablets and he had to mouth at her and point at the cupboard where they were kept. Digger was loitering at the open door, the dog jumping and barking behind him. She rattled the tablets on to his plate next to his cup of milk and he lifted them one by one to his mouth; as soon as he had taken the last and brought the cup down from his lips, she pulled it away. Then she left, telling him she wouldn't be long and he'd be fine.

She didn't tell him to finish the milk or wipe his mouth. She didn't wait to see that he'd managed to swallow the pills. When the dog's barking at last grew faint, Howard emptied the bitter, chalky spittle into his hand and wiped it down his thigh. He ate the last piece of banana on his plate and finished the milk: children's food. In the quiet of the kitchen, the empty space of the morning ahead opened up, wide and uncrossable. He heaved himself up to his walking frame and pushed it along toward the sitting room. Behind him, the clock spat out a tick between each shuffling step. Between each step he stopped and waited, longer each time; with every tick and every step, he wanted to be dead.

When she came in later she stank of sheep. He wouldn't look at her and wouldn't eat the sandwich she made for his lunch, because it also stank of sheep. She told him he was tired and helped him to bed. He could tell she was excited about something; there was life in her, maybe because today she was doing what she liked doing, keeping away from him. More and more, she wanted to keep away from him. He lay awake on his bed while the sun's blaze filtered through the drawn curtains and his lips worked in silence, forming unsayable words of pleading. A memory of his own voice droned in the warm air over his head. A little later when she looked in on him he pretended to be asleep, and after a while he heard the back door shutting and the van starting up in the yard.

There must have been a time that afternoon when he did fall asleep, and there was a time when she came back and got him up and fretted around him and made him another sandwich, which he ate. He couldn't be sure of the order of those times or how long any of them took. Later, he was back in his chair in the sitting room, that much he knew; also that she switched on the television and went out again.

The room was stifling and dark. Noise, color, and also, it seemed to him, heat radiated from the television. Since the bedroom partition had gone up there was only one window in the sitting room and he'd wanted it opened but hadn't been able to say so. Why hadn't she opened it before she left? She knew he couldn't do it; it took two good arms to lift the sash. He could die in here like a dog in a car. She was trying to kill him. If he could hurl a shoe far enough to break the glass, he would. He'd enjoy the sound of shattering glass. He remembered that she'd promised that morning to trim his hair; that, too, she had forgotten. It was simple fury that gave him the strength to grasp hold of his frame and go to the kitchen drawer where the scissors were kept.

Deborah always cut his hair in the kitchen, so he would not; besides, he didn't want her or Digger barging in on him before he'd finished. For no reason but to hear the words aloud, he tried, and managed, to call out "Cut hair!" and then his voice cracked with laughter. "Too hot, cut off!" he cried, but on the *ff* he bit down on the moist flap of bottom lip that was caught between his teeth and drew blood.

Sucking on his mouth, he shuffled back to his chair in the sitting room. He turned up the volume on the television—it was necessary to create a distraction of some kind, he felt, from his act of self-sabotage—and began to cut.

The first snip of the scissors loosed and let fall a shockingly large amount of hair. He lifted out another handful from his head and snipped again; the dry whisper of the blades right next to his ear was beautiful. He began to cry, and went on cutting, and cutting.

Much later, when she came in and said, "For God's sake, Howard, what have you done? What the hell have you done?" he could not begin to speak of his gratitude for her return.

She prised his fingers from the scissors calmly and snapped them twice in the air. With a touch that made his neck tingle she pulled the tufts of hair that were left through her fingers, drawing them out straight.

"Oh God," she said softly, "what a mess. You only had to wait, you know, I would have done it for you." She sighed. "You've made such a hash of it, all I can do is cut the rest off. Finish the job." She sighed again; she was considering the risks of cutting it, he knew, so close to his head. Then she began to make her way, it seemed by feel more than sight, scraping her nails gently across his temples, ruffling the clinging hair free from his damp skull, and raising the overripe smell of skin and sweat. She laid the scissor blades close, metal against scalp, and snipped. She pulled the cut fronds away with her other hand and opened her fingers. With solemn slowness, his hair fell in strands to the floor. She clipped again. Howard sat up very straight, swaying with each push of her hands, while from his mouth issued small noises he could not control. She shushed him and began to work faster, as if hurrying to outdistance a rising desire to hurt. He thought he heard a sob, and fancied that a mild trickling sensation might be not a bead of sweat but a tear dropping on the crown of his head. Nothing was said. After a while she put down the scissors and sank into the chair opposite.

Drifts of Howard's hair sparkled unevenly on the floor between them, where the setting sun, slanting through the window behind her, caught the copper and silver strands among the dark. With her back to the light Deborah appeared to him black and solid, a rounded, human wall between him and the burning bright outdoors. Although he could not make out her face he knew from her perfect stillness that she was gazing at him, and could not bring himself to wonder what she saw. He could feel the beat of his own blood in his fingertips, in his throat and his sore lip, as if it were her eyes fixed upon him that kept his heart pumping. He felt himself aging before her, as if time itself, with infinitesimal, delicate footstamps, were crossing the room and entering his body.

Deborah stood up, scraping the scissor blades clean along the edge of her thumb. "Well, that's that," she said. "Here's supper. You must be hungry now." She placed the remote for the television in his hand and moved across to the tray she'd brought in. She started talking in a casual, wavery voice about the food: cheese and ham, tomatoes and mustard, what did he want?

So this was how they were to go on. She had decided that nothing had changed. But Howard knew that something had happened, beyond a mere haircut and the removal of a beard, although not something sudden—for all that it had been accomplished in a few minutes with the scissors—but no, it was something gradual, working between them perhaps from the very beginning, out of focus but present nonetheless. Something that had been happening for years had been brought into the light, maybe at last its time had come, this shared dread—eventually a realization—that one day she would see him for what he was. Howard stroked his good hand across his forehead and back over the new stubble on his skull, and switched on the television.

From: deborahstoneyridge@yahoo.com

To: <adam.morgan@logisticsomnicorpsystems.com>
Sent on wed 27 july 2011 at 11.28 GMT

Hello darling – nothing from you today, I suppose you are frantically busy! Or probably away again somewhere.

Big surprise last week, Dad got hold of the scissors somehow and gave himself a shearing! Not to be outdone by the sheep, he wanted a summer haircut too. He's absolutely shorn, beard and all.

I did my best to tidy up his efforts at coiffure and now I must say he does look a bit cooler. Takes some getting used to, though. The beard is so "him" and would you believe I've never EVER seen him with short hair?! Makes his face quite different.

Everybody used to remark on Dad's hair. Did I ever tell you about the time years ago we were in Honiton one day and we were meant to meet up at that little gallery upstairs from the gift shop because Roderick (Dad's old pottery teacher) had an exhibition? You were with me of course but far too young to remember. Well I was late and a bit flustered and worried I might have missed him so I said to the girl Oh I'm looking for my husband I wonder if he's here? She said I don't know, what does he look like and I said Oh, well, actually he looks like God. And straightaway she said Oh, yes, he's just gone upstairs.

I've never seen him like this. He looks SO different! You'll get quite a surprise when you see it though I'm hoping it'll have grown back a little by August!

No other news. Veg garden gone crazy, it does creep up on you. There's been a bit of drought so I lost the tomatoes, they don't stand up to much and a lot of the lettuces have bolted.

Darling you can have no idea how much I am hoping to see you.

Lots of love M xx

AUGUST 2011

<adam.morgan@logisticsomnicorpsystems.com>

To: deborahstoneyridge@yahoo.com
Sent on mon 1 aug 2011 at 16.45 EST

Dear M – weird about Dad's hair!! Way to go, sounds cool – in both senses. Tell me more when we spk, wish you could take a picture and send it as an email attachment.

Reminds me, did you find out any more about that course you thought you could do at the library for IT beginners? I really think you should do it, you'd see how simple most of it is and make life easier for you. And me!

Sorry no way can confirm dates yet but it's ages yet, will let you know. More soon, take care love A xxx

Sent from my BlackBerry

From: deborahstoneyridge@yahoo.com

To: <adam.morgan@logisticsomnicorpsystems.com>
Sent on wed 3 aug 2011 at 11.28 GMT

Ok darling but do let me know about dates soon as poss, ok? So looking forward. Today I'll grab my chance and get walnuts and stem ginger at the Spar, so birthday cake and cookies will be done and in the freezer. (Yep, picnic menu under control!) Seems ages since I got out on the moor to do more than count sheep. It's been rainy since the shearing so that doesn't help. For fresh air I only go up the track as far as the field, wouldn't be fair to go much further, Dad would worry. He's lost all confidence in his walking, the nurse at Stroke Club says he might well improve if he did more but it's hard to make him. Still doesn't seem to get much out of Stroke Club though they've got quite a lot on offer. Oh well. It's hard for him. Must go he's waiting in the van. Take care darling, keep me posted re your flights Mum xxx

On his good days, Howard could tell what Deborah was thinking, in the old way he believed he'd been able to before the stroke. When his eyes and his mind worked together and fast enough, and if she remained still for a moment, he could, fleetingly, read her face again, and what she was thinking, he knew, was that she hated looking at him now.

But he was determined not to let his hair and beard grow back. He'd become quickly accustomed and then addicted to the half-hour of every day she now had to spend, with slow care, shaving and trimming him. At first she'd tried to find excuses: she hadn't time, his hair was much nicer long, his beard suited him so well. But he was having none of that. He'd gone rigid, refused to move or eat, scratched his chin and scalp raw. He did the same on the days she'd tried to skip it with a promise to do a proper job tomorrow.

Now it was a daily ritual. There was no space to do it in his shower room, so a pink washing-up bowl from the Spar in Bridgecombe, in which were kept a plastic jug, brush, soap, towel, and a collection of disposable razors, had been given a place on a shelf in the kitchen. Every day Deborah brought it down, used the jug to fill it with warm water, placed the towel around his shoulders, and set to work at the kitchen table. She was new to it, as he was, and not very skilled, and he liked it that they shared this new undertaking in which they were both novices; it was as near as they'd get to taking up a hobby together. It was delightful to him that she had to come so close that he could make out the frown on her face as she soaped and scraped and wiped. And keeping his chin and head smooth couldn't be done in the usual snappy way she had of dispensing tablets, doing up buttons or mashing food. She was forced into slow motion, which Howard believed was good for her; the concentration and effort slowed her breathing. He was a model of co-operation, allowing her to tip his head up and down, to one side and to the other; he pulled his neck skin taut and grimaced and tried hard not to cough or swallow. He loved it that she couldn't hurry without cutting his throat.

She complained, of course, in her habitual manner, with continual but mild little eruptions that were no more than a kind of accompaniment—the soundtrack of her stoicism—to all that she had to get through in a day. Oh, the fetching and carrying, the paraphernalia of the soap and razors and water and towels, her own lack of skill, the risk of cuts: Howard did his best to look sorry but he enjoyed listening to her making it sound so bothersome and hazardous. Because once she took the razor in her hand and began to concentrate—and she seemed unaware of this—she stopped talking. In silence he could contemplate the sensation of her breath on his skin, her hands traveling over the folds of his cheeks, the rasp of the blade against stubble. Sometimes she sighed, and occasionally in her sighing he was aware of a slight grunt, and now and then he caught on her face a turning down of the mouth. Don't be that way, he wanted to tell her. Willing or not, she had no choice but to perform this prolonged, daily act of tenderness, and although he knew that a performance was what it was, he hoped that in the exercise of the care necessary for the simple avoidance of bloodshed—for reasons of practical efficiency she would avoid bloodshed—she would in time acquire a trace of true tenderness. Meanwhile, until she might come to feel a little of the emotion he forced her to enact, he didn't care that it was undignified of him to crave the measured half-hours when she was her old, gentle self.

But afterward, time would hang heavier still. Left alone, he would haul himself up and hobble to the sitting room window overlooking the yard and the side of the property that sloped down the hill toward the road, and there he would lean, peering across at the spot where he knew the edge of the vegetable garden to be but seeing only dark shapes and patches of light. Sometimes he thought he picked up

a slight movement but then would suspect he'd imagined it altogether, hoping for it too much because Deborah might have told him
that the vegetable garden was where she'd be spending the next hour.
Or it might have been a rabbit or a badger, or one of the hens, strayed
from the run he'd built at the far end of the vegetable garden, under
the shadow of the hill and out of sight from the house. He didn't
remember how many hens they had now.

He remembered the long-ago past more vividly, how it had taken
them over six weeks to clear the ground for the vegetables from the
bare hillside, working by hand with mattocks and crowbars. The use
of machinery for cultivation he'd regarded almost as cheating, an
affectation that seemed incredible to him now. Then, he'd wanted to
feel the earth between his fingers, to get dirt on his hands and mud
on his boots. They'd planted spindly hawthorn cuttings for a hedge
and put up a flimsy boundary fence; both were trampled within three
days. They replanted and rebuilt them twice again that spring as
deer, sheep, rabbits, and the wild ponies and then Exmoor's April
winds kept Stoneyridge's small bit of land under siege. In the end
they had to surround the vegetable garden with cinder blocks and
barbed wire. It was hard to tell, looking at it, that the whole point of
the place was harmony between Man and Nature.

Every summer the thick-rooted ground weeds returned, sprouting
up among the vegetable seedlings. He and Deborah weeded and
hoed, weeded and hoed. In later years even Adam weeded and hoed
in his very own patch, until the child-sized tools Howard had made
for him rusted from neglect and the patch reverted to scrub; Adam
wanted a bike, not a rake and spade. With a regret he was unable to
express, Howard gave up trying to interest him in growing food.

Yields were usually small; the surpluses they'd planned to barter
or sell for money appeared only when there were seasonal gluts of
the same tomatoes, marrows, runner beans all over the county, and
then they could scarcely give them away. They cleared more ground.
He stopped Deborah from growing flowers, even to sell, saying they
needed all the space for food and garden flowers were phoney and
suburban. Go out on the moor, he told her, if you want to look at
flowers, the moor's covered in them. One June day she picked every

single one of the orange flowers on the runner bean plants and arranged them in a jug on the table, and he lost his temper. Didn't she know the bean pods grew from the base of the dead flowers, didn't she know she'd sabotaged the entire crop? But she had to pick them, she said, collapsing in tears. She so badly wanted some flowers for the house, just a jug of flowers on the table, she *had* to have them.

Howard could no longer bring to mind what she'd been wearing that day, but if he blinked he could almost conjure out of the dark behind his eyelids a flashed imprint of the tiny ringlets of bean tendrils spiraling up among the brilliant orange blooms in the jug. He'd felt a brute. He was appalled that he'd had no idea of her need for flowers. But, determined to remain angry on account of the lost bean crop, he hadn't said so.

Now Howard watched from the sitting-room window and wished his eyes could distinguish genuine signs of life from imagined or reflexive blinks and flickerings, from mere tricks of the light. He wished he'd tried to understand his family better. He thought of bringing flowers to Deborah now—he'd plant her a garden full of them if he could. He'd learn a hundred things about her, he'd memorize all her small desires and strive to meet them, every one.

Well, he couldn't, of course. But they would go on. Days would pass, and probably he and she would appear to each other ever more oblique and pitiful; more would be asked of them both. Though it was too late to earn her forgiveness he would try to reach out and touch her when she leaned close to wipe his face with the corner of a towel; he might be able to lift his hand and stroke her arm when she was tired and when the bad shoulder under her hanging-off clothes was causing her to stoop. Which of them was the more ravaged, or if one of them were more needful of care than the other, he found it impossible to say; what was important was that for each other's sake they garner some kindness from somewhere, amid such cruelty.

<adam.morgan@logisticsomnicorpsystems.com>

To: deborahstoneyridge@yahoo.com
Sent on sun 7 aug 2011 at 21.23 EST

Hi Mum! might be looking good for end of month if still ok with you?
hope you're ok
    more soon

A xxx
Sent from my BlackBerry

From: deborahstoneyridge@yahoo.com

To: <adam.morgan@logisticsomnicorpsystems.com>
Sent on wed 10 aug 2011 at 11.03 GMT

Adam darling

Oh, that is great news!! Let's have the flight details please!!! I wish I
could meet you at the airport but the van doesn't like long journeys
these days (let's face it, it never did!) In any case I probably shouldn't
be away from here that long anyway, and if I brought Dad along it'd
be difficult for him and then you'd have to ride home in the back
which would NOT be comfortable!

BUT please DO be a love and let me know the details. Sorry to nag but I'll be waiting!!! Will you be hiring a car? Don't forget once you're here you won't really need it, the van's still fine on short journeys and you can have it any time. The shop, library, prescriptions, stroke club etc on Wednesdays is all I use it for.

Adam, you won't get a taxi all the way from the airport will you? Whatever they're paying you that would be terribly extravagant and if Dad got wind of it he'd have a fit.

Come to think of it best thing would be to take a train to Taunton and I'll pick you up there. Or even Exeter. AS LONG AS I KNOW WHEN AND WHERE!

Dad's dying to see you, I tell him every day you're coming! Adam, you mustn't be upset if you see a change. It's not just the beard and hair gone (yes he still insists he isn't having them back again!). The thing is he's speaking a bit less. After he got some speech back initially he's gone back a bit since the last time you saw him. The stroke nurse says that can happen, and we have to remember it's not necessarily a problem inside his brain as such, it's the ability to communicate. I think emotions especially. Maybe it's just too exhausting. So he might not seem thrilled to see you, it might look as if it hasn't even registered, and there's the added problem of this vision problem – he can only register about half his normal visual field even though his eyes still work so it's very confusing, you can never be sure which half he sees and which he doesn't.

But he can be as bright as a button on his good days, he takes in everything! Though to be honest he can be naughty, he'll just switch off when it suits him, for instance I can't get through to him about the shaving, how it just adds to the list of things to do. I did try once or twice just not doing it but he got his message across! Not to worry.

Main thing is FLIGHTS!!!

Love
Mum

Ps please ring the house with flights as I won't get to email again till next wed

<adam.morgan@logisticsomnicorpsystems.com>

To: deborahstoneyridge@yahoo.com
Sent on thurs 11 aug 2011 at 21.23 EST

Mum hoping to make it but nothing's definite yet, you know what it's like ok?! Still working on it, but it's pretty crazy round here! Out of office rest of week Will keep you posted. Luv xxx

Sent from my BlackBerry

From: deborahstoneyridge@yahoo.com

To: <adam.morgan@logisticsomnicorpsystems.com>
Sent on wed 17 aug 2011 at 11.47 GMT

darling do what you can!!! Freezer's full and fridge will be groaning! I can't believe they can't give you a week off. Five days even, whatever you can manage. Email's great but we haven't actually seen you for ages! Will be tackling your room tomorrow, not that it's all that bad – rest of house will get a once over too, the B & B rooms could do with a spit and polish. I haven't really advertised this year so we've had nobody to speak of, just a handful using last year's Staying on Exmoor leaflet – it's really a tall order on top of everything! Do so hope you'll make it somehow, I know you'll do your VERY best…
ALL fingers and toes crossed you'll be here by 28th, – we're expecting you! Lots of love and can't wait Mum xxx

<adam.morgan@logisticsomnicorpsystems.com>

To: deborahstoneyridge@yahoo.com
Sent on wed 17 aug 2011 at 06.48 EST

Out of office reply: Hi I'm out of the office right now and checking emails infrequently. If your inquiry is urgent please contact my colleague nicky.ray@logisticsomnicorpsystems.com.

<adam.morgan@logisticsomnicorpsystems.com>

To: deborahstoneyridge@yahoo.com
Sent on sat 20 aug 2011 at 06.48 EST

On all day site meeting, am checking with office asap

Sorry, dealing with major issues here, our new demand signal model's throwing out forecasts by over 30% and that means major knockon effect on entire process integration. Will call. A xxx

From: deborahstoneyridge@yahoo.com

To: <adam.morgan@logisticsomnicorpsystems.com>
Sent on wed 24 aug 2011 at 11.41 GMT

Lovely to talk for a minute on Sunday, shame the signal went, I tried a few more times but you'd switched off or something. Landline still plays up here sometimes, maybe it's the council digging up the roads or something – anyway maybe when you get back to the office they'll let you know about the leave. Haven't you told them you're booked and everything?

It sounds terrible, all the problems – hope you're sorting every-thing out ok. hope you're getting my emails!?! As we haven't heard we're assuming you're still booked and arriving 27th in time for 28th?! If you CAN give rough time of arrival it helps! See you soon!!
Lots of love Mum xxx

W e got through the day somehow, with no idea of when Adam was going to arrive. By four o'clock Howard shuffled away to lie on his bed, shaved and combed and quite cowed by all the expectation and preparedness. In the kitchen the large joint of pork was waiting, its hide slashed and salted, leaching watery pink blood into its dish. At half-past four I put it in the oven, as if doing so would somehow draw Adam here in time for dinner at around eight. I'd picked the vegetables in the morning and they were sitting in a bucket in the yard, and although it was really far too early, I brought them in and washed and peeled them and put them in cold water. I had managed to get potatoes, carrots, some leaves of chard, all a bit stunted and nibbled, so I cut everything up small. By then I was too restless to remain where everything was ready for Adam but where there was yet no Adam present. The rest of the house was so tidy I couldn't set about doing anything else without spoiling the order and polish I'd achieved. I walked from room to room, seeing the place through Adam's eyes, disparagingly.

It had always been a musty house, too cool in summer and with that soft grip of damp and a sodden, mineral smell about which I had first felt when I lived here slight consternation, but finally helpless-ness. Howard and I didn't use any of the other downstairs rooms now, and the Bed and Breakfast trade was too sparse to dispel the unlived-in stillness that waited behind their doors. I hadn't cleaned the ashes from the stoves in the dining room and front sitting room since they were last lit over two years ago, so those rooms smelled sooty as well. A grainy mesh of cobwebs and wood ash and bark crumbs lay at the side of each fireplace where the logs used to be. Every year at the end of May I used to sweep everything out and stack the logs up neatly and place bowls of fir cones on the hearthstones, but nowadays I never found the time or saw the point. Whatever I did, it was a house that seemed always to be waiting for the next winter.

The day before, I'd stacked the small Bed and Breakfast tables up at one end of the dining room and laid the large table in the middle for three. I straightened the cutlery again and polished the glasses against my sleeve. Once Adam was settled in we would probably eat in the kitchen as usual, but for his first evening, even though the formality of it wouldn't be very comfortable, I wanted us to claim the whole house for ourselves.

In the hall, I'd cleared away the tourist leaflets and Visitors' Book from the sideboard and put a copper jug of dried grasses on it instead, but the place still had a look of institutional gloom, like a run-down sanatorium. Howard's folded wheelchair stood between the fire extinguisher in its bracket on the wall and the table with the bookings diary and telephone on it.

I couldn't do anything about the carpet. It had been here when we moved in and wasn't very old at the time, so we'd kept it until we could afford something we liked. It was of that dark red, drenched-looking kind you see in pubs and it had a pattern of small swirls that reminded me of mince. Now it was worn through in several places and shedding long fronds of black underlay that were always getting caught in the wheelchair, so I'd covered the worst patches with doormats and rugs, which crossed the floor like oblong stepping stones. On both sides of the hall, above the yellowish oak wainscoting, the walls were still hung with the mismatched antlers that also had come with the house. I'd never exactly liked them, but of course I'd gone along with Howard, who said they "belonged" here. Or, put another way, I liked the idea of us as respecters of our predecessors' history, which for some reason sat quite comfortably with my zeal to supplant it with our own. In those early days we were too romantic to point out to each other that the history of Stoneyridge's former owners was unromantically recent, or that the farmhouse wasn't old or at all pretty, having been built in 1924 of red brick and pebbledash to the same design as hundreds of suburban villas going up at the time in Minehead and Exeter. Digger had showed us round. Although unoccupied for the five years since his grandmother had died, the house was, he said, a "rare opportunity," available on a long lease and protected rent to tenants who'd make good the fabric of the building, and it came with two paddocks and twenty acres of grazing on the surrounding moor. I was too young to bother that Howard's money wasn't enough to buy us a place, or that Digger was getting his redundant farmhouse fixed up at our expense. Neither of us paid much attention when he told us that the protected agricultural tenancy was only valid while we worked the land. If we gave up our smallholding, the tenancy would be void and he'd be entitled to sell or rent out the place as a holiday home. So what, we thought; what else were we here for but to make a success of everything? I remember the surge of protectiveness I felt, seeing the look on Digger's face as Howard, reassuring him on this point, actually used the phrase *going back to the land*.

But for that lapse, Digger put on the charm. I let him entrance me with the story he spun, about the house being built for his grandmother Elsie who'd come to Stoneyridge as the twenty-year-old bride of the second Diggory Bickford (Digger himself was the fourth, he told us), a man of property nine years older than she was. He was a great catch, he said, for a butcher's daughter from Minehead, especially one who served behind the counter. It was Elsie and Diggory's three sons—and the notion of three sons also played nicely into my yearnings for the folkloric life we would lead here—the eldest of them Digger's father, who started the collection of cast deer antlers they found on the moor.

So the antlers stayed, and some years later when we were painting the hall (a pale shade of orange that time, to stimulate optimism and sociability) and I said I really didn't want them anymore, Howard was ready with another reason to keep them. They were naturally shed antlers, he said, as opposed to whole mounted stags' heads, so symbolically they represented the superiority of Nature over the "outdated macho trophyism" of deer hunting. But we eat venison, I said, when there's been a cull and it's cheap. Howard said that wasn't the point, although I didn't really grasp why not. Perhaps I wasn't listening properly. By then, things were already quite badly awry.

Five o'clock came and went and still there was no word from Adam. I'd been maintaining an attitude of mild rebuke for his casualness about the arrangements; in my head I could hear the sharp remarks he deserved but which I must not say, for I could not have borne to see on his face a look that asked why he had bothered to come if, once he was here, all I did was complain. So I rehearsed the mock scolding I would give him that would conceal my real worry, and dialed his number. Calls to his mobile were terribly expensive but this felt like an emergency. I was close to losing hold of my good mood. He didn't answer. Of course—he must be still on the plane. That meant he would be hours yet. He hadn't let me know a train time so he must be hiring a car and would just turn up. I had to be patient. I wandered upstairs where there was still an air of ill-ease that wouldn't shift.

I made my way to his room and checked again that the bedside lamp was working. I wiped a finger along the window ledge and straightened the curtains. Since the only thing to do next would be to return to the kitchen, I stayed at the window and did nothing. Adam's room was one of the two bow-windowed ones at the front, with a view looking down to the road; I stood and watched one or two cars go by. Even in summer very little traffic passed this way, another factor we'd overlooked when we tried to sell the weaving and pottery, and later in desperation also garden produce and afternoon teas, from the "gallery" that was only an old farm shed.

I turned away from the window. I'd kept the room clean and aired since Adam's last visit not long after Howard's stroke, although it had been unchanged for much longer than that. He'd depersonalized it completely when he was fourteen, just before he went to lodge with Mrs. Dobbs and go to school in Exeter. As a boy he didn't have much in the way of possessions; we didn't give him big expensive toys or gadgets and he didn't keep treasured collections or make things. But he'd taken such as he had—posters, books, dart board, a few broken homemade toys—and piled them in the yard for burning.

Without a sigh, over the course of a single day he'd tried to expunge all evidence of his life here as if his presence had never been more than a temporary arrangement—and worse, as if he never intended to return. After he'd gone I brought it all inside again and fixed the room up as if he'd never left. Howard thought I'd gone mad. I hung the dartboard back inside its circle of pockmarks on the wall and remounted the posters of places Adam had never been to—Paris, Madrid, Moscow—telling myself he'd regret it one day and be grateful that I saved it all. Well, even if not exactly grateful, he hadn't minded, or at any rate not enough to chuck the stuff out all over again.

Fourteen years on, the room hadn't changed except that now the wardrobe held the new clothes I gave him as birthday presents and that he kept here because they were really only suitable for the country. (I liked the idea of him stepping into clothes that were here, ready for him when he arrived.) Although he seldom slept in it, the room was still his and would remain so. Even if he only ever came back for a few days at a time, his room would be always waiting.

I smoothed the bedspread and adjusted the angle of the towels over the back of the chair. I gave a pointless quarter-turn to the pottery dish on the chest of drawers. It was one of Howard's pieces, neither bowl nor plate. I lifted it and considered it in my hands: its thickness, the partial, globular brown glaze that adhered like an obstinate gravy stain. Howard had only ever made stoneware, heavy and cold to the touch, like concrete, and he never deviated from a palette of dun-colored glazes, which he described as natural. What was *un*natural, I used to wonder, about the green of new grass, the orange of egg yolk, the red of blood?

I replaced the dish on the chest of drawers. That was when I had the idea of going to pick some heather to put in a vase beside it, and a thrill of excitement ran through me, because Adam *was* coming back. He would love the moor when he saw it again, and the heather in a vase in his bedroom would remind him we were going there for the birthday picnic. I was elated to have something to do to pass the next hour or two. I went quickly downstairs and looked in on Howard. He was lying on his back, deep asleep with his mouth open. I basted the pork joint, put it back in and lowered the oven, and left the house quietly.

I took the bridleway that led from the side of the house and followed it to the first gate into the fields. I walked up between the hedgebanks and across more stiles until I was high on the moor, on the very top of the ridge beyond the stand of hawthorn where the sheep gathered on warm days. I paused to get my breath back.

Far below me and away to the right, Stoneyridge looked, as ever, misplaced, towny and foursquare in its recess dug out and leveled from the squally moorland hillside. I used to come up here sometimes and look at it as if it had nothing to do with me, trying to puzzle out, from a distance, if it were a place I'd choose to live in if I didn't already. I would get to thinking about Digger's grandmother in 1924 coming as a twenty-year-old bride to the house just built for her. Elsie the butcher's daughter from Minehead, how had she fared, actually? I always wondered if Minehead was where she'd really hankered for her new house to be; maybe she'd had Stoneyridge's front garden walled and laid to lawn and planted with those bitter-leaved town shrubs, laurel and privet, with her heart yearning for suburban orderliness, for the company of women at tea in the afternoons and, beyond her garden gate, for a pavement to walk on rather than the wide moor and the steep, wooded combes where, out of sight of everybody, a person could easily stumble on thorns and rocks, break an ankle, and entrap herself. Now, as then, the house itself and the hill behind it cast Elsie's front garden, or the remains of it, into shade; it was always chilly and unvisited, its shadows damp, its greens too dark. We'd dug beds in the lawn and tried growing cabbages there that had brought a plague of slugs, and potatoes that came up wet and hollow.

It was on the other side of the house, at the back, where the life of the old farm had come and gone, and maybe Elsie got used to the tides of mud at the doorway, the yard shared with poultry, the pig with her endless litters in a shed a few feet away. I wondered if her spirits ever sank when one of the three boys presented her with yet another set of mite-riddled antlers that she would have to boil in brine in the washing copper and mount with the others in the hall. If ever she did come up here to get away for an hour or two, maybe she, as I did, took a little secret pleasure in flinging any antlers she might come across into the impenetrable gorse bushes. She, too, might have thought how brittle and ancient they looked no matter how freshly cast they were, and how wintery, jutting from the walls of the hall like thorns from a thicket of dead trees behind the wainscoting. Yet she'd stayed, caring for the ugly house for over fifty years until she died there at the age of seventy-two. I learned from Elsie that, at least when it came to houses, it must be possible to love the unlovely, and I set my own mind and heart to it.

But in our time, Stoneyridge's decay advanced roughly in step with our attempts at transformation; we never got on top of it. We underestimated many things: the cost of repairs to the house and outbuildings and drains, the labor of clearing the rooty, low-yielding land, the attrition of the spirit wrought by winter after winter of rain and fog. Set against all that were the things we overestimated: our own skill, certainly, our power to learn from our mistakes, and, ultimately, our resilience to the drudgery of it all.

We seldom managed more than short bursts of energy or success at anything and so after a while we came to expect bad luck, and then, of course, bad luck was what we got. A new hen came to us with bronchitis that spread and killed the whole flock (antibiotics were out of the question), and the flock after that we lost all in one night to a fox. Roof repairs one October were undone in November by the worst storm that anyone could remember. I managed to get some of my weaving into a decent craft shop in Honiton, which went bust without paying me. One year I discovered a profitable flair for making green tomato chutney that for some reason I couldn't repeat; the two following years it turned out runny and bitter. And the one summer we managed to get enough bookings, mainly from Howard's old London friends, to launch the Alternative Spiritual Retreat (four weeks of meditation, yoga, pottery, weaving, and whole-meal food) turned out to be also the summer Adam was teething. He roared the house down night and day. Somebody wrote "Alternative, all right, but not in the way I was looking for" in the Visitors' Book.

The year after the teething disaster Howard spent a lot of money on a Hindu mystic. He came from Portsmouth, which struck a false note with me from the start, and turned up with two young robed followers who also exacted a month's bed and board from us. Only a handful of people attended the Stoneyridge Spirituality Summer School, advertised "with resident guru." The year after that Howard introduced earth healing and crystal therapy, but bookings were down again. We had yet to turn a profit on the smallholding produce or on my weaving or Howard's pots. After the following penniless winter we faced the necessity of opening the next year just for the holiday Bed and Breakfast trade, and although that brought us the custom, before the end of our first season I suspected that we weren't naturally hospitable people at all. By then our mediocrity was an entrenched and settled thing, our attempts at self-sufficiency a doomed round of chores. But we went on trying, growing wormy vegetables among the encroaching gorse and ragwort, keeping and losing livestock, turning out rough cloth and pottery, and painting our rooms with murals in harsh, desperate colors. Adam grew.

Now the vegetable plots we'd dug and redug stretched away from the far side of the house and down the hill, and with every year they retrenched a little, as more of the moor's thorn and reeds crept across their broken borders and rooted themselves where once we'd planted lines of brassicas, beans, and chard. Sheep and deer and ponies still tried to trample the fences, and rabbits and moles colonized the soil. I'd sown some lettuce seed this year and put in a few tomatoes, but I would forget about them for days on end and come across them parched and wilting or gone to seed or eaten by invaders. The out-side painting of the house never had been finished and the walls were strangely brindled where the newer patches of white were daubed against the old, unpainted pebbledash.

I walked on and over the ridge to the far side of the hill, and picked the heather quickly, tearing it up because I'd forgotten to bring cutters. The flowering season on the moor was ending early because of the drought; I pulled out the scorched and dead brown sprigs from the rest of the bunch, and threw them away.

When I got back to the ridge from where I could see the house again, I caught the glint of a silver car down on the narrow road. It slowed, then turned up our track. From there to the house took several minutes along nearly a mile of rough stones and ruts; even so, Adam would be at the house before I was. Though I knew it was pointless I waved and shouted, and I tried to hurry, but the ground was boggy and bumpy with tussocks and I kept looking up to see the progress of the car, and of course I fell, dropping all the heather in my hands and soaking myself in the oily, peaty water that lay in the deep cups molded in the mud by the hooves of sheep and ponies. I didn't care. Stained, stumbling all the way, not bothering to dodge the mud anymore, I got down the hill as fast as I could. Laughing and crying and terribly out of breath, I ran into the house by the front door.

In the sudden dark of the hall I could see only his silhouette, the head bowed and haloed against the half-glazed door at the back that led through to the kitchen. He was leafing through the bookings diary.

"Adam! Oh, Adam, darling, you're here! I'm so sorry, I was up on the moor! Look at me, I'm filthy, never mind, oh, Adam, give me a hug!"

The stranger stepped back. I pulled my hair away from my eyes, and my vision adjusted to the dimness. He wasn't and never could have been Adam, even in silhouette. He was shorter and probably around Howard's age. I saw that he looked antiseptically fastidious; his skin was taut and pink, the steely hair corrugated and obedient. He wore a cravat inside a standing-up shirt collar under a sweater with buttons along one shoulder.

"I'm sorry? Excuse me?" he said. He removed his glasses and stared at me. His lips twitched, then tilted into a smile that suddenly showed me to myself: a large middle-aged woman, ludicrously inelegant, panting and unkempt in a mud-spattered homemade dress.

I wiped my nose on my sleeve and tried to stare back. "I'm sorry, I was expecting my son," I said. "For a minute I thought you were him." I raised my hands to tidy my hair into a twist at the back of my head and a rank smell from my underarms escaped into the hall.

"I'm sorry, but the door was open. And I did call out, you know, a number of times, but I'm afraid nobody came." The man's voice was precise, the accent deliberately exquisite. He was smirking. His enlarged, capped teeth were a little yellow, but polished to a carnivorous sheen. "I'd like a room, please," he said. "Plus dinner, supper, whatever you call it. Anything as long as I don't have to get back in the car. I really cannot face any more driving today."

"I'm sorry. I'm expecting my son."

"Yes, yes—understood. No need to apologize. I hope you've got a double but a twin would do. I'm assuming it's en suite?"

"No, the thing is, I'm expecting my son. And you haven't got a booking, have you?"

He was surprised. "No, I haven't got a booking," he said. "But I only want one room. And you're not full." He nodded at the diary, open on the table.

"I'm expecting my son. We're closed."

The man looked down at his feet—he was wearing highly polished loafers—and pulled in a quiet, dramatic breath. "Madam," he said, looking up and straight at me, "the sign at the bottom of your drive says bed, breakfast, evening meal, and vacancies. It doesn't say *closed,* it says *vacancies,* and your book here is empty. It's nearly seven o'clock, and you are my last hope. I've driven the entire length of the coast from Minehead to Bideford and in circles over most of Exmoor, and everywhere else is full."

"Well, you'd expect that," I said. "It's the Bank Holiday weekend. It's always busy on Bank Holidays."

He raised his palms defensively. "I realize it's the Bank Holiday. I realize *now* I should've booked somewhere in advance. But I didn't. I had no idea it was going to be this difficult. And I cannot— I *cannot*—drive back to London tonight. My companion's going to—"

"There's two of you?"

"He's in the car. Didn't you see him?" I shook my head. He rolled his eyes. "Yet another cigarette. I suppose I should be glad he doesn't smoke in the car. He's in a foul mood."

He wiped a hand across his eyes and smiled a small smile that I sensed was supposed to make me complicit in some not very pleasant truth. I said, "I'm sorry, but there's nothing I can do."

"Madam, forgive me," he said with the same unfriendly smile, "but there *is* something you can do. You can please take pity, and let me have a room for *one night*." He tapped the open page of the booking diary. "Which you are able to do, aren't you? Oh. Wait. Oh—*oh!* Oh, I see." Suddenly he was gazing at me with open distaste, nodding his head. "I *see*. So that's it. Good God. Of course."

"I'm sorry, what do you mean?"

"Of course." He took a step toward the door. "Amazing, how it can still take one by surprise. One forgets, in London. Still plenty of it around, though, obviously, in the sticks."

"Plenty of what? What are you talking about?"

"Oh, come *on*." His pompous manners failed him for a moment and his voice turned harsh and shaky, as if he were speaking to someone who'd threatened to hit him. "Homophobia, that's what I'm talking about. I should've known. Good to see that rampant bigotry is still alive and well." He recovered himself. "Well, thank you. And good day."

"It's not bigotry!" I said. "It's not that at all! Look, I'm sorry—"

He shrugged. "It was only for one night." He looked around at the antlers overhead with their festoons of spider threads, the carpet dotted with mismatched rugs. "Still, clearly business is booming. Obviously you're in a position to turn away undesirables."

"Look, you're completely wrong. *Please*," I said. "We're not like that. It's only because my son's expected today. That's all it is, honestly. Please don't think we're like that here."

He paused. "Really? So what is your usual rate? Oh, no, don't tell me, you don't take one-night bookings on Bank Holiday weekends? All right, I'll pay for two. Come on, what do you charge?"

"The double's seventy-five pounds a night," I blurted. I'd added ten pounds to put him off but out loud it sounded so outrageously high that I added, "Of course that includes breakfast."

"I'm serious," he said. "I'll pay you for two. A hundred and fifty. All right?" I couldn't reply. The man sighed, pressed a thumb and forefinger against his closed lids and rubbed his eyes, then looked hard at me. "Please, just help me out? I'm exhausted. My companion's upset—so *I'm* upset. Please."

I still wanted to say no. He was still being condescending, and I didn't want him here, so dapper and looking down on everything, never mind his invisible, bad-tempered companion. But a hundred and fifty pounds. And Adam would help me with everything; with Adam here, it would even be fun. I'd spent a lot on the joint of pork, and the picnic, and a sweater for his birthday present and all the rest of it, it had added up. A hundred and fifty would set me straight for the month, with a little over.

"And you'll charge for dinner on top, of course," he said.

"Dinner would be eighteen pounds. Per person," I said. I never charged more than twelve. "And I could only do table d'hôte, I'm afraid. I'm not geared up for much, not tonight."

"Table d'hôte will be fine," the man said. He smiled genuinely for the first time. "Something smells delicious, anyway."

The scent of the roasting pork was filling the hall, and for a moment I wondered if, actually, our place could seem quite welcoming in a shabby, out-of-date, misleading way. I could hear this man, back in London, saying in his clippy voice, *Oh, and we ended up in a hilarious little place—complete time warp, run by some mad middle-aged hippie in a purple dress!*

"I'm afraid that's not on the table d'hôte," I said quickly. "That's for something else. And we're not licensed."

"Then I'll expect to pay corkage," the man said. "We have some wine with us. I'm in the trade, actually. I'll get the bags."

While the man was out fetching his luggage I checked the answering machine for a message from Adam: nothing. I hurried upstairs and changed out of my muddy dress, and when I came back the man was in the hall with a small suitcase and a backpack. There was still no sign of the companion. I showed him up to the double room at the front with the bay window. He tested the mattress, pressing his fingers into it a couple of times, and he raised an eyebrow when I showed him that the bathroom was next door and not en suite, but he didn't comment. He must have been pleased with the view from the window. I told him that dinner would be served at a quarter to eight.

I took the pork out of the oven. It was the largest piece of meat I'd cooked for years and it spat and gleamed in its tin, filling the kitchen like a personality, some exciting, extrovert guest of honor. It was almost done and smelled wonderful. Howard had got himself up and was watching television with the sound down, and even though he didn't take much interest in food anymore he craned round in his chair and gazed through to the kitchen, so he must have been hungry. But the connection between his stomach and brain didn't always work properly and he could be hungry without being fully aware of it, and I was glad about that because he was going to have to wait. It was just after a quarter past seven and in another hour the meat would be perfect, by which time Adam would be here. I turned the oven down as low as possible, covered the joint with foil, and put it back in. What I had to do next was get the two guests fed and out of the way. I loaded a tray with a paper cloth and cutlery and glasses, and took it to the dining room.

I opened the door to silence. They were both there, sitting at the big table in the middle. *Our* table. The man's companion had his back to me. A bottle of wine stood open, and already they were using the glasses. "Oh, I'm sorry," I said. "This isn't your table. I'm afraid I'll have to move you."

I dragged one of the small tables from the stack at the far end and set it on its legs in a corner of the room, and started laying it. Before I had finished, the older man got up, took the wine bottle and both glasses, and seated himself at the new table. His companion didn't budge.

"Our hostess prefers us to sit here," the man called over to him. "So perhaps you would be good enough to move, and thereby oblige her. I realize that obliging *me* is out of the question."

The young man pulled himself to his feet, crossed the floor, and threw himself into the other chair without looking at either of us. He was tall and rangy, and might have been rather strongly built but it was difficult to tell from his baggy clothes. His straight dark hair fell forward and across his face; all I could really see was a jutting chin and a grim, unhappy mouth. He took a long swig from his wineglass, sat back with his eyes closed, and began an exaggerated, regular nodding of his head; I saw the white strings of his iPod snaking down from his ears. He was behaving like a teenager but could have been any age between twenty and thirty.

The older man reached across and lifted the wine bottle. "A Tempranillo and Tinto Fino blend," he announced, "from the Toro region of Spain. Pintia 2006." There was no reply. "This is a pretty good wine. You might take some interest."

The young man opened his eyes. "What does it matter where it's from?" he said. He drank again from his glass. "I'm not that bothered about wine," he added, unnecessarily.

The man sighed, poured the last drops into his own glass, and handed me the empty bottle with a half-smile that showed his big teeth and the inner edges of his lips, stained dark. From a carrier bag on the floor he drew another identical bottle and a corkscrew. As I finished laying the table he pulled the cork and passed it slowly under his nose.

"I suppose it's too much to hope this could be decanted," he said to me. "But it should at least breathe for twenty minutes. Perhaps you would set the bottle on the sideboard?"

Before I could take it from him his companion grabbed it, filled his glass fast, and thumped the bottle back on the table. He took three or four hard gulps.

"There you are," he said, wiping his mouth. "I'm taking some interest."

I didn't dare look at either of them. I hated them both; what were they doing here at all? I carried the new bottle to the sideboard and took the empty one back to the kitchen.

I opened a tin of sardines and a jar of cockles in brine, and sliced a couple of tomatoes, then arranged everything on two plates with some lettuce and slices of lemon. I sprinkled on some dried marjoram; there were chives and a woody bit of parsley in the garden but I hadn't time to go picking herbs. I couldn't have taken more than fifteen minutes over it, but when I took the plates to the dining room the bottle from the sideboard was on the table and had been started.

Both men were slumped back in their chairs, but at least they weren't arguing.

"Marine medley," I said, setting down the plates. Neither of them spoke. Just as I reached the door, the older man called, "Oh, bread! May we have some bread?"

But when I went back to the kitchen, Howard was on his feet. He needed to pee and wouldn't go by himself, so I had to attend to him first. When I got back to the dining room with the bread, the second bottle was nearly empty. The food had barely been touched.

By now Howard was getting confused and restless. Usually I fed him around six o'clock, in front of the television, and he had got up again and was trying with one hand to pull his tray table across in front of his chair. I tried to reassure him that Adam would be here soon; I told him that he'd have to be patient a little longer, that I was busy with some last minute B & B guests, but he just shrugged my hand off his shoulder and refused to let me help him settle back in his chair. He lurched and lowered himself into it and sat glaring. I put our potatoes in the oven to roast and made him a banana sandwich to keep him going. He flicked it around on the plate and looked at me as if I were trying to poison him.

I'd been going through in my mind what on earth I could produce for the guests' dinner. It was a long time since we'd had much passing trade and I didn't keep big stocks of food. There was plenty of pork, but it was out of the question that I should give them that and so present Adam with the joint already carved into, in less than its full splendor. I defrosted some chicken joints in boiling water and put some rice on. I found peas in the freezer, too, so I cooked those while I sautéed the chicken in a frying pan with a shake of Worcestershire sauce, for color. There was a can of condensed mushroom soup that would do for sauce, with a knob of butter. When it was ready I served it all up as nicely as I could and told them it was chicken fricassee. There had been a long wait, but most of the marine medley was still on their plates. The room reeked of alcohol; one of them had knocked over a glass and their twisted napkins lay sodden in a pool of wine where the paper cloth had disintegrated. I didn't comment, nor did they. For dessert I sliced two bananas and stirred them into custard out of a tin, and sprinkled some crushed biscuits over the top. When I took it in, they were still sitting in front of their plates of chicken, so I set it on the sideboard. It was a quarter to nine and I didn't have time to waste attending to them any longer. Just as I was telling them to help themselves to dessert when they were ready, the telephone rang. It would be Adam, needing a lift from Taunton station. I rushed out to the hall and picked up.

Adam was in Barcelona.

"Mum, I just got your email. Look, I'm really sorry. You obviously took it the wrong way about me getting the time off, it doesn't work like that. I've got no choice in the matter. I'm sorry but I thought you knew the score."

I couldn't speak, except to say, "Barcelona? *Barcelona?*"

Oh, hadn't he said he might go? He was sure he had, maybe some time ago. It was never really on the cards he'd get a whole week off, he certainly had told me that. They would only give him four days in the end, he went on, so he'd grabbed the chance and gone off to Barcelona with a couple of guys from the Marseilles office. They were staying at this cool place just off the Ramblas. One of them knew someone with a yacht.

"Barcelona's amazing. You ever been? You really should go," he said.

"Adam, we're expecting you here. I thought you'd be ringing from the station. We've been waiting all day. Everything's ready."

"Oh God, Mum, look, I'm sorry! I really am. But I don't understand how you got the idea it was ever definite."

"You never said it *wasn't* definite."

"Sorry, Mum, but yes I did. I did say I wasn't sure I could make it."

I didn't reply.

"Mum, I've had site meetings back to back for three weeks, I'm going from one place to the other, I'm on five planes every three days, I couldn't ring before, okay? Plus the backlog in the office is worse now, they very nearly didn't even give me the four days. Four days isn't worth the hassle of getting to the UK, is it?"

"Isn't it?"

"You know it isn't. It's practically another whole day just to get to you from Heathrow. Look, I *am* sorry, really I am. It would've been great to catch up with you guys. I worry about you, you know. I worry a lot. But I never promised, I *couldn't* promise. Maybe later in the year, okay?"

"I hope so, dear. I do hope so. Maybe Christmas?"

"Yes! Yeah, Christmas might be *very* possible. I'll try and swing it, I'll really try. Mum, I'm truly sorry, okay? I'll ring you tomorrow. Love to Dad. Take care now, okay? Talk soon. Bye!"

It was after nine o'clock by the time I was able to go back and clear the dishes. The third wine bottle was empty and the older man was slumped forward at the table, too drunk to care about pretending not to be. I think the younger man might have been crying; he turned his face away from me as I came in. The unfinished chicken lay on the plates cut open to the bone, the flesh pink and injured-looking. The bananas and custard were untouched on the sideboard. I didn't offer them coffee or wish them goodnight. Back in the kitchen I gave Howard a slice of the pork and some roast potatoes, cut up so he could manage with a spoon, but he didn't eat much. When I told him Adam wasn't coming he behaved as if he hadn't heard. I got him to bed without either of us speaking again, and went up to my own room.

ADAM'S BIRTHDAY 2004

On the morning of his twenty-first birthday Adam stayed in bed, intending to shorten the day by avoiding his parents for as long as possible but unsure if the effect wasn't actually to lengthen it. For ages he'd lain wide awake but now was tired again. He yawned, pulling the cool of the room into his mouth and catching a web of mucus in his throat that made him cough in a way that reminded him of his father. His teeth were furry. It was after eleven o'clock and he hoped he'd lingered long enough to undo his mother's hopes of a birthday breakfast; he didn't do breakfast, at least not here and least of all the birthday kind. He remembered other birthday breakfasts, being expected to smile before he was properly awake, eating through gritted teeth the porridge made "special" in some awful way, mixed with nuts or rhubarb or something, and never being able to show he thought his presents "special" enough to see the worry clear from his mother's face. Hardest of all was pretending not to notice how uncomfortable everyone was with the whole idea of "special." He couldn't face any of that today. He'd only been here two days and already he'd run out of energy for play-acting the prodigal son. But he ought to get up.

From downstairs he heard his mother treading through the hall from the kitchen, then a click as the front sitting room door opened. In a moment he would hear triple clunks as (one) she dropped the vacuum cleaner, (two) plugged it in, and (three) switched it on, followed by the rising drone as she went scraping along the carpet. In advance, his heart sank with the predictability of it, this series of familiar, comfortless sounds from childhood that meant B & B guests were booked in that night. The extra work for his mother always made Adam feel unreasonably guilty, as if the general atmosphere of reluctance that hung around the very idea of B & B guests came only from him. He yawned again. Just then his father's voice rolled through the hall, calling out to her. Something about the pottery kiln, something not good judging by the peeved, high pitch of his voice. Probably another complaint about Digger, most likely over the logs for the firing he was supposed to be doing today. His mother's answer sounded breathy and clipped as if she were talking to a child with the last remnant of her patience, and although the problems with the firing weren't Adam's fault either, her sad, even voice made him feel guiltier still. The vacuum cleaner started. Downstairs, the conversation seemed to be over. He ought to get up.

Instead he tried to turn his mind to Melanie and interest his penis in the attentions of his right hand, but the sounds that had intruded into the room intensified the idea of his parents, and threatened to bring an image of them—each alone, not together—almost before his eyes. He worked his hand harder. Then, as if from a distance, he saw a picture of himself—a young man sprawled on a heap of bedclothes with his eyes closed, trying to induce a forlorn, masturbatory oblivion that would postpone for a few moments longer the dismay of his twenty-first birthday. Instantly, he went limp. He rolled over and swore, hating the way he could ambush himself like this, by simply holding up an imaginary mirror that confronted him with his own lonely, overwhelmingly pathetic reflection. All at once he seemed even more lonely and pathetic than his parents, and his cock, flopping in his hand, even more lonely and pathetic than the rest of him. Melanie vanished from his thoughts, at least the carnal ones; they'd broken up weeks ago, anyway. She wasn't really the point. If he was being honest, for the first two months they'd been together he'd been a bit bored except when he was in bed with her, and for the final two he'd been bored there as well. And guilty for the entire four, because she was a genuinely nice person and deserved better. Beyond the four months, he'd gone on feeling guilty because he'd been too busy working for his finals to miss her all that much, and by the time they were done with, too tired.

Now feeling self-conscious and a little disgusted, Adam withdrew his hand and cupped the back of his head on the flattened pillow. Could he go back to sleep? He closed his eyes and exhaled. But he heard the vacuum cleaner stop and the clump of his mother's footsteps, and could not help seeing in his mind her leathery bare feet as she trudged in her clogs back to the kitchen and set about another of the jobs she would have liked him to be helping her with. He ought to get up.

As well as the clogs, she'd probably be wearing the same mottled brown skirt as yesterday. He hated the skirt, which she'd sewn from a bit of her home-woven fabric that she said was "naturally slubbed." It looked like sackcloth dotted with rabbit droppings. The weave was so uneven and loose it bagged at the back where her buttocks strained and rubbed it to a brown sheen, and in front it made a sling for the crescent-shaped pillow of her stomach and dropped like a curtain over her knees. He wondered why he could imagine her in expensive, beautiful clothes when he'd never seen her in any, and why the thought made him feel like crying.

Now he could hear a van straining up the track, probably Digger's pickup with the logs in the back. Adam yawned again. He should go and put in an appearance in the yard and back his father up when, as almost certainly it would, some spat started, about the price of the logs, the late delivery, whatever. Or he should go and feign some interest in the firing, at least; he hadn't even asked Howard last night what he had ready for the kiln because the firings were so hit-and-miss it was better not to get any hopes up. Adam had heard enough about the fickle variables of clay and mineral quality and ambient temperature to last a lifetime, and as for his father's experimental modifications to the loading, fueling, timing, and cooling of the kiln, never mind his specific errors—the blistered glazes, the vessels exploding because he'd trapped a bubble of air inside— well, it wasn't unknown for those to cost him every single piece in the firing. Adam had found that the less he heard about the technicalities the easier it was to commiserate with genuine sympathy for all the wasted effort.

Now Digger's dog started barking and Adam heard the rumble of the logs sliding from the pickup into the yard. The van coughed and revved, turned, and chugged back down the track. After that, silence. Adam knew that from his room at the front he would not hear the soft thuds as Howard lobbed logs into the wheelbarrow, nor the squeak of the wheel as he trundled it round to the outbuilding behind the studio that housed the kiln, nor the returning squeak, and more thuds. It took one person two hours to shift enough wood for a firing. Adam got up.

His parents came in and drank coffee while he opened his birthday present, a thick check shirt from the outdoor shop in Exeter where his mother bought him the clothes and boots that he only ever wore when he visited and that stayed in the house when he left. Didn't she ever notice that his own clothes were completely different, that he was never going to feel comfortable in the things she gave him to wear? No, she really didn't, he thought, listening as she told him she'd spent forever choosing the color and was wondering if the dark green was right, she could change it if he wanted. She never did seem to realize the effect of what she was doing, that it so often produced the opposite outcome to the one she hoped for.

"No, I really like it," he said. "Thank you *very* much."

She smiled, and poured him more coffee. The trickle from the pot drew too much attention to the sudden silence among them.

"Oh, Adam, twenty-one!" she said wildly. "Where's the time gone? Flown by! All grown up! I can't believe it. Howard, can you believe it?" Howard, as if he'd been a bystander at the past twenty-one years, shook his head.

Adam could believe it, though. What he couldn't believe was that his mother could come out with such remarks without irony or embarrassment. It would shock her to learn how very *long* in passing the twenty-one years seemed to him, how far away and aloof from his childhood he felt and had perhaps always wanted to feel. But then, pretty much everything shocked her, because she hadn't a clue what was really going on half the time, not even in her own mind let alone anyone else's. She had no idea, for example, that he hated the big fuss she made of his birthday, that he couldn't stand the way she acted all incredulous and relieved as if it was a surprise to her that the date came around every year—what else did she expect? But she'd always been like that, taken aback by the obvious, never knowing with any conviction anything beyond the obvious. Never really *thinking*, because that way she could let the stupidest things go on appearing to be important. Birthday picnics, for example. It made him furious that she would go to all that trouble when, with or without B & B guests, she was always busy and mostly tired. No, that wasn't the truth; what made him furious was that all the effort she made forced him to be spectacularly grateful, when all he wished for was that she would just stop making it. He couldn't find it in himself to tell her that the birthday picnics were pointless, that even when he was little they hadn't been that much fun. Instead, year after year, overwhelmed by the same paralyzing surge of tact, he went along with the fucking birthday picnic, furious that his gratitude made him complicit in the pretense that everything was lovely.

It wasn't even that he *wasn't* grateful, exactly. It just took it out of him, the strenuous show of appreciation for the dredged-up "favorite" picnic recipes, the clumsy baking, the finger-crossing for a fine day; it all brought a lump to his throat. But he could never withhold his gratitude. She would be hurt. Another thing for which Adam had always felt unreasonably and painfully accountable was how easily she was hurt.

At least this year the picnic would be short, because the firing that should have got under way first thing still hadn't been started. With a bit of luck (or mismanagement on Howard's part) there might not be enough time at all. That would be easiest, really. He couldn't quite picture himself giving them the news he had to give them up there on the windy moor; the kitchen with the flat ticking clock was a more amenable setting for difficult news and of course would allow him a quicker getaway than the desolate trudge back down from the picnic. He watched his mother clear away the paper she'd wrapped the shirt in, folding it to keep, and bit his lip to prevent any observation about another of her futile little economies. He merely vowed privately, sucking in his breath, that never, ever, no matter how poor he might be, would he recycle a bit of wrapping paper.

Adam heaved himself from his chair, carried their coffee cups to the sink, and made for the door to the hall.

"You will wear it today, won't you?" his mother said. "I'm dying to see it on."

Adam returned and picked up the shirt. "'Course. I'll put it on later. Don't want to get it dirty helping with the logs, do I?"

She didn't reply. Both his parents had weird and awkward smiles on their faces.

"What?" he said.

"Surprise!" his mother said. "Birthday surprise! Picnic surprise! Nobody's doing logs. We're going for a lovely *early* walk up on the moor and the birthday picnic!"

Jesus Christ, he thought, does she think I'm ten years old? "Mum, really, as far as I'm concerned the birthday's no big deal, honest," he said. "I mean, it's great of you to do it and everything but there's lots to get on with here, isn't there? Dad's doing a firing. We can leave off the picnic, can't we? I don't need a picnic. I'm twenty-one, not twelve."

"But that's *why*," she said. "Twenty-one! Of course we're having a birthday picnic! Oh Adam, your face! Howard, tell him!"

Howard ran his fingers through his majestic hair. "I'm not doing a firing. There isn't enough stuff ready to fill the kiln," he said. His voice was heavy with resignation at his lack of productivity. "I'm not in the studio so much these days." He lifted his eyes and stared nobly out of the window. Jesus Christ, Adam thought. He's actually proud of how little he does, he wants me to applaud it. How does he do it? How does he turn making nothing into something more significant than making a lot?

He asked, "Really? So if you're not in the studio, what *are* you doing? You can't be hoeing lettuces the whole time."

Howard removed a beard hair from his mouth. "Your mother wanted you to think I was doing a firing so the picnic would be more of a surprise," he said. "Even though there's always a picnic on your birthday."

"I wanted it to be a *special* surprise!" Deborah said, laughing.

"Oh Mum," Adam said, smiling as hard as he could manage. To his father he said, "So, no firing."

"Well, indeed, no. A firing's a firing. And a picnic's a picnic," Howard said slowly and expectantly, as if some point to the words might occur to someone once he'd spoken them aloud.

"And the sheep are the sheep, remember," his wife said, sighing and rising from the table. "They need checking. You didn't go up yesterday."

"They're fine now they're sheared. I'll check them today. You still haven't washed the fleeces."

"Well, anyway," Deborah said, "thank goodness Digger's brought some logs up at last, in case you *do* do a firing."

"I'm not in a position to do a firing."

"But if you were, now you can."

"I don't know I can, even if I did do one. No two firings are the same. And I'm not doing one, so either way it's the same, there's no difference. Any more than you haven't washed the fleeces yet."

"What's no difference? The same as what? You just said no two *were* the same."

"That's not what I mean. It was you that brought up the fleeces. Anyway, of course they're never the same."

All this was conducted in a placid, secure shared rhythm, as together Deborah and Howard washed and dried the coffee cups. Adam gazed from one parent to the other and wondered how long it had been since either of them had spoken more than a couple of words to anyone but the other. He began to wonder if they were going mad. Certainly they were becoming the kind of people who use words without meaning anything by them at all, people whose conversation, to the ears of any sane person, was a doomed verbal chase down a rabbit hole after sense and understanding.

Later, walking up the track behind his mother, Adam tried to collect the words he would need to tell her he was leaving that night. He knew from the way she was walking, in slow easy strides, her head tipping now and then upward to the sky, that she was for the moment happy; he yearned to keep her so and at the same time wished that her happiness had nothing to do with him. His bag was packed and waiting in his bedroom, his clapped-out old Nissan was in the yard. Let his father, lagging some way behind, take care of her happiness.

Each of them walked alone and spaced out from the others. After an hour or so they'd gone as far up the moor as they usually went, to the old stand of trees under the ridge. Deborah threw down the rug on a patch of grass and Adam kicked away a few thistles and the scattering of rabbit and sheep droppings nearby. Over the ridge and away to the left, their sheep grazed the edge of the damp wooded combe that ran downward, slicing deep into the hill. The afternoon had clouded over and the trees sprouting in the crack of the gulley were almost black in the shadows.

The wind was too brisk for wasps or mosquitoes but also too brisk to sit in comfortably for long. It was also, to Adam's relief, too windy to light the birthday cake candles, though his mother went through a whole box of matches in the attempt. Eventually she handed out slices of cake with her large cold hands and they ate fast, with a pretense of appetite. Deborah had brought ice cream but didn't have any herself, and Adam discreetly tipped most of his into the ground. Howard fed his into his mouth without a glimmer of pleasure. His silence had deepened into a sulk; it occurred to Adam that his father never did enjoy anything that was somebody else's idea. Within twenty minutes the picnic was over. Adam, in a show of tired contentment, leaned back and closed his eyes, wondering how soon he could decently begin his leave-taking speech. Howard murmured something about checking the sheep and wandered off. A few moments later when Deborah let out a long, stagy sigh and said wasn't it all lovely, Adam pretended to be asleep.

Another picture of Melanie flashed into his mind, and for a moment he imagined bringing her up here and fucking her on the picnic rug. It was the sort of thing that would make her laugh. Maybe he'd text her later. Maybe if they got together again he'd be able to like her properly—after all, she was great, really. Thinking about it, fucking anybody up here on the rug would be pretty good, wouldn't it? But the idea would not take hold, or rather everything about the idea except the actual fucking depressed him. The rug depressed him, the surrounding thistles and animal turds depressed him. Being up on the moor depressed him. It bored him. He sat up and looked around. He hated the whole place. His mother was sitting on a rock with her eyes closed, clasping her bent knees and smiling up at the sky. Her lower legs were veined and hairy. The brown skirt had ridden up and Adam could see the backs of her thighs, somehow vulnerable for all that they were so big. Didn't she know she was revealing all that flesh, or did she know and not care? How did she manage to make such a thing of sitting and saying nothing, being so carefully quiet as if she were a child and still making up her mind how to behave?

Howard had stopped on the moorside several yards away and taken up a shepherdlike pose, staring across the ridge at his sheep, one hand folded over the head of his stick, the other stroking his beard. He was wearing a baggy smock that flapped girlishly around his body and his long hair streamed out behind him. Just then Deborah opened her eyes and called out to him, and he raised a hand, turned, and made his way slowly back. Maybe I am not normal, Adam thought. Maybe something in me is distorted. I am twenty-one years old, not a resentful adolescent anymore, but it really could be the case that I hate my parents.

After Howard sat down again Adam waited another ten minutes, during which there was a bit more offering and taking of picnic food. Nobody spoke much.

"Listen, I'm sorry it's a bit of a flying visit, this," he said. "I did tell you, didn't I? I need to be off a bit later."

"Off? Off where?" his mother said. "You don't mean *today*? Where are you off to?"

"I have to go back to Leicester."

"But you've just finished at Leicester," Howard said.

"Oh, you mean go back to pack up your things? Will you get everything in your car?" his mother asked. "Shall I come up in the van as well? We could all go up!"

"No, I mean I'm going back properly, to stay. For another two years. I'm doing an MBA." His parents didn't speak. "It's a postgraduate degree. Master of Business Administration. It's all sorted, I've been accepted. Term starts last week of September."

"Another degree?" Howard said. "And what would be the point of that?" The question wasn't neutral, of course. Part of Howard's credo of the general fucked-up-ness of the world's systems and institutions was that formal education was shallow and overrated. Adam knew that when he'd demanded to be allowed to go to school after ten years of home schooling, he'd defected from one of his father's core beliefs. He also knew while anger was against Howard's principles (all those negative energies), he'd never really got over it.

"A master of what did you say, *Business Administration?*" his mother said. "But you've just spent three years doing *Business Studies*. Won't it just be more of the same thing?" She picked out the words as if she were naming a disease, or a vice.

"Look, there's no point arguing about it. I'm doing an MBA. I'm not asking you for anything, I'll be paying for it."

"But what for, Adam? *Why* do you want to do it?" Deborah asked.

Adam ground his back teeth. A typical Mum question, while what she would never, ever ask was *how* he was doing it, how he would manage to pay for it all. She wouldn't be interested that he'd be working his arse off for the next two years to earn enough to live on as well as study. He said, "Mum, the MBA—it's a recognized thing. Everybody knows about the MBA. It's a . . . a sort of passport, okay? It helps you get a better career." He cleared his throat. "*Everybody* knows that."

"I've never heard of it," his father said.

No, you wouldn't, would you, Adam thought. You make certain you never hear about anything real, anything that's part of the real world. He shrugged. "Well, just about everybody else has. Everybody but you and Mum knows an MBA gets you a higher starting salary, for one thing. Faster promotion. An MBA,"—he paused to draw breath for the next bit—"an MBA represents a high-recognition, value-added skillset with high transferability potential across a wide range of industry sectors."

That struck them dumb, as he intended.

But only for a moment. Howard snorted. "Oh, I see, a higher starting salary. Money. Of course," he said. "An MBA—Money Before Anything. Eh? Big salary, flash car—oh, yes. Thoughtless consumption, is that what you want? Selling your soul in the process." He paused. "One day, Adam, I hope you'll find out there are more important things than money."

"Oh, yes? And what would they be?" Adam said. "Really. What things? I mean, for instance, what have you got that's so much better than money?"

"Adam!" his mother said.

He stood up. "No, really. Go on, Dad, tell me. What? Your mangy sheep, your dump of a smallholding?"

Howard had assumed the stillness of a stone figure, staring into the wind, and did not look at him.

"Adam, please—don't," his mother said.

"It's okay, forget it," Adam said. "We've had this conversation before, anyway. We'll never agree."

He meant it. He'd always known his own attitude to money to be unromantic, unlike his parents'; even as a child he could see that nothing worked without it. Whether you liked it or not, money was necessary the way oil was necessary to the working of all machines, from a jet engine to a door hinge. On a personal level you couldn't get moving at all without at least some, and plenty of it made things run nice and smoothly. Adam intended always to have plenty. He'd tried explaining this. But his parents, even though they were too short of money to be casual about it, went on behaving as if it were somehow optional to survival, never mind happiness. Later, he tried to put what he was learning at university into practice and intervene in the finances of the smallholding, but he couldn't get them to grasp even the basics; they simply didn't believe anything he told them about markets, or product development, or demand and supply. They went on regarding earnings from their handicrafts as a kind of tip, a bonus awarded in recognition of some superior moral quality that they felt attached to them because they didn't set out to make big profits. They were chronically puzzled that more people didn't appreciate that their pottery and weaving were "worth" the prices they asked, and of course they were chronically poor.

Adam didn't ask any more how much they had to live on, any more than they asked him how much his student loan came to now he'd graduated or how he'd managed to put in thirty hours a week behind a bar and still work for his degree. The loom shed and pottery were virtually derelict now, though they kept on with the vegetables and the sheep and hens and sometimes a goat or two. Well, God help them. All along his parents had aimed to live on as little money as possible, so they'd got what they wanted.

"You're entitled to your opinions," he said. "And I'm entitled to mine. And now I'm sorry but I have to go."

Deborah was snatching up the paper plates and spoons and cups and jamming them into the bag. She began to cry. "Adam, please. It's all right. Surely you don't need to rush off today. Don't go. Adam, it's your birthday. Please . . ."

"Sorry, Mum," Adam said. "Thanks for the picnic. I'm really sorry but I have to rush. I'll be in touch. See you."

No, I don't hate them, he thought as he strode off down the hill, but I cannot stand being with them a minute longer, and I have to get out of here before I start crying, too.

I didn't put on a light or undress or draw the curtains. I was glad to be tired, and I climbed in under the quilt and after a while I managed to fall asleep and did not wake until around five o'clock, when the birds started up. I lay with my eyes closed, trying not to hear them and listening instead to the house, tuning in to the lonely acoustic of the time before the day began, its echoes and rattles: the dawn wind that swept between the hillside and the back of the house and around its north-easterly angle, a fresh resonance over floors and walls. A series of coughs like the crushing of dried leaves came from Howard's room directly below mine and I waited for his voice, calling to me. But he just stirred a little and settled, and my heartbeat softened. From the double room at the front, far away down the corridor and around the corner on to the landing, not a sound came.

I'd thought it was the birds that had woken me. But then I heard two or three furtive thuds—quiet footsteps, a downstairs door closing—and they were familiar, a reprise of sounds of movement that must have broken my sleep in the first place. Outside, at the front of the house, a car engine started.

I got up and hurried round to the landing. Through the wide-open door of the double room I could see towels and bedclothes strewn over the floor. I knocked, but of course the room was empty. From the window I watched the silver car bump away down the track. On the mattress, placed inside a folded sheet of paper, were two ten pound notes. On the paper was written:

Madam, notwithstanding the unexpectedness of our arrival, your standards of accommodation, food, and, in particular, welcome and service have been deplorable. Enclosed is what I in a generous mood consider the stay with you to have been worth. It was an appalling experience. Goodbye.

I returned to the window and watched the car, now almost halfway to the road. It took the sharp left turn in the track and disappeared behind the line of wind-tormented hawthorn trees that clung in a ragged line down the hillside. I sank on to the edge of the bed and read the note again, trying to be angry but just feeling ashamed. What he'd written was true. I'd been so anxious about Adam I'd made no attempt to look after the guests well, I'd done nothing to make them comfortable. And Adam was not coming. He never had been going to come. I'd wanted so badly something I never was going to get, I'd poured all that effort into trying to make it real. I'd wasted money, too, and now I didn't have enough to see us to the end of the month.

Another day alone with Howard was beginning. Beyond this one, countless more stretched ahead. I began to cry. One of Howard's nurses had told me once it was common, only natural in fact, for caregivers to give way now and then; it helped to have a little cry. But there was nothing little about this. My whole body began to shake. Great sobs burst from me; I crossed my arms and clutched my shoulders tight to try to hold them in, I gulped mouthfuls of air, but I could not stop them. I mashed the heels of my hands against my eyes but more tears spurted from them. I could scarcely get my breath. I was afraid the noise would wake Howard and upset him and we would start the day badly, and three hours too early, yet I could not stop.

Howard knew he hadn't lost his mind, but he also knew bits of it had been mislaid. He did think of it as in bits. The idea of damage to his actual brain he found quite unmanageable—squeamishness alone prevented him from thinking about the soft wet ropes inside his skull—so instead he pictured his mind as a clean, glass globe, like an old-fashioned fisherman's float, that once had been buoyant and shiny and cool to the touch but was now broken, its pieces scattered. He would imagine himself trying to sweep them all up in a pile and glue them back together using only one hand, a Sisyphean labor of atonement for his failure to appreciate how fragile a thing it had been in the first place, and how fugitive now its millions of shards and splinters.

So bits were missing, still precious and searched for daily as if lost under furniture, and every day losing a little more luster and sharpness under gathering dust. Some days he could summon one faculty but not the partnering one that was needed to make it work: he might have ready in his head all the words he wanted to say but be unable to make his tongue deliver them, or he might feel himself quite able to talk, but not to chase out even the simplest words from his memory and bring them to his lips. His right hand and leg worked only when they felt like it, his left hand and leg hardly at all. Without warning, his guts seemed to forget what it was they were supposed to do with food and would create urgent and chaotic stomach upsets, at other times his jaws refused to chew. His sight could no longer be trusted; gathering information from his eyes and ears and making sense of both at once was seldom successful. The world had

rearranged itself into two continents, and each eye scanned a different, opposing landscape, each ear was tuned to a different time zone;
most unnerving of all, each continent had a habit of slipping out of
existence while he was attending to the other. Moving objects, especially people, startled him with their arbitrary flitting between the
two, and sometimes they disappeared altogether, making a fool of
him for having thought them real. He wept copiously and often, and
sometimes he laughed when nothing was funny. He was angry nearly
all the time.

Then there were what Deborah called his shut-downs, days when
he would sit in his chair worn out, saddened, afraid to move or eat
or to hear or say anything at all. It was impossible to explain that he
wasn't being "difficult," but simply could not face being present in a
world so unreliable and alarming. With his eyes closed, and keeping
very still, he would try to hold himself aloof from all the humiliating
lapses and betrayals of his body and mind and by so doing, he hoped,
stave off any fuller comprehension of the disastrous turn his life had
taken.

After a while I stopped crying but I stayed where I was, sitting on the bed with my eyes closed and my hands over my face. It struck me much later that I must have sat there for a long time, waiting like a child hoping for a surprise, as if I knew he would make an appearance. (I didn't, of course; how could I?) And how strange it was that he made not a breath of sound. He approached so silently that not even the air stirred, yet the moment I became aware of him, I wasn't surprised. He must have entered the room on bare feet without touching the open door, and he sat down next to me on the bed so softly as to cause not even the slightest shifting of the mattress. I knew of his presence by neither sight, sound, nor movement, nor any other measure of the senses, but only by his presence, about which there was something pure. My breathing eased a little but I kept my hands over my face. I knew he was there without having to turn to look at him.

"I was in the other room. I heard you crying," he said. He hadn't spoken to me at all the night before and his voice, while not familiar, was exactly as I knew it would be: young but not boyish, and shy. "I slept in the other room. I hope that was all right."

"What other room? Not the one next door? That's my son's bed-room! How dare you!"

"No, no, the back one. That little one past the bathroom, at the back. I'm sorry if I shouldn't have."

"Oh, well. No, I suppose that's all right. That's the other Bed and Breakfast room." He said nothing to that. "But you only had one room booked," I said.

I felt him shrug beside me, not by a touch but by a faint warmth, both male and childish, as if he'd moved fractionally but tentatively closer. Still I had not turned to look at him.

"I'm sorry. But I had to go and sleep somewhere else."

I didn't want to hear any of this. It was all quite irregular, sitting here on a bed with a Bed and Breakfast guest. "Even so. You can't just go using unbooked rooms, you know. Just because you fell out with your friend." I wanted a response, but none came. "He's gone, you know. Your friend, he's gone without you."

"Good riddance," he said. "I'm glad. I told him to go."

"He went without paying properly. He only left twenty pounds."

I waited for an expression of some sympathy, if not outrage. But the voice was calm. "Yes, he said he was going to do that. That's why I wouldn't go with him. It's so unfair. Really unkind."

Downstairs, Howard coughed again and called out for me in a sleepy, strangled voice. I stood up, yet I did not go to the door. I moved away to the window and remained there, looking out.

"I have to go and attend to my husband," I said, almost to myself.

But I did not go, and for a while nothing more was said. Below the house, the track, fringed here and there by twiggy trees, slipped in a loose zigzag between the contours of the moor, all the way down to the road. Today was Adam's birthday and again, Adam was not spending it here. I never should have expected him to. The last time he'd come for his birthday was in 2004 and it had ended badly; perhaps he'd resolved then never to be here for another. I felt a sudden stab of anger that if that were so he should have told me, instead of just leaving me to engross myself in futile attempts to make amends. I'd give him bloody Barcelona. In fact, what about all those other birthdays, all those efforts? Every year I'd tried to turn it into "a lovely day," filled with celebration or at least a kind of exuberant disturbance, anything to deflect attention from memories of the actual day of his birth. Now I had to face this one alone, with Howard. How was it to be borne this year, how was it to be managed yet another time? I wanted the day and all days henceforward to be held back, to be prevented from happening. The odd thing was that even as all this was going through my mind, I felt the stranger knew my thoughts already. I went over in my head all the words that we had actually spoken, and without turning round, in a whisper I repeated them, and the cool room seemed to answer back with a silence that stretched itself out until it lay, numinous, like a grace, across the space between the stranger and me, and over all that we had said. Also, over all that we had not said; the pauses between our thoughts were no less an exchange of understanding than the thoughts given voice. In this stranger's presence, silence and speech were equal and precious gifts. Then Howard called for me again, more urgently. When I stepped outside this room, I would be once more alone. I did not know how I was going to go downstairs and carry on as usual.

The voice from behind me said, "My name's Theo, by the way."

It was a good voice, almost accentless; I liked the voice. But I had to get downstairs. I shook my head, as if the sound was a buzzing in my ear. I tried to remember Adam's voice, and Howard's, but could not recall them clearly. Why did this person want me to know his name, anyway? Did he think I'd respond by telling him mine?

"We'll discuss the balance of the bill downstairs, if you don't mind," I said. "You should pack your things and then you can be on your way."

He didn't reply to that. I didn't expect him to. I waited a few more moments at the window, until my breathing returned to normal. Then I turned around, and I was alone again, of course. The room was empty.

On the morning of Adam's birthday Howard was awake too early and Deborah came to him too late, by which time he'd wet the bed. After that it was inevitable that the day would be one of his shut-down days even if, while she was pulling off the sheets, Deborah hadn't also given him the news that the overnight visitors had cheated them. What overnight visitors? And where was Adam? Howard really could not have any part in a day like this, with its bewildering absence of routine, Deborah's distress about the comings and goings of strangers, the confusion of Adam. Let these events happen if they must, but let them come to him as events unreal and happening to made-up, invented people, like snatches of a radio play sounding in a room on the other side of the house. He wished she would shut up. But all the time she was dressing him and helping him to his chair at the kitchen table she went on talking, and it was all, all beyond him. Secretly, his eyes followed her, the lumbering shape of her, as she carried the bundled-up laundry past him out of the kitchen to the passage that led to the scullery, leaving in her wake an ebbing torrent of words.

In the silence after she had gone, his mind cleared enough for him to wish that understanding only a little of what was going on around him amounted to feeling only a little. He had never quite believed in Adam's visit, he now realized, but the sight of the barely touched pork roast on the kitchen counter and the picnic flasks, unearthed from under the stairs, standing newly rinsed on the draining board, left his throat tight and aching.

He heard the washing machine in the scullery begin to whine, and then she returned. With listless hands she scraped back the loose hanks of her hair and twisted them into a dry rope on the back of her head, and went about getting breakfast. The kitchen, like all the rooms at the back of the house, was close against the hillside and almost always dark, and Howard watched her movements silhouetted like shadow play against the window as she filled the kettle and reached for teabags and milk. She hauled herself through her tasks, going between fridge and cupboard as if her feet were chained. Already the annoyance of the day, or the disappointment of it, had used her all up; she was capable of only the weak gestures of the habitual morning routine. She poured milk on his cereal, placed the bowl in front of him, and turned away to switch on the kettle. Howard could not see her features clearly but the back of her neck pushing up from her sweater looked pouchy and swollen. Now she was scrubbing at the sink. The body that he used to think of as generous looked lopsided and unloved; its bulk shifted and sagged unevenly under her clothes.

Howard felt his throat tighten some more. One thing at a time, he thought, and concentrated on getting his fingers to close around his spoon. But tiny unobtrusive jolts were thudding up through his chest into his throat and gathering force, and soon tears were splashing on to the back of his worthless hand. Deborah did not notice, or chose not to, and now to him she was no more than a watery blur drifting across the center of the permanently tunneled dusk of his vision. But at least there was no more talking. Much as he hated her angry outpourings, even more he hated her special invalid talk with its jovial insincerity and vacuous aphorisms about cheering up and taking one day at a time. He was grateful she could not summon the energy to try fooling him with any of that today.

But he could hear that she was speaking again. Not to him, because her tone was guarded and formal. Someone must have come to the kitchen door from the scullery passage. Howard managed to raise his hand and wipe his eyes, but still everything around him was a fog of grainy, mingled shapes. If it was Digger he'd have come into the yard and through the back door, and Howard would have heard the Land Rover and the dog and Digger's voice that would, even just saying hello, sound sarcastic. So who was here?

He—I would not try his name, Theo, even to myself, inside my head—hovered in the scullery doorway while I was putting the powder in the washing machine. He must have wandered into the passage from the door at the back of the dining room, which meant he must have gone in there and been waiting for breakfast. The nerve! How could he think I would be willing to give him breakfast? I stopped what I was doing and stretched up to look at him properly, or at his eyes, at least. They were a non-color, a sort of gray, paler than Adam's. They were also full of calm, and I wondered why. Could he actually be feeling calm about being stranded here? I looked at him harder to see if he might be just stupid, and he smiled as if he guessed what I was thinking. Then he came right into the scullery and bent down to the pile of laundry on the floor, moving in the nonchalant way of all tall young men with long limbs, as if the smallest movement might be the last before his arms and legs ceased to bend at all. He started feeding the sheets into the machine. The urine stains were obvious, yellow and hard-edged.

"Don't. There's no need for you to do that."

"I don't mind. Is your husband ill?"

"He had a stroke. Really, there's no need. I can do it myself."

But it was done. The drum was loaded, the door shut with a *clack,* and all I had to do was switch the machine on. When it ticked and clicked and then trickled with incoming water, I looked up and saw that he was smiling at me as if between us we'd achieved something remarkable. All at once the grinding of the washing machine felt like some delightful, secret cleverness that was the unique outcome of our combined talents. I noticed he had young, strong teeth. There was something both formal and grown-up, but also childlike and mischievous about him. Neither of the words *man* or *boy* would adhere to the idea I was forming of him, but in any case I wanted his mild, visitor's face to stay undefined; too unarguable an identity would lessen the gentle force of the atmosphere around him. I could not find a trace of the sulky, graceless companion he'd been yesterday. Yet I did not smile back. I waited for him to speak, but he said nothing. The washing machine thrummed and gurgled, the twisted sheets began to churn around.

"Well," I said. "Thanks for your help."

Theo shrugged. "I'm sorry. I haven't got any money. I can't pay the bill."

I shrugged, too. "Please just go. Get your luggage and go," I said. I returned to the kitchen, closing the door behind me, hardening myself for the day.

I didn't say anything to Howard about it. What good would it do to explain that one of the hateful visitors had stayed behind, claiming to be penniless, and had been loitering around me all hangdog, pretending to help with the laundry? He would probably barely follow what I was saying, which would upset him, and if he did understand, he'd be embarrassed about a stranger seeing his soiled sheets. Anyway, I couldn't speak; I couldn't have stood the sound of my own voice, all flat and airy to conceal how desperate I was feeling. Howard's eyes followed me as I got his breakfast, dumped the bowl in front of him, and switched on the kettle. When he began to cry I was relieved he did it quietly enough for me to pretend I didn't know about it. The Stroke Club nurses were always saying Howard's ability to do things for himself might improve if he tried more, although that was not the reason, this time, that I left him to it. I returned to the sink and wiped round it unnecessarily. I'm afraid I just didn't feel like helping him.

I was thinking about Theo. I supposed he'd gone back upstairs, but I couldn't hear any footsteps overhead. How could he be taking so long to pack a few things? Would he just leave, or would he come to say goodbye? I wanted him to go; I did not care to have in my own house a man of my son's age looking at me with what could only be pity, and at the same time exuding some kind of aura that all would be well. What did he know about me, about Howard and Stoney-ridge, about anything? I truly did want him to go. I had no idea why I wanted to see his face one last time. He really didn't look in the least like Adam.

I listened for the sound from the hall of the front door closing and instead heard again his feet on the floor of the scullery passage. I went out to deal with him before he could barge his way into the kitchen; Howard didn't respond well to strangers. Theo was stand-ing there in silhouette, stooping in the slanted light shining into the passage from the scullery. He had no luggage.

"I thought you had a backpack," I said. "Has he taken it with him, your friend?"

Theo shook his head. "I'm really sorry about the bill," he said. "I've only got eleven quid."

"You'll want to be on your way. You might pick up a lift on the road," I said.

"But I can't pay you."

"No, well. I didn't really expect you to," I said. I intended to sound bitter, not forgiving. "Anyway, I'm cutting my losses. I haven't given you breakfast."

"I didn't really expect you to," he said, and smiled. The smile was another secret offering to me, and this time I accepted it. I returned it. Behind me, through the open kitchen door, steam plumed out from the kettle and the automatic switch clicked off. Looking past me, Theo smiled again, and then his eyes were on my face.

"Well. I could manage some tea, I suppose," I said. "I expect you could do with a cup before you go."

"A cup of tea would be great," he said.

I turned away, expecting him to turn also and go to the dining room to wait for his tea. But he followed me, scraping his feet over the threshold, and suddenly there he was in the shabby kitchen, looking around at the homemade plyboard shelves that were never finished, the scabbed and blistered paint, the curling pictures and notes stuck on the walls and cupboards. And sitting under the overhead light that shone down on the table was Howard, crying and fighting with his cutlery.

"How do you do," Theo said, smiling at him, which made me wonder if I had smiled at Howard even once since the day began. Howard lifted his face and peered in the direction of the voice. Then he switched his attention back to fitting his spoon into his hand, folding his sluggish fingers around the handle, panting with exasperation, still half-sobbing. Theo watched for another moment, then pulled out the chair next to him and sat down. I couldn't believe my eyes.

"Some days you take ages, don't you, Howard?" I said. "Some days it's harder than others, isn't it?" But neither of them was listening. Already the spoon had been prised from Howard's hand and then I heard soft, ridiculous crooning and clicking noises that usually would drive him mad. Now the spoon was being loaded, and directed full to Howard's mouth. I looked away. I didn't need to see the malty spray of milk and saliva and the pulpy scraps splatter over the table and floor.

It wasn't as bad as it might have been. When I did look, I saw that Howard had just let his jaw fall open, and with his tongue he'd flipped the contents of his mouth down his chin. A glistening blob of mashed cereal sat on his jumper at the end of a string of slime attached to his bottom lip. Theo scooped it up in the spoon and pushed it back in Howard's mouth. Howard ate it. Not a word was said. He ate the next mouthful, and the next.

Still, it was a nuisance, Theo being here. Disruptive. Because I had my routines: I made tea with a single teabag in a cup of hot water for myself and then squeezed the bag into cooler water in a mug with a special handle for Howard. Now I had to make it properly in a pot, but not one of the metal Bed and Breakfast ones that might make Theo think he was indeed a guest. He was an intruder, I reminded myself; my offering of tea and his presence in my kitchen did not mean he was not, essentially, uninvited. I got out the folding steps and heaved myself up and lifted the old teapot from the top of one of the cupboards. It was a misshapen thing made years ago by Roderick, a fat-fingered Welsh potter Howard had gone to for some lessons, who could at least do spouts. It was coated in a sticky gray down of grease and dust. I washed and dried it, hoping it would break apart in my hands from its own dirt and ugliness. I wasn't aware that Theo was watching me until I heard him say, "You've got a bad shoulder."

My shoulder wasn't an injury anymore, it was a disfigurement. I believed I managed to hide it pretty well; I should have been annoyed that he'd mentioned it. But I wanted to thank him for noticing. I felt grateful to hear him state a fact so long unthought of that it was a sort of rediscovery to have it spoken aloud. Yes, I *have* got a bad shoulder, I was going to say. But I didn't answer at once because I wasn't sure my voice wouldn't waver. I was also curious about what else he might find to say about me. I wanted him to go on observing and telling me things about myself.

Anyway, before I could speak he said, "You shouldn't be lifting that heavy kettle. Let me." He rose from his chair, filled the teapot, and brought it to the table. He fetched cups, spoons, and milk, then sat down again and went back to helping Howard, who had not so much as blinked. Theo made every operation so easy, so fluid; I stood mesmerized, long since unaccustomed to displays of effortlessness. In the scullery the washing machine rose to a diabolical, high-pitched whirr. Theo nodded toward the door.

"Wet sheets. They're heavy, too," he said. "I'll get them out. Put them in the dryer for you."

"I haven't got a dryer. They're against my husband's principles."

"He's against dry sheets?"

"He's against the unnecessary consumption of resources. We do everything as naturally as possible. I dry the washing outside."

"What if it's raining?"

"I wait until it stops. Anyway, it's not raining."

"Then I'll hang it out for you."

I wasn't expecting that. "It's on the hot wash," I told him. "It won't be finished for at least an hour. You'll be gone before it's done."

"An hour? In that case you might as well sit down and have your cup of tea."

I had no reason not to do as he said. He poured out two cups, for himself and me. As soon as I sat down I knew I should get up again and find the mug with the special handle and pour some tea for Howard, but I waited. Why worry? He didn't seem to mind not having any. Theo went on feeding him his breakfast until the bowl was empty, and then Howard belched peacefully and closed his eyes. It was not yet eight o'clock. Outside, the sun had traveled far enough around the house to shine into the rooms at the back, as it did only at this time of year and for a short while in the mornings. It slanted in through the window and the glass pane in the back door and set the kitchen ablaze. Theo and I sat in a vibrating, yellow pool of light.

"Your friend, I suppose he's on his way back to London, is he?" I said. "Will you make it up with him when you get back?"

"Nicholas? I doubt it," Theo said. I waited for him to say more. "He goes to this bar where I used to work, that's how I know him. I didn't even want to go away for the weekend, he more or less made me. Insisted."

"He seemed very upset."

"Not as upset as me. He's a complete control freak."

"Even so, how could he *make* you go away for the weekend, if you didn't want to?"

His face turned red. "He's sort of persuasive. You know." He drank some of his tea, looking at me to see if I did know. I didn't. "I had a room in this flat for a while," he said. "Only I lost my job, the one at the bar, so I had to move out. Nicholas knew I was stuck so he said I could stay at his place while I sorted myself out. That was a couple of months ago. Then all of a sudden he said he was going away this weekend and he wasn't letting me stay in the flat on my own, and if I came with him he'd see me all right. You know, with a bit of spending money. And if I didn't want to come, I could get out." He sighed. "I didn't have anywhere to go. Didn't have much option, did I?"

"Not very nice of him to turn you out of the flat when he'd invited you in the first place."

He looked sheepish. "It got a bit nasty. He said I was sponging off him. It was because I didn't really fancy him. That's what it was all about, to be honest. He took it very personally."

"Well, it is personal."

"It is and it isn't. The thing is I'm not really gay. Not that gay. So he was pissed off with me."

I didn't know what to say to that except, "You're well out of it, then. Except he's left you in the lurch."

"Yeah. And you didn't get paid."

"Well, the dinner was terrible."

Theo smiled, and shivered. "I hardly ate anything." He glanced at Howard's empty bowl. "So now I'm starving."

I realized then that he'd helped Howard with his cereal thinking I might offer him some, too; there had been no real kindness in it. Still, he had done it. I filled a bowl for him and brought a spoon and hoped he'd take no more than five minutes over it. It wasn't that I didn't like him being there, but since he must go, I wanted him gone. I had not yet had time to think properly about Adam, and I did not know if it was his absence or just my anger with him that lay like a weight inside me. So I was surprised at the way my heart lifted to see Theo eat so ravenously. I poured him more tea, and then more; he drained the pot. I gave him another bowl of cereal. When he'd finished, he looked up and saw I'd been watching him. His face was friendly but still somehow neutral, a mask of almost android mildness and adaptability, upturned and waiting for experience to come and draw lines and press shadows upon it. And until that happened, I thought, those well-composed features, handsome as they were, were probably forgettable. There was a shred of cereal stuck on his top lip. I didn't tell him about it. I let it stay there, a detail I'd be able to bring to mind later, when I had trouble remembering his face. For the sun was rising up the sky and over the roof, and soon would be too high to reach into the room anymore; soon the angles of light would sharpen and retreat across the floor and Theo would be gone, leaving me in the shadow of the hill and alone with Howard asleep in his chair, his bald head crooked on his shoulder.

A long time passed in silence. I didn't want to say anything that would begin the inevitable leave-taking.

Then Theo said, "Listen, I mean it. I feel really bad about the money. Maybe I could stay and do a few jobs for you—you know, work off the debt? I mean, there's a few things need doing around the place, isn't there? I'm pretty handy."

"Oh, I'm sure I can manage," I said, intending to put a stop to it all and be rid of him; he was taking a friendly conversation too far. "I've been managing for many years. And my son helps, when he's here."

"Are you sure? Well, I'll leave you the eleven quid, anyway." He stood up. "If you do want me to just go."

That was when, without pausing to think about it any more, I told him I didn't want him to just go. I was still in the clothes I had slept in. I wanted him to help Howard give his face a quick wipe (since he'd done so well helping him with breakfast) and keep an eye on him while I got myself bathed and dressed and ready for the day, and then I wanted him to take us up on the moor for our son's birthday picnic. We went every year, I told him, even the years Adam couldn't be here. Lately, since Howard's stroke, I would even go alone, just to sit. But Adam had been so looking forward to it this year, I said. He'd been desperate to get back for his birthday. He'd be thrilled to know we made it on to the moor and had the picnic, even though he couldn't be here himself.

Howard awoke to the feel of hands cupping his cheeks from behind, large hands that were cool, and rough. It registered with him that they were Deborah's hands—who else's?—although maybe today they smelled a little different: newly washed, giving off a whiff of something from a bottle, grassy with a hint of tar. A voice, which also could only be Deborah's—although there was something different about it, too—said something he didn't catch, and then his head was tipped back and a wet cloth came down over his eyes. He tried to claw it away but the hands were heavy and quick as well; in one movement they seized and covered his own, and lowered them to his lap. The cloth was replaced over his face. Howard tried to shriek but no sound came, and for a while nothing else happened. The voice spoke again; again he could make no sense of the words, and he couldn't see anything through the cloth. But from the echoey drop of the voice into silence and the watery smell he knew he was still in the linoleum-floored kitchen, where he half-remembered he'd been having breakfast not very long ago. Usually he was moved right after breakfast. He tried to lunge out of his chair but was forced back. The cloth slid off his eyes and around his cheeks and was gone. Howard blinked and strained his eyes for a glimpse of Deborah coming to him with a towel to dry his damp face, but at the corner of his eye he caught only a movement, a stirring of air following someone's departure from his line of vision. He was alone, in silence.

Silence—that was it. He wasn't in the sitting room watching television, as he ought to be. He shivered. No wonder he'd fallen asleep—he'd been left in the kitchen, where there was nothing to

watch. He rummaged at the sides of his chair as if he'd find the remote control there, but of course he wouldn't, he knew that was
stupid, it was all wrong. Things were going wrong. He tried to call
out and this time from his mouth there came a shriek, and with an
explosion of spittle he almost managed the word *Deborah!*

The voice, out of nowhere, spoke close to his ear.

"It's all right, Howard. Quiet, now. Guess what, we're going for
the picnic. All of us. That'll be fun, won't it, Howard?"

I was always quick in taking my bath because the bathroom was drafty and the tap ran so slow the water would be tepid before there were more than a few inches of it. There was never any possibility of soaking in deep warmth, not for someone my size, so I sat up straight like a fleshy, rounded inversion of an iceberg, nine-tenths above the surface. Anyway, I knew if I tried to lean back, the cast iron slope of the bath would feel uneven and I would begin to hurt, as if there were an extra, tender little spur of bone sprouting under my left shoulder blade, which, for all I knew, there was. So I sat with my knees drawn up as I always did, and washed my body up and down, clasping myself in long, slippery hugs and pushing into my folds of flesh with a nugget of soap in each hand, while the water ran in trickles down my back and cooled around my haunches. Even so, I liked the novelty of a morning bath—I usually bathed at night, after Howard was in bed—and even though it wasn't very comfortable I thought of it as a treat, as if the day were *my* birthday. Then I put on my dress of dark blue and white checks that I used to love but hadn't worn since Adam was last here and told me it looked like a tablecloth. It was years since I'd used perfume but I put some on anyway even though it had gone syrupy in the bottom of the bottle and smelled like sherry.

When I came down Howard was still in the kitchen and had retreated into a doze. There was no sign of Theo and his absence hit me hard, until I realized that he must be in the scullery, emptying the washing machine. I left him to it. It was strangely enjoyable and relaxing, the thought of someone out of sight but somewhere in the house, helping to get ordinary things done. I had decided in the bath that the less chance I gave Howard to make a fuss about Theo being here the better, so I told him about the picnic but didn't mention Theo directly. If I assumed that Theo's presence was going to be fine with him, then surely it would be. In fact it must be already, or he wouldn't have been sitting so extra quiet and docile.

I took the carving knife to the cold pork and made big sandwiches with thick slices of meat and bread swabbed with warm butter. I wrapped the birthday cake in some old newspaper, filled two thermoses with tea, and slung everything in the basket that hooked on the back of the wheelchair. I brought the wheelchair from the hall, unfolded it, and parked it in the yard, just over the threshold. Howard came obediently enough. He was tremulous and unsure, but at least he didn't try to ask silly questions. The main thing was that there was no struggle in him. I didn't know if he understood entirely what was happening, and I didn't altogether mind if he didn't; the outing never had been for his sake, and now it no longer felt as if it was for Adam's. It was for mine. Just by remaining here to carry out my wishes, Theo made it so. Beyond that, he was making a gift of the event to me, bestowing upon it a worth it would never possess had I simply claimed it for myself. I tucked Howard's legs in safely under a blanket, and we set off. The weather looked uncertain.

Howard's bulk, the weight of the picnic, and the uneven ground made the going very heavy. But before we'd cleared the yard Theo was pushing alongside me, saying nothing but taking most of the load; the new ease I felt in my arms and shoulders made me smile over Howard's head. I was carrying the walking frame lightly hooked on one arm because the wheelchair would be useless once we'd gone through the gate into the first field. If we made it across the field, following the hedgebank on the far side, Howard might be able to get over the stile into the next field. With Theo to help, I was confident we would. Farther than that, we'd have to see.

It was rough going on the track. Howard shrank himself up small and yowled going over the bumps, but then Howard always did complain about doing anything at anyone else's speed. I signaled over his head to Theo to ignore him and keep going. It was important to keep going. Everybody at Stroke Club said Howard must be encouraged to move and do things for himself and get out as much as possible. Immobility therefore depression, depression therefore immobility, they warned, without explaining how we were supposed to stave off or withstand either one. Well! Here we were managing to do both, and all thanks to Theo. With him beside me, we set a rattling pace along the track, quite drowning out Howard's whimpers and yelps. Now and then I got tired of pushing and we paused for a short rest, and then I would wander away out of earshot of Howard's complaints on to the verges and pick flowering weeds that wilted at once in my hands. Soon I got to thinking how pointless it was to pick them because back at the house they never lasted in water anyway, so I stripped off the leaves and flower heads and dropped them, and carried on up the track clutching the bare stems and then chucking them away, too. I didn't know why I'd picked them in the first place or why I was so profligate with them. It might have been simply that in the company of this new person, Theo, I could try out the idea of myself as fickle and faintly irresponsible; maybe I could be one of those careless women who idly pick flowers and lose interest in them and throw them away.

At the end of the track Theo set down the brake of the wheelchair, pulled off Howard's blanket, and helped him to stand up and grip the walking frame. I opened the gate into the field. Howard shuffled forward, staring at the ground. Behind his back, Theo and I smiled, and then I remembered suddenly that I hadn't brought my camera so I wouldn't be able to take pictures from the moor to show Adam. I thought about running back for it but instead I waited, and once Howard and Theo were through the gate, I followed and closed it behind us. This was not really Adam's picnic, after all.

Less then half-way up the field, Howard planted the walking frame in the ground, slumped over it, and wouldn't budge. It had taken us nearly half an hour to go fifty yards and now he was sweating and moaning, and if he hadn't already wet himself, he probably needed to pee. I should have thought of that. Also, although the wind was always blowing up here the sun was hot, and I should have thought to bring his hat and sun cream. One way and another I was being unforgivably careless. The field we were stuck in was thistly and dirty with cowpats and there wasn't a view—in fact, we were no distance from the house. The thought that this was as far as we would get filled me with despair and rage. I wanted to scream at Howard for just standing there as if rooted, his nose turning pink in the sun, his bare head glistening. I looked around for Theo, feeling suddenly deserted; this promise of release from the house held out, only to be snatched back—I did not know how I would bear it. He'd vanished. But just as I was about to call to him and cry out that we would have to go back, he loomed into view from the direction of the hedgebank beyond; he must have gone on ahead, perhaps scouting out the least boggy route for us up on to the moor.

I watched him glide toward Howard, and I swear that, even through the trembling haze of wind and heat across the field, what I then saw happen was incredible. Theo turned the frame away from Howard and dipped forward, shoved his head under Howard's arm and hoisted him over his shoulder. Howard's body bent in the middle like an understuffed toy, arms dangling, legs flopping disjointedly. I held my breath and watched, aghast and unbelieving. Theo staggered under the weight and bulk; his knees locked and then wobbled, and locked again, he struggled for balance, stamping one foot and then the other down hard on the uneven clumps of grass. Howard shrieked in terror and I cried out to Theo to put him down. They were both going to crash to the ground, and only Howard's bones would break. But Theo steadied himself like a weightlifter, took a wide sideways step. His eyes were bulging, spit sprayed out from between his bared teeth. His feet snatched at one spot, then another, then he managed to plant one foot in front, and he started to tread uphill, pausing every few steps. I followed.

Eventually, with a great bellowing sigh, he set Howard down on the step of the next stile and bent over double, panting and blowing out his cheeks. By the time I reached them, there was Howard standing at his frame (I suppose Theo had carried that, too, somehow) as if he'd never really budged, laughing breathlessly. Theo was delighted because Howard seemed to be enjoying himself. I didn't like to tell him about Howard's crying and laughing fits which were like involuntary spasms, just muscular upheavals caused by his misfiring brain that might not have anything to do with his feelings at all. So I made a show of delight and laughed, too, and told Howard he was doing fine.

After a long rest, Theo lifted the basket and walking frame over the stile. Then he stood on the first step, and between us, pulling and pushing, we got Howard up and standing on the stile, hanging on for dear life to the top bar of the fence. Theo stepped over, and I stepped up behind Howard and held on to him. Theo coaxed his good leg over the stile and took his weight while I bundled the bad leg across. Howard's eyes were closed and his jaws were working fearfully, and he was almost a dead weight, but he didn't panic or resist. I don't know how it happened, but then Theo, holding Howard under the arms, toppled backward off the stile, taking Howard down with him. Howard landed heavily and was winded. His legs were scraped and bloodied, but we were over. Once he was hauled back on his feet he locked the fingers of his good hand on to his frame and clung on, bent and trembling. The ground was soft, I pointed out, so no bones were broken, he was fine; there was nothing to worry about.

Anyway, Howard had to be fine, because we could not go back now. I was too elated. The wind was pulling up from the ground where he'd fallen the raw smell of broken grass, and letting loose all kinds of sounds that went tumbling over the hillside: the bleating of sheep and lapwing cries, and from deep in the combe at the far edge of the field, the hissing of leaves in the alders. We cut a diagonal path, making for the remains of a gap between a stone dyke and some bigger beech trees. There was a channel of water to cross in the middle of the field, no more than three inches deep, but Howard looked alarmed. Theo took him on his shoulders again, and under his weight his feet sank deep into the streambed and turned the glassy surface of the water into chaotic swirls of mud and grit. I took off my shoes and waded across. The water was so cold and the shale so stinging underfoot that for a moment I felt sick, and then I wanted to pee so badly I was afraid I would wet myself. This feeling almost, but not quite, wrecked my elation, until I decided it was almost funny, really, for such an accident would only happen because I was overweight and getting older, but in fact the sudden panic and shame at even the possibility of it was making me feel very young, reminding me of the way children keep hidden from the grown-ups all those secret, trivial little scandals that feature themselves and nobody else. When I'd got my shoes back on I stopped for a rest, and to watch. Theo's grace was quite unreal; in the distance he moved as if born of the wind or the sky. With his hand pressed into Howard's back, he was making him take minute steps forward. But Howard was about to give up. The ground was uneven and the walking frame listed and began to sink, and Howard uttered a cry that turned into a fit of coughing. Theo moved fast, and hoisted him once more over his shoulder. I followed, picking up the walking frame on the way.

After an hour and a half we had crossed three fields. Neither Howard nor Theo could go another step, so we settled ourselves a few yards from a line of alders sprouting from a broken hedgebank, some way under the crest of the rise. Along the ground a blue plastic hose snaked down from the moor around the tree roots and fed into an old metal bath that overflowed at one end; all around it the mud was choppy with hoof tracks where the sheep came to drink. At first Howard was unhappy about sitting on the rug but we helped him down and after a moment he looked comfortable enough, lying flat on his back. I sat with Theo on the edge of the rug to look at the view; behind us, Howard went quiet. He might have been thinking about Adam's birthday, but most likely he wasn't.

We were within sight of the ridge of the moor. A way over it, on the far side, was where I'd found the dying sheep that day. I hadn't been up here since. I considered, and dismissed the idea of telling Theo about it, and about the floating figure I'd seen through the rain clouds, treading the air yet staying distant. It wasn't just that I didn't know how to describe that day, or perhaps was afraid to, it was that today was so different. The horizon was clear and the only clouds were high-up, wavy veils across the blue; sunlight glinted on the other side of the moor that sloped away from the ridge. The harvest was almost in, and for miles around, the acres of arable land claimed from the wild furze and made fertile were buzz-cut into thick, fawn-colored stripes. A combine was flailing across one faraway, vanishing yellow square of field and raising a cloud of wheat dust, and a tractor pulling a load of grain trundled through the lower pastures that rolled down to the barns. A languid pair of buzzards floated in stiff-winged circles over the stubble.

I could tell that Theo had turned to look at me, but I went on gazing out across the moor and pulling at the little tufts of grass under my hands, which tore with a soft creaking sound. A banal remark about the wild ponies and deer and how we were almost certain to see them today was on my lips when I heard Theo ask me abruptly if I liked coming up here. I glanced behind me. Howard had managed to turn on his side and I couldn't see his face.

"Of course I do! It's beautiful, isn't it? The moor's so beautiful!" I said.

"You don't have to like a place just because it's beautiful," Theo said.

I thought about that for a while. "But it is beautiful. And it's important to me," I said. "Don't you have any place that's important to you?"

There was no answer. "Where have you come from, Theo?" I said. "The place you're from—is it important to you?"

He waved the questions away. "Some places I like, some I don't. Why do you have to come up here? Just because it's your son's birthday?"

I got up and attended to Howard, who was asleep with his mouth open. His head looked so small now his hair was shorn, and the gusting wind was teasing the remaining strands, exposing his bumpy yellow scalp. He looked cold, a little blue around the mouth and nose, and his hands were blotchy. Poor Howard, he could have been asleep in snow. I took off my cardigan and placed it over him.

When I sat down again I told Theo that in the early days we loved coming up here, Howard and me. On afternoons like this I would bring a rug and flask of tea in a sling strapped to my back and Howard would carry his shepherd's crook. I'd pour Howard's tea into a cup and sip mine from the lid of the flask. He'd sit whittling sticks with a penknife and talking about everything to do with Stoneyridge, the reasons we were here, how it would all come right. He had it all worked out. Such wonderful summer skies, at the beginning. I had thought of painting the sky, or putting the color of it into my weaving. I never managed to do either, not after I had Adam.

"But you still came every year, on Adam's birthday?"

I remember Howard took up woodcarving the year I was pregnant, I said. He was always whittling away at something, he always had something green and half-done. He never made money at it, of course. Even a simple little figure took so long it wasn't worth it. When I first knew I was pregnant I asked him if he might make toys and he even began something, a rattle I think it was, though come to think of it, it never got finished. But he was never idle.

"You mean he always had a knife in his hand," Theo said, looking at Howard's sleeping face. I laughed to show I wasn't taking his remark the wrong way. "He was always busy. We both were. There was the pottery and weaving, and the animals, and the garden, and the spiritual retreat," I said. "And then, of course, Adam." And I laughed some more. "As a matter of fact, I came up here on the day he was born. I didn't want to, I was so heavy by then. But Howard brought me up here." Theo didn't reply. "Then, do you know, he actually suggested I should stay and give birth up here!"

I knew I'd said too much; I knew Theo was silent from shock, not indifference. "Do you know, I've never told anyone that before? So, anyway! It was all a long time ago," I added.

I went to the basket for the package of sandwiches and we began to eat. Theo fed bits of bread and meat into his mouth and gazed around calmly, but his silence somehow demanded something of me. It was interrogatory, pushing unspoken, impertinent questions in my direction. Why did Howard bring me up here that day—two steep, uphill miles? I didn't want to think about it, so I started talking again.

"You may have a point there. What you said about not necessarily loving beautiful places. I don't always love the moor. It can be bleak. Dangerous, too—the weather can change just like that. That's well known around here."

Theo didn't respond, which I took as an invitation to continue. So actually, I then wondered aloud, did we really love it up here, the two of us, as much as all that? In truth, how often did we, committed as we were to our drudgery, allow ourselves to while away time that could be spent working? And did it really never rain? I wanted to think that in those early years there had been many, many afternoons on the moor, but I had to accept that maybe there had been no more than two or three. Maybe I'd torn up my memories of those few like photographs and was feeding them back to myself in scraps, pretending that each fragment came from a different picture in an entire album of pictures that, if it existed, would be evidence of a whole season of happiness, when in fact all we'd ever had was a handful of fine days caught in a handful of snapshots. The very idea that we made our way on to the moor and wasted whole afternoons up here, like people given to even mild pleasure-seeking, was absurd. There was always work to do, something that couldn't wait, and the impulse for simple fun was never very strong in us, anyway. What was certain—although I did not say this aloud—was that I really did come without fail every twenty-eighth of August, on Adam's birthday. I couldn't keep away.

I woke Howard by tapping on his cheek, and I hauled him gently to a sitting position. He ate his way through a sandwich, pulling strings of meat through his teeth and even getting his left hand as far as his mouth so he could lick his fingers. Then, with a look of disgust on his face, he brought out of his mouth a long flap of pork rind that he couldn't swallow, and dangled it in front of me like a dead flatworm. Theo reached over his shoulder, took it from him, and flung it hard into the grass. With his index finger Howard hooked a lump of bread out from his bulging cheek and tried to copy him, but he hadn't got the strength in his arm to throw it anywhere and the ball of sodden dough dropped on to the rug. Theo flicked it away before Howard could grab it back, and pushed another sandwich in his hand. Howard whined and rolled over, Theo eased himself away and helped Howard until he was lying on his side, in the recovery position. It occurred to me to take the sandwich out of Howard's hand because there was a risk he might choke if he tried to eat lying down, but he was showing no interest in it anyway, and so I left him alone. Theo handed me another sandwich and I crammed it into my mouth, conveying appreciation. There was nothing wrong with the food on this picnic.

"So when was the last time?" Theo asked. "The last time he was here with you for his birthday. When you were all up here together."

"Oh, the last time?" I said, my mouth still full. I waved loosely around and about in the air with the sandwich in my hand. "The last birthday picnic all together?"

I glanced at Howard still sprawled on the rug and was pleased to see he wasn't following the conversation, and his eyes were beginning to close. I got up and knelt beside him, and lifted his small, cold head on to my lap. I stroked the side of his face and made a show to Theo of dredging up the recollection, as if our lives were so crammed with incident, so hectic with visits and parties and picnics that I had to sift through a hundred memories of past amusements to pinpoint a particular one.

"Must be a couple of years," I said. I hesitated; I had to prevent my memory of it from altering the expression on my face. I wasn't going to tell Theo it was seven years ago. Why spoil the day? Today we were up on the moor, the wind was rattling through the bracken, the grass was silvery under the sun, and we could see for miles. I glanced down at Howard's face. He remained quite still amid the waving grass, as if fallen on a battlefield. I knew better than to wonder if he remembered it as I did. Our shared history had become mine alone, since long before the stroke.

"Adam's firm keeps him terribly busy. They send him all over the place, so he can't always get here," I said. "But oh, how he would love this! Isn't it all just lovely!" I leaned across and pushed the open packet of sandwiches toward Theo. "Have another!" I cried. I took one myself and bit into it.

But why did even a simple pleasure have to be forced in this way? When did enjoyment grow so elusive that I had to chase after it and pin it down so desperately? Even more desperate was the sudden knowledge that I wouldn't be enjoying any of it at all if it weren't for the presence of Theo.

"How old is he today, then? Older than me?"

I had to chew for a long time before answering. Though it might have been a little tough for some tastes, the pork meat was delicious, dense and fibrous and salty, and the skin was soft and thick.

"Twenty-eight," I said. "How old are you, Theo? When's your birthday?"

"I'm twenty-seven," he said. "My birthday's next month. The twenty-eighth."

"Oh, my goodness! September the twenty-eighth? That's the day Adam was due! He was born nearly five weeks early, you see," I said. "He wasn't meant to come till September the twenty-eighth. But I went into labor."

"Wow, we were nearly twins, then, me and Adam," Theo said. "Can I have some birthday cake?"

SEPTEMBER 2011

<adam.morgan@logisticsomnicorpsystems.com>

To: deborahstoneyridge@yahoo.com
Sent on thurs 1 sept 2011 at 08.23 EST

HI Mum – sorry about mix-up. Am back from Barcelona in one piece (a bit burnt tho, my back's peeling!). I'm sorry if you got the idea me coming over was a done deal. You have to realize working for an American parent company it's not the same as a UK company, you don't get long holidays, it's a whole different attitude. Back in office now. Shame I couldn't get to see you but honestly it wasn't a viable option. Hope you're both ok. Next time!
Love, A

<adam.morgan@logisticsomnicorpsystems.com>

To: deborahstoneyridge@yahoo.com
Sent on sat 3 sept 2011 at 15.44 EST

Hey no email last week, you're not mad at me are you?!? that would be pretty random, after all it really wasn't my fault and I have said sorry!!! Hope you're ok, maybe you just didn't make it to the village last week. But usually you ring instead if that happens, but I don't think you've tried to get hold of me? No missed calls. Sorry if you tried and the mob was switched off… I'll try and call tomorrow. Love A

September is never my favorite month. The weather turns colder before I'm ready to let go of hope for a few more summer days, and at dusk, which also comes too early, a wind particular to the change of season blows through the laurel and privet around the house and whips the trees on the moor with lonely, whining strokes. This wind comes from the west and beats the land with slanting rain that carries in it the tang of seawater. It reaches inside the house, where familiar, faintly acid drafts reveal themselves anew. I tear up old bits of cloth into strips to stuff the gaps in the window frames, and I fit wedges of folded cardboard to silence the rattling of the upstairs doors. The Rayburn starts up with puttering noises that fill the kitchen with coal smoke, and I worry that this year, once again, we can't afford a new stove. I wear my everyday, year-round dresses as always, but with sweaters on top, and long, thick socks, most often Howard's old outdoors ones that he doesn't need anymore. There is nothing golden about the autumn here. Beyond the quagmire of the yard, gray oily puddles form in the mud where deer and sheep browse the trees and hedgebanks. On clear days the sky is a flat, opaque blue. The sere green of August bracken on the moor turns almost overnight to brown, and with the first frosts, to black.

I am harvesting the last of everything in the garden. The lettuces are gone to seed and leak a pungent white juice like dandelion milk when I break them off their stalks close to the ground. The leaves are as tough as cabbages and lacy from slug damage, and I wonder about making a sort of end-of-season soup with them, picturing a pale green broth in which the last of the runner beans, so dry and woody, might also soften enough to be edible. There's one last courgette that has swollen unseen under its own leaves and is now a marrow, torpedo-sized. I tap my knuckles on the side of it, enjoying the hollow knock against its dark green wall. It's yellow and wormy on the bottom where it's been sitting in wet soil, but most of it can be used. The tomatoes that haven't rotted on the stem cling on in green clusters, and I wonder why it is that Nature lets them survive so long past the time they should have ripened. I start to pick them anyway, trying to remember a recipe for fried green tomatoes I read in a magazine at the library and knowing that no matter what they taste like Howard will make out he doesn't care for them. Although I'm quite alone out here, as clear as a bell I hear him saying it. *American food—it all tastes of death!*

He must have really said that once, years ago, for his voice to come into my head now, and so forcefully. What doesn't come to me at all is what I replied to it. At the time, probably nothing out loud. Almost certainly I didn't give it much thought; in those days such sentiments were throwaway assumptions among the kind of people we were. Or, I wonder, were his actual words, *Fast food—it all tastes of death!* I can hear his voice in my head saying that, too. Or maybe it was something else entirely that tasted of death (battery chickens?) and when, exactly, in the chronicle of the nigh-on thirty years I spent listening to him, did he say it? Standing here on a damp afternoon in this twenty-ninth Exmoor September, my hands sticky with clay and sap, I'm amused to find I can't recall, and Howard's voice in my head falls silent and suddenly I feel sad and guilty, wishing for his sake that back then I'd been a person who could have helped him laugh off that kind of thing. It has taken me all these years to understand that ideas, even Howard's, have a lifespan. Like clothes or anything else that goes in fashions, they're only right for a while and then they turn wrong or plain ludicrous, a lot of them, anyway. Some ideas, of course, come up again and again, like vegetables left in the ground. But nothing much I can think of holds true forever. Maybe even what Howard called his principles were only ideas that survived a bit longer than the others.

But how dare I think these things? I stretch up and gaze at the dusky sky that's decorated with a high, silver-edged bank of cloud and I wait for Howard's voice to come again and fill my head with his thundering objections. But I hear nothing, as if even my imaginary, long-ago Howard is struck dumb by my heresy. I'm smiling. So minds—even mine, it would appear—may change, and the sky stays right up there where it belongs. And while it is terrible that the stroke has robbed the real, still-living Howard of speech and he is incapable of claiming or declaiming anything now, I'm relieved I no longer have to listen to the stuff he used to come out with. It's a thrill to admit it: I'm not sorry that the death of part of Howard's brain has silenced his ideas. The thought sends a shiver running through me. I don't want to think about what else must have died to let me even think this way and so I concentrate hard on the picking, fingering my way through the pungent tomato foliage and feeling on the backs of my hands tiny prickles from the sharp hairs on the stalks and undersides of leaves. I strip every plant and I'm pleased with the size of the crop. Theo might like fried green tomatoes.

Yes, Theo is still here.

When we came back down from the moor on Adam's birthday it was late and we were soaked and shivering; it had rained long before we reached home. Howard was exhausted from the walking and I was, too, from so much heavy lifting; in fact I couldn't understand where I'd found the strength for it all. I couldn't quite believe what had happened. But I was quite clear that now the picnic was over Theo would—and probably should—go and leave us in peace.

So I parked Howard in the kitchen and went to the scullery to find towels to dry him off and then I saw that the laundry from that morning was still in the washing machine; of course it hadn't been emptied. In the excitement of the picnic I'd forgotten all about the soiled sheets and Howard's stripped bed, which I hadn't made up with clean linen yet. I wanted to cry. I was so tired, my shoulder was aching, yet I could not delay; Howard was fretting and probably getting a temperature. If Theo were just to leave now, if he left me to tackle this all on my own—if he was to enter and exit my life within the space of a single day—it would be as if I had never had him here at all. Yet I could not very well beg him to stay. So I will always be grateful that as I bent down to open the door of the washing machine, I simply sensed him at my side, as I had first thing that morning.

With a lot of tugging, out came the heavy wet sheets into a laundry basket. "It's still raining hard out there," I heard Theo say. With some more effort, the sheets were hauled up onto the drying pulley that hung from the ceiling until they filled the scullery like hanging sails. "There won't be many cars on the road. I might not get a lift," he said. I held my breath. "So would it be all right if I stayed another night? I'll work off whatever it costs. Whatever I owe you."

I gathered up a couple of dry towels for Howard. "Thank you," I said. "That's fine with me."

For the first few days after that I was a bit jumpy (and probably a bit short with Howard), expecting Theo to go at any moment, but he didn't, and now I am no longer uneasy in his presence, or anticipating that he's on the point of taking his leave. He says he'll stay and do chores for me until he's worked off the whole of the unpaid bill his unpleasant friend left behind. Even though I have confessed I was overcharging in the first place, he insists on it. I am touched that he wants to stay (and I sense that for him it's not just about paying off the bill) but I have no idea how to calculate how much time he might owe me. By now it's even possible I owe him; in any case, I don't want to put a price on having him around the place.

It's several days, actually, since money was mentioned. I shan't raise the matter. Any talk of money would signal a tallying of the account that could be followed only by his departure.

A little more about him is clear now. He does look something like Adam after all, with coloring a bit like his, and of similar height and build and almost as good-looking. He's unaware of how very pleasing his appearance is. I dug out some photos of Adam for comparison although there are none very recent. Actually there are only a few of Adam past the age of fourteen, the year he went to school in Exeter, and none at all since Howard's stroke.

I dug out the old album, too, to show Theo; it was in a box of junk under the bed in one of the Bed and Breakfast rooms. *The Year at Stoneyridge Farm 1981–82.* I was expecting to be rather proud of it. I wasn't; I doubt Theo or anyone else would be interested.

In the early days I kept the camera with me and took photographs all the time—that's another thing that fell by the wayside. I mounted them all in order with dates and excited little captions, intent on making a complete record, an album for every year; I thought I might try to get them published one day as a guide for other people like us, trying to be self-sufficient. I was taken aback, looking at it again, to see how very long ago all this was. Howard's hair is still dark, and the one or two pictures with me in them that Howard took show me standing straight and tall, my body emanating youth and vigor. But nearly all the pictures are of Howard: Howard with a broken fence, Howard with the mended fence. Howard with the first flock of hens, with the kiln, with the beehives, Howard in various yoga positions with beads around his neck. In all of them, of course, he is Howard with hair, which was even longer in those days and sometimes tied back or in a pigtail, and he is Howard thickly bearded, like some figure from an epic. I took the pictures with the certainty I was capturing a success story, one that featured our integrity and determination and ingenuity, but looking at them again I see they're simply vain and dull. We were so busy observing and recording ourselves we didn't see our pioneers' foolishness all over our own faces. Howard stares at the camera with a look of humorless infallibility. I imagine myself behind the lens, meticulously laying down an archive of my adoration of my husband as if I knew one day I should need reminding of it.

After Adam was born, the times I couldn't be bothered to fetch the camera began to outnumber the times I could. Eventually there came a day when I saw no point in yet more pictures, not even with Howard in the foreground, of another pile of sheared fleeces, another batch of hens, or more cracked pots warm from the kiln.

So I haven't shown the photographs of Adam, or the album, to Theo yet. Anyway, it's an evening activity, looking over old pictures, and evenings are when he tends to take himself off, leaving me with Howard in the sitting room or, after Howard is in bed, alone there with the television volume turned down. Out of habit, I'll sit in front of the screen for another couple of senseless hours with the feeling of waiting for something better to happen, or just for enough time to pass until a normal person's bedtime comes around. Now I wait for Theo, and am disappointed, because he doesn't come into Howard's sitting room in the evenings.

However, out here digging over the emptied vegetable garden as the afternoon light fades, I'm quite content, because most of the time I no longer feel alone. In fact, I feel very much less alone than I do when I'm with Howard. A few hours spent out here is not loneliness anymore but just a measurable interval between spells of Theo's company. As I strip beans off the wigwam of canes, I am storing up things to say to him over a cup of tea. When I left him in the kitchen I think he was just about to fill a basin with warm water, so by the time I get back he'll be finished with Howard's shave. (I would be so relieved if shaving Howard were to become one of Theo's regular jobs.) I heave the basket of pocked and blighted vegetables on to my hip and set off with it to the house. Theo rather than Howard might be at the window, and I compose my face so that as I enter the yard I am wearing an expression that nobody could possibly describe as lonely.

I swing the basket off my hip as I come in. I feel Theo take the weight of it from me and set it down, and then the kettle goes on. I tiptoe into the sitting room, just far enough to see that Howard, his face red and shining, is slumped sideways in his chair with his eyes half-closed. Light from the television screen flickers over his face. I don't disturb him. He doesn't look well, but that's because this room is always dark. By September, as the day wears on it takes on an even worse, dull, orangey pall from the hessian-shaded lamps. In fact I very much dislike the evenings here, though I've never said so. I return to the kitchen table and suggest to Theo that we might start lighting the stove in the front sitting room in the evenings, after Howard is in bed. I don't say that for me the foremost pleasure in this would be that Theo might stay up a little longer and sit with me. I'm delighted when his face lights up and he says he'll bring in some logs straightaway.

From: deborahstoneyridge@yahoo.com

To: <adam.morgan@logisticsomnicorpsystems.com>
Sent on wed 7 sept 2011 at 11.12 GMT

Hello Adam – things been a bit hectic, I'm a bit disorganized at home as Dad came down with quite a bad cold that went to his chest. I think he's on the mend but we skipped shopping and stroke club last week. Anyway I wasn't sure when you were back from Barcelona so I wasn't sure if you'd get an email. Still plenty in garden and anyway Dad isn't eating much.

Nothing else to report and there's someone waiting to get on here (as usual!) so will sign off now. Take care, lots of love

PS – I must be going nuts! The big news is D and I went up on the moor on your birthday anyway. We had a great time. Sandwiches, cake, everything! Sun was out though it was windy. D enjoyed being out even though it was hard going, especially coming back – sudden rain shower, it came down in sheets, typical Exmoor weather!

PPS – You should have been there!!!

Noises from outside woke Howard, and brought him to the kitchen window. Although his legs were still sore from the day on the moor (how long ago had that been?), he almost enjoyed the effort required of them to move him across the sitting room, through the door, and into the kitchen. Without his frame, walking was laborious and demanded his full concentration, but before he reached the window he realized that it was years since he'd been curious enough about anything to get up on his feet and move.

Crashing and splitting and tearing sounds were coming from across the yard, from the old pottery workshop, whose long, bulging brick wall he could see only because he knew it was there. What was she doing, in *his* workshop? As he peered, an object came flying through the open door and skeetered to a stop on the yard cobbles. Another followed it, and another. The sounds of breaking went on and more bits of wood came flying through the air. A loose, zigzag pile of sticks was accumulating in the yard. Howard tapped weakly on the window and tried to shout out, but the agitated string of swear words that was in his mind got tangled in his mouth and came out as a spitting, angry screech. He lurched to the door but couldn't get it open; hauling at it with a shaking hand, he overbalanced and nearly fell. He had to get outside, but to do that he needed his walking frame. He turned, as fast as he could, and staggered back to the sitting room. By the time he'd got his frame and come back to the window, Deborah was in the yard. He watched her fill the wheelbarrow and trundle it calmly up to the door. She opened it and came in.

"You're up and about, are you?" she said, stepping past him.

With his good hand he managed to take hold of the edge of the door before she closed it, and to make a sound that directed her attention to the barrow outside.

"What? That? I need some kindling, that's all. There's no decent dry wood around here," she said. Howard wanted to ask what the hell she thought she was doing. He did his best with a sentence about destroying furniture, about *his* workshop, but wasn't sure if he got it across. She stared at him.

"Those rickety old things, the old workshop stools? Is that what's bothering you?"

Tears began to run from his eyes. He nodded, and tried to wipe them away.

"Don't be silly, Howard, they haven't been used for years. Not since the last pottery weekend, remember? They were falling to bits, like everything else in there, the place is full of junk. Come on, let's get you back in your chair," she said, taking him by the arm. Her voice softened a little. "They're no use to you now, are they? And I do want some kindling."

Howard allowed himself to be led back to the sitting room. She switched on the television for him and placed the remote control in his hands. Over the thudding soundtrack and screaming tires of a car chase, he thought he heard her say, as she left the room, "Anyway, it wasn't my idea, it was Theo's."

<adam.morgan@logisticsomnicorpsystems.com>

To: deborahstoneyridge@yahoo.com
Sent on thurs 8 sept 2011 at 08.23 EST

Nothing in post from you! Tried to get you on phone, no answer and there was no answerphone yesterday afternoon – were you off on an outing somewhere? If you go out, remember to switch it on!!! Hope you had a good time wherever you went.

So does that mean Dad's ok in the van now or does it still make him feel sick? How is he, how's his cold? Hope it hasn't gone to bronchitis, it did that once, remember. You haven't got it as well, have you? Tough call, looking after him if you've got it too. There's something going round here as well, a stomach thing. I'm OK so far touch wood, only with loads of people off I'm here till after eleven at night then if I'm lucky I get about six hours sleep and am back in for 7 am! Nightmare, plus I know for a fact at least three of those people are skiving. Sacha my boss has got it and feels terrible (looks terrible too but I don't say that!!) but she struggles in and keeps going, there's not many like her.

Mum have you put my mobile number into yr phone yet – 04779 690323. Remember I showed you how to do it – then you only need to press 1 and the phone will dial my number automatically. So CALL ME if you need to. Will try and get you on Sunday again though I'll probably have to go in to the office for at least a half day to catch up on stuff.

Can't believe you went up on the moor! How the hell did Dad make it or did you have to carry him?! It's amazing he got that far and back. To be honest I don't really see the point of all that effort just to go up there but whatever makes you happy I suppose! …☺

Mum it would have been great to see you last month. sorry again. I really wish I could have made it. Say hi to dad, lots of love Adam xx

PS when will you get this, I suppose on Wednesday? When you do ring me and I'll ring you straight back ok?

From: deborahstoneyridge@yahoo.com

To: <adam.morgan@logisticsomnicorpsystems.com>
Sent on wed 14 sept 2011 at 11.12 GMT

Dear Adam, sorry I missed talking to you when you rang and sorry I didn't write last week – can't remember where we were last wed, don't think we were out – I will check phone and make sure it's working ok. No need to worry.

I hope you haven't gone down with the bug! Hope everyone's better now and back at work and giving you a bit of a break. Poor Sacha, she does sound hardworking. Like you!

Probably I missed your calls because I was outside, I'm getting on with some jobs now. I've got a bit more energy from somewhere these days! Eg the pottery studio's a disgrace, am burning a lot of the old junk and it's nice to use the sitting room stove again, it's ages since we did that and I like to have a proper fire. Makes a change of scene for me in the evenings. I think it's taking the chill off the front of the house as well, fingers crossed it might even keep the damp at bay this winter.

Nothing more to tell, really – business as usual. Talk soon. Take care, don't let them overwork you! Lots of love, Mum xx

PS – sorry! Posting your birthday card asap!

It's too late for Howard's silly objections. The old pottery stools are now a heap of sticks so we may as well get some use out of them. So in comes the kindling, in barrowloads wheeled through the kitchen, down the hall, and into the sitting room at the front. While this is being done, and Howard sulks in front of the television, Theo makes a suggestion that is a little presumptuous and comes out of nowhere. He says now there's a bit more space in the old workshop he could set up some drying lines. He ought to do a proper clear-out in there, get the lines up, and then the washing would get dried even when it rains. And it rains an awful lot, he notes, and it's not as if anybody wants to make pots in there anymore. I see his point and I'm touched he's remembered what I told him that first day about wet washing. It was Adam's birthday, and with a shock I recall I still haven't posted him his birthday present! But he wouldn't wear a thick jumper where he is anyway, so I suppose it doesn't matter. On the matter in hand, I don't suppose Howard will like the studio being given over to the drying of washing, but I've struggled long enough with no proper place to do it. I expect he'll come round, but even if he doesn't, there's nothing he can do about it.

Meanwhile, the stack of kindling looks nice stored by the fireplace, next to the place for the logs, as if this is a well-run and well-provisioned house.

Even so, I have to wait a little longer for my fires in the evenings. The logs piled at the side of the yard have been there for years, waiting for Howard's next kiln firing, which never came and never will. They are saturated and mossy and it's more than a week after they are stacked indoors before they will catch fire at all, and another before they burn evenly, but dimly.

But once they do, we fall happily into the new pattern. Theo turns pyromaniacal, testing this and that theory about how much and what sort of paper to use for lighting, how and when to use the bellows, how to lay the wood—in tripod or crisscross formation—to achieve optimum ignition, air flow, and flame. He likes a proper blaze. There aren't any fire lighters in the house so he experiments with methylated spirit and kerosene, though I absolutely forbid him to try turpentine or petrol.

So now he sits by the hearth in the evenings, feeding the stove, and I sit in an easy chair and do—well, nothing, really. There is no television in here, and I do not wish to read or knit or sew. I do not even think; best of all, I do not worry about Howard.

But I do talk about him. There are things I want Theo to understand, perhaps because I do not fully understand them myself; perhaps Theo's perspective will help me form my own. For instance, there's the way Howard can't make sense of what he sees. He's still afflicted by this mysterious, half-world blindness that they told me sometimes happens after a stroke and that has a name—*hemianopia*—which I think nevertheless is a beautiful, mysterious word, evoking a kind of sorcery that I take the condition to resemble, rather than the condition itself. Because, I tell Theo carefully, it's as if dark veils have been dropped by magic down and across the edges of Howard's eyes. Half of his visual field on both sides has simply vanished. But the black mischief is in his brain and not his eyes, and so he only partially understands that this has happened. He isn't aware, or he forgets, that half of the world doesn't exist for him anymore, and so he doesn't know, until he stumbles and falls, that this hidden half is full of obstacles. He doesn't know why voices without faces suddenly start talking at him, or why dangerous hands apparently unattached to human beings loom out of nowhere and push pills in his mouth, and wash and shave and dress him, and guide him from place to place. Often if he's in a room with more than one person at a time he gets confused and doesn't know who's saying what; then he'll just ignore everything, or cry, and then there's no getting through to him.

I tell Theo I think it must be like being asked to understand several conversations in different languages all going on at once. Poor Howard, no wonder he gives up. At the hospital, they also told me that the condition improves over time, in some cases. Which can mean only that in others, it doesn't.

As I was explaining it all, the sound of this wafting, magical word—*hemianopia*—made me nostalgic for that time at the hospital, before I knew what the future would be like. Even while I was being told what it meant, I could not associate such a lovely word with the benighted life that would lie ahead for Howard. I tried to explain that to Theo, too, and it's possible I lost my thread, because I'm not sure how much of it he understood or even took in. I'm sure he's intelligent enough, and anxious to share in my practical, day-to-day concerns, but I keep being surprised at a way he has sometimes of turning very still and not reacting to what I say. At such times, I can almost see my words fly toward and through him and away again in another direction, as if they were moths or butterflies and he were a column of pure light or spinning air. I will keep explaining it to him, the *hemianopia,* and how it affects Howard. How it would upset anyone. Although, of course, it's Howard who really needs to understand it, but fails to.

Since Theo's attention span—his very presence, actually—is a fragile thing, I decide in the end against showing him the Stoneyridge album, and the photographs of Adam. What could he be expected to make of them? Instead, I go through them again several times alone, in my room late at night, and then I put them by with an idea I won't want to see them again for a long while.

Another reason it wouldn't be fair to foist a load of old family snaps on Theo is that he has no pictures to show me. Any question of where he himself is from is impossible for him. His accent isn't distinctive, but I haven't much ear for accents, anyway. Over several evenings his story emerges; he tells me, poor boy, that he doesn't really belong anywhere. He doesn't know either of his parents because he grew up with several sets of foster parents, none of whom he cares to describe. He says he has no family except maybe a brother somewhere (or a half-brother, it's rather vague) who was born sometime after Theo was taken from his mother. He's never met him and he doesn't know where he is; he may not even be alive. As for friends, he has none to speak of. That's because he never learned to mix, he says with sadness, and it's quite true that living with other people, even just me and Howard, doesn't come all that naturally to him. Sometimes during the day he vanishes without warning. It seems related to the way that, at intervals, he tunes out of a conversation. But at least these days he doesn't disappear off to bed so early, right after Howard's settled for the night. The evenings are less quiet than they were, and not nearly as long.

I didn't let Howard see the photographs either, because as long as there's no improvement in his sight he can't make sense of pictures. Besides, they're old; what's needed around here are new pictures. When I next email Adam I may tell him I'm going to get back in the habit of taking photographs. I dismiss at once the wild thought of taking some of Theo and sending them to him. I haven't mentioned Theo to Adam. There's no particular reason why not, except perhaps that Adam is equally capable of interrogating me on some minor detail of life or completely passing over something important, and either way making me feel half-witted. Most mothers endure that with their grown-up children, I suspect. But there must be new things to photograph, if I only look about me again. It's Theo's presence that enables me to raise such a possibility; it's another of the things I think about now, in the evenings. I feel encouraged, in the literal sense. It could really be that I am finding courage.

Theo likes it when he finds a log with a slug on it; he opens the door of the stove, delivers it with a flip of the little brass shovel into the jaws of hell and with glad horror reports how it writhes in the heat, discharges its bubbling goo, and shrivels to nothing. He times it. Some evenings he runs contests, searching with the poker through the logs for a batch of slimy contestants and using the hearth brush to sweep them along and into the shovel. Then he tips them all into the flames and watches. He awards points for wriggle performance, slime leakage, and length of survival; last one to die is the winner. Some honor, I say. Several times I complain it's cruel. I tell him I don't want to see them suffer.

"They're slugs. They don't suffer," he says.

"How do you know that?" I say.

"How can they? They haven't got any nerves, so they haven't got anything to suffer with. And even if they did have nerves they've got no brains, so they've got no way of *knowing* they're suffering."

"How do you know they haven't got nerves, or brains?"

Theo giggles and says, "Because all they are is gloop. Ergh, did you see that one?"

I continue to object, in an offhand way. I loathe slugs. Howard would only lift them out from the vegetable garden and fling them away, but I used to slice them with the spade. Is this any different? Mostly I just smile at Theo's childishness and don't pretend anymore that I care. I fancy there is a new, mushroomy, almost meaty smell in the room when slug-roasting is in progress, but I keep this to myself. I'm a little ashamed that I'm not altogether disgusted by it, and that I am enjoying in the back of my mind the knowledge that Howard would be horrified, and also that he never found out what I did with the spade.

The water was often cold and the bristles too sharp, especially when, as happened more and more often, the shaving brush was jabbed into his face and neck rather than stroked across. The soap was greasy and astringent and made his nose and eyes prickle and run. Every one of the nicks from previous shaves, which never had time to heal, sang with pain. Howard squeezed his hands into fists inside his sleeves, and he closed his eyes and mouth tight and tried to keep still and quiet, but the smell of the soap brought on hard, stinging sneezes that he was always afraid would cause the razor to slip. Struggling against it all, he couldn't remember why he'd cut off his beard in the first place, and every time he tried to find words to explain that he'd changed his mind and wanted his hair and beard to grow back—that he wanted, above all, to be left alone—there was even rougher zeal in the shaving and trimming, and harsher warnings about being difficult. But he wasn't trying to be difficult.

He remembered that getting rid of the hair had had something to do with the heat, although he was no longer sure exactly what, nor how long ago that had been. But as the days wore on—he knew they were now in September—he could hardly bring to mind what heat had ever felt like. Instead he was absorbed by a new misery, quite apart from the fear and pain of the shaving sessions, because without his long thick hair and beard his head was never warm. His skull ached with cold, drafts blew down his neck. His earlobes and the tip of his nose turned numb, and then sore. Cold traveled down his limbs and trunk and seized his fingers and feet. One morning, left alone in his bedroom, he managed to reach the chest of drawers where he thought his sweaters might be but he couldn't open the drawer with one hand, and ended up falling. To his own surprise, the crash didn't bring Deborah running—though he didn't remember her saying she was going outside—and he'd managed to get himself up unaided. He hadn't really hurt himself, so she never found out. If she'd noticed the bruising on his hip the next day, it hadn't bothered her enough to put two and two together. He was afraid of what might have happened if she had.

The autumn days, though shorter, took longer to pass. He spent longer spells alone, he thought, stretches of time broken less often than before by some interruption from Deborah with a few words he strived to catch, some attention to his comfort such as a cup of tea. He was very sorry that he got fewer cups of tea in the course of a day than he used to; he might at least have warmed his lips and hands on them. To keep his legs from seizing up altogether, and when he knew Deborah to be out in the garden or checking the sheep on the moor, he took his walking frame and made little tours of the ground floor, pausing to rest in the cold, quiet rooms he no longer used. The front sitting room, for years kept spruce and untouched as the "Residents' Lounge," was now hazy with old fire smoke and had a rumpled look, like a carelessly vacated bedroom. The hearth was powdered with wood ash, chair cushions lay squashed and awry. In the hall he stopped under the broken and jagged honor guard of old antlers and shivered in the drafts blowing down the staircase. Once or twice he thought he heard someone upstairs. But the creak of a bedroom door or some small, muted cracking noise could be only the sounds of the ninety-year-old timbers of the landing over his head shifting infinitesimally with another change of season.

Most days he tried but couldn't manage to get his frozen mouth to articulate the word *hat* in Deborah's presence, and when he managed to pat his head to convey what he needed, the gesture was waved away and he was told there was nothing to get agitated about. One desperate time, patting his head with both hands, he was asked if he thought he was conducting along to the music on the television, and there was laughter.

Night-times were a little easier. He often looked forward all day to getting back to bed. He was grateful now for the thick, warm pajamas Deborah made him wear; as soon as he was lying in the dark, he would curl up small and draw the bedclothes over his head until morning.

One day, he was woken by the rasp of the curtains being opened, followed by a clutching and shaking of his shoulder. He felt a smack on the back of his hand as the blankets were prized from his fingers. The covers were ripped back, creating a chill that made him draw his legs up to his chest. He tried to keep his eyes shut but as he was hauled upright felt so dizzy he had to open them again. The room was full of dark shapes, and the window and the world beyond it an empty, blinding square of brightness. It was early. Or perhaps it was late; perhaps that was the reason for the roughness and the hurry. He was led to the bathroom cubicle in the corner of the room, where his pajama trousers were yanked down and he was plonked on the lavatory. A hand pushed his cock between his legs, a voice told him to get on and do his best. As he finished urinating he felt his pajama jacket being tugged off, and he heard the fizzing of the shower. No time was being allowed, then, for the matter of his bowels, which always took longer. Next, he was pulled up, turned around, and deposited on the cold plastic shower seat while a jet of water, almost warm enough, played up and down him. He peered through the curtain of water for a glimpse of Deborah's face, and tried to speak. But what could he have said? That he was still half-asleep, that he simply couldn't bear this? That he craved to feel the accidental touches of her arms or her breasts when she brushed against him? That he ached to be handled kindly again? Water poured down his face and into his mouth. Squeezing his eyes shut somehow made him unable to hear as well as unable to see, but over the rushing and gurgling he heard the voice again.

"Picnic today, Howard! Aren't we lucky? Up on the moor again. Another birthday. Another treat!"

He tried to reply.

"Yes. Twenty-eight today! Remember the twenty-eighth of September, Howard? That's the day Adam *should* have been born."

A flannel was slapped into his good hand and he began listlessly to rub his belly, while other hands pushed against and into him with a cold bar of soap.

"Remember the twenty-eighth? Adam was already more than four weeks old. Still in a hospital incubator. Do you remember that?"

Howard opened his mouth to cry out above the rattle of the shower, and was at once gagged with the flannel.

"Do you? Do you remember anything, Slug Brain?"

Howard spluttered, and swallowed soap. Nothing more was said. The flow of water stopped, he was pulled around by a cold towel and dried, more or less, and dressed. Then he was chivvied along in his walking frame into the kitchen. He could tell that the vague, dark disturbance that fell across one eye was the back door, ajar and swinging in the wind. Some dead leaves had blown across the threshold and a hen had wandered in and was pecking at the scraps bucket next to the pedal bin.

From nowhere, Deborah's large body loomed in front of him. She shooed the hen outside and rubbed the sole of her sandal on the curl of shit it left behind on the floor. Howard was put at the table in front of a plate with pieces of peeled banana on it. She placed a slice of bread and butter on his plate and cut it into fingers.

"Come on, Howard, quick now," she said. "I need you done with that before I go. I want to get on and get to Bridgecombe for the shopping and library. You're staying here, all right? I haven't got long and you'd only slow me down. Besides, if you went to Stroke Club you'd be too tired to enjoy the moor."

Howard began, laboriously, to eat. Deborah, with her back to him, did not notice when, after two or three mouthfuls, his hand grew too tired to lift anything more from the plate, and dropped into his lap.

"Theo says we have to set off for the moor by eleven, because later it's going to rain."

She was writing a list, and arranging and rearranging the picnic basket, all the while singing under her breath and looking up from time to time to pause and gaze through the window as if the familiar view of the yard were transforming before her eyes into something wondrous and new. She did not see that Howard was shivering in the wind that blew in through the door she had not closed after the hen.

"Like fried green tomatoes, a plate of mashed potatoes, a scoop of ice-cream on a steamin' apple pie," she sang, scraping Howard's plate into the hens' bucket and rinsing it under the tap. She took the van keys from their hook, picked up her list, and left, with a slight wave and backward glance. Howard waited for her to go, so she would not see his head slump forward and his lips search along the tabletop for the piece of banana that had fallen from his plate as she snatched it away.

<adam.morgan@logisticsomnicorpsystems.com>

To: deborahstoneyridge@yahoo.com
Sent on thurs 15 sept 2011 at 08.23 EST

What jobs outside, do you mean the sheep or the hens or what? Don't tell me you've started on the weaving again? Mum??!?? But the point is when you're outside doing stuff what's Dad doing? Has he got better about being left by himself? You said he got upset on his own. Is the nurse still coming?

Anyway apart from all that, you know I've got various issues about this flat, I told you about it a while ago? I'm seriously thinking of moving now. Twice last week it took me an hour **and a quarter** to get in – the whole transport situation's getting worse if anything and it's not as if there's anything to actually be there for, there's basically no incentive to live there, the area's totally dead on the weekends. So I am basically just going back there to crash out and it's not even convenient to do that, it's a nightmare. So I'm looking around for somewhere else, I've put the word out round the department and a couple of feelers, shouldn't be too much of a problem, hopefully I'll get it sorted. Mind you I really haven't got any time to flat-hunt but you never know something might come up. We're flat out at the minute because the Q4 assessment round kicks off in ten days and there's stuff backing up from the regions that has to be signed off before we can progress any of it!

Anyway sorry to go on about my stuff. Is it cold there yet, have you got the heating on? I know what you'll say about the expense but you must put it on, ok? I can help with that, you know I'd be only too glad to contribute, I mean it Mum.

Give my love to dad and take care, both of you A xxx

<adam.morgan@logisticsomnicorpsystems.com>

To: deborahstoneyridge@yahoo.com
Sent on sun 18 sept 2011 at 08.23 EST

Hi Mum, Chill-out Sunday here, doing nothing because nothing's going on! Thought I'd give you a ring but can't get hold of you – you did do the phone stuff like you said? And the HEATING?? Will try again later A xx

Sent from my iPhone

<adam.morgan@logisticsomnicorpsystems.com>

To: deborahstoneyridge@yahoo.com
Sent on sun 25 sept 2011 at 23.10 EST

Hi Mum good to hear your voice a little while ago, hope you really are ok, you sounded good but kind of different! Maybe it's because we haven't talked last couple weeks – we should do the Sunday call every week (OK my fault I know I missed a few) – I promise to do better from now on! ;-) Lots of love Adam xxx

Sent from my iPhone

From: deborahstoneyridge@yahoo.com

To: <adam.morgan@logisticsomnicorpsystems.com>
Sent on wed 28 sept 2011 at 11.12 GMT

Gosh, a torrent of emails! It's a shame I won't have time to do them all justice because the plan for today is to get out on the moor again.

We're making the most of any dry weather we get, so I've just dashed in to do shopping and check emails – D's at home, skipping stroke club because that PLUS moor would be too much for one day. Adam darling I'm sure you're right about the flat, good luck with it all.

Nice to talk last Sunday – not sure what you mean by different! I am a bit taken up with things now I've got the bit between my teeth to get on with them. Dad is on his own more but I'm not sure he's really noticed, which is good. I think he might be a bit keener to move about which is exactly what he should be doing.

The evenings are quite cozy now I've got the stove – I quite look forward to the evenings these days.

Don't let them overwork you!! I always say that but I mean it. lots of love Mum xx

It was probably going to be even worse than the last time he'd been dragged up on the moor. This time the weather was colder, and she was more hurried, less friendly. But there was something familiar about her, though familiar from so long ago it was like discovering something new: it was the way she'd had, once, of being wide awake and easily delighted, ready to be surprised by new things, always on the point of bursting out laughing. But it no longer pleased him. Her mood was altogether too zesty, almost demonic. She larked and spun about, like a child in a story left outdoors too long and gone wild following the wind, turning over rocks and gulping water from streams and pools, wayward and half-possessed. In fact she was ridiculous.

Even as she pushed him toward the hill she was straining to get away from him. Now she was talking again in a distracted, breathy voice to, as far as he could make out, nobody at all; she had broken off her commentary to *him* before they'd left the house. She prattled on, making no sense. Her words were in a hurry, too, flying on past him before he could snatch at their meaning. Howard was incidental to whatever was going on, he gathered that much, sitting in his wheelchair in the lane while she hoisted armfuls of gear over the stile and dumped them in the field. He was so tired. And what was the point of it anyway, another escapade on to the moor where there was nothing to see or do? He looked up and saw Deborah standing in front of him, breathless and glaring as if he'd complained aloud. There was no appealing to her today, no getting around her.

"Howard, please try! Make a little effort, can't you?" she said.

There was a slight screech in her voice. "I just don't think you're try-ing at all!"

He managed to shake his head, but could not ask what she meant. Trying to do what? He waved his arm and whined, "Why? Why go . . . up there?"

His voice angered her. "Why?" she said. Her face loomed in close to his, her teeth slightly bared. "Stop it! You love the moor!" she said. "Stop pretending you don't understand! Today's a *birthday*!"

She turned and looked across the stile into the field. The wind had pulled her hair loose, and he could not tell if it was lighter or darker than it used to be, only that with the years it had grown crinkled, and moved stiffly in the wind. When he thought of reaching out to touch it, a tremor started up in his hand. He began to cry, shaking his head from side to side. "No, no, no, no . . ." he whispered.

She turned back to him. "Oh! Oh, Howard, you're *determined* to be difficult today," she said. "I can see that! Well, you can just wait here."

She rolled the wheelchair on to the side of the path until it sat, not quite level, in the shadow of the hedge and partially out of the wind. She stabbed the brake down and arranged a blanket around him. Then she pulled a filled feeding cup, a cheese roll, and two chocolate biscuits from the picnic bag and placed them in his lap. "Here! Here, Howard, take it. There you are," she said. "A nice little lunch! Re-member to take little bites, all right? Because if you choke I won't hear you. So!" She produced a tissue and wiped his cheeks and nose. "There. You'll be all right, won't you! I'll be back in time to take you back for your nap."

Howard watched her haunches rise and wobble and turn as she swung herself up and over the stile. After she had gone he sat very still for a long time, afraid that the wheelchair might tip over. In the shade of the hedge he felt colder than ever and he clawed at the blan-ket to draw it closer around himself, forgetting about the food in his lap. All of it tumbled to the ground and everything except the cup disappeared beyond the periphery of his vision. The cup landed where he could just see it, on the edge of the lane. It rolled away along a stony rut, sprinkling milk as it went, and came to rest against a tuft of couch grass, its spout still spilling gently. Howard watched the trail of white drops behind it soak away into the ground. He moaned and started out of the wheelchair, but collapsed back. His walking frame was several feet away, at the base of the stile. If he tried to stand up, here on the rutted track, he would surely fall. In the house he could move about more or less, using walls and furniture as handholds and leaning posts; out here there was nothing to help him. He gazed miserably around. It was worse than that, it was actually dangerous; a deep uneven ditch ran along the back of the grassy verge and the hedge was a prickly, swaying web of thorns. Bones would break, skin would tear. He would just have to wait.

Howard tipped his head up to the sky in an unconscious search for an idea of the time of day, but could not locate exactly the position of the sun. Anyway, Deborah would be hours. Perhaps he could sleep, if he got warm enough. Or if he just sat very, very still in his wheelchair, the time might pass quickly. He'd be all right until she came back, as long as he didn't think about her.

But this was not possible. He found he could easily put out of his mind all thoughts of her as he had just seen her, heaving her bulk over the stile, but his head swam with glimpses of her as she'd been when he knew her first. He could not believe that the Deborah who'd clambered down into the field and disappeared was not the Deborah of thirty years ago whom he now saw clearly in his mind. He could remember only with effort a day ago, and a week was almost impossible, but now the faraway past was as vivid as if that life were all still playing out a few feet away and he'd just moved into the shadow of the hedge for a moment's peace and quiet and a chance to think about it all.

Memories much more real than the day he was living through came back to solid life. Past conversations with his wife poured through his ears, with the sounds of not only their voices but their breathing and their laughter as well. He heard them both groaning with cold—it was a freezing January that year—but still laughing, on the first day they awoke in the house and their breath vaporized in the air over their heads. There were ice patterns on the inside of the windows. Later that day she slipped and fell, running across the yard to see if the hens "had had a good night's sleep" in their newly built coop. He could smell again the aroma of clean frost in her hair when he helped her up. But he had not the slightest recollection of how he came to be an old man trapped in a wheelchair, unable to follow his young wife in her swinging walk up the field toward the moor.

With a sob he pulled the blanket away from his knees and let it fall. Then he planted both feet on the ground and with his good arm on the armrest, pushed himself up. The wheelchair began to skid away from him but he held on, steadied himself, and slowly inched his way around, hand over hand, so that he had a grip on the handles. He couldn't risk balancing on one foot long enough to release the brake, so he pushed and leaned forward, shoving the chair's locked wheels along down the cinder track until he reached the stile. Carefully and gradually he set about transferring his grip from wheelchair to walking frame. When he finally let go of the chair it toppled over.

There was no going back now.

Sweat was breaking on his forehead and drying cold on his skin, and he was badly out of breath. He tried to lengthen his gaze across the field but could see no sign of Deborah, or of any movement at all. She would be much too far away to hear him anyway, were he to shout for her. But if he could only make out her retreating figure and call across the years she would, he felt certain, stop and turn to him, all at once transformed. The Deborah he'd brought here, whom he'd refused to notice fading and slipping away from him, would return, he was sure of it.

He jerked the frame around and turned, and began to move along the path that led all the way back down to the corner of the Stoneyridge yard. If he got that far, once there he could lean on the wall of the old pig shed and rest, and then when he felt ready he might venture on to the brick cobbles and make it to the door and into the house. He'd be pleased to make it all the way to the house. But he felt no triumph in the prospect of undertaking the journey without help, only an aching sadness that his condition placed such an eventuality as walking with an aluminium frame as far as his own door in the category of an achievement. He kept going, pausing every few steps to calm himself and recover his breath, but could not bear to look back, even once, toward the moor.

He made it. The door was unlocked, as always. Howard took several minutes to turn the handle. When he finally got himself into the kitchen he was trembling with tiredness, but with exhilaration, too. He had no idea what time it was, and did not care. Pushing his frame along, he got to his room and lay down on his bed, fully dressed. For several minutes he felt his head on the pillow thump with the same fast and desperate beating of his heart, and then it quieted, and he slept.

It's only when I'm away from Howard that I can breathe freely. This has been the state of affairs for some time but it's only now, trudging away from him up the hill, with Theo a little way up ahead, I finally admit it—whether just to myself or aloud I'm not sure, and it doesn't much matter, because all this, and more, Theo already knows. He can see it, and through his eyes I can see it, too. Howard chokes off my life in my throat as surely as if he clasps his hands around it and day by day squeezes a little tighter. Only in Theo's presence can I breathe, and think, and speak. Only to Theo can I put such questions as these: What are you supposed to do when you are very angry with a person you have loved? How are you to go on when his helplessness doesn't make your anger go away? I do not voice the questions aloud, for now; all I hear is my own uneven breathing and the sigh of grass under my feet. It is enough for the time being that the matter has been broached at all, that it is in the air.

I spread out the blanket on the grass near the top of the ridge, and flop down, lie back, and close my eyes. Damp presses through the blanket and the wind is blustery and cold, but then sunlight splashes unexpectedly through a gap in the clouds and warms my face. I think of Howard dozing in his wheelchair down on the path, way below the brown expanse of moor, and wonder if he feels the warmth, too. This late in the year the sun shines in such unpredictable and fleeting patches, flaring across one field in a moment and extinguished by cloud shadows in the next; it can't be trusted. Theo draws near. Even with my eyes closed I know the moment when he drops on to his knees beside me.

Nothing is said, but I am not surprised when I feel his hand touch mine, clasped across my body. How strange it is that for a long time our hands remain like that. I smile, that's all, and keep my eyes closed. Still I feel no surprise, but rather a kind of discreet, delighted acceptance that he chooses to place his hand upon mine and leave it there. (I do believe absolutely that, though he may have sensed something of my need of him, he has *chosen*.) I find myself thinking again of the walking figure on the moor that stormy July afternoon, and conclude quite calmly that of course it was not real. How could it have been? What else can gods and ghosts and angels be but apparitions, conjured from the force of our yearnings? That figure was a pathfinder, a Gabriel, coming in advance of Theo's real presence. There is no other way to explain why Theo's touch brings, among many sensations, the same pleasure of recognition and blessing that I felt around me that day. And now with his hand touching mine I feel again, even more intensely, the pleasure of the silence between us that I felt on the morning he stayed behind and came quietly to sit by me on the unmade bed in the room of the departed guest. So deep and still is our silence I don't move my hand or turn to look at him for fear he may not really be there after all, or that he may melt away under the warmth of my gaze. There is no need to open my eyes, anyway. I trust him to be more than a mirage. For if he is not, I will be alone again, and that could not be borne.

As we lie here, Theo does not ask a single question, yet I begin to tell him things. I can't remember being in such a hurry to be heard since I met Howard, and that was only ever up until the point, quickly reached, when we both preferred to hear him talk rather than listen to me. Theo is different; his silence becomes a plea for words that brings more and more of them out of my mouth. I tell him small, silly things—for example, that since the day of my father's funeral when Auntie Joan tried to stop my sobs by making me suck on a Fox's Glacier Mint, I cannot abide the taste of peppermint—as well as the big things, about Howard, Adam, all of that. Theo listens as if he has renounced words himself and came here, an abstinent pilgrim, precisely so that my words may flow out and into the air and light of the moor for him to catch and make sense of, for both of us. I talk and talk. Many hours go by.

Eventually, I tire of speaking. Theo slips his hand away gently, and moves off through the grass. Perhaps he's gone to count the sheep. The day is wearing on and it's long past the time I should have gone back. But we haven't had the picnic yet. I sit up and open the basket. There are sandwiches again and another cake, of course, which I set out on a plate, and a flask of tea. Theo wanders back and stands watching and smiling.

"You've gone to a lot of trouble," he says, after cake has been eaten and tea drunk, hands clasped around the cups for warmth. It's very cold and there's a spit of rain in the wind now.

"Well, of course! It's your birthday," I remind him.

"And it was *supposed* to be Adam's," he says.

"But it wasn't," I say, handing over the parcel from the bottom of the basket, "and it isn't. Happy birthday, Theo."

There's no need to tell him, because he already knows, that this parcel was brightly wrapped and beribboned weeks ago to give to Adam, who was not here to receive it, and that my offering it today to Theo instead makes it a greater, not a lesser gift. The paper and ribbon tear and fall away, and the sweater inside releases the smell of new wool, clean and oily, like unused rope. It's a practical garment for country wear, rough but warm. He is quietly pleased, lifting it to his face to feel its wiry mesh against his cheek. I fancy I can feel it against my skin, too. It will actually suit Theo rather better than it would Adam.

"Does it fit? Try it on," I say. Then I find myself on the point of adding that the sweater will serve well against the coming winter, which is always hard on Exmoor, and I realize we have come quite far enough for one day. Where does it spring from, my assumption that Theo will still be here when winter comes? But how could I survive another one here without him? I gather the picnic things together and stand up. I'm rigid with fear and cold, and fighting a need to cry.

"You're cold," Theo says. He hands me the sweater. "Here, you put it on. It'll keep you warm till we're back at the house."

"But it's yours. You should wear it," I tell him, but he insists. He says he's fine, quite warm enough, and obviously I am not. When I put the sweater on, he smiles and says the color suits me. My body softens in its instant warmth and I like feeling its prickly fibers through the dress I am wearing. But I say nothing, and set off quickly down through the mud and bracken. I'm suddenly upset that Howard is stuck in his wheelchair over a mile away; he might have choked on his lunch or tipped himself over. He's bound to be cold, and he's overdue for his tablets, and he hasn't been shaved. Even as I'm muttering all these things I can't decide who's responsible for the lapse of routine, me or Howard. Or Theo.

The next day, or perhaps it was the day after, brought Howard another shock. Somebody else was in the house. He heard a car—not Digger's Land Rover—drive into the yard, and now Deborah was talking to somebody in the kitchen. From the polite tilting of her voice he was sure it wasn't the same person he'd heard her talking to every day for weeks now, to whom her tone was both changeable and extreme, either high and excited, or low and thoughtful, sometimes secretive. No, she was speaking now to yet another person, somebody whose voice he could actually hear, somebody whose voice was familiar and a little on the loud side. He switched off the television and peered around the sitting room and found it, too, familiar; to his relief, what he could see of his surroundings was solid and unchanged. But something was wrong: the voice talking to Deborah from the kitchen did not fit here at Stoneyridge. The voice did not belong here.

Then he heard the laugh, and knew at once who it was. He craned round in his chair toward the kitchen. Though he couldn't see anything through the glass pane in the door he knew it was her: Stroke Club, nurse, laughing, nice, kind—Jenny. The door opened, and Jenny came in, followed by Deborah. Although he now knew who the visitor was, and knew she was in the room, he still couldn't really make her out in the way he had once been able to. It was as if one day when his back was turned the world had reconfigured itself and was now operating in accordance with new, tricksy laws of geometry and space that broke up rooms and faces and bodies into sudden angles and jutting planes, so that now a great deal of what went on right next to him seemed to be happening off-center, or behind a partition, or in a mirror. Not only that, the world was simultaneously emptier and fuller than it used to be. Every day, sounds and movements, shapes, smells, and tastes hinted at but did not yield their meaning, reducing him to a state of almost permanent distraction. Every day wore him out with numberless inexplicable sensations and unanswered clues. But he didn't need to explain any of this to Jenny. She knew.

"Hullo, Howard! Thought I'd just drop in for a minute, seeing as I was passing," she said. "We've been missing you at Stroke Club. Thought I'd come and see how you're getting on." She laughed some more, and Howard smiled broadly in the direction of the voice.

"Hullo, Jenny," he said. He raised his hand and felt it gently clasped and held.

"My goodness," he heard Deborah say. "You *are* honored!"

Jenny laughed again, and Howard could smell something lovely and lemony, and then he heard her voice, now close and soft. She was sitting beside him, practically visible. "How're you doing, Howard? Deborah tells me you've been getting out nearly every day. That's progress. That's excellent!"

Howard knew that Jenny would wait for as long as it took him to speak, which made it worth his effort. Besides, he wanted to please her. Slowly, slowly, he made his mouth produce words. "Yes, out. I have been out. Left, out." He squeezed Jenny's hand, hoping she'd understand how seriously he felt about it. "Not, no—no good. Out. Left. I'm bad, left."

"His left side's still bad. He still struggles," Deborah told Jenny. To Howard she said, "But you managed it very well, Howard. Didn't you? When you were out. You did really well. And you had your chair right there for when you needed a rest, so it was fine."

Jenny said, "Your hand's a bit chilly, isn't it? How's your appetite, Howard, are you eating all right?"

Howard shook his head vehemently. "No. No food. I don't like."

"He's a bit hit-and-miss with his eating at the moment," Deborah said. "He's quite fickle."

"I think we'll just pop you on the scales next time you're at Stroke

Club, Howard, would that be all right?" Jenny said. "I think you might have dropped a bit of weight, I'm not surprised with all the exercise! Tell you what, suppose you try having a couple of milky drinks a day in place of your tea or coffee?" Howard shook his head again; she was missing the point. Even if he couldn't be given food he actually wanted to eat, he had to be allowed enough time to force it down. Jenny's voice faded as she turned her head to speak to Deborah, and he strained to hear the words.

"Plain milk if he likes it, full fat preferably. Or hot chocolate made with milk, that'd be a good idea now the weather's turned. Does he mention feeling the cold at all?"

Howard tried to speak, and Jenny turned back to him. "I think you might be feeling the cold now you've lost a bit of weight, mightn't you?"

She spoke again to Deborah, confidentially. "If you can keep an eye on his hands and feet and pop a blanket or an extra layer on, that'll help. And wrap him up extra warm to go out, of course. Plus *hot* milky drinks especially if he's not eating much."

"I do my best with his food," Deborah said. "And there's the palaver of getting him out. And now the shaving on top. There's a lot to do. I don't mind, of course, but he's difficult to please sometimes. He still gets very down."

"Oh, I know. I do understand. All these things, they're so variable. It's very frustrating for the person doing all the looking-after. Maybe you could try giving him smaller amounts at mealtimes and top up his plate a little at a time—it takes longer but it usually pays off. Anyway, very nice to see you both. Better dash, got four more visits before lunch! Ring the clinic if there's anything else we can help with, don't hesitate, all right? Thanks for letting me pop in."

Howard felt her hand tighten around his. "Bye-bye, Howard. Keep up the good work. See you at Stroke Club next time? I'll be looking out for you!"

She waited until he was able to say, "Goodbye, Jenny." Then he felt her hand withdraw, and she was gone from his side.

"No need to see me out," she said to Deborah.

"It's no bother," Deborah said. "Anyway, I'd like a word."

Some time later he was subjected to another new sensation; another texture, of alarm and strangeness, was brought to bear upon an already unpredictable day. Rough fingertips poking out from a scratchy, strong-smelling sleeve darted at him from nowhere and began stroking the side of his cheek.

A voice said, "It's all right, Howard. I'm going to shave you." The hand—or, at any rate, the sleeve—was unfamiliar. He couldn't join up the voice with the face it belonged to, he couldn't see the face at all.

"You're all right with that, aren't you, Howard?" the voice said, from behind him this time. "We've got to make sure we don't do anything you're not all right with, haven't we, Howard? Very important. Here we go, then."

All at once he felt a cold, slippery cloth sliding around his face as if, despite the words, it wasn't in the least important that he should be all right with it. As if there were already some easy fellowship between himself and the owner of the hand that presumed the granting of his consent to be shaved, which there certainly was not. He opened his mouth, found the cloth jammed between his teeth, and held on, shaking his head. The cloth was wrenched away. Howard felt a light cuff against the side of his head, and yelled out.

"Listen, Howard," said the voice. Warm breath wafted over his face. "Don't. Don't mess around with me, all right? I'm going to shave you. Then we'll be going out for a walk. All of us."

The sharp-smelling, prickly sleeve scraped against his cheek, and Howard sneezed. He tried to focus his eyes but could see only the outline of a dark figure now leaning over the low table where the pink plastic shaving basin was set. Again he wanted to say he'd changed his mind about the shaving, that he wanted to grow his beard back, but the words wouldn't come. Next, a towel was placed around his shoulders and his chin was raised. Howard gulped and closed his mouth as the fat brush pasted the soap across his lips and down over his neck. He had to stop his chin from trembling. Because if he went on trembling like that, the voice told him in a calm, private whisper in his ear, it would be his own fault if he got cut.

OCTOBER 2011

<adam.morgan@logisticsomnicorpsystems.com>

To: deborahstoneyridge@yahoo.com
Sent on sun 2 oct 2011 at 17.23 EST

Hi Mum just tried to catch you in, missed you again, left a message! Hope you were out because you're still having great weather and making the most of it!

You ok? I'm fine. Hope you didn't send a parcel for my birthday because nothing's arrived?

Although the whole flat scenario is still a big problem, I haven't found anywhere else yet so basically it's the same traveling nightmare and it's really getting me down. Also I don't know if I told you about Sacha (my boss, she didn't get transferred in the end which was good). Anyway a while ago she was ill with that bug or so we thought, but then she was out of the office for the last two weeks, we didn't know why and we thought it was really weird.

Well she came back in on Friday afternoon and looks totally different and she got us all in the meeting room and basically told the whole team she's been having these tests and she's got cancer. She hasn't been feeling well for a while but nobody knew. She was really brave about it. Really brave. She's already had this massive surgery and just started chemo but she's coming back into work starting Monday so as of tomorrow she's carrying on as normal except for the chemo appointments, she said when they were but I've forgotten. She's going to lose all her hair apparently so she said our main job is going to be getting used to her in a wig a couple of months down the line. Or she might do hats, she might start a collection she said, definitely NO baseball caps though. She was actually laughing. She said she's fine with it and doesn't want any sympathy, it's just an illness that can affect anybody, it doesn't make her different she's still just Sacha, and she's going to beat it. They told her she might feel pretty rough with the chemo so she might need the odd day off to rest but the best way we can help is if we just all get on with it and forget about it, like she's doing. Then she started talking about our Q4 targets.

Nobody knew what to say. The girls were in tears and I nearly was too. I never minded having Sacha as a boss, I really like her actually. I found out afterwards she's only thirty six and she's got two kids, six and three. I didn't even know that and I wish I'd noticed she was ill. Mum it's incredible how brave she is. I felt like going in and telling her that but you can't, can you? I can't even tell her I think she's a brilliant boss, it would sound cheesy or morbid or whatever. It's funny (not!) how the minute you really want to tell someone what you feel is the exact same minute you know you can't.

Sorry to be a bit depressing! Hope you get to library this week and make sure you email me back, I need cheering up! Are you and Dad ok? I know a strokes bad enough but thank god you haven't got cancer either of you! I could never be as brave as Sacha. Stay well.
Lots of love Adam xxx

Theo's the perfect person to talk to. He doesn't mind if I ramble, he may even like it. When I contradict or repeat myself he never points it out, and just by saying nothing he allows me to pause and reflect and put my story together so it makes sense to both of us. I need his patience, because I am out of practice at thinking and speaking for myself. I feel a little guilty about that, because the way I followed in the wake of Howard's momentum through all these years can only have been a form of laziness, or dishonesty. I thought of it as my duty, but that wasn't it; Howard may have been a little bullying in his opinions, but my torpor was all my own. It was easier to echo his convictions and philosophies than find things of my own to believe in. Perhaps also I had an inkling that if I were to question, even to myself, Howard's right to assume my concurrence in all matters, the chaos would be limitless. Theo says I shouldn't worry about all this. But there is much to blame myself for.

The act of retrieving my pride, let alone my opinions, from these years of deference feels like building work, or sculpture. It's not effortless by any means, but because the material I am using—words, nothing more, nothing less—is pleasing and weightless and mine to assemble however I wish, I go to the task with energy, even excitement. All this flowing of *my* words, on every subject I care to think of, after so long! Theo brings them spilling out of me. I garble away most of the day as if making up for the lost time, fashioning sense out of what has lain for years unspoken. It's exhilarating.

I tell him all about the bread, for instance. I haven't made bread for years. I gave up on it not just for lack of time or energy, or even because of the pain in my shoulder, but out of superstition, no matter that long ago I grew privately dismissive of superstition in most of the forms it took. I'd held on to an early notion of Howard's, though, at first because I enjoyed believing in it back when I also believed I was happy, and later because it served as confirmation that I wasn't.

This notion was that there is such a thing as the spirit of the dough. Yeast is alive, and so bread dough, according to Howard, like any living creature—hens, sheep, children—is happy only when its life force is acknowledged and respected. If you treat the dough right, it behaves right. (For a person who didn't actually make any bread Howard was very clear about all this, although it was, he said, only in a trivial way about *bread*.) So the dough called for a nimble but not fretful hand, a hand light and gentle but also with a certain firmness. Above all, the hand must be benign, because the tiniest malevolence that I might be harboring inside myself would contaminate the energies that flowed from me, down through the heel of my hand and into the kneading. And by pressing and pushing bad energies into the spirit of the dough, I would impart sourness to the loaf and turn it heavy, and in turn the people who ate it would be sour and heavy, and they'd pass that on in all they did. What a responsibility. But I listened complacently. How could I, married to Howard, bake anything but happy bread?

I did, a number of times, but after Adam was born it got to be a bit hit-and-miss. I was rushed, harassed with everything; I tried more yeast, molasses, a pinch of soda, less salt, more salt. Nothing worked for long. So I baked only on dry days, or on rainy ones. I meditated beforehand, I played music, I sang kneading songs. For years I went on like this. Adam grew up thinking bread was never the same twice, except in its tendency to disappoint. Howard muttered soothingly about energies. It was the Rayburn's fault, I told the Bed and Breakfast guests, who didn't ever quite acquire the acquired taste of my fusty, beery-tasting seed breads. To hell with my energies, I seethed to myself, when instead I made toast with white sliced shop bread which the guests thought much nicer. I lost confidence, and deeper down was actually ashamed: I was too flawed a person to make a good job of bread-making. When Howard's stroke gave me a reason to give it up altogether, I felt I was being relieved of a task to which I'd proved myself inadequate. Besides, my bad shoulder would sometimes ache just at the thought of all the kneading.

However, with Theo to think about, that is changing, and I turn my mind to bread-making once more. And while thinking, unselfishly, that it is something I can do that might give Theo pleasure, I admit that I am, by planning his, attending to the neglected matter of my own. It's enjoyable to conjure up my very first, early bread-making days and falsify them into silvery, soft-focus memories that are treacherously fine and good, too good, of course, ever to have been true. But it's lovely to think of them and to long for them all the same, for October afternoon hours in a kitchen filled with new loaves and baskets of blackberries and jars of jam. I dream of a man alight with love and with autumn gold on his skin coming indoors from a blustering wind to the scent of hedgerow fruits and baking bread, and of course to me, smiling.

In a burst of desire and hope I pull out the old kneading board and all the mixing bowls and baking tins and packets of nuts and seeds. I have no yeast, and there are black specks and silver-backed mites crawling in the flour; a dab of it on my finger tastes sharp and dusty. I throw it all away and explain to Theo I will have to take the van to do a big shop at the wholefoods place just outside Taunton. It's years since I've done that; we've been getting by on what I pick up in the village on Wednesdays. It will mean driving a long way, and I will be far from Howard for several hours, which has not happened since the day Theo came.

I'm thinking all this aloud, sitting at the kitchen table. My hopes begin to ebb, and I wonder if there is any point in even starting the shopping list. "Howard cries, you know," I remind Theo. "If he's left alone for any length of time he just cries, and I can't bear it."

Theo doesn't think that will happen this time, because of course he'll stay with him. "You must go," he says. "If you want to go, why shouldn't you? It's not asking for much, is it? It'll be fun. You could do with a little outing."

Then I explain again about Howard and the spirit of the dough and why I gave up on bread-making. Theo laughs.

"For God's sake, bread has *feelings*? You think you can make a loaf of bread happy or sad?"

"I suppose I am being silly," I say. "And no, not happy or sad, exactly." Theo says nothing to that, but in a way that tells me he wants me to go on. "But when the dough gets sticky and tight and won't rise and it tastes bitter, it is sort of sad," I say, and I pause to write a few more things on my shopping list. "And then when it's all frothy and you get these great big air bubbles in it, it's happy, in a way. Sort of excitable, at any rate. Do you understand what I mean?"

I carry on with the list, speaking my thoughts aloud as the washing machine sloshes away in the scullery down the passage from the kitchen. When I look up I realize Theo's not here. I feel momentarily deserted, until I realize that he'll be flitting to and fro seeing to the laundry, obviously thinking over what I said.

"I mean, people *do* have good or bad energies, don't they?" I call to him. "You put either negative or positive energy into a thing. Everything's got an energy. Including bread." His silence makes me doubt this for the first time in at least thirty years. Where does my certainty about it—about anything—come from? What use is it to me now, what use was it ever?

Theo returns. He does not ask if I want any, but tea is made, my cup is placed on the table. He goes about it not knowing that this isn't the small thing he may think it to be. Having my mind benignly read—my need for a cup of tea noticed and met—charms me more than I can say.

"So if you're sad, you make sad bread?" he says. "So it's all your fault if it goes wrong? But suppose it's not your fault. Suppose it's nothing to do with you at all."

"But Howard says . . ."

"Howard says, Howard says?" Theo swallows some tea, then cocks his head and smiles. "He says what? I don't hear anything."

Howard is in his chair next door, possibly asleep. There is nothing but silence.

"You see? Howard says nothing. So why don't you just make some bread, and enjoy it?"

"I'll try. That's what I want to do."

"Get on with it, then. Go shopping. Make bread. You *are* a silly woman."

He speaks like that in a joking way, of course. I laugh and finish my list, and then he sends me straight off before I can change my mind. He doesn't stand at the door, he doesn't wave. He doesn't even let me say goodbye to Howard, though I want to. Much better this way, he says.

He's right. The longer I'm away without Howard knowing, the shorter the time he'll spend crying. I may be there and back before he's any the wiser if I just get on with it. I do as I am told.

<adam.morgan@logisticsomnicorpsystems.com>

To: deborahstoneyridge@yahoo.com
Sent on tues 4 oct 2011 at 23.34 EST

You should get this tomorrow, hope you will anyway!

   Mum, I can't ever get you in so when you get this will you please ring me and I'll ring you straight back. I'll leave my phone on 24/7 so you'll get through, ok? Unless I'm on the metro or something but if so I'll ring you back the MINUTE I get your message so don't just hang up because then I won't know you tried. Have you tried in past couple of weeks? If so and you didn't get a reply I'm really sorry – must talk soon! Xxx

For maybe half an hour after the van chugged out of earshot Howard sat quietly waiting, until the silence felt safe. When the house was quite still he got up and went to his bedroom.

He had it all planned. First, he used the legs of his walking frame to bat his outdoor shoes out from under the wardrobe into position at the side of the bed. Then he sat down, eased his slippers off, and worked his feet into the shoes. It was too bad about the laces but it wouldn't matter; the shoes would fall off only if he lifted his feet as he walked and he couldn't do more than shuffle. All he had to do was be careful not to trip on the trailing laces. He stood up, got his balance, and set off for the kitchen.

He hadn't in fact got it quite all planned. The cold hit him as soon as he tugged the door open. He hesitated, wondering if he should go back for another sweater, but remembered in time to save himself the effort that the last time he'd tried to open the drawer with the sweaters in it he'd fallen over. On the back of the door hung his old waxed jacket, hard and dirty with years of mud and dried-on rain and kitchen smoke. Practically invisible from years of hanging unused, it was half-hidden under a dirty towel, a bag of clothes pegs and a plastic bag stuffed with other plastic bags, and it was also too high for him to reach. He moved across the floor, stretched over to the mustard jar crammed with kitchen utensils that sat next to the Rayburn, and picked out the longest of the wooden spoons. He edged his way back and used the spoon to knock down the things draped over the jacket. The clothes-peg bag fell open and spilled its contents, littering the floor with a hundred hard, hazardous, sliding obstacles, like dead scorpions. Howard let out a howl, which made him feel dizzy and suddenly afraid. He took several deep breaths, let the last one out slowly, and tried to get a grip on himself. If he didn't start getting things right, there was no saying what might happen; he had a vision of just how badly he could end up, stranded here for hours with broken bones while the wind blew in through the open door.

Raising the spoon again, he brought the jacket down from the hook and caught it against his chest. He dropped the spoon, got one arm into one sleeve, and heaved it up as far as his shoulder, but he couldn't manage the other, and used up too much energy trying. After waiting to get his breath and balance back, he slid through the rattling sea of clothes pegs and negotiated the two steps down into the yard.

Suddenly, there it was, a beautiful autumn day, a small miracle: the sun hanging like a gong in the sky and the air hitting his face and filling his mouth, wide open with concentration, with a sharp cleanliness like mint, or alcohol. Howard inhaled and shivered, felt the air slip down his throat and into his chest. The cold was suddenly lovely. It reached his arms, trembled through his legs, and prickled at his fingertips. All the solid, perpetual aches of his body, all the stiffness in his joints seemed suddenly vaporized, lifted away from him into the rich, coppery, cold sky. Even the rasping calls of the crows flickering in and out of the bare trees against the hillside sounded joyous. He looked up and started forward, feeling that the sparkling day and bird-filled sky were granting him a kind of pardon, as if the choice, obliterated by his stroke, of whether and how and where to move every part of his body, had been restored to him.

It hadn't. He caught his toe on a cobble, the walking frame skidded on the damp stones, he grabbed it hard, gasped, and tottered. The bones in all his limbs jarred painfully. His half-on, half-off jacket slid down his arm; he shook it off and let it fall to the ground. He was going to get very cold, but at least he'd managed to stay upright. The crows above croaked and flapped; two of them landed on the ridge of the pig shed roof and gloated down at him. Across the yard, an incredible distance away, sunlight stretched in through the open door of the pottery studio. He set off.

After what seemed like hours, he reached the doorway and shuffled inside. Exhausted, he slumped against the workbench and looked around. There was no sign of the new drying lines that Deborah had been so excited about. Howard didn't altogether believe there ever would be; one thing he'd noticed about Deborah's excitements—so many of them, recently—was that they flared for an instant and fizzled out, like matches struck in the dark. But just in case the place was going to be gutted, hosed out, and set up for drying laundry, he had to retrieve the things he'd come for before she discovered them. Just as soon as he'd had another moment's rest.

Slow though the journey across the yard had been, he found he was waiting, as he recovered his breath, for his feelings to catch up with him. To begin with and a little to his surprise, it came as neither consolation nor sorrow to be back here. It was simply cheering to remember how his feet had once worked the pedal that turned the wheel still on the bench, how his hands really had thrown pots. That they never would again was a sadness that, even as it swept over him, he tried to dismiss as irrelevant; that the pots had been invariably drab or flawed he wanted to overlook. But the years—the expenditure of years. Howard gazed, seeing himself engrossed in the work, his shoulders hunched over the bench and outside, the weather at the window, another day slipping by. Time he'd never get back. The numberless hours he'd spent here trying to improve, driven by the drawn-out, irreversible error of mistaking all that propulsive vanity and industriousness for talent. How to justify so much misdirected effort? His failure weighted the air with the density of grief.

The place had changed color by losing color, its surfaces turning pale and powdery like disintegrating paper, its edges softened by a pall of clay dust. But tracks on the floor from the door through to the back were darker where someone had recently gone to and fro, and a tracery of scrapes and smears near the middle marked the spot where the old work stools had been broken up and splintered for firewood. Howard's eyes scanned the shelves on the back wall. All his tools and jars and tubs of glazes stood under a fuzzy coating of dust; to his relief, all looked untouched. The large biscuit tins he was looking for were there, too, stacked as before. He scraped forward.

The immediate difficulty, which he'd anticipated, was reaching the tins at all. In the past he would stand on a stool to lift things off the shelves; now, even if there had been a stool left in one piece, he wouldn't be able to manage that. But he knew there was a pair of tongs somewhere in the studio, left from the time he was experimenting with raku ware, and he found them where he hoped they'd still be, on their wall hook above the glazing bench. The handles were fashioned like a pair of shears, requiring one hand each, so he held the tongs by their closed flat pincer ends, designed for lifting newly fired pots red-hot from the kiln into tubs of sawdust. Howard winced, remembering how he'd botched it, the sooty black smoke that had filled the air as the sawdust ignited. The place might have burned down, and when he'd brought out the blackened pots and dipped them in the vat of water that was supposed to wash the smoldering sawdust ash away and reveal the crackle pattern of the raku glaze, they'd shattered to pieces.

With the tongs, there was no question of lifting the biscuit tins from their shelf; all he could do was dislodge them. They were seven of them, all rectangular and sitting one on top of another. The one he wanted was at the bottom, where for years its contents had been safe from Deborah's eyes; she had no cause to go looking for anything in the pottery, least of all something in a biscuit tin at the bottom of a stack of seven; she seldom even went in the place. Howard poked and nudged at the tower of tins until it came crashing down, banging the lower shelves, shedding lids and raining an assortment of pottery tools: cutters, pins, scalpels, looped wires, sponges, kiln props. The tins, lids, and contents hit the floor in a cacophony of clangs; objects rolled and tumbled away. Howard squeezed his eyes shut and waited for his ears to stop ringing. Then he went searching about the floor, stooping only when necessary, holding on to his frame with one hand and bending his knees cautiously, then stretching upright very slowly so that he didn't get dizzy and keel over. In this way, painstakingly, he found everything that had spilled from the tin he was interested in.

He came across the T-shirt first: it seemed to have shrunk and was of no real color anymore, though he remembered its being yellow on the day he wore it last. He flapped it against the wall to get rid of the clay dust it had picked up from the floor, which brought on a fit of coughing. When he'd recovered from that, he stroked the T-shirt across his chin and felt it catch on his stubble; it still carried the slight pungency of his sweat and maybe the animal scent of birth blood. The nurse had tried to take it away but he'd closed his eyes and clung on to it, afraid to ask her if he could keep it in case she failed to understand that he *had* to keep it, and told him no. He'd rolled it up when she left the room and sneaked it under his sweater to bring home. Now he placed it again under his clothes, and tears broke from his eyes at the sensation of it, the cotton flattened and cool against his skin.

But breaking down would stop him doing what he had to; he braced himself next to pick up the bracelet from the floor. The plastic was yellowed and splitting and the words in faded ballpoint were hardly legible under the clouded name panel. He understood what the label said more because he'd so long ago memorized it than by recognizing the letters. He closed his hand around it and pushed it into his pocket.

The last thing had landed on the floor some way away, blown perhaps by the breeze from the doorway. Howard shuffled through the spilled litter and picked it up. The little hat, shaped like an acorn cup, had been fashioned from a tubular length of muslin, cut and knotted at one end. He brought it to his face and squeezed the tight cloth button of the knot in his good hand; he breathed in the scents trapped in its fibers. It was too much; quickly he bunched the whole thing in his fist and stuffed that, too, in his pocket.

Howard pushed himself on his frame all the way back to the door. He was shivering now, and the return journey across the yard took even longer. He did not notice the sun again, and did not have enough strength to make the small detour to retrieve the waxed jacket; he left it flapping on the ground. The back door stood open—deliberately he had not closed it behind him—but once inside he could not keep hold of the doorhandle to bring it to again. When he made it back to his chair in the sitting room he pulled out the T-shirt, identity bracelet, and muslin hat. Without looking properly at them again, he stuffed the T-shirt and bracelet deep in the upholstered crevice between the seat and side cushions of his armchair. They'd be safe there. Nobody in this house had any reason to lift chair cushions from their places. But he kept for a moment in his hands, before pushing it also into the depths of the chair, the muslin hat. He brought it to his face and held it, dabbing it against his eyes as he wept. Because although after all these years it couldn't be possible, he thought he could still smell in the soft bundle of cloth the new, damp hair of a baby.

Hi Mum will you be at the library today, did you get the email I sent yesterday? I'm guessing you didn't because you haven't called. If you get this wed morning you can call straightaway from the library, I managed to get a few hours to be at a desk so I can take a call, so I hope to hear from you.

Please call because from tomorrow I'm on the road again and I know you won't even leave a message because you think I'm too busy for phone calls. I'm not!! I can't always answer but you just have to leave a message and I'll *always* get back to you.

I wanted to tell you, things are a bit different round the office, it's a completely different atmosphere. Sacha's boss (guy called Cy Chambers he's about 45) is around this week which is usually a total nightmare but it's ok – he's changed, like he wants us to like him, he's been actually talking to people, he knows our names now. He told somebody off for not taking all their holiday, it's a bit weird!

I was talking to Sacha about it after. She's really white in the face and wears this sort of turban, I told her she looked cool and I hoped it was ok to say that, it felt a bit awkward but she didn't mind. Anyway I also mentioned to her I didn't get to see you last summer and she just looked at me with this really sad look. Then I said something about maybe I could manage it this Christmas and she said if I wanted her to she would personally see to it there was cover for all my deadlines over the break if I wanted to take a week off!!

To be honest I do NOT fancy Christmas in this flat on my own and nobody I know is going ski-ing anywhere I fancy going, so I might as well come and see you guys. Just kidding!! Seriously I really just want to come and be with you. Sacha says she's staying home and not budging, she just wants things nice and normal. I totally get that, I probably want the same.

Lots of love Adam

CALL ME!!!

A few years back I forgot to renew the tax disc and insurance on the van. It was an oversight that first time but since then I've let the whole business slip. The older the van gets the more it's a waste of good money to insure it, and I resent paying out tax to the government just to drive four miles to Bridgecombe once a week on a frost-cracked road that's all but deserted. Even in summer there are more sheep and wild ponies wandering along it than cars and I don't notice them paying road tax, and my little bit of wear and tear on it can hardly make any difference. On top of that they never grit the road in winter so it's not as if they're spending a penny on it. Theo and I are of one mind on this. So inside my week-in, week-out orbit from Stoneyridge to Bridgecombe I never really think of myself as breaking the law, and even though I am, who's to know? I don't think I've once seen a policeman in Bridgecombe. But once I'm outside my safe orbit by even a few miles, I can see that if I'm stopped by the police I will be considered a cheat or a petty crook, or merely feckless and slightly nuts. That's not how I am, and Theo confirms it. I don't accept that picture of myself. But being stopped would be troublesome.

And out here on the main road the van shows its age and takes all my concentration. On the Bridgecombe journeys I don't much notice the scraping gearbox and how the steering pulls to the left. The accelerator pedal is worn silver-smooth and when I try to get up any speed it rattles so hard it nearly shakes my foot right off. The passenger's window judders down every few minutes because the winder's broken and then the wind and road noise roar in, spinning my hair across my face and making me deaf even to the rasp of the engine. Going up the hills I mash my foot down but the van just slows and slows so I have to pull over to the left and crawl along. Then I can see it all as if from the outside and at a great distance, a metal box scabbed with rust shaking along the smooth black sweep of white-striped tarmac, its tires snapping through the gravel on the shoulder while shiny cars and trucks whip past. And all around, the shoulders of the wind are pushing, pushing, pushing at it because it's going slower than everything else on the road, and slower even than the great plumy clouds up above that are racing over the empty hills on either side and going higher still, way, way up to where there's nothing but weather and huge sky and the streaks of plane trails. Down here the van scuttles along like a tin cockroach. I feel small and out of place and afraid. It's a mistake, I should not have come. All my truant's joy at the idea of this expedition has vanished. What does bread matter? The van breaking down will bring a heap of woe, and all for a few bags of flour. But I can't return with the task abandoned for want of a little courage. If I do that it will mean that yet another thing—in this instance, Theo's encouragement—will have failed. I don't want him to feel failure of any kind. So I keep on driving, holding on tight to my plans for the bread-making and to my dreams of an October kitchen with Theo in it, because I don't know what else to do, and besides, those plans and dreams are what I want.

At least I don't have to go all the way into Taunton. I pull in to the farm shop and health foods co-op just off the roundabout where in summer *Welcome to Taunton* is spelled out in geraniums among white petunias in a long curving flowerbed. On this autumn day it's an empty brown rectangle. I haven't been here in over three years and it's a little disorienting to find there's now a children's play area and a fancy sort of shed selling garden pots. Across from the co-op a new cinder-block building is going up and bulldozers are leveling the ground all around it, pushing the smashed turf and roots and chalk-smeared clay into a low, thick wall.

It's even more disorienting to find that inside the shop, Christmas has arrived. I haven't given Christmas a thought, but as the tinselly banners over my head point out, it Is Coming. However, the dread that usually comes with the idea of Christmas begins to fade as I push my cart around, because of course it will be different this year. Theo will be with us, and so it cannot fail to be delightful. (I don't have to ask if he'll still be here. I know he will.) So when I've got everything I need for baking every conceivable kind of bread, I go on buying, piling the cart with dried fruits and brown sugar and mulled wine spices and nuts, which are all on special offer. I am going to make plum puddings, Christmas cake, mince pies, everything. The prospect of being really busy is exciting in a way it hasn't been for years. I shall make it a Christmas to remember.

The bill at the end is a dreadful amount, but I won't need to come back here anytime soon. Apart from the expense, the thought of repeating this expedition is unbearable. I have been stuck at Stoneyridge for so long that leaving Howard to drive twenty-six miles to go shopping is a momentous and fearful adventure, and no wonder I'm anxious to get back to him. But the fact is, although I am concerned, it's got nothing to do with Howard. It's Theo I'm anxious about. Of course he had to stay behind, but I still wish I'd been able to bring him. I need him with me. Shopping for the special Christmas baking and imagining his pleasure at the lovely things I'll make has me missing him all the more, and now I have to face the return drive on my own before I'll be back with him. I push the cart out to the car park as fast as I manage and start loading everything into the van. Then I hear my name.

"Deborah?" It's spoken like that, as a question. I know the voice. I hate the voice. More than ever I wish that Theo were with me. I keep my head down and go on with the packing.

"Deborah, hello! It *is* you. Gosh, hello!"

"Oh, Pat. Hello," I say. "What a surprise. Didn't see you there, sorry!"

"It's lovely to see you! How are you? How's everything? Been stocking up? Here, let me give you a hand." She pushes her empty cart out of the way and starts loading my things in.

"It's fine, honestly, don't worry. I'm fine."

"So, how's Adam doing? I don't hear from him so much these days. What's he up to?"

"He's fine. Very busy, he's got big responsibilities now. His firm think the world of him. Still based abroad. Going from strength to strength."

"It is lucky, bumping into you like this. I only came in to get stuff for the Christmas cake. I always get the fruit and nuts here. They're Fair Trade."

"Are they? They're quite expensive," I say. "Still, only once a year," I add, realizing in time this is the correct attitude. "So, how're Vince and Flora?"

"Oh, they're both fine, thanks. Vince is a bit tired, looking forward to the end of term. Flora's in great form—she's still teaching in Gambia, goes traveling when she can, she's in Cape Town at the moment. Home for Christmas. Gosh, look, you've bought half the shop! Are you about to hibernate? What about Adam, is he getting back for Christmas?"

We finish the unloading and I have to turn and face her. She isn't wearing her dog-collar and her hair is springier than ever, but she hasn't changed. She still thrusts her goodwill at you like a yapping puppy she thinks you want to hold and have lick you. She still has those gleaming eyes like gray-flecked whirlpools that pull you in and make you tell her things.

"Adam? Oh, yes. He wouldn't miss Christmas at home."

"You'll be looking forward to that. You must miss him. How's Howard? Are things still okay, all by yourselves up there? There's a caregivers club in Taunton now, did you know?"

"Actually, we're not by ourselves anymore." I don't in the least mean to tell her this, but I have to put an end to her patronizing. "I have someone to help now."

"Oh? That's great! That's *really* good to hear. So, do you have a, is this . . . what, someone in the family, a nurse, or —"

"He's a volunteer, sort of. Theo. He's marvelous, just like family. He's Adam's age, so it's a bit like having Adam around all the time, that's what I tell him, anyway! He's so willing and practical."

"Gosh! He sounds amazing. How wonderful!"

There's a note in her voice I don't care for. "Yes, it is wonderful, especially for Howard. He seems ten years younger."

Then Pat says the coffee at the whole food café isn't bad (and is, of course, also Fair Trade) and it's her day off so she isn't in a hurry as she usually is, so would I like to have coffee with her. I smile, and she keeps on smiling. She has no idea how the thought of being detained long enough to drink a cup of coffee with her appalls me. I don't need her sympathy about coping with Howard and I don't want to waste time listening to her reminisce about Adam's schooldays and how well things have worked out for everybody—she has a way of refusing to take any credit for it that somehow causes all of it to attach to her. I don't want to observe her tact as she skirts around any precise mention of how and why Adam came to fetch up in her vestry and get taken under her bloody wing, and did so well in his A levels he got into his first choice of university. More than anything, I don't want to be reminded of the way Pat still wants to belong to us in some way, or us to her.

"I can't, sorry," I say. "Theo's expecting me back. It's not fair to him if I'm not back when I said I'd be."

Pat tips her head to one side. "Not even a quick one? I'd love to catch up properly. Use my phone if you like, ring and say you'll be a bit late."

Use her phone? How little she knows.

"No, there's no point, he won't hear the phone if . . . if he's out, taking Howard for a walk. We can't really use mobiles at Stoneyridge."

"Oh, variable signal? We get that, too. Well, that's a shame. But it's good to see you again, Deborah. Hang on, let me give you the club details. If ever you can make it you'd be really welcome. It's every second Wednesday. I've got a pen somewhere."

"Thanks very much, Pat, but I never come to Taunton. There's no need now I've got Theo."

"Oh. Are you sure? It's great fun if ever you do fancy it. Just give me a ring, all right? Great news about Theo. He sounds great. Just what you need."

I get myself into the driver's seat but she keeps a hold of the door and stops me from shutting it.

"It would be good to catch up properly sometime. I'd love to see

Howard. I do pass your way from time to time, maybe I could drop in."

I'm trying to turn the ignition so I pretend not to hear this. The van starts on the third try. "Well, take care, then, Pat. Bye, now. Happy Christmas!"

Pat straightens up and lets go of the door. I slam it shut and drive off without looking back, knowing she will be standing waving.

I am now in a great hurry to get home and tell Theo about bumping into Pat, how it has brought rushing into my mind that long-ago time when Adam was a teenager. I haven't spoken of it before now and I'm nervous; I'm pretty certain I'm not up to the test of courage it will be to dwell at any length on those two awful days when he went missing. I need to try the story out on myself first, to check that the words it requires won't solidify into dumb, unsayable blocks in my brain. As I'm driving along and sifting these thoughts around, I almost hear Theo telling me to take my time, to find the words and the courage little by little. I can skip any bits I wish, he's saying, I can come back to them later or leave them out altogether. I don't even have to start at the beginning.

So I decide I will start at the end: that nowadays Adam does a job I don't understand in a terribly complicated business I don't see any need for, called supply chain management, and he got this job because he is very good at mathematics and logic and very interested in how big businesses work and make money. As I'm saying all this aloud, as if Theo is with me in the van, I'm listening out for the customary note of awe in my voice as I explain that Adam is much cleverer than I am and, I go on to say, I'm afraid that consequently my mothering has always been a little nervous and possibly overloaded with respect. I sense Theo nodding and waiting to hear more, and I drive on, now in silence, thinking.

I am forcing myself to recall Pat's breezy way of telling me her news of Flora; she gave no hint that she's in any way impressed by her daughter's brave, bold doings in Africa. By comparison, I speak of my son as if my feelings for him verge on the idolatrous. I imagine Theo weighing the possibility that, as I put it to him, it's as though Adam's being born to me was a gift I didn't earn and that therefore

demanded, as propitiation, that I fasten upon him a meek, even ob-
sequious kind of love. For his part, Adam probably considers my
being his mother a handicap. Even when he was very little, if I
scanned his face for signs of a child's affection I observed something
more like fatigue, or at best a composed, possibly intellectual fond-
ness. I wipe away the tears that are beginning to fall; I won't be able
to drive if I can't see properly. Go on, Theo's voice urges softly.
"There's more."

What is not in doubt is that Adam is qualified to do his inexplica-
bly complex job because, when he was fourteen, Pat and Vince arranged for him to lodge on weekdays with Vince's recently widowed
mother and go to a school in Exeter, where he was immediately
picked out as an academic high flier. None of that, nor his determination to go to university, nor his ambition to make a lot of money—
and least of all his fascination with supply chain management—has
anything to do with his parents. Except, perhaps, that he set out to
realize an ambition to become as unlike us as possible in every way.

Then you needn't feel guilty about not liking Pat, Theo would
reply to that. It's no wonder. Even if she is a genuinely good person.

This is the beauty of talking with Theo. He understands everything I say and also what I don't say. I wasn't talking about not liking
Pat. I did not even know I was in need of reassurance on the matter
of not liking her. In the juddering van I say "Thank you," and shove
my foot down on the accelerator. The engine strains. I pump my foot
up and down; Theo's patience may be infinite, but mine isn't. I can't
wait to get back and tell him the rest of the story. I have a strong
feeling he's going to encourage me to conclude—although I am re-
sisting it, even now—that Adam hasn't always been a very good son.

From: deborahstoneyridge@yahoo.com

To: <adam.morgan@logisticsomnicorpsystems.com>
Sent on wed 12 oct 2011 at 11.12 GMT

I'm so sorry Adam, I didn't make it last week, Wednesdays not always so easy any more.

I'm not sure the stroke club's really worth it anyway, it's a hassle getting him up and ready if he's not in the right mood.

I think I told you about that nurse turning up here a little while ago? Right out of the blue, very inconsiderate, it put D off for the whole day. There was no need, either, she was just dropping in because Dad had missed a couple of stroke clubs. You'd think she'd have enough to do! Anyway I told her on the QT we don't welcome surprise visits, proper notice is preferred. I have plenty to do without having the routine thrown out – she seemed to take my point.

Anyway, then they rang up just because he wasn't there last week! He doesn't need weighing, he's eating as much as he wants and he hasn't said anything so I don't think he's missing out by not going.

Talking of unannounced visitors I saw Pat the other day. I don't mean *she* dropped in unannounced (though she's been known to), I saw her when I was out. It's been at least three years – last time was quite soon after the stroke, she turned up here, I think I told you. I've nothing against her in the least and I know she did a lot for you but I can't say I'm sorry she hasn't been back – that last time Dad got very agitated, you know how he hates organized religion. I still think there's something odd about a woman in a dog collar. But Pat and Vince were good to you.

Seeing her got me thinking about your fourteenth birthday. Well, I'll never forget THAT one. It all worked out fine in the end but oh, if you could have just talked to us!! Who knows I might have been able to persuade Dad about school and everything without all that drama! OK I know, useless to go over it now, and I'm not really raking it all up again, it's over and done with. Are you still in touch with Pat, I think she said not. She moved to a different church didn't she?

What a shame about your boss Sara, that is sad. She's young to have cancer but she had her children quite late didn't she? She's the same age I was when you were fourteen, that's another reason I was thinking about it again I suppose. Speedy recovery to her, anyway.

Re your visit – oh yes it would be lovely but how can you be sure about getting the time off because Christmas is still months away!!! You never know where they're sending you next so I definitely won't get my hopes up too much! (eg won't mention it to D). The shops are full of Christmas stuff already of course, I was at Food For Thought last wed (hence no email) and it was just as bad there as anywhere else.

D's really getting around the place and doing more for himself at home eg when I got back from FFT he'd been all over the place making a terrible mess. Kitchen upside down and the old studio a bombsite. I'm getting rid of everything in there, did I say? It never occurs to him somebody's got to clear everything up after him – he is the limit! I tell him I'm going to have to start treating him like a bad boy if he behaves like one and we'll see how he likes that!

Talk soon lots of love Mum xxx

ADAM'S BIRTHDAY 1997

Adam flung his backpack on to the shoulder where the track from Stoneyridge met the road, and crouched down opposite the log slice sign on which his father had burned the words FOR SALE POTTERY WEAVING TEAS BED & BREAKFAST. Another board propped against it read EGGS FOR SALE. His backside sank against a wet, frondy nest of couch grass and the rain came down harder, rolling through his scalp and dripping on to his shoulders, drenching his back. Getting soaked was part of all this, he supposed. It kind of fit with the rest of the crap.

It was the ninth day of rain, his fourteenth birthday, and the first day of his freedom. Around him, through his half-closed eyes, the green landscape glittered. Past the bend in the road and in the distance the fields and the moor were misty, the sky over them gray and sodden. He wondered if, supposing a rabbit ran across that field right now, he'd stand a chance of getting it with the shotgun. He raised a hand, closed one eye, and scanned the width of the field, squinting down the barrel of his forefinger. Probably. He was a pretty good shot—not as good as Kevin but way better than Kyle. If he got the chance to practice he'd be excellent, probably he'd end up being able to shoot just about anything, if he got the practice. It was a skill, you'd think Dad would *want* him to get a skill like that. It was unbelievable—what was his *problem*? What was wrong with getting a shotgun for your birthday when it was only for rabbits and pigeons? It wasn't like he was going to shoot *people,* it wasn't like he was going off and joining the fucking army. Kevin and Kyle and their dad knew there was nothing wrong with it, that was why Kevin and Kyle gave him the gun today for his birthday, an old one reconditioned but practically the same as theirs and they'd had theirs for years and Kyle was still only thirteen. *You're best learning young to use a gun properly, you country lads*—that's what their dad said. Then you grow up respecting it, that's the way you stay safe. Adam pushed his fingers into his scalp and tugged, ready to tear his hair out. His dad couldn't be like that, oh no. His dad had to wait until they'd gone and then take the gun off him. Just like before, taking stuff off him. *No, Adam. There will be no guns in this house. That's final.* The only stuff he ever got that he really wanted, his dad took it off him, and he had no *right.*

Adam filled his cheeks with air, held his breath, and shot his plug of gum hard across the tarmac. It came to rest in a puddle bubbling with rain. He put two more sticks of gum in his mouth and chewed fast. Once the flavor went he'd shape them into another ball against his teeth and shoot that out, too, see if he could get it farther than the first one, maybe across the white line. Or maybe he'd wait for a car to come snaking along the road and he'd stick his thumb out, and if it didn't stop for him he'd time it so either the gum hit a wheel as it fizzed past or shot right underneath and bounced out on the far side. Hunkered on the shoulder, he smiled and looked up and down, hoping for a caravan—he might actually get the gum to stick on the side of a caravan—although he knew the road was too narrow and hilly for many of those. Not even that many cars came.

Adam pushed his tongue through the gum to test it for stretch and blew a pathetic bubble. He gazed at the first rising bend over to his left and imagined it all: some tosser coming down with a caravan in tow, going too fast, squeal of brakes, caravan swings, car veers, skids, loses it—*wham!* Car's crumpled in the ditch, caravan's on its side.

What would he do?

He runs to help, obviously. What if the tank's burst? Whole fucking thing could go up in flames! He takes charge, gets them all out.

There's three of them, a pair of stupid arguing parents and their daughter. She's about sixteen, but he's so tall everybody takes him for sixteen too, or older. The parents are tossers. They ignore him, they're too busy shouting at each other. The girl's slightly hurt but it's only a bump on the head. Mainly, she's pissed off. He knows this because the moment he sees her he understands her. For once he's not afraid (this is new, this has never happened before). He tells her *Look, you don't have to take any more of this. Fuck, you could've been killed! This is their shit, not yours. Mine are just the same and I'm not taking any more, I just fucking walked out.* Then over her shoulder he'd see another car approaching down the hill. *So can you. You're sixteen, aren't you? They can't stop you.* And she looks him hard in the eye. Just as he's waving down the car he notices properly how gorgeous she is—long hair, long body, short skirt, great tits, golden skin—and what's more, she sees him noticing, and she's cool with it. Now he, cool but determined, talks to the driver. His voice does not yodel like it sometimes can in real life. The driver talks back to him like he's an equal, not a kid. *Yeah mate, lift to Exeter? Sure, no problem, get in.*

You coming or not? he says to the girl. She really is gorgeous. She gasps *Oh, yes,* he grabs her hand, and they're off, laughing.

Adam spat the ball of gum across the road. It landed short of the first. He had no more gum and now his thing was swelling in a familiar way; the girl had been featuring in his daydreams for a few months now, though she was occasionally displaced by more pressing memories of some pictures Kevin had showed him in a magazine he'd found crumpled in the storage box under the seat of his dad's tractor. Maybe there was something wrong with him, the way the same girl kept appearing, but mostly what felt wrong was the emptiness he was left with when she went away and ordinary life took over again. How then he almost hated her for real for not being there, like she actually did exist or something.

He was feeling the emptiness yawn open right now. He let out a minty belch, stood up, wiped his hands down his backside, and wandered a few yards along the shoulder, kicking methodically at the heads of drenched cow parsley and showering the air with seeds and cold drops of rainwater. He heard a car coming, turned, and stuck out his thumb. It didn't even slow down.

In the next hour a dozen more passed him in the same way. When he wandered back and hunkered down again, he found a snail on his backpack. He picked it off and kicked it across the road, enjoying the intimate tap it made against the toe of his sneaker, the tiny rattle as it rolled. In the grass next to his foot he found another one and kicked that after it. Then he remembered a joke Kevin once told him about a snail getting kicked off somebody's doorstep and couldn't help smiling as he went hunting for more along the shoulder. But already he was sickened by what he was doing to them, and he was sickened by the rain, and most of all he was sickened by the knowledge that he was so wet and pissed off that if he hadn't stolen his mother's egg money from the box on the hall table he would probably go back up to the house. The thought of stepping out of the rain into the warm, empty kitchen wouldn't leave him alone. But fuck it, as if he could. Anyway, the kitchen never was empty, and if ever it was warm enough the Rayburn stank.

He slid his fingers over the notes and coins in his back pocket, trying to make them feel like his. Because they should have been. He'd asked specially for a bit of money (he knew it couldn't be a lot) for his birthday. Just a bit to do what he liked with, to go and buy something normal with. A wooden seagull carved by his father out of a twisted bit of dead tree was what he got instead, together with another scarf knitted by his mother with wool from the manky sheep. *You can hang the seagull from your bedroom ceiling,* his mother said, when the crap presents lay unwrapped on the table. *And the scarf's from Celestia, her wool's got a lovely touch of auburn, hasn't it?*

Fuck Celestia. Fuck the seagull. Adam pulled the money from his pocket and counted it, a month's worth of egg money, just over twenty pounds. A lot to his parents. They were always going on about money. How it wasn't important, but also how it wasn't important that they didn't have enough of it to buy the things other people did. Making out it didn't matter, as if the things weren't worth buying in the first place, the liars.

He wasn't fooled. Since he was a kid he'd been clearer about money than they were. To begin with you needed it to get stuff you wanted, and yes, he did want stuff. Normal stuff. He wanted computer games and a video player, never mind that they didn't have a computer or a television. But beyond that he understood money in a way he couldn't put into words. He just knew there was a feeling that having money would give you, a safer, nicer feeling than the excitement of wanting and getting stuff. You wouldn't even have to spend the money, you'd just have to know you could. Maybe it was a feeling of freedom—the wanting freed from the awful, dragging ache of not getting. However you defined it, Adam knew that money was a kind of enchantment that could settle over a person's life like a magical form of dew. It was impossible that his desire for it, a feeling so pure and yearning and private—so spiritual—could be the ugly impulse his parents called greed.

He put the egg money back in his pocket. Serve them right. It wasn't like he'd been expecting a PlayStation, never mind an airgun, he knew they weren't rich. The bit of birthday money he'd asked for wasn't even the point either, not the whole point anyway, because more than anything what he'd wanted was for them just to listen. Just for once hear what he was saying. Then they'd see he was different, that he wasn't like them. Actually, nobody else he knew (apart maybe from Callum and Fee but they'd gone away) was like them.

Kevin and Kyle's mum and dad weren't rich either and Kevin and Kyle still got normal stuff, they had a PlayStation and a telly and computer games. They had takeaways and holidays and their house had proper carpets, and radiators that got warm. And their farm had sheep and stuff but it didn't make their dad weird like his dad, their dad didn't go on about fucking earth harmonies all day.

He had to get out of Stoneyridge. And it was only twenty quid, for fuck's sake.

By the time a car stopped for him nearly two hours later—a white Volvo estate with two slavering dogs in the back, steaming up the windows—Adam was almost tearful. He was damp, shivering with cold, and also miserable with hunger. He'd thought of bringing some food but the idea of standing in the kitchen making sandwiches to run away from home with felt stupid and weird, the kind of thing his mother would think of. He'd left the house with only a hunk of bread, which he'd eaten on the way down the track.

The man driving the Volvo didn't speak but the woman was nice. She said, "Oh, look at you, you're simply drenched, are you heading for Exeter?"

Adam said yes and climbed in. As the car drove off, he turned back to look at the hillside but could see nothing through the steamed-up windows. He thought about his parents going on with the day at Stoneyridge, unaware he'd left home for good. He pictured his father too busy counting sheep on the moor to notice the absence of his only son, his mother rolling out brown pastry to make three disgusting pasties lumpy with potato and carrot, her face a blank. He couldn't eat his mother's pasties unless they were smothered in ketchup, but nonetheless his cheeks watered at the thought of them. She'd be looking out at the pouring rain and hoping it would ease off enough to let her insist on the birthday picnic. Well, there wasn't going to be a fucking birthday picnic, and for the first time that day Adam felt a wave of joy. He sat back in the Volvo and tried to concentrate on the journey.

He couldn't. The joy didn't last. His parents would notice he was gone sooner or later but what if they never *got* it, what if they never really grasped how infuriated he was? He was angry not only with them, but also because it felt so bad to be invisible to them *and* on his birthday, and he was afraid that caring about that might mean he was still a child. He didn't understand why, when he was the one who had left, the thought of them up at Stoneyridge without him made him feel so locked-out and lonely. Most of all he was angry that once again (and it kept happening) he found himself unable to feel the same way about anything long enough to know what his true feelings were.

When the woman turned and beamed and said she'd made her husband stop, she just couldn't think of driving past him in this weather, he gave her a faint smile and said nothing. He was horrified that tears were rising in his eyes. She asked him if he was a student and did he live locally, and he told her he was a bit hungover from celebrating his seventeenth birthday and didn't mean to be rude or anything but he wasn't really up to conversation. The man cast his wife a look and they drove on in near silence for over an hour. When they stopped for petrol at a service area seven miles from Exeter the husband told him this was as good a place as any for him to hop it. Adam took his cue.

There was a café, where he wolfed down the all-day breakfast. Afterward he sat on, unable to think of moving without wanting to cry. He tried, and failed, to bring back the dream girl from the overturned caravan and place her in the seat opposite him and looking at him with love, trusting him to know what to do. Outside, the rain had stopped and beyond the canopy over the forecourt the sky was turning pink and silky with sunset clouds. Adam stared through the window as cars pulled in at the fuel pumps and drivers filled up, paid at the kiosk, and drove on again. He envied everyone he saw. They were all people who, he could tell by their careless way of walking back to their cars, had proper destinations, places they wanted to go and where they were expected. Next to them, his plan to find Callum and Fee's house and stay with them began to look really stupid. He remembered how great they were, much younger than his parents and always nice to him, but suppose they'd changed? Or suppose they hadn't: they'd done the same kind of smallholding stuff on Exmoor until they gave it up and went to live in Exeter, so were they really going to understand why he couldn't stand it at Stoneyridge? They weren't expecting him. They could be on holiday. They could be dead.

Eventually he had to get up from the table to go and pee, and afterward he wandered into the games arcade, where he wasted money on Ace Driver. Feeling even more stupid and wretched, he latched on to three lads who came in and started playing some war game. They were loutish and friendly, and over the thumping of simulated rocket fire and planetary annihilation he learned they were on their way back to Exeter after a day delivering white goods in a radius around the city. Their van was empty now and the one who was driving told Adam he was welcome ("welcome" meaning it didn't matter to them one way or the other) if he wanted to string along with them.

The journey was raucous, the driving alarming, and when they reached the outskirts of the city the lads were in too big a hurry to go and get drunk to bother with him and left him in the car park of a floodlit, red-brick pub on a roundabout. It was a humiliation to Adam that they didn't invite him along for a drink because that could only mean he looked his age. And he was slightly shocked they didn't ask where he was going or if he'd be all right. He had a line ready about looking up old friends, a spur-of-the-moment thing. But they hadn't even asked his name.

He watched the pub door long after the lads disappeared behind it, trying to find the courage to follow them. But he couldn't, and after a while turned away. He wasn't in any part of Exeter he'd been before, and the picture he'd had in his mind, of arriving in an understandable, familiar sort of place that was somehow ready to welcome him, was suddenly absurd. It hadn't occurred to him to buy a street map—he wasn't sure how good he was at reading maps, anyway. If he'd thought about it at all he'd sort of imagined jovial strangers giving him directions to Bouvier Terrace, as if everybody he encountered would be friends of Callum and Fee's. He hadn't seen them himself since he was about ten; now that he thought about it, maybe there'd been no more than a couple of visits after they gave up their Exmoor place. And supposing he found the house, and even if they hadn't moved, the idea of them taking him in would dissolve on the doorstep. How would they even recognize him? Why couldn't he have seen all these problems earlier, when he was copying their address from his mother's address book? His belief in the past was evaporating, the mirage of a welcome at Callum and Fee's house vanishing before the hard churn of traffic on the roundabout, the garish pub, the dark pavements. In its place he saw how complete the world was, how perfectly well it turned without him—he wasn't at the center of anything except his own failures. He saw with horror how childish he'd been. It was another example of how his mind changed itself, without his consent, and how he never thought things through in time to stop himself from fucking up.

He left the roundabout behind, and making zigzag turns through the streets, headed deep into a suburb of terraced houses bordered by low hedges and shallow front gardens. It was dark now and curtains were drawn across lit rooms, and he thought of home with dreadful, false longing. He thought of telephoning. Do that, he told himself fiercely, and you're stuffed. Give up now and it will *matter*. This night was going to be a test, it would prove something or other. How he handled it would be important for other nights to come, maybe for the rest of his life.

He carried on walking, first of all to keep warm and then because he was afraid to stop, and beyond that because there was nowhere he could stop. He walked to get away from the strangeness of walking, to outdistance his panic, telling himself he'd be all right once he got his bearings. He didn't, of course, get his bearings, and the strangeness and panic dogged him. It was weird that there was nothing to stop him walking anywhere he wanted, but he still felt cornered. The suburb grew darker and the houses bigger; they receded now behind high walls. After an hour or so he had the idea it was just as well he was wandering God knows where because he should be avoiding the main streets and the city center anyway, where he might be stopped and challenged by the police.

Although the wind had dropped it was much colder. A smoky, orange night sky roared softly above him and through the trees bordering the long front gardens. Adam saw lights behind curtained windows go out. From a driveway ahead of him a fox appeared. It stopped, a front paw raised, snout in the air, and looked at him unafraid; its black lips wore a raddled, delinquent smile. Then, judging Adam no threat, it turned and carried on without hurry, looking back at him from time to time and loping casually into the middle of the road. Adam followed, feeling befriended at last. When the fox disappeared into another garden he loitered at the gate hoping to see it again, until he was too cold to go on standing there and went on his way, crestfallen.

He was hungry again and berated himself for not having had the sense to buy food at the service station. There wasn't going to be anywhere round here to get anything. It was unthinkable—although he did think of it, and then his innards burned with fear as well as hunger—that he might go up the driveway and around the back of one of the big dark houses and try a few doors in the hope of finding an unlocked one leading into a kitchen with a loaded fridge. But then he imagined alarms going off, security lights, people shouting, and if any of that happened he'd never be able to run away because his legs would seize. They were already heavy and stiff—fear and cold had him in irons—and if he stopped walking he might not be able to move again. He'd had no idea, he realized as he trudged on, just how many freezing hours were contained in a single night. But he *had* to stop being so afraid, he had to find a place safe enough for him to lie down and sleep. He saw himself, oddly, cartoonishly, on a park bench under newspapers. Was that what he was now, a tramp? Where *did* tramps sleep? Then it came to him, his first good idea for hours if not all day—a church. He could sleep in a church.

So his walking took on purpose. He'd passed a church ages ago, not far from the pub. After a few wrong turns he found his way back to it, but it was locked. He went all around the building looking for other doors; everything was locked. His good idea was beginning to look really stupid. He was beginning to find the thought of lying under a bush not unbearable, and certainly better than walking through the night.

He felt like crying again. Only because he couldn't bear to retrace his steps, he slunk along the pavement and took a different turning. The houses thinned out. He passed a school with railings and padlocked gates, a few playing fields, and after more walking found himself on an industrial estate. There were lights shining in some of the low buildings and he began to make his way cautiously from tree to tree, afraid there might be security guards or, even worse, guard dogs.

He had to find somewhere he could stay hidden until morning. One of the buildings was unlit and surrounded by an overgrown hedge; he ventured near enough to peer through it and discover that the whole place was boarded up and derelict. The doorway wasn't too filthy and at least looked dry, and it was deep enough to give him a little cover. He tucked all his money against his chest under his T-shirt, shucked off the backpack, and put on almost every piece of clothing he had with him. Then he lay down, pushed both hands high into his sleeves, and curled himself into a ball in the corner with his head on his emptied backpack. He couldn't believe how cold it was for August; he wondered how *really* homeless people survived in winter.

He couldn't sleep. Whichever way he lay the concrete pressed into his bones as if he were naked, and his back felt open to attack even when he squeezed up against the door. Eventually he got so cold that his shivering broke into loud, distressed sobbing and he got up and paced around until he got a grip on himself and quieted his panic. Afterward, he could not bring himself to lie down again. Instead he hunkered in a corner and waited, and when the first birdsong started, long before it was properly light, he rose and moved off.

He discovered he'd come almost in a circle. The edge of the industrial estate was only a couple of streets from the locked church. It was still locked, so he started again to walk, this time following the way he'd traveled before, sharing the streets at first only with seagulls. The white, cold early light softened as he went.

Eventually he found himself back at the roundabout with the pub. He supposed it was too early for buses, especially as it was a Sunday, so he walked from there along a dual street into the city. Thinking vaguely that he might find a map there, he followed signs to the railway station, and next to the entrance there was a café open, one of those new places with armchairs and newspapers. He drank coffee, which he didn't usually, with a lot of sugar heaped in, and ate a huge sandwich. Warm at last, he lay back and slept. Later he was woken by the woman who ran the place who told him he had to leave or buy something else. So he ordered more coffee and a piece of cheesecake, and after that he felt properly awake and able to think straight. It was now half past nine by the café clock. It was Sunday, not the day he would have chosen if he'd planned things properly, but too bad. He just had to get through the day—it was only a day, plus another night—and then it would be Monday and everywhere would be open again and he could sort himself out. He wasn't sure what he meant by "sorting himself out," but it would become clearer. It certainly had to involve sorting out money because he'd got through almost half of what he had, and another thing he'd definitely changed his mind about was trying to find Callum and Fee, because even if he did they'd take his parents' side and drive him straight back to Stoneyridge.

So, he would return to the church. Because churches were open on Sundays, right? No question of not getting in. First he'd buy some food, then he'd go back to the church and sneak in when the service was on. He'd find somewhere inside to hide and then all he'd have to do was keep quiet. Somebody would lock up after the service and he'd stay locked in until the morning when someone—a cleaner or somebody, it didn't seem important who—came to unlock it again. Adam felt clever at last. He was getting on top of the game, figuring out how these things worked. And it was a comforting idea in itself, being locked in.

He washed himself in the station toilet, peeled off and repacked his extra layers of clothing, bought some more sandwiches and two bags of crisps, and left.

But when he walked all the way back and came within the sound of the church bells, he discovered there were far too many people around, straggling along the pavement and lingering on the church path. He walked on, past the entrance, cursing himself for not thinking about the problem of other people. He wandered along the surrounding streets until the bells fell silent. But when he returned to the church, the sight of its closed doors made him feel even more lost and hopeless. Of course he couldn't go in. If he did he'd find himself standing in a packed church with everybody staring at him, and that would be even worse than if he'd followed those lads into the pub last night.

He walked back to the empty industrial unit where he'd slept, but now there were cars going in and out from the unit two doors up that fitted tires. He settled himself on the ground behind the overgrown hedge, exhausted. When he heard the church bells once more he returned to the church gate, against the tide of people leaving the service. He stood at a bus stop across the road, from where he watched the vicar, a short woman in a white robe, shaking hands with everyone as they left. Eventually she went back inside and for the next few minutes Adam waited in despair, wondering what to do. Then the vicar reappeared with an elderly man; she set off, her vestments flapping round her legs, along a path leading around the side of the church and the man, carrying a sheaf of papers and a music stand, left by the gate to the pavement. Adam watched him get in his car and drive away, and then he walked quickly up the path. He entered the porch, opened the inner door, and stepped inside. He halted, realizing immediately that the church was not empty. A muted scraping and banging was going over a loud staccato conversation between two women apparently at opposite ends of the church from each other. The talking continued; they couldn't have heard him come in. He slipped round the door and closed it quietly, then he squeezed in behind a thick brown curtain drawn back and hanging at one side. The talking women would have to leave sometime, wouldn't they? But the conversation and the sounds of their work went on; they must be collecting up hymnbooks or something. The curtain was scratchy and smelled of dust and also something warm and unclean, a bit like sheep fleece, that immediately made Adam think of his mother and the birthday scarf. He also, suddenly, needed to pee, probably because he couldn't. How long could he stand there not moving and not sneezing? What a stupid, *fucking* stupid place to hide, because even if he managed to stay still and quiet, when they did leave—*if* they ever fucking did—they'd have to walk right past him. They might see at once there was somebody behind the curtain. Or they could pull it across the door all unawares and discover him that way and scream the place down. And any of that might happen after he'd stood there for fucking hours and wet himself. Again Adam had to swallow a terrible need to cry, for feeling stupid and lonely and displaced, but just as much because he simply did not know what to do next.

But after a while, the voices stopped. Adam waited. There was no sound of any movement at all. He waited some more, and then very carefully pulled the curtain aside a little. Still no sound came. He drew himself out and peered around, as far as the pulpit and choir stalls and altar at one end, and the font and display boards and tables at the other. Keeping close to the wall he made off down the length of the church. His feet made a dry, high-pitched squawking noise on the waxed floor and after two or three steps he halted, terrified he'd been heard. Nothing stirred. He walked all around the font, made his way up the middle aisle until he stood at the base of the altar steps, then turned and faced the empty pews. It was surprisingly pleasurable, he found, being alone in a place built for hundreds of people, especially a religious place. Some discovery that he couldn't put into words was nudging at his mind, something about a church being both less and more of a big deal when you saw that it was just a building where a lot of people could sit and listen to you if you were standing where he now stood, and that was whether God existed or not. He was tempted to stretch his arms out wide, imagining them enrobed in deep, wizardly sleeves, and if he were to try his voice, he was sure it would resound with depth and power and not break into one of its uncontrollable warbles. But he did not quite dare do either. Instead he circled his hands around his mouth and made a *tock* with his tongue, and followed it with a soft *woo-ooo*. The echoes made his heart beat harder.

The sense that he was alone was now exhilarating. Adam crossed to the brass lectern and stepped up behind it. A huge black Bible lay open; he had never before seen such an object. Light from the stained glass window above the altar caught the smooth gleaming gold of the edges of its pages, and he could not resist lifting and dropping them, loving the regular, liquid whirr of the membrane-thin leaves flickering through his fingers. Down the middle of the book, in the shadow between the opened halves that sloped in matching curves toward the spine, lay a bookmark of embroidered white satin. Adam lifted it and weighed its corded tassel in his palm. He raised it to his mouth and passed its scratchy, gold wire embroidery over his lips, tasted its metallic sting with the tip of his tongue. His eyes skimmed over the double columns of text without special interest; he had never thought of the Bible as a book anyone might actually read. At the top of the page he took in the words:

> And Jesus saith unto him, The foxes have holes, and
> the birds of the heaven have nests; but the Son of man
> hath not where to lay his head.

He sucked in his breath. He read it again. Weird, like somebody knew he'd be here and had opened the page for him. And too fucking right—he did hath not where to lay his head. He dropped the bookmark. It was time he got a hold of himself; he had to concentrate. He walked down the church again and all the way back up, searching from side to side. There was nowhere to hide except on the floor between the pews and that would be useless; there was barely enough space to lie down, and anyway, he'd be discovered by anyone walking past. He'd always thought of churches as places full of secret nooks and crannies, but this one wasn't much more than a big stone hall. He inspected the organ and choir stalls, then moved across to the pulpit; nowhere offered a hiding place. Behind the pulpit was a piano, and next to the piano, in the gloom of the side aisle, was a sloping wall of dark wood paneling with a door in it. Adam opened the door and found himself in a room with a high mullioned window. It was churchy but also homely, much warmer than the church and fusty with kerosene fumes and a clothy smell that came from the worn-out carpet. Plastic chairs were stacked along one wall; along the other hung several blue robes on a row of pegs. In the far corner, an area of floor was covered in red padded matting on which sat a kerosene stove, two large plastic boxes marked SUNDAY SCHOOL and several floor cushions in bright colors. Beyond the window was a door that led outside. It was locked; the two women must have left the church this way and locked it behind them.

The kerosene smell and the muffled stillness: these things, as if coming from a place and time of warmth too distant for him to recall exactly, soothed Adam, suggesting an unreliable, half-dreamed kind of bliss, but bliss nevertheless; he could feel himself slowing down, he could not help thinking of safety and sleep. And all at once he was thinking of nothing, or thinking at least how much he wanted to empty his mind and think of nothing. He could not bear to do any more planning, or walking, or going anywhere at all. It amazed him that he'd ended up here, but now that he had, the echoing church and windy path and the streets beyond this friendly room were receding fast and becoming unreal; it was quite beyond him to negotiate any more of them today. He felt it happening again; he was turning numb and giving in, going down, down, down—down past thinking or caring. Using the last practical corner of his mind, he dragged the floor cushions together into a sort of nest in the corner, and pulled down the blue robes from their pegs. He bedded himself down under them and, with childish pleasure, turned on his side, opened his backpack and ate all his sandwiches and crisps. After that he felt warm and full. He lay back, stretched, then curled up and drew the blue robes over his head. Once he'd rested for a while he'd go looking for a better place to hide. He wouldn't fall asleep, he'd just lie quietly.

When he opened his eyes there was a woman standing with her hands on her hips, looking down at him. Her unsmiling face was familiar but he couldn't place her. She was wearing a fleece and jeans and the stupid kind of shoes that look as if they're on the wrong feet. He scrambled to his feet and started mumbling but had no idea what he wanted to say. He realized that now he really did need to pee.

"Ah, so you're alive," she said. "Lucky for you there was no Evensong today or they'd have woken you up ages ago. That's the choir's cassocks you've got all over the place. Come on, let's get them hung back up. Can't leave them on the floor, can we? Then I expect you could do with a cup of tea."

Adam thought of diving for the door but with his bladder so full he didn't trust himself to move fast enough. He stood with his backpack tight against his chest, trying to speak. But the woman didn't seem interested in anything he might have to say. She was hanging up all the cassocks, moving the cushions back to the corner, and now she was picking up the litter from his sandwich and crisp picnic, tutting loudly. Then she opened the outside door. "Come on, then," she said. "I have to get back to do supper. They'll be starving. They're always starving. Oh," she added, "I should have said. I'm Pat. The Reverend Pat Dobbs. I'm the vicar. This is St. Mary's. I'm locking up now so you've got to come along out of here, you can't stay. But you can come back home with me for a cup of tea, all right?"

She walked extremely fast. Adam followed her almost at a trot along the path around the side of the church and through a gate into the back garden of a modern, semi-detached house. Pat stepped into a kitchen in which everything seemed to be hanging up: socks and underwear from a drying rack on the ceiling, mugs and pots from hooks under shelves, cooking utensils from a metal grid on the wall. Curling postcards and photographs, coupons, takeaway menus and notes clung to a noticeboard next to a calendar covered in scrawled writing; a pink sweater was slung over a chair back, a satchel gaped open under the table. On the table were a dirty mug, an empty yogurt pot with a teaspoon in it, two or three open books, and a pencil case with its contents spilling out.

Pat binned the sandwich wrappings and crisp bags, filled the kettle, and walked with it in her hand to the door leading to the hall. She yelled, "Flora! Vince! I'm here!" and then turned to Adam. For the first time she smiled at him. "And you are?" she asked.

"Adam. Er, please can I use your toilet?"

He'd just use the toilet and leave. But when he came back into the kitchen from the cloakroom under the stairs there was a girl sitting at the table, and a tall stooping man in slippers over by the sink fishing teabags out of three mugs. Pat turned from chopping onions and introduced Flora and Vince with a wave of her knife. Over the top of his spectacles Vince raised a friendly eyebrow in his direction, and Flora swung a languid hand at him without taking her elbow off the table.

Adam gawped at her, and blushed. Give or take her glasses, and the clothes that were not hot at all (and maybe her hair was darker), Flora was as near as he'd seen in real life to *his* girl, the girl from the overturned caravan. Older by a year or so as well, but still. Flora. He realized he'd never even given a name to his girl. Flora wasn't a bad name.

"Shift the junk off that chair and sit down, Adam. Make yourself comfortable," Pat said.

"Oh, okay, uh, thanks," he said. He lifted a pile of folded laundry on to the table and took the chair opposite Flora.

"If you're okay with spag bol, you're welcome to eat with us," Pat said, turning back to the chopping board. "That's if your mum isn't expecting you back straightaway. Where do you live?"

"Oh, uh, no, I'm fine. Thanks," Adam said miserably. He was ravenous. "Thanks a lot. It's fine."

"Fine your mum's expecting you or fine you'll stay?" Vince said, mildly. "D'you take milk? Sugar?"

"Oh, uh, yeah and one sugar, please." He took a deep breath. "And I meant, if it's okay with you, yeah, it's fine. To stay. Thanks." He'd had no idea before he said it that he wasn't going to refuse the offer, drink his tea, and go. He felt himself blushing again.

"I guess you'd better ring and let her know you won't be home for supper," Pat said, adding the onions to a frying pan on the stove. "Phone's in the hall."

"Oh. Uh, no, no, it's fine," Adam said. "My parents—they won't be bothered. They're cool about stuff like that."

Vince put the mugs of tea on the table, ruffled the back of his wife's head, and left the room. After two or three sips, Adam dared to look up. The girl was looking at him over the top of her mug. Through the steam on her glasses, her eyes looked friendly.

"Hi," he said.

"*Hiya,*" Flora breathed. Then she put down her mug, sighed, took off her glasses, and threw them across the book in front of her. She leaned back, tipping her chair on to its back legs. "Do you have to do Biology? I hate it."

Adam shook his head.

"See, Mum? See?" she said, swinging back farther. "You so do not *have* to do Biology. So why do I? Why, Mum? I really hate it."

"I know, Flora, Biology is awful but you just have to get on with it. And please don't do that with your chair," Pat said. Flora sighed again and glared at the ceiling. "Or you could go and lay the table." Pat was stirring meat into the onions now. "Actually, darling, please would you go and do that? Adam and I are going to have a word."

The front legs of Flora's chair crashed back to the floor. Behind her mother's back she cast her eyes upward and threw Adam a look that said *God, parents.* Then she got up, clattered about in a drawer, and left the room with a handful of cutlery.

Over the soft fizzing from the pan, Pat said, "So, Adam, what's going on, that you bedded down in the vestry? And don't want to talk to your parents?"

"Going on? Oh, nothing's going on!" he said. "I'm fine. I suppose I was just tired." He shrugged with embarrassment at how bad a liar he was.

"I mean, I don't get the impression it's drugs. Or drink," she said. "I can usually tell."

Adam swigged some tea and said nothing.

"Okay, so how many nights have you slept rough? You're, what, about fifteen? They'll want to know you're safe, you know." Adam squirmed. "Unless they're *really* not interested in you. Some parents don't care. Not many, but some."

"No! They do care, of course they do! But there's no point talking to them. They don't listen. It's no big deal. Anyway . . . thanks for the tea." He got up and reached for his backpack. "I gotta go."

"Whoa, there," Pat said. "Hang on a minute. Adam?"

"I'm not talking to them. It's none of your business. I'm not going back."

"Adam, it's okay. Sit down."

At once, Adam did sit down. He wiped a hand over his face. As soon as he'd got to his feet he'd realized he could hardly bring himself to leave behind his half-finished mug of tea, the smell of frying onions and meat, the cluttered, safe kitchen. He couldn't bring himself to leave behind Pat's offhand kindness.

"So, want to tell me what's so terrible?" she said, glancing up from the stove. The meat was sizzling now, sending wafts of steam through her hair.

"They don't listen. They don't care what I want," he said, staring at the table. Tears began to roll down his cheeks.

"Well," Pat said, more gently, pulling the pan off the heat, "even so, we can't have them worried sick. Suppose I ring them, just to let them know you're safe. That okay?"

Adam raised his face and wiped his eyes. "No! I don't want you to, I never asked you to! I don't want to go back. I just want to—"

"Adam, it's okay. Finish your tea. Then suppose you tell me what you think I should do. Tell me what it is you *do* want."

While she waited for him to answer, he looked around the kitchen, at the scrawled wall calendar, Flora's books and pencil case, the photographs, the washed and folded clothes. He hadn't worked it out for himself yet, the way these ordinary things—just *stuff*, after all—were different, somehow, from things at Stoneyridge, and for that alone were already precious. They just made a kind of clean, cheerful sense to him; they belonged to a family life so much lighter-hearted than his own. He wanted to tell Pat about the Stoneyridge kitchen, just as cluttered but where the stuff was always wreckage of some sort and always grimy or broken or scavenged, and where his mother worked from half-empty sacks on the floor to make pots of bulky, joyless food that always lacked something she couldn't grow or afford to buy.

Most of all he wanted to tell Pat that because the rest of their house was always freezing it was at the kitchen table that he'd endured as much as he could stand of his father's scattershot and wayward home schooling: the abacus maths, the clumsy models and futile experiments, all of it stuff that somehow he'd always known wasn't the kind of thing he had to learn if he was going to get anywhere. He'd had it with woodcraft and pottery and the pointless collections of fucking bones and feathers, but he couldn't tell her that.

Pat had turned back to the stove. She opened and tipped a tin of tomatoes into the pan, sprinkled on some herbs from a jar, stirred some more, and tasted. "No hurry, Adam. Drink your tea," she said. He obeyed. "Most things can get sorted, you know," she added.

He didn't believe that for a minute. And where to begin? He wanted to tell her about his parents' worn-out commentaries about themselves—the number of times they came out with statements beginning "Well, we happen to believe . . ."—and he wanted to tell her about the even worse silences between, about the tarnish of monotony and tension and unspoken fury that lay over everything around them. He'd walked out of there in the nick of time, he felt, carrying with him the whole of his life so far: the worry that he was backward or strange compared with other people, his fear of real girls, his rampant curiosity about them. He'd walked out carrying, barely intact, the few things for which he felt an excited, secret, and uncertain love: the beauty of numbers (it was a mystery to him, where that came from), cities he'd only heard the names of, music so loud it made his teeth buzz. But most of all, and harder to carry than all of those, was the craving to become the person he was meant to be. He did not know how he came to be a misfit in his parents' lives, only that he was, and he did not wish to live another day feeling also a misfit in his own. He didn't know how to lay claim to the kind of life that could be lived in a kitchen like Pat's, only that he had to try.

"I want to be normal," he said. "I want ordinary stuff, I want to be ordinary. I want to go to school."

From: deborahstoneyridge@yahoo.com

To: <adam.morgan@logisticsomnicorpsystems.com>
Sent on wed 19 oct 2011 at 11.43 GMT

Hello Adam this will be very quick, I will tell you why.

10.30 this morning I was in the yard, I had just got D out of the back door and was locking up – D went on without me on his frame, he doesn't stand about waiting for me these days, just heads off under his own steam, not exactly speedy but he does all right. Anyway he was half-way to the van and I was locking up and suddenly CRASH the most terrible noise like an explosion and I turned round and there it was, the most ENORMOUS lumps of pebbledash coming away from the wall and smashing into the yard all over the place, it was a great big bit of the render it just came loose off the wall and came crashing down, bits of concrete and dust everywhere. It could have killed somebody. Under the upstairs window you can see all the brick now, it's the little B&B room at the back, the single.

I didn't know what to do, go back in and ring somebody but tradesmen don't answer their phone in the daytime do they – and I stood there for a minute thinking anyway who would I ring, the nice builder that used to be on the other side of Bridgecombe is no more and I don't know anybody else. Then D started gibbering something and pointing at the wall instead of hanging onto his frame and I could just see where that was heading, him sprawled in the yard with a broken hip. Plus if we didn't get to stroke club this time no doubt there'd be more grief from that quarter.

So I told him not to fuss and got him to stroke club and then came to the library. Just as well I did because when I had 5 mins to think about it of course it's Digger I should get hold of. He's responsible for structural repairs though he'll argue about it of course. But I'm not putting up with any more bullying or his nonsense about the lease. For some reason I feel quite equal to him. Makes a change!

He'll try and say it wouldn't have fallen off in the first place if the painting had got done but I shall point out that doesn't mean it's not structural. Need to go as only have five mins before stroke club finishes. Lots of love Mum xxx

When I go to collect Howard he's one of the last ones there but not yet ready to leave. He's sitting at a table in front of a plate of biscuits with his cheeks bulging, and he barely looks up when I come in. Jenny's also there, all smiles and asking if I have a minute for a word with her and Dr. Armistead.

In Dr. Armistead's clinic they sit me down and tell me Howard has lost over five kilos. I'm looking at the walls where drawings done by Dr. Armistead's children are stuck in between a watercolor of Fountains Abbey, a poster about washing your hands, and a scroll in fancy writing of that thing that starts Go Placidly.

"That must be because he's more active," I say. "He's getting around much more. Doing more for himself. That's good, isn't it?"

They fall over themselves to assure me it's good. "It's very good. And he's got a bit more motivated with his speech, too, hasn't he? We noticed that," Jenny says. "He's talking much more, really *trying* to communicate."

Dr. Armistead nods. "And his appetite's good today, in fact he's been quite hungry this morning." She looks at Nurse Jenny, nods, and goes on, "So we've had a little word together and as he's due for a review anyway we thought what we'd like to do is get him in for forty-eight hours or so—you've not had him in for respite care before, have you, that means you've earned a break! We're just a little bit concerned about the weight loss and I'm sure you could do with a few days' rest."

"Especially as you've been managing everything on your own,"

Jenny says. "We do understand the burden on lone caregivers. So we see this as being very much for both of you."

This statement doesn't require any reply, least of all the reply I could easily give about lone caregivers. They wouldn't find it acceptable.

"Respite care? You mean take him away?"

"What we'd do is arrange to get him into Jocelyn Lodge, you see, not Taunton General," says Dr. Armistead. "So he'd be very comfortable, not in a big hospital ward at all. There's a bit of a wait for a bed, usually about three weeks, and you needn't worry he won't like it, they *love* Jocelyn Lodge. It's very relaxed, very homely, they've got some single rooms and the garden's beautiful. And they've got a hydrotherapy pool."

Jenny takes over. "It'll give us time for a full care review and you get two maybe even three days for a proper break—you might even want to get away somewhere. People say what a difference it makes, it recharges the batteries so you can carry on, that's what most people find." She beams at me. "It's win-win. He'll have a great time at Jocelyn Lodge and you get a bit of time for yourself. And when he's in, you see, we can get a snapshot of where we are with everything, so we'll review all the medication and it gives the physio and the speech therapist a chance to give a bit of help with his movement and speech, plus we'll work with the nutritionist on a plan to get his weight back up."

"Would you be happy with that?"

All this said, and with a pleased glance at each other, they both stop to rest and look at me with smiles on their faces, and we all wait until I realize they want nothing except my agreement, which I give. I don't know what I think about it yet, but it's a less pressing matter than the state the house was in, crumbling before my eyes, when I left this morning. I haven't yet seen Theo today. I fancy he was sleeping when the render fell off—there was no sign of him—so I need to reassure him on the matter of the repairs to what is, after all, his bedroom wall. And of course I must ask his advice about how to proceed.

By the time we get back to the house I am feeling unsettled and so is Howard, but fortunately he's also tired and takes himself off for a nap before lunch. I won't wake him. He's stuffed with biscuits so he probably won't need lunch, and besides, he's increasingly picky about eating my bread and the chutney stuff I made with the big marrow and some curry spices that needed using up. More often than not there's cheese to go with it (but not today—I was too distracted by events to think of shopping) so he can hardly complain.

Theo never complains about food. Not even when it's unconventional and last-minute, which it often is now that life is much fuller. Theo has a way of holding my attention, which means I'm slower over some of my chores and sometimes I will idle away whole hours in conversation and then just fling together any old thing to eat. Given the choice, I might well have given up on cooking altogether by now and gone on to convenience foods and takeaways (the very thought makes me giggle). That's if I had the money, or a microwave, which I don't. Actually there's less money than before. There's been no Bed and Breakfast cash for ages now so I'm getting meals out of anything I can salvage from the garden and cupboards. It's fun, experimenting a little. I'm using all the flour I bought, of course, but keeping the special nuts and fruits for Christmas. I'm well aware that some of the results may be strange to some tastes but everybody likes dumplings, don't they? It's amazing how filling they are and how easy to make. Also, a big marrow goes a long way.

I find Theo in the yard and ask him what to do. He comes straight to the point and tells me to ring Digger straightaway and says there's no need to be afraid of him because Theo will be right behind me (in the background, of course—neither of us needs to spell out the necessity for that). The yard is a shambles, he says sternly, and the extra mess from the fallen masonry makes it look as if the whole place is falling down around us. If Digger's coming, I have to spruce up the yard a little. He is right. Digger hasn't been here since the shearing and already I can hear what he'll say in that loud voice of his. Come to think of it, what if he demands an inspection of the whole place, pretending to check for other repairs? I wander around, doing my best to pull the weeds out from around the doorways but most of them are nettles so I'll have to come back later with gloves.

It's good to have Theo's perspective on things. I've grown used to what an eyesore the yard is, I suppose, but now I see it through his eyes. Howard's shaky scaffolding is still in place against the house and now looks more like homemade buttressing, shoved up to keep the walls standing. I won't go up those ladders again so the painting is still not even half-done, and I can't get the scaffolding down on my own. But maybe the point of leaving it up has been that I liked to think of Adam coming back and getting the job finished. I see now how silly that is. Adam never comes, and even if he did he wouldn't think of offering and I wouldn't dream of asking. Theo murmurs, reading my mind, that in due course we'll get something done about it. I don't know if by *it* he means the scaffolding, the painting, or Adam's visits, but I am reassured.

I poke around some more, going into all the old places I've ignored. The pig shed roof is worse; the pinholes between the slates have multiplied and in one corner the beams curve toward the ground like the bow of a ship and will soon collapse. Some lengths of rotting timber from the dismantled and broken pigpens still lean against the back wall. Patches of black and green fungus are sprouting everywhere, and as I walk around scraping my fingers along the cold stone, my feet kick up a musky smell from the earth floor. It's a dump. I'm truly glad I don't have to hear Howard describing it to our Bed and Breakfast guests as "the potential yoga studio" anymore. It always was perfectly absurd to think he would ever do it up and run classes in here. But, I remark to Theo (who has followed me in), when I realized it would never happen, I kept quiet in case Howard took my point and went back to using it for pigs, which I really couldn't stand. Right up until Howard had his stroke I went on pretending it was going to be a proper yoga studio one day.

From across the pig shed Theo gives me an old-fashioned look and says, "Have you ever considered that maybe Howard was pretending, too?" His impertinence takes me by surprise and I refuse to answer. He adds, "Maybe he knew as well as you did it wasn't going to happen. Maybe he was trying not to disappoint you."

"You make me angry sometimes," I tell Theo, "throwing questions at me that are none of your business." He offers a mild apology, saying he didn't really mean it. Then he imposes one of his small silences, which are painful, and always up to me to break, which I won't do before I'm good and ready.

I've seen all I want to see in here and I make for the doorway, but then I turn for a last look. Yes, you do make me angry, I confess aloud to Theo, but not as angry as Howard makes me. It's true; in my mind's eye I can still see Howard standing here, and his lips, encircled by moustache and beard, pursing up with an infinitesimal, *almost* concealed smirk of self-satisfaction and—as I perceive it now—self-delusion, and forming the words "the potential yoga studio." And then, I whisper to Theo, I could hit him, I really could. And for something that's all over and done with and in the past. Isn't that terrible? Theo bestows another silence.

"Not really," he says, following me out and across to the pottery studio. "Some things never really are in the past. You can't help it if some things go on mattering." I walk on ahead of him so I don't have to think of a reply to this.

My onslaught on the pottery shed has stalled, because I don't know how I'll ever shift enough of the dust to get it usable for drying laundry. The trouble is that anything damp dropped on the floor (or anywhere else) will instantly need rewashing, because every surface and implement lies under a matt, pinkish coat of clay powder. The thought of the mess I'd make trying to hose the whole place clean is appalling: I imagine the blasts of water drumming into the corners and knocking things off shelves, the drenched and dripping walls, the tools and objects tumbling and rolling in a running river of mud. Then, even if I got the place clean, would it ever dry out? I explain this to Theo and he tuts in recognition of what a tremendous task it would be. "We'll address it in due course," he says, and tells me not to worry.

Next, I peer in through the broken panes of the loom shed window. I'm not surprised to see that the floor is dark and grainy. House martins have been flying in and out all Spring and Summer; they've migrated now, leaving their nests on the crossbeam and the floor spackled with droppings. My last piece of weaving is still on the loom from nearly three years ago. There's bird shit on that, too, and something's been eating it, but the truth is it was a pebbly, dun sort of cloth anyway so it isn't as shocking to see it spoiled than as if I'd been weaving, say, tinselly swathes of pink or turquoise or lilac. It makes me smile to think of such colors anywhere near this place. I don't want to go in. "Come away, you've seen enough," Theo says.

Back in the house I telephone Digger and leave a message for him to come as soon as he can, then I make scrambled eggs for lunch, which Theo and I both like. A modest enough little pleasure in a demanding day, scrambled eggs for lunch, I venture to say, and Theo agrees and compliments me on my cooking.

"Not everybody can make good scrambled eggs."

Simply said, simply meant. I bask in it.

Howard doesn't stir, and I don't wake him up. I do the dishes, and then Theo suggests we check over the rest of the house so that if Digger does get nosy we won't be caught on the back foot.

But we don't make it any farther than the room that Theo occupies, the single Bed and Breakfast bedroom from whose wall the render fell. As soon as I walk in I'm ashamed. It's freezing. I've never given a thought to the ice-cold radiator in here (even if the heating worked properly it's too expensive to run) or checked the number of blankets Theo has. Have I ever offered him a hot water bottle? I've never even wondered if he has anything warm to wear in bed. I have neglected him.

Even worse, I discover why the pebbledash fell off. It must have been cracked and letting the rain in for months, which has soaked the brickwork right through. While the outside mortar perished and the pebbledash fell off in lumps, the plaster on the inside is soaked and the wallpaper under the window lies in long, peeling-off tongues. The room is uninhabitable, like the third Bed and Breakfast room, which I closed up last winter when a bit of ceiling plaster came down and some black stuff started growing out of the skirting board. (I did mean to get someone to see to it but three Bed and Breakfast rooms were too many to manage, anyway.) Theo has never complained, but I resolve that he will not spend another night in here.

"But where will I go instead?" he whispers. "Do you want me to sleep in the other B & B room?"

The other Bed and Breakfast room hasn't been occupied since Theo's companion left it almost two months ago. There might not be any more guests until next Spring—I get very few after September—but I'm not putting Theo in there. I tell him I need to keep it ready on the off-chance of passing trade over the winter weekends. He doesn't challenge that, but asks again in a small, rather frightened voice where, in that case, he is to be put. Or am I telling him to go?

Go? I hurry to correct any misunderstanding. That is the last thing I want. Theo must be assured that he is welcome, that his remaining here is necessary. So the only and natural course is to move him into Adam's room at the front.

The rest of the afternoon is spent clearing out Adam's belongings. I take down the dartboard and the old black-and-white posters of Paris and Madrid. There's a third poster, another cityscape but I can't recall which city; certainly it's not anywhere I've been although Adam probably has by now. It could be bloody Barcelona for all I know. "You sound angry," Theo observes, and I realize I am, even though it was months ago and I thought I'd forgotten it.

It's not important, I say, meaning it, but nevertheless I'm pleased when I hear Theo demur and tell me that he understands how I feel.

I empty the wardrobe of the clothes I've given Adam over the years, making myself notice that he has never worn any of them for more than a day. The stoneware dish of Howard's goes, too, along with a driftwood carving of a bird that looks both clumsy and malevolent. I dump everything in the room Theo is vacating, where it won't be in the way. Then I bring all the bedding and add it to the covers already on Adam's bed, so Theo will surely be warm now. But in case not, I point out the corridor off the landing that leads to the door of my room and tell him he must let me know if he needs any more blankets. To my annoyance the telephone rings downstairs before I finish speaking, interrupting my flow of thought, and when I've dealt with the call and am finally able to think straight again, I move Adam's clothes back again, from the little damp room into the wardrobe in Theo's new room. Because of course Adam won't be needing them, but Theo does. Also, Theo's much more appreciative. Warm practical jumpers, thick shirts, outdoor trousers, country socks. And a pair of sturdy boots, and would you believe it, they're the right size! I leave him to settle in and tiptoe downstairs to put the kettle on. Howard's prowling around the kitchen, foraging in the bread bin. Not so fussy now. I make him a nice cup of tea, too, and he's grateful.

Later that evening, in front of the fire, I apologize to Theo for not giving him the clothes and his own comfortable bedroom much sooner, and his smile tells me it's all right.

<adam.morgan@logisticsomnicorpsystems.com>

To: deborahstoneyridge@yahoo.com
Sent on thurs 20 oct 2011 at 14.22 EST

Mum it was really good to talk yesterday but I want to check you're really ok. You sounded pretty out of breath! Think I must've caught you at a bad moment even though you said it wasn't? I didn't really get the point of all the shifting and sorting you've got going on, sounds like you're going nuts over a bit of clearing out! Don't go lifting heavy stuff, though, will you?

Don't mean to sound negative, it's good you're thinking about decorating but Mum, shouldn't you get the rendering fixed and the outside painting finished first? Also if you need a hand with money for stuff like that I can probably help out – I've got quite a bit saved up but I don't necessarily need all of it for a deposit plus I don't even know yet where I'm going to buy. Mum, you just have to say.

Also you need to talk to Digger about the repair to the wall, he'll do it at cost even if he won't pay for it. It's in his interests plus he knows you can't do it yourself. OK? DON'T just leave it, ok?

Hopefully I'll be able to sort some stuff out for you when I'm there at xmas. Lots of love Adam xxx

On Sunday I'm up and dressed by six o'clock. I go out to check the sheep at first light and the world seems full of good, ordinary things, the cold little birds sitting in the sun on the roof ridge, the smell of clean earth. An overnight freeze has cast a sheeting of thin ice over the pools of groundwater around the stiles and the going is easier where the tussocks of reeds are stiff with frost, but on the lea of the hill the dead moor grass has rotted and is slippery now. When I get back, Howard comes half-dressed to the door of his bedroom. He sends me a crooked wave to let me know he's been waiting, and his face bends into a funny attempt at a smile. I smile back, momentarily fond of him, fonder than I have been for years. I am fonder of myself, too, though for no real reason. Theo slumbers above our heads, oblivious of the necessity in a long marriage for the sharing of apologetic little smiles. I give myself over to helping Howard with his socks.

That's when Digger turns up. It's just gone eight o'clock so he wants to catch me in my dressing gown again, I suppose, and I am glad he hasn't.

I make him wait in the kitchen. When I've got Howard dressed and ready and lead him in, Digger's leaning in his usual place against the draining board. He watches me help Howard to his seat at the table. Not for the first time, I can tell he's thinking about sex. I know it from a musk he gives off, from the occluded, cloudy look in his eyes, and where he allows them to travel. Or rather he's *wondering* about sex, and probably making a number of assumptions. Such as, Howard's incapable now. Such as, she must be desperate for it. He's correct about the first, the second I would deny, and he has no idea, none at all, how angry his speculations make me. Nor that, in revenge, I, too, am speculating about how—or whether—he can heave himself on to the mountainous form of his sullen wife Louise, mother of their two boys (who take after her in solidity and dullness rather than their cunning, stringy father). Smiling at my own daring, I imagine Digger and Louise's coupling performed to the sound of hippo grunts and the slap of slack flesh, and concluded in a collapsed, silent sadness.

I say, "I thought you were going to ring before you came over, to make sure I was in."

"Sunday morning, reckoned you would be," he says. "Anyhow, I been up the ladder and looked at your wall. Wear and tear, that is. Tenant's liability. You're in breach. I could have you out."

Howard rocks forward and manages to produce a few words of protest, but in no sensible order. I stroke his hand and shush him gently. "Surely it's structural damage," I say to Digger. "And I don't think we should discuss it here."

Digger glances at Howard and then fixes dull eyes on me. "No skin off my nose where we discuss it," he says, lowering his voice. "Anyhow, it's going to cost. Got to be paid for whatever way you look at it. Nothing free in this life, eh?"

"It's structural damage," I say, in a way that shuts out Howard, who's struggling to speak again.

Digger snorts and swings himself forward from the draining board. "Got to cover it somehow, Missus. I do you a favor, you does one back."

My heart is beating hard. Howard has closed his eyes.

In the same quiet voice Digger says, "You says on the phone there's damp come through on the inside, didn't you? Want me to take a look upstairs, do you? Whenever's convenient."

Theo hasn't been around all morning and I know he will not appear while Digger's here, even if I want him to.

"Thursday," I say. "You can come on Thursday. In the afternoon."

From: deborahstoneyridge@yahoo.com

To: <adam.morgan@logisticsomnicorpsystems.com>
Sent on wed 26 oct 2011 at 11.12 GMT

It's all in hand, Digger came on Sunday and he's seeing to it.
Love, Mum xxx

PS Dad's going to Jocelyn Lodge tomorrow, did I tell you? We got the
letter through last week. They want to change his drugs and get him
walking more and so on and it'll give me a break.

He watched her packing his things, trying not to show the hurry she was in. His clothes, mainly pajamas it looked like, were folded and placed neatly in his case, washbag on top; there wasn't much. For once she was quiet; none of the babbling she was in the habit of, none of her whispery remarks into the air, or her jerky laughter. She got the zip of the case whisked round and the buckles done and had him sitting in the freezing hall hours before it was time, and when the ambulance men came they said he wouldn't be needing his own wheelchair. They helped him out by the front door to the ambulance. Deborah followed with the case. When she climbed into the ambulance to say goodbye, it was as an afterthought.

He knew. Even though when she kissed him she didn't keep her lips long enough against his cheek for him to reach out and stroke her face, he knew that if he were to touch her—not as an invalid reaching for support but really to *touch* her—her skin would feel alien. Its warmth would be no longer her own but would emanate, somehow, from some other source; it was the thought of someone else that put the life in her these days. She couldn't wait to be rid of him.

I could say it's none of my doing, or out of my control. Or a necessity—that I have no choice but to give in to whatever brought him to me, or me to him, in the first place. I could say I didn't look for it to happen, that I haven't consciously brought it about in any way. But the truth is I allow it. I'm ashamed.

I could claim not to understand it, as if that would make any difference, for who's to say there's even anything *to* understand, that there's a mystery to solve or some elusive truth to expose? Maybe I'd only be casting around for a hidden meaning because that's what I do, and am always doing—looking for reasons, looking for something I need to understand, when the thing itself is enough. And surely what the thing is—pure sensation—*is* quite enough. I really shouldn't be fretting as though the *why* matters when the *why* may not exist at all, never mind be unknowable. All that really matters is that I submit to it and that it consumes me. That each time it burns me up and leaves me with nothing. Needing and wanting nothing.

It happens like this. To begin with there has to be the *yes,* a decision of sorts: to let go, to let it happen, to concede to myself I have the desire, the will, the temerity to do this. In my son's bedroom, his former bedroom, that is. In the daytime. Like this.

There is the arranging of myself on the bed, with a secret intake of breath as if this will make me a little lighter and less of a creaking burden on the springs. I allow some time to elapse: time enough to roam, of course only in my mind's eye, all through the rest of the house, peering across rooms and checking behind doors, interrogating and then establishing as actually true the extraordinary notion

that Howard really is not here. Oddly, it's only when I've given myself reassurance on this point, which I already know to be a physical
fact, that I can leave go of all self-consciousness.

Then I breathe more easily, the mattress shifts under my weight; I
spread my limbs across the covers and roll my hips, raise my pelvis.
I yawn and hum and sigh, just for the sake of making sounds of
heedlessness and pleasure. Outside, the wind catches this exposed
corner of the house and rattles the window; the curtains move. Perhaps there's a moment when I could—am even tempted to—return
to the winter's day and the kind of thing women like me are supposed to do on ordinary afternoons at home: read a magazine, bake
a cake, watch an old film. Women like me seldom even use the word
sex. We're not supposed to think about it. I'm heavy and middle-
aged and out of practice at it; even so, was it ever any easier? But
although I may be out of sympathy with my body I'm slightly impressed, and no longer embarrassed by its uncomplicated readiness,
by the audacity of its little cues and prompts. The very thought that
I'm considered too old for all this makes me inclined—though I never
give in to it—to giggle.

Instead I concentrate on the pricking of air on my skin as clothes
are peeled away in this cold room, and I no longer want to laugh;
there's a seriousness now, an intent in it. The shivering and tingling
as my body is exposed is like fingertips playing on the back of my
neck, the draught from the window like the edge of a single nail
drawn lightly down my spine. I shiver also with the awareness that
the same undressing and the same stroking gesture, performed with
less patience, would alarm me. This revealing of myself is never total,
however—I think through modesty, although for whom should I be
modest? But being entirely naked would be an ordeal, so I clutch at
folds of cloth and wrap them around my breasts and press them between my thighs. At this point I don't look at my discarded clothing,
which is worn-out and ugly, or at myself. Too much of my skin is like
a plucked chicken's, pale and clammy and loose over the muscles and
bones. In the hinges of my joints it crimps like glove leather and the
pores are dotted red from years of washing in cold water and the
abrasions of rough towels.

I don't look at the spread of tufted, graying thatch at the base of my belly, either. I don't need to, because recently—appalled and delighted, equally, at my own nerve—I took a hand mirror and examined the wet gash beneath and between my legs, just to see what he'd see, perhaps to understand what all the fuss is about. I still don't understand it, really, but now lying back I can imagine it, the rose-pink envelope exuding its warm gloss and opening under his tongue. Another thing I don't need to understand: whether this is seducing or being seduced.

What I do understand is the polished tightness of skin over fingertips, poised for the gliding in. And my own salt-sweet emulsion licked from them. This whetting of my body is a little clumsy, somewhat mechanistic, but always assiduous, and so quite soon after the excitement comes the solid ache all the way down from the neck of the womb, and the want. The change from want to need, for the hardness pushed inside me, a kind of desperation. The soft-throated groans I hear in the room sound like the sobbing of the lost, and the found. There is plenty of time and yet there is also hurry. Tendons, in one movement, pull tight and dissolve. His name slips like liquid from my mouth, but no other word is said. Afterward I realize my eyes have been closed since I lay down.

I turn on my side so I can't see the door. My arms are empty and I need a long time to recover. My body feels scuffed and sore. But I have the whole day.

Until Howard comes back, whole days slip past me in this manner. Tasks lie undone. The telephone rings a lot but answering it is out of the question. Yes, I am ashamed. But not ashamed enough to stop it.

<adam.morgan@logisticsomnicorpsystems.com>

To: deborahstoneyridge@yahoo.com
Sent on sat 29 oct 2011 at 14.22 EST

Mum where are you, where's Dad? Is he still at that place or is he back? Is he any better, have they sorted out all the medication and stuff for him? I didn't think there was much they could do, or can they?

I think you must have gone with him in the end. They've got facilities for family in some of these places, haven't they? Hope you get a break anyway.

Is the render fixed yet?

I'm always asking you questions, you could ask me a few now and then! Well I'll give you my news anyway though there's not much. Office has gone back a bit to how it was before (but it's still ok for time off over Christmas, don't worry, I'm booking flights this week probably).

Sacha's doing really well considering. But I was going through a final sanity-check on a couple of inventory schedules the other day with Gemma and she showed me a couple of photos Sacha sent round of her son's birthday, he was seven last week. Just ordinary photos, him opening his presents plus this Lord of the Rings cake and him and his little mates going mental playing with the Wii – it looked manic! Apparently when Sacha showed them to gemma she said it was really hard just doing the birthday as normal and not turn-

ing it into a really, really big extra-special deal, like taking him to Dis-
neyland or something. So I said why what's the problem and Gemma
said Sacha doesn't even know if she'll be around for his birthday
next year. Her other kid's only 3. Mum, I can't get my head round it.
It's so unfair.

Hopefully you're okay, I think I would have heard if you weren't?!
Let me know anyway. I'll send you the flights when I've got them
sorted. Remember I can do some stuff round the house for you when
I'm there. Lots of love Adam xxx

ADAM'S BIRTHDAY 1990

"Adam, how many times do we have to go over this? One of the reasons you're being home educated is precisely because we don't believe in that kind of institutional straitjacket. It's not about holidays versus term-time. You should be learning *every* day of your life," his father said, with his wise eyes fixed on the wall behind and above Adam's head. As usual, he sounded sad.

"Yes but I just want to be off school at the same time as Kevin and Kyle," Adam said. "Please, Dad. It's my birthday."

He held his breath. His father began to knock rhythmically on the kitchen tabletop with his knuckles. "In fact, we *reject* that kind of regimentation. It's archaic, outmoded, and discredited. Do you understand?"

"Yes but it's my birthday."

His father sighed. "Listen, Adam. In the past, children only got the summer off because they had to go and help their parents bring in the harvest. Not even *their* harvest, the landowner's! And the whole system supported it. We don't have to follow those rules anymore."

"Yes but they've been off five weeks already. They're going back soon. And it's my birthday."

Howard sighed again and smiled. "Oh, all right. We'll just do two hours and then you can go. But remember, getting six weeks off in the summer isn't really a holiday, it's just a remnant of oppression.

You shouldn't think of it as a good thing. Wait, where do you think you're going?"

Adam was already at the door. "I'm just going to tell Kevin and Kyle to wait," he said. "They're outside. Back in a minute."

When he went outside he found Kevin and Kyle slouched in the yard, peering through the windows of the weaving studio where his mother, with her back to them, was bent over the loom.

"All right?" Kevin said. Adam kicked at the ground, and a sudden flutter of knowledge came to him: *there's nobody watching us.* He gazed back at the house. Then came a second one: *I am not going back in a minute.* Kevin and Kyle caught on at once; glances were exchanged; the agreement to flee was made among them with eyes alone, not a single word said. With no other signal they took off running out of the yard. Kevin, the oldest and biggest, hit the track first and with a long skid turned left up toward the moor. Kyle followed, skinnier and faster than Adam, who panted behind. He didn't think to shout to them to wait, or to drop back and let them race on without him. In permanent and abject need of their company, he'd chase after them anywhere. He was afraid they knew this.

By the time he caught them up at the stile, the brothers' mood was already changing. The wind off the moor blew through the silence that descended. Kyle wanted to go home and play on his bike and Kevin suddenly didn't feel like doing anything. Adam felt his morning of freedom drifting away with them, and he had nothing with which to lure them back. He tried, nevertheless.

"My dad, he's got all these knives for wood-carving. They're dead sharp. If we go back to my place he might let us have a go of them. Anyway, I know where he keeps them."

Kevin considered. "So what? My dad's got a gun."

"Two guns," Kyle corrected him. "He's got this really big one that's just for deer. If you tried to shoot a rabbit with it"—he made a loud exploding noise—"you'd blow it to bits. The rabbit wouldn't even 'xist no more."

"Yeah, and we've got to come back to yours this afternoon anyway, haven't we," Kevin said, wearily. "My Mum says. You're having a *party* or something."

The way he said *party* conveyed the inferiority of any party of Adam's in comparison with any of theirs. It was obvious. At their parties there were always lots of kids their age making lots of noise, and proper party food from a supermarket, the kind you actually wanted to eat, and their mum shrieked a lot and was funny. They didn't have homemade decorations and nobody asked you to read a poem or sing a song. Best of all, their parties were indoors. Gloom swept over him.

"It's not a party, it's a picnic," he said.

"Don't you want a proper party, then? Aren't you allowed one?" Kevin said slyly. He knew. Adam's parents didn't do proper stuff.

"There isn't any girls going, is there?" Kyle said. Kevin gave his brother a shove and they broke into squeaky laughter.

"My mum bought you this present we've got to give you when we come to the picnic," Kyle said. "Want me to tell you what it is?"

Adam did want to be told, but he shrugged the question off. Any talk of presents might lead to questions about what else he'd had for his birthday, and he was so ashamed of the homemade wooden scooter he'd got from his parents he had to keep it a secret. For the rest of his life.

"'Course there isn't any girls coming," he said.

Kevin didn't say any more, but Adam had lost ground and he knew it. There weren't any other people coming on the picnic except for Callum and Fee, friends of his parents who talked and dressed the same kind of way, and they didn't have kids. They always came on his birthday. Adam had the feeling that Callum and Fee were sorry for his parents and his parents were sorry for them.

Kevin spat out the grass stalk he was chewing. "Okay, gotta go. See you later. C'mon, Kyle." He set off down the lane and Kyle shambled after him.

Adam climbed up and sat on the stile and watched them go. They conducted a kicking and tripping-up contest as they went, which had Kyle upended and yelping on his back every few yards. Back at their house the telly would be on. They were allowed to have fizzy drinks and help themselves to Pop-Tarts whenever they felt like it. They were so lucky.

Adam couldn't go back to his house and the moor was too boring to absorb the next four hours, so his pride would have to give. He ran after Kevin and Kyle and tagged along behind at a distance, saying nothing. They didn't object, and after a while he drew level again. Then Kevin took them on a detour up the fields to see if they could find the place where his dad had turned up a rats' nest the day before, but they couldn't. When they got to the boys' house an hour later their mum, Louise, was in a bad mood. She told Adam his dad had been on the phone three times and he was to go straight home.

Back with his father, Adam tried to work some more on his model of a dinosaur but no matter what he did to it, it still looked like just a lump of clay. He'd forgotten the name of the dinosaur he was supposed to be making and he'd stopped looking at the picture he was supposed to be using for inspiration ("And don't just copy it, Adam, try to be *original*"). He sneaked a look at his father working at the pottery wheel, his hands wet and gray and gnarled, cupped around the clay. Like a dinosaur's, he thought, staring with pleasurable disgust.

His father looked over and frowned. Adam dropped his gaze. Running away from lessons had been the biggest act of rebellion of his life so far and, although it hadn't felt it at the time, a calculated one, trading on the birthday goodwill and cheerfulness that had to be kept up for the picnic. Inside him there burned a lovely, hot little bead of satisfaction that his father was angry with him today and could not show it.

"Adam. You're not concentrating," he said.

Adam picked up a fork and drew a few squiggly tracks down the dinosaur's back.

"I can't do dinosaurs," he said. "Can't I make a Teenage Mutant Ninja Turtle instead?"

His father sighed. "What, imitate some American mass-market commercial rubbish instead of creating a figure from your own imagination? Is that what you'd rather do? Really?"

Adam nodded slowly. "They're only turtles," he said quietly. For the first time, he was beginning to think he could get to enjoy wanting the wrong things.

His father sighed again. "Oh, all right, then, Adam, we'll leave it for today," he said. "I suppose you want to go and play on your scooter, eh? Off you go, son."

Adam was glad to be reminded about the scooter. If he played on it now he stood more chance of not being made to get it out and show it to everybody when they arrived for the picnic. He wheeled it outside and made at least twenty circuits of the yard on it, in view of his father, who remained at the pottery wheel, and his mother in the kitchen. It was more fun than he thought it'd be. Then he pushed it into the old pig shed and propped it against the pile of old timbers that filled one end. The back wheel was already wobbly.

It was still only about eleven o'clock. His mother came into the yard with the hens' bucket and the egg basket and he followed her down the vegetable garden to the poultry pen. As she lifted the latch of the wire gate and stepped in, he stayed outside. She emptied the bucket into the feeder and at once, as he knew they would, the hens came shrieking at it with smacking wings and stabbing beaks, their eyes unblinking in their jerking heads. He watched, fearful for his mother, as she collected the eggs from the coop and waded back through the cackling mob around her bare legs. She was actually laughing and clucking back at them. Couldn't she see they hated her for stealing the eggs?

"If a hen pecked you really hard would it make an actual hole in your leg?" he asked on the way back to the house. "You'd lose loads of blood, wouldn't you? You'd have to go to hospital."

"What? *Oh*—oh, Adam, I don't know. I'm not sure about that," she said. "Look, we got five today. Do you want to help me hard-boil them and make sandwiches for the picnic?"

He didn't. He couldn't bear the smell of hard-boiled eggs, he reminded her. He didn't like egg sandwiches. Also, if they were made with her brown bread (which they were going to be), he didn't like *any* sandwiches. She smiled vaguely and went back inside.

Adam got the scooter out again and trundled round and round the yard, thinking. His mother had always been that way, ignoring or forgetting things, never being sure what she knew or didn't know; it didn't bother her that she couldn't untangle even the simplest thing for him. When he was five they'd found all the hens dead one morning and he'd cried and cried and asked why foxes didn't sleep in the night-time like everybody else. *Oh, they're just not sleepy, I suppose.* Another time he wanted to know why they couldn't get a tractor, so he could have rides on it. *Oh, well, imagine! Then we could grow a whole field of beans instead of just a few rows. But maybe it'd be unkind to the earth.* When he asked what was unkind about growing a lot of beans instead of a few, she seemed not to hear and only much later, half in a dream, said, *Well, a field of beans. What harm could that do?*

Now there were times, like today, when there was no point in asking her anything. He could see from her face she couldn't really see *him;* she seemed to be elsewhere, listening to a conversation he couldn't hear. When she did pay him some half-attention she'd only say more of her stupid things that were vague and prone to her sudden changes of mind, that began *Oh, I'm not sure* or *Ah, though maybe* or *Well, I just wondered.* Sometimes she'd read her poems aloud at the table, or worse, try to make him write some. Adam sped angrily around the yard. She did it on purpose, making everything wishy-washy and slippery so that nothing she ever said was really true or not true and you couldn't ever argue about it. When he took the scooter back to the pig shed, he flung it down and let it fall over.

Later, he was pleased that Kevin and Kyle's dad brought them to the picnic instead of their mum—Louise hadn't been very nice to him that morning—even though Digger stayed on the edge of it all, pouring out most of his tea on the grass and saying he only had time for a half-cup. Then he stood in the bracken instead of sitting on a rug with the others while Adam opened his presents.

There was a bag of marbles from Callum and Fee—they were nice colors, and Fee said they were made of special hand-blown glass; Adam wasn't sure what that meant or that he knew how to play marbles. But Kevin and Kyle's present was brilliant. Just *brilliant,* so brilliant that at first all he could do was gasp. Then he tore the rest of the paper off so fast that Callum had to go off down the hill after it. It was a M.A.S.K. vehicle, one of the best ones, the Razorback—it

turned into a mobile weapon platform and it came with a Brad
Turner figure *and* an Eclipse mask. Adam yelped with delight. Kevin
and Kyle were grinning. He did high-fives with them, and the excitement spread—Kevin turned red and whooped and clapped and Kyle
made both his hands into fists and shook them around his head as if
they held dice. Adam had seen the M.A.S.K. videos at their house;
Kevin and Kyle had loads of the other vehicles, too. They, or Louise,
must have seen how much he absolutely loved them. He'd been given
something he really *wanted*. Suddenly he wished everybody could
disappear. He didn't want them to watch him gazing at his Razorback and touching it and getting used to it being *his,* in case he cried.
Then his mother broke in with one of her *Well, now!*s and told him
to say thank you. Then she went very quiet, and he could not look at
his father for the rest of the picnic for fear of catching his eye.

After that, doing the cake was real fun, even though the cake had
dried apricots in it and his mother and Fee clapped their hands a lot
and made too many thrilled noises. Kevin and Kyle's dad had gone
by then. Everybody else huddled up together on one side to keep the
wind away from the candles and he pretended he couldn't blow them
out without making loud raspberry noises that made everybody
laugh, especially Kevin, until his father told him to get on with it or
they'd still be there when it got dark. On the way back down the hill
he ran around shouting and chasing Kevin and Kyle and laughing so
hard he felt sick by the time he reached the bottom.

That night he lay awake in bed, amazed to think he'd been so
happy. He wondered how it was possible that a day could be as
happy as that, and yet before it was over turn into the complete opposite. Because after everybody had gone home and he was sprawled
on his front in the hall playing with the Razorback, he was suddenly
aware of his father towering over him. Adam shrank back; for a moment his father's head, silhouetted against the antlers behind him on
the wall, sprouted a gigantic, jagged halo of thorns. All at once his
Razorback was scooped off the floor. Adam scrambled to his feet
yelling, but it was already beyond his reach.

"Adam," his father said, in his deep calm voice, "I'm sorry, but

I'm afraid it doesn't matter how much you object. No thinking father would let his son play with a toy that glorifies bloodshed and violence."

In the dark, Adam broke into high, squealing sobs that shook the bed. Tears poured down his face and into the pillow. After he'd watched him break the Razorback in two and put it, along with the Brad Turner figure and the Eclipse mask, in the recycling bin, he was so weak with hatred and grief that he hadn't the power to stop his father drawing him on to his lap and holding him for a long time. He remained rigid in his father's arms. "I'm sorry you're upset, Adam," he said. "But never mind, eh? Tomorrow you can finish your dinosaur and play with that."

NOVEMBER 2011

From: deborahstoneyridge@yahoo.com

To: <adam.morgan@logisticsomnicorpsystems.com>
Sent on wed 9 nov 2011 at 11.32 GMT

Hello Adam, it was nice to talk to you at the weekend, so you caught me in, finally! I was out and about quite a lot seeing as Dad was at Jocelyn Lodge and there was nothing to hold me back. They kept him there a few days longer as he was doing so well, he does look as if he's put on weight but that could be the beard growing back because they didn't shave him there. He doesn't seem to mind so I think that little phase is over.

It did seem he was away ages! He's been back a week already, it doesn't feel like it. He is definitely a bit brighter and more on the ball. He's at stroke club now, was keen to go this time. He's talking more. Love, Mum xxx

PS This morning he managed to say to send you his love, at least I think that's what he meant!

To: deborahstoneyridge@yahoo.com
Sent on wed 9 nov 2011 at 09.23 EST

Mum that's great! Give me a bit more detail, how far can he walk now

– do you mean with the frame or with a stick? Or can he manage without?

Glad you're ok – flight details soon.

I'm actually in a meeting right this minute, emailing under the desk ;-) more anon. love Adam xx Give D my love too, ok?

The evenings by the fire are no more. The logs are used up and I haven't the strength to chop more and bring them in, and naturally Theo doesn't offer. It means I retire earlier and earlier, even though it's cold upstairs. I slip into Adam's old bedroom, lie down under the covers, and wait for the moment when Theo comes through the door. Sometimes he does, sometimes he doesn't. No matter; the privacy of waiting for him in the dark is enough. The waiting's more necessary to me than the moment itself, and that's what I look forward to all day; his arrival, if it comes, is all the more thrilling for it. I do not feel guilty, although I never put on a light. By and by I get up and go to my own room across the quiet hall, my movements loose and easy. I can relax. Well, not relax.

It's too strange for that. And so unexpected, when I am so much older than he is, and looked upon his presence here as filling the place of a son, not a lover. I had no inkling that was what I would allow him to become. Is that what he is? I do not feel I am in any way betraying Howard. I'm not hiding from him anything more than I hide from myself. I have hidden much from myself. Theo understands I've had to, over the years.

But now that Howard's back from Jocelyn Lodge, the practicalities take over. I'm swamped with things to do—I didn't use the time he was away to get on top of the jobs at all, so I'm a little overwhelmed—and Theo is keeping his distance. I get hardly a glimpse of him or a word all day, especially as Nurse Jenny keeps coming by to check that Howard is settling back in all right. I see her eyeing the house for signs of mismanagement. She leaves a sheet called "Dietary Guidelines for Mobility Impaired Patients" and a leaflet about getting help with your shopping. She asks if I've had time to stock up, because Howard's really found his appetite again. Howard's very chirpy and agrees, in whole words. He even gets up and sees her to the door. I think he winks at me on his way, slow but unaided, back to his chair in front of the television, but it could be accidental. I find myself smiling, anyway. Something to tell Theo later.

But with all this commotion going on, I grow afraid. Usually it's only in spells of tranquillity that Theo will emerge at all, and he only speaks in an atmosphere of perfect safety.

But, to my relief, he is back, and now there's a new side to him. He's playful.

Bread-making, for instance. It's fun now in a way it never used to be, although I still make terrible bread. I don't eat it (nor does Theo). It's for Howard. He likes it, or he should, since I am making it to his old requirements. At least more or less: that's where the fun comes in.

When he was away, I went through some of the junk upstairs looking for stuff to burn in the stove now that the logs are used up, and I came across his "Bread Is Life" poster with the list of Rules. It's vital that the Bed and Breakfast guests understand the philosophy here, was what he said, quite defensively if I remember right, when I questioned the wisdom of putting it up in the dining room. I showed it to Theo. He says it's nuts, and he says it in a tone of voice I maybe should have used to Howard in the first place.

It's not just the bread. Theo now admits he has never even heard of most of the things Howard considers important (or considered— it's anybody's guess what matters to him now). He asks what Howard thinks he's trying to prove, and I do find that a little shocking. My loyalties are divided. Well, I tell him, Howard would say it's about living modestly and naturally and responsibly, he would say that Adam and his generation should be grateful to people like us. "For what, exactly?" I hear Theo ask. I see the friendly bewilderment on his face.

For the way we tried to live, I repeat. For what we tried to be. Frugal. Responsible.

Theo has nothing to say to that. Then I feel sad and angry, thinking of all the self-sacrificial years I let Howard persuade me I was making a difference for my successors on this greedy planet, and it turns out, guess what, all the while the planet was filling up with Theos, millions upon millions of them, a whole generation of unblemished souls who don't want a shred of sacrifice from me after all, not a single thing, not so much as a passing thought. With or without my sacrifices Theo reckons things might get patched up all right, planet-wise (he does use such phrases). Not perfectly, obviously, but when was the world perfect? It's a little patronizing of people Howard's age, Theo murmurs, to suggest the world might not go on turning if it was left up to people *his* age.

Anyway, he finds Howard's Bread Is Life rules hilarious. He has taped the poster up on the kitchen wall under the shelf where I keep the scales and mixing bowls. Just putting it there turns the whole idea of bread-making into a joke. I shouldn't laugh. But the kitchen is now full of fun.

DEAR STONEYRIDGE GUESTS

BREAD IS LIFE

1   All our flour is organic and whole grain. We sometimes add seeds and nuts to the Bread mix but we DO NOT sprinkle them over the top. Bread is Life, and it is Beautiful. It needs no decoration. Does a sunrise need diamonds?

2   All our Bread is made by hand. No machines are used. We believe kneading is a beautiful act. It is an act of love that transfers part of the World's ENERGY, through the person kneading, to the Bread, from which it is passed on to those who eat it. None of the World's Energy belongs to us, we are only the channels through which it passes.

3   Yeast is alive. We use only new fresh Yeast, which is strong. Old Yeast, even if it is fresh, has no vigor. WE NEVER USE DRIED YEAST, which is dead. BREAD IS LIFE!

4   To make the Dough we use only the Rainwater of recently fallen Rain, which comes to us fresh from the Sky, still holding some of the Sky's Energy. If fresh Rainwater is not available we use freshly drawn Spring Water, which holds some Energy from the Earth. WE NEVER USE TAP WATER.

5   Dough is alive. We use only wooden bowls, boards, and spoons for Bread-making, which are made from a living material. No lifeless materials such as metal or pottery are allowed to touch the Dough before it is baked into Bread.

6   All our loaves and rolls are shaped by hand and baked in rounded natural forms which reflect the shapes we see all around us in the Hills and Rocks and Fruits of the Earth.

We have kneaded and baked this Bread as a gift for you.
Pass on its Goodness in the form of your Gifts to others.
We are together in the Oneness of Energy.
Use it well!!!

No sooner is the poster on the wall than a line appears through the *h* of *Dough* in Rule 5.

Theo says, "Who's Doug, anyway?"

And I say I have no idea, but at least he's alive.

It's just a silly joke, but it sticks. Now we have this banter going all the time.

Is Doug still in bed? No, he's just risen.

What's Doug trying to prove? Maybe just that he's alive?

Soon enough, all these exchanges appear scribbled on the margins of the poster along with little naked podgy cartoon figures—Doug the Dough. They make me laugh every time I look at them. It's just a bit of harmless fun.

I rinse my hands at the tap and shake my wet fingertips at Theo, who's watching from the big kitchen chair. Drops of water glint on the floor. *We use only wooden bowls, boards, and spoons,* I sing, setting the cold weight of a stoneware dish on the counter. *No lifeless materials such as metal or pottery are allowed.* I tip the flour into the enamel scales and add extra bran (Howard's bowels being a law unto themselves), and with a teaspoon I measure out the dried yeast from its packet. It's good and dead; it runs into the spoon like pulverized bone, and smells of meat. *No machines are used,* I say, fixing the dough hook into the electric mixer.

In the past, when the bread took me half a day and tired me out and still failed to rise, Howard would ask me why I ever expected it to be easy. Bread called for the labor of fingers and hands, and wouldn't I have to admit that what I felt was a *good* kind of tired out? Well, all I do now is flick the switch. "And you know what, Howard?" I say aloud over the noise of the mixer, answering his question at long last, "this feels better." There's an uncertain laugh, and I make out Theo's voice, talking to me from the big chair.

He's always asking me about my life. Anything can come up.

The hens, for instance. "What's the point of keeping them? We don't get more than a couple of eggs a week now. Why not?"

I go through the reasons. It's getting dark earlier, and hens need daylight to lay. Or maybe the feed's not quite right; they only get scraps, after all. But probably they're just old, I tell Theo. They're all old ladies now.

"Get some new ones, then," Theo says.

I'm surprised at how definite he is about this. I can't, I say. I can't bring new birds in without upsetting the old ones. It upsets the pecking order. Anyway, there's only room for about six.

"Then let's get rid of the old ones," Theo says. "Eat them. Make room for new ones."

I decide not to take this seriously. Besides, I don't want lots more eggs, I say. There's no passing trade for them in the winter.

"Are you fond of cats, would you like to have a cat?" he asks next. His voice is drowsy, and hard to make out under the drone of the mixer.

A cat might get in and kill the hens, I say back, as I watch the dough forming. And, I go on, even if it didn't, we couldn't let a strange animal anywhere near them—then they wouldn't lay at all. They could die of fright. Anyway, Howard's allergic.

"Too stupid to live, then," Theo says, "as well as useless."

You're in a funny mood today, I tell him. Quite often, he's in a funny mood. It's as if he doesn't know his own mind, comes out with one thing, then the opposite. The mixer is whipping the dough up into a fizzing swamp of lumps and farty gray blisters, the beater hurls and thumps it against the side of the bowl. I smile; this is how it's done. There's a crazy, necessary violence in it.

"Maybe we'd get a dog, then?" Theo says, ignoring what I just told him about bringing strange animals into the yard.

I don't like dogs.

Theo goes on as if I haven't said a word. "A dog trained up, that'd be useful. I could shoot rabbits, easy, with a dog. You need a dog, the right sort of dog that'll fetch them off the moor in his mouth and drop them at your feet, not a tooth mark on them, just a clean hole through the head."

I hate dogs. And Howard hates guns, I tell him. He won't allow a gun on the place.

"Oh, won't he, indeed?"

Digger gave an old shotgun to Adam once and Howard took it away from him, and Adam ran away. He went to Exeter. I was so angry with Howard I couldn't speak. I couldn't say anything to him for weeks. Months.

My eyes fill with tears, remembering. This could be the first time I've said this aloud. I stop the mixer and lift the dough hook. I scrape the bowl's contents into the loaf tins, spoon in the next batch of flour, add the yeast and water. There's a long silence now, as if Theo is taking in what I've said and weighing it for truth.

Howard told me to return the gun to Digger but I didn't, I kept it. I went behind Howard's back. I thought it might bring Adam home.

I hid it upstairs and I got Digger to show me how to keep it clean and oiled, just in case. I wrote to Adam that if he came back, somehow I'd talk his father into letting him keep it.

"Then what happened?"

I lower the dough hook and switch the mixer on again.

I needn't have bothered. It wasn't really about the gun, you see. Adam wanted to go to school. He wanted to get away from us. He never really came back here to live.

I let all these disclosures float and flow around me as the food mixer churns. It amazes me that such dangerous words can come up out of nowhere, proving they were sayable, after all, and fill up the place with not just sound but, if I close my eyes, with restless lines of light or movement. I find myself thinking of Howard's half-world blindness and wonder if he sees them, too, these freshly agitated, peripheral little specters of so many awkward truths and unburied grievances.

Theo, there's more, I say. There's more to tell you. Other things.

But Theo's mood won't allow for any more confessions. He changes tack again. Really and truly, there's no predicting him today. "So Howard made you angry. Why, because he got a few things wrong? Wasn't perfect? Wasn't it a bit much to ask of him in the first place, that he never make a simple mistake?"

A simple mistake? I whisper. Oh, Theo, you have no idea of the mistakes. Mine, too.

I stop the mixer. Silence. Then he says, "I'm sorry for Howard. I'm sorry for you, too. But the point is, even after all the mistakes, you have to look at what you're left with. Each other."

I open my eyes again, to the pricking of the harsh kitchen light. Theo's words are like paper chains flown up to the ceiling in the beaks of magic birds, and fastened there in hanging festoons of all colors.

Do you know a lot about guns? I ask him, to change the subject.

"Not really," he says. "Just enough to fill the pot, and keep down the pests."

Every day at Jocelyn Lodge was packed. Howard had a timetable of exhilarating, exhausting sessions of walking and turning, going up and down stairs, sitting and rising from chairs. He kicked and stretched obediently in a pool of very warm water; he practiced doing up buttons and slicing bread and using a pencil. There were hours spent trying to tame his voice, during which he followed instructions about breathing and swallowing, repeated staccato syllables, and sang through them when they jammed themselves in his throat. After his meals—hot platefuls of stewed meat and mashed potatoes, bowls of sweet puddings with custard—he lay down and slept, pleasurably sabotaged by his full stomach. Each morning he awoke in his warm, clean bedroom with scarcely a pain in his body, his limbs heavy, but stronger. Every face he could make out smiled at him, every voice he heard was musical and cajoling. When he contemplated all this cheerfulness, all this devotion to keeping him comfortable and happy, the gratitude he felt toward every person charged with care of him, tears ran down his cheeks. Not for a single moment did he stop longing for Deborah. If only she could be treated like this, too, the strangeness and remoteness and cruelty would melt out of her, he was sure of it.

After a week in the central heating he'd forgotten all about cold; he'd forgotten about weather. He'd almost forgotten the time of year, and on the day he went home was mildly shocked to see a frost like powdered glass on the drive. They set down a pathway of rubber mats for him to walk the few yards from the door of Jocelyn Lodge to the ambulance. On the drive back he tried to brace himself to withstand the cold again. Stoneyridge was a house with the flimsiest of seals against the seasons, and winter would be reaching into the rooms already: ice on the windowpanes, his breath forming vapor clouds as he lay in bed in the early morning.

When he got back, he found that Deborah was different. How long had he been away, surely only a few days? How could that be long enough to change her, or was it he who had changed?

As he was able to study her more closely, the more she puzzled him. The more carefully she tended him, the more she receded. In her treatment of him she was less rough but no kinder, merely abstracted. Her eyes when she looked at him were distant, as if already fixed on the yard that she would suddenly say needed sweeping, or on the moor where she must go again to check the sheep. He struggled to show her that he was capable of performing little tasks to help her—he would get up and take cups in a shaking hand to the sink, and even wash them—at which she might smile disinterestedly. One afternoon when she was up on the moor late in the day, he managed to pull on boots, cross the yard, and go down the garden in the twilight to close the hen house. She came back after dark and planted a kiss on his forehead, but gave no other sign that she had noticed.

She was unfathomable. Howard would hear her talking to herself in the room next door, her tone of voice settled and conversational, even dull, but he missed too many words to make sense of what she said. And although she still roamed about the place, tidying up here or clearing out there, her routines had slipped; just as often he would come across her sitting at the kitchen table long into the morning, frowning and alert, as if absorbed in some complex mental puzzle. When she did rouse herself, the motivation for her dithery little homemaking gestures remained opaque; her way of moving, once eloquent of her state of mind, was now so self-possessed it evaded any interpretation except that perhaps she did not care to have her feelings known. She left him alone for longer and longer spells and he could not get used to it, although he was managing, more or less, to get used again to being cold and always at least a little hungry. Howard took all these changes as signs that in his absence she had developed a taste, amounting to an aptitude, for being alone.

Grateful that he seemed not to make her angry anymore, he felt nevertheless more afraid of her, for under her new calm flowed a trickle of something tense and potentially hazardous, which he could not pinpoint. He sensed it all the more acutely when she was out of sight. So he took to following her around, stumbling after the sound of her voice or the noises of vacuum-cleaning or furniture moving; it was like trying to trace a leak. Often as he roamed the house seeking a sign of her presence and finding none, it occurred to him that nowadays she frequently went out without telling him, and he wondered if she was actually giving him the slip. And sometimes he would creep upstairs and stand silently at the door of Adam's bedroom, where, for reasons of her own, she often went to lie down in the afternoons.

She never mentioned Adam. At night in bed Howard practiced his name aloud and put together sentences about him, asking when he was coming to visit. If he managed to deliver the sentence the next day, Deborah's answer would be huffy and inconclusive. Every day he struggled to tell her, when she next emailed him, to give Adam his love.

From: deborahstoneyridge@yahoo.com

To: <adam.morgan@logisticsomnicorpsystems.com>
Sent on wed 23 nov 2011 at 11.45 GMT

Hello Adam, nothing to report really – D doing ok. I'm busy as always. The days are so short now. Queue of people waiting, they really need more computers in this place. Looking forward lots to
seeing you!! We both are. I'll sign off, bye for now love Mum xxx D
sends love too

To: deborahstoneyridge@yahoo.com
Sent on fri 25 nov 2011 at 12.02 EST

Mum you didn't answer any of my questions in my last email OR that
I asked you on the phone on Saturday – what was the assessment in
the end, after D was at Jocelyn? Don't they give you a sort of report
and work out what to do next?
    Sacha's great uncle had a stroke too and that's what they did with
him, there was this special stroke nurse. Or is that what they do with
him at stroke club? It's good he's going to that.
    So the flights are all booked and here they are, since you didn't
have a pen handy when I rang:
    Thurs 22 Dec   Arr Heathrow   08.35
    Tues 3 Jan Dep Heathrow 19.20
    Can you stand me for that long?!

I don't want you getting anything special ready, do you hear?? I'm coming early so there'll be time for us to do Christmas shopping together. In fact I've ordered a hamper with some stuff which will arrive 18th or 19th so keep an ear open for a delivery van (they should ring you the day before) you'll have to sign for it. Mum, I really am sorry about not making it in the summer – hopefully we'll have lots of time to catch up over Christmas.

Love A xxxx

Ps – next round of site visits coming up so on the road for next 2 weeks, will keep in touch via mob. You can still email, remember I get them on my phone.

From: deborahstoneyridge@yahoo.com

To: <adam.morgan@logisticsomnicorpsystems.com>
Sent on wed 30 nov 2011 at 12.22 GMT

Hello Adam, still not much going on, we're very behind today — nearly didn't make it to stroke club!

Days very short. Digger appeared the other day with some pheasants, he said they were going spare. Some of these people who come out for a day's shooting, they don't even take the birds. They don't want to eat them, only kill them.

I'm not sure I'm up to the plucking and drawing any more, it's so messy. There was a recipe I used to do once but I wouldn't know where to find it now. The other thing is D might make a fuss, he was never very happy about it, them being shot for sport and everything. It's hard to tell what's going to bother him these days — maybe it was always hard! Still it's a terrible waste if they don't get eaten and I don't see the harm in it — they're bred for it aren't they and Digger says it's a better way for them to go than getting caught by a fox.

They're hanging in the pig shed while I decide.

Exmoor must be overrun with pheasants this year, I hear the shots from all directions and I can just imagine them all at it, people paying a fortune to get a gun in their hands. It goes on all day.

Digger asked about you and were you visiting, and I said yes, but it's hard for you to get away. He said we could well be in for another bad winter, all the signs are there. So we'll have to keep an open mind about it, you won't make it if there's snow, as you know all the roads round here get cut off.

Lots of love Mum xxxx

Once the bread's out of the oven I put on my boots and coat. I have to go off up the hill to check on the sheep. I'm late in going; it's a morning job, but on these late November days I don't get to it until the afternoon's on the wane, because with one thing and another the morning routine's gone to pieces. I hang on at the breakfast table talking to Theo, to begin with. Today we were late for Stroke Club so Howard only got the last half hour. They glared at me, those bloody women, Jenny and the other one, but I didn't much care. Really, they have no idea. I told them that since Howard was struck dumb (a stroke really does *strike*, and do they begin to grasp what that means?) I've gone without the sound of another voice for such a long time, and I'm making up for it now.

They pretended to understand. Yes, keep talking to him, they said, it's important you keep talking to him. Involve him. It'll stimulate whatever speech he has, you must keep talking to him. They have no idea what they're asking. Howard's voice going on about this and that, booming about the place all those years, so loud and certain, and then suddenly there's no sound at all but your own little bleats of desperation? Weeks, months, years of hearing only yourself, trapped in your unrelenting false brightness, and getting scarcely a sound back? You'd do anything to hear another voice raised in reply, whatever it might be saying.

Also, although dealing with Howard's speech affliction may be a little easier since he came back from Jocelyn Lodge, every other thing that needs to be done for him takes just as long as before, possibly longer. Theo's around to help, in theory, but I can't say he makes a practical difference, and it wouldn't be reasonable to complain about that. I admit there are times when I come across things left undone: Howard shivering and patient on the side of his bed waiting to be dressed when I believed him sitting content in front of the television. There are times when Howard simply gets mislaid; I might find him stranded at the end of the hall clinging to his walking frame and the overhead light left on from the night before casting the shadows of the antlers across his face. I'll hear Theo's voice at my ear saying he'd like to see the last of those bloody antlers and would I like that, too, to which my answer is a whispered, yes I bloody would.

Howard, meanwhile, is blinking and mumbling and about to keel over. Come on, Howard, what are you doing wandering about here? I'll say, and then Theo sniggers over my shoulder and says something so sly I would have closed my ears to it if I'd had any warning he was about to say it.

"Useless eyesore," he says, after I've watched poor Howard turn from me and shuffle away. Of course he means the antlers. He's heard my views on the antlers. "Any more useless eyesores you'd like to get rid of?"

Then I'll smile, thinking of Howard's earnest philosophy about the antlers and what they stand for, and I'll make out I didn't hear what Theo said. He has no right to be expressing such thoughts in a house where he is, after all, a guest, I wish to remind him. Or if I've really had enough, I'll tell him to leave me alone.

The pity of it is that when he does leave me alone, when it's just me and Howard in all this great echoey prison of a house, it's unbearable.

When Theo is nowhere to be found, my faith in him falters, and I curse this way he has of vanishing. But wherever it is he goes, whether it's into outbuildings or his own room or the attic or up on the moor, I imagine him curled up asleep and hidden under a heap of sacks or behind a wardrobe or in the branches of a tree, like a boy in a nursery rhyme. Then my heart melts. For Theo did arrive here an orphan and runaway, and is no more to be scolded for being a little bit in disgrace than is Tom the Piper's Son or Little Boy Blue, whose faces in a nursery rhyme book from the library Adam, when he was four years old, obliterated with a black crayon because, he said, they were naughty. And, after all, Theo is here, and Adam is not. I think of Theo as a lost boy who happened by chance upon my life here, and I remind myself that he does not have to stay.

So I forbid myself to mention how he tends to go absent when I most need him, and I'll get busy rescuing Howard from this or that small predicament, and in due course Theo reappears. If I then confess to him whatever little lapse of care I discovered, he gives me a mild ticking-off and says I have to accept that I'm growing forgetful as well as slow. I say nothing, for beyond the mild unfairness, there's a blessing in it all. While Theo speaks I see his eyes settle on me and then, however dark the world around me, I stand in the light. I don't fret as much, and nor does Howard. Howard doesn't object at all.

That's not to say I want Theo around all the time. When, as he does increasingly, he oversteps the mark with one of his crueler observations, I want to get away from him, too. I think up new and especially difficult chores as a way of getting a rest from him, because, after all, chores are chores and have to be done. (For example, the pottery workshop did get a hosing-down. The water forced out some loose panes of glass so these days frost forms inside on the workbench that runs under the window and the old wheels have all rusted up.) Perhaps this is one of the reasons why I leave going out to check the sheep until so late in the afternoon.

It's a squally day and I wear my oilskin that's permanently damp and so stiff with age it's like wearing a piece of old tarp. I also put on a tweed hat of Howard's that's gray and waxy with dirt but at least keeps the rain off and doesn't blow away in a high wind. Nobody in her right mind would go out on a day like this but I can't put it off because I skipped checking the sheep yesterday. Now that the mornings fly by, I tend to go only every other day. This isn't how it should be, but when Howard was away I felt terribly tired and went to bed in the afternoons. Once I went to lie down forgetting that I hadn't checked the flock, and when I got up again it was too dark to go up on the moor. The next day when I saw the sheep they were perfectly all right, so it hadn't mattered. Now I have a nap nearly every afternoon. That's another thing. I suppose I need a little sleep in the daytime because conversations with Theo can go on long, long into the night.

I'm used to my nap now, and come three o'clock or thereabouts, I crave the curtained dark and thick bedclothes. Today under the cold oilskin coat my flesh is full of its own, heavy warmth and feels too soft for the work of walking up the moor. It's after half-past three and the sky is gray with rain clouds and the coming dusk, and I would do anything to stay in and light the fire and sit by it as the day fades outside. But I drag myself out and trudge up the muddy track. Theo, as I expected, has disappeared. I climb the stiles between the fields and carry on up through the bracken and heather. I'm too tired to walk fast, although I ought to hurry as there isn't much daylight left. Lighted windows in the farms over on the far side of the moor make me feel excluded and rather feckless; my distant neighbors have attended to their outside work at the proper time and are now indoors. I tramp knee-high in the wet bracken and over clumps of reeds and brambles. Up on the moor top the grass shivers all around me and the wind bullies me along, shoving at me sideways, slapping my raised collar against my face. The rain rattles into the hard folds of my coat; it tastes metallic. I move in close under the line of rowan and alder that straggles across the crest to try to get out of the wind but it's too boggy here where animals have huddled for shelter, and the rain drips thicker and colder on my shoulders from the bare, waterlogged trees. I move out again, into the open. All around me I hear the reedy sighs of dead grass, and tatters of fog, paler than the sky, are uncurling across the moor.

Not a sheep in sight. When the weather's this bad they tend to cluster over on the other side, in the lee of the slope. They'll be standing close in by the combe, one of the deep stony gullies formed by ancient landslides of rocks and torrents of meltwater that runs down the hill from the moor top, where the ground is always boggy and treacherous. It's as well the gorse there grows too densely even for sheep to break through to the fissure in the hillside, where they would stumble and hurt themselves on the boulders and slide down the scree of prehistoric rubble. I hear them through the noise of the weather; their small, dry bleats rise and break in turning gusts of wind. It's too dark to count them from here; I can't make out their shapes from the scattered boulders against the hawthorn scrub and thickets of gorse. I have to get nearer to them, close to the combe, and hope they won't scatter. I jam my hands hard in my pockets, sink my head deeper into my collar, and set off going crosswise from the moor top.

Maybe it's the change of direction that does it. The ground beneath me seems to tip under my feet. It loosens, shifts, my front foot slides along a hank of wet grass, the ankle wobbles then bends like a hinge and tips me over. There is enough time for me to know I'm falling and also enough to know that I didn't know it fast enough to get my hands out of my pockets. There's time to know I'm going to land hard and get hurt. I crash over on my left side and I feel grazing and stinging and I hear my voice sending a ludicrous "Ooh-ooh-oh-oh!" into empty air. I scrape and bump down the hillside and when I come to a stop, again comes a strange expansion of time. Much more time than I feel I need is now available to me, in which I come to understand, slowly, that I'm flat on the ground and winded, and my upper body and face are trapped in a cage of biting bramble strands. I resist an urge to try to thrash my way out; I get one hand free and unpick the thorns from my skin and hair and clothes, and I manage to sit up. I'm scratched and punctured in several places, pain is starting to throb in my neck and shoulder, and my hands are shaking. I'm wet through and I've lost the hat. My left side landed hardest and I can't use that arm to push myself up. The left leg feels useless. My mouth is warm to the touch and there's a tinny taste on my tongue. I don't know how long I spend taking note of these things, but eventually I'm aware that time has speeded up and is running along again as normal, and with it has come rain that is dropping like pebbles on my oilskin shoulders. My head pounds. There's a panicky, animal command shouting in my brain, telling me to move. It is not all right to remain here. I must get up from the ground. Here, down on the ground, is where hurt creatures lie until they die. I must free myself from the damp pull of the earth and *get up. Move.*

I don't move. My face stings with rain and tears. Although there is no point or sense in it, I lift my head and roar, "Help! Is anyone there?! Helloo?! Help!" and the wind whips the sound away and the air soaks it straight up so that even if there were someone within a mile, they wouldn't hear. Anyway, I know there isn't. The effort of shouting makes my head swim. I can't help thinking about Howard dozing in his chair or lying on his bed in the dark back bedroom, and the mayhem there will be if I'm not back soon to look after him. I'm not so far gone as to imagine Theo's attentions are any sort of substitute for my care. Or to think it's not up to me alone to get myself out of this mess. I'm on my own. I think wildly that if I had a phone, or if I had a gun I could fire to raise the alarm, or a dog who'd run back barking to Stoneyridge—but what use would any of those be when there's no guarantee they'd bring anyone to the rescue? And the sheep, the bloody sheep. I still haven't counted the sheep. And I cannot move.

I lift my bad leg in both hands and try to make a circle with my foot, inside the boot. The ankle turns in a gritty, muffled sort of way that tells me worse pain is lying in wait, but it does move, so it can't be broken. I haul myself around and get on to all fours and then upright, taking my weight on the right leg. I hobble a short way, dragging the left foot. It feels cased in lead. After about twenty steps I collapse against a low boulder. I'm breathless and my heart is thudding in my throat. The light is almost gone; I can see, but in an adaptive, nocturnal kind of way. I make out another boulder, and a little way off is a long, flat stone rising out of the ground at a shallow angle. It's not familiar at first, but then I know it. This is the place. I'm back.

On some summer afternoon Howard sat on the grass here and whittled sticks and I lay back on that stone and pretended to be asleep. Now and again I opened my eyes and looked up at soaring birds, and I stroked my pregnant belly and I longed for poems, that would make everything clear, to suggest themselves. I waited for words to descend. I wanted to catch them and rearrange them and write down what they would surely say: that there could be heaven on this earth. That believing in Howard as I did, there was nothing impossible in the idea, nor anything childish in wanting it, as long as I accepted it had to be earned. Motherhood would be only the beginning. I wasn't impatient; in fact I took it as a measure of my maturity—I never really enjoyed being young—that the last thing I wanted was that the perfect life should be easy to accomplish. I was prepared to wait for Howard to bring to fruition, with my help, all that he promised.

I can't start thinking about that now. It doesn't matter. What matters is that I am back here in pouring rain slumped at an awkward angle against a rock on a wintery evening nearly thirty years later, that I've fallen on my bad shoulder and injured my ankle. The pain has lessened, though, but this may be because the night air is stealing all heat and sensation from my body. Only my face burns, under the cold rain, from the lacerations and the effort of getting this far. I realize I'm desperate for some water to drink; I lick the rain off my hands and hold out my palms to catch more. I start to shiver. Deep in the stone of the boulder that's pressing into my back through the oilskin there's a presentiment of ice. I think about lying down and waiting patiently, as if I'm still here on a summer afternoon. All I need do is wait and that single cloud will pass across and clear the sun, and perfect light will shine down on me once more. I close my eyes, willing the scene into life and myself into the center of it. Howard yawns and stretches and is murmuring something to me; I'm watching skylarks while baby limbs bump gently under my ribs. I'm here with Howard and everything's fine. There's no hurry to go back. It's fine for me to lie here and simply wait for the next thing to happen.

Nonsense. There is sleet in the wind now, and I open my eyes. It's Theo's voice. Nonsense. Who do you think you're fooling, all this stuff about Howard yawning and stretching, all that "all's well with the world"? Face it. That's not how it was. That's not what happened.

Theo is not even *here.* I shout at him through the rain to be quiet, but he goes on. No, and Howard's not here, either, he says, and the way you think of him, he never was. Your perfect sunny day, all the perfect sunny picnic days, they never were like that. I tell Theo again to shut up and I berate him for his uselessness in practical matters, most of all for his languid way of coming and going, that is no help to me now.

And he does shut up. In the silence I hear the wind again, and I am left considering his face, and the expression in his eyes that, gentle as it may be, requires me to use every grain of strength I possess to get myself up from the ground and back home to Howard.

In the end, every grain of strength is required. I stumble and crawl my way down, stopping many times to rest. But the rain and wind prove a blessing; for a while all I can think about is how cold I am, and later I am too numbed by it to feel much pain in my ankle and shoulder. By the time I reach the back door and get inside, my left side is useless. The kitchen is empty. Howard will be asleep in the sitting room in front of the television; I make out the flickering of the screen through the glass pane in the door. I manage to get myself into a chair at the kitchen table and for a few moments all I can do is rest my head on my arms. I can't stop shivering, and my face is hot. Sensation, in the form of pain, begins to return.

To: deborahstoneyridge@yahoo.com
Sent on wed 30 nov 2011 at 23.43 EST

Hi mum got yours from earlier, tried to call a few hours ago. I think Dad might have tried to answer!! but not sure – couldn't get a response, might have been him breathing or maybe just static, I just called down the phone to say hello and send love. Anyway where were you when it was gone 7pm your time, were you shutting up the hens or something?

Anyway re Christmas Mum I"M DEFINITELY coming, I gave you the flights – am all booked. Here they are again in case you didn't make a note.

Thurs 22 Dec   Arr Heathrow   08.35
Tues 3 Jan   Dep Heathrow 19.20

But I'll be keeping you posted anyway. I'll rent a car at the airport, if weather looks bad might even get a 4 x 4 so don't worry about snow.

Visit round going ok, the usual stuff, am stuck in boring hotel, got two reports to file, double boring!!

Hope you're ok. lots of love A xxxx

He awoke suddenly in his chair, aware of the back door opening and commotion spilling through. He got up and went to look from the doorway into the kitchen. With the stirring of air came an exchange of smells, between the musty whiff of coal smoke and burning bread from the kitchen and the earthy frost vapors blowing in from the hillside. There were noises, unintelligible but human, and troubled: the sounds of stumbling and pain and shock. Howard turned his head this way and that, trying to make his banded stripes of vision coalesce into a coherent image. It was her, of course, or the shape of her, that came within his sight at last, solidifying out of an impression of movement in the room that to begin with was not quite convincingly *her*. The words to explain this, even to himself, swilled around his head, defying order.

She crossed the room and collapsed jerkily on to a chair, the noises of distress following her in a haphazard wake. She didn't seem to see him. She slumped over the table with her head on her arms, and the room's stillness returned. But Howard began to shake, and he struggled for a moment with the idea that he had to get moving or the shaking would never stop. He shuffled back to his chair in the sitting room and got both hands on his frame, and walked back to the kitchen.

When he got over the threshold and peered round again, he saw at once that the black, freezing rectangle on the opposite wall was the back door, wide open to the night. As he caught hold of it and pushed it shut against the wind with his good arm, he was aware he was moving faster than usual. At the sound, Deborah lifted her head and gazed at him without speaking. A further thought, sparkling and lucid, came to him. He was the man of the house. He needed to lock up. The key was in the door. Turning it was difficult, but he managed it, finally.

She was trying to get out of her wet oilskin, and had begun to cry. The weight of one arm was pulling her shoulder down, and she couldn't lift it to get rid of the sleeve. With one hand on his frame, Howard used the other to ease the oilskin off the shoulder, and pulled at the collar until it came free of the other shoulder. Then he sat down and reached for her boots. One came off easily, the other took a lot longer and she wouldn't let him help her. She was in pain; there was something wrong with the ankle.

Howard moved over to the fridge, stooped down to the icebox, and brought out a bag of frozen peas. As he was trying to rise and turn around, it slipped from his hand. He let out a howl; the small green marbles rattled over the floor. Deborah pulled herself up, hobbled across, and scooped up the spilling-out bag, took her seat again, and sat hunched over, holding it against her ankle. Then Howard had another good idea. He found his shoebox of drugs on the kitchen worktop, brought it to the table, and tipped its contents out. He couldn't read any of the names on the dozens of blister packets, but he waved a hand over them and managed to say, "Here. Take . . . something. Tablet. Take tablets, for pain." Deborah nodded and began raking through them. He managed to fetch her a mug of water and she chose what he supposed was the right thing, and swallowed them.

After that she just went on sitting, as if she didn't know what to do. She must be hungry, he thought. He found the bread knife in a drawer and with a surge of Jocelyn Lodge confidence cut clumsy wedges from the loaf she'd baked that day. He remembered something particular about this kind of bread, how sour it tasted when he'd last eaten some of it a few hours ago, but even so his mouth flooded with saliva. There was honey somewhere, he remembered. Did she like honey? He got it down, and carried plates, knives, and their food, one thing at a time, to the table. They ate together, smiling at the first burst of honey sweetness on the tongue, coughing on the crumbs, until the loaf was finished and the honey jar empty.

Afterward, he stood up, took one of her hands, then the other, and helped her to take hold of his walking frame. She didn't need him to direct her; neither of them had to point out she wouldn't be able to manage the stairs. She leaned forward on the frame and edged toward the door, keeping the weight off her bad foot. She wasn't as skilled as he was and once nearly fell over, but Howard knew that a bit of practice would deal with that. He could show her a few tricks. The thought made him happy. She followed him across to his bedroom. He always slept at the side near the door and next to the bathroom, and again without any words being necessary she made her way to the far side. Howard closed the door behind them and pushed one of his pillows across to her. Still dressed, she lay down stiffly on top of the covers and closed her eyes, as if allowing herself to rest for only a moment before rising to deal with her next round of tasks. Howard ached to help her. Moving silently, he came and stood at the end of the bed. Her feet poking out from her baggy men's trousers looked impossibly naked, white and cold with blotched sore patches; the toes were knobbly and squashed. The bad ankle was puffy and beginning to bruise. She lay quite still; he wondered if she could feel it throbbing and could not bear to move at all, or if she could possibly be already asleep. He wondered if he could bandage it or replace the bag of frozen peas without disturbing her. Probably not. Gently, he pulled at the rug that was folded across the end of the bed and managed to arrange it over her body. It was more important that she rest, he decided, liking the strangeness of his being called upon to make any decision, even the smallest one, about what was best for her.

He shuffled round, got himself out of his slippers and into bed, and lay down. His mind ran over the evening routine, as far as he could remember it: his nightly dosage of pills that he would never get right by himself, a wash, the brushing of teeth, pajamas, bed. Well, a little slippage wouldn't hurt.

A horizontal bar of light at the bottom of the door shone across the carpet; he had not thought of switching off the lights or the soundless television. An odd picture came into his head, simultaneously reassuring and alarming, of someone else in the house still up and about, perhaps stepping in from the dark after one last check on the henhouse, clearing dishes in the kitchen, wiping over the surfaces and yawning, someone who might later turn the door handle in the dark and come in to look at them both lying in bed half-covered, asleep at a strange angle. But his mind was too tired to accommodate the idea seriously, and he let go of it, and his thoughts swam toward sleep. With one last effort he turned and drew the blankets across so they covered Deborah, who didn't stir.

He lay back, feeling dizzy. When he closed his eyes he felt as though he were falling, spinning and spinning away into darkness. But he could not fall or escape; he was caught and pinned down, staked to the mattress by his exhausted, invalid body, scarcely less by his wildering mind. His heart raced, his breathing was shallow; he should have emptied his bladder. Yet, he wanted to be who he was. He was happy to be himself, this man Howard Morgan—now—here—lying next to his wife. He wanted there to be no end to it; even his remorse he would bear willingly forever more, if he could just be allowed to go on living in the knowledge of this moment. In the dark he raised his hand and placed it on Deborah's head, and let his fingers rest lightly on her hair.

DECEMBER 2011

In the morning she was up early and already hobbling around in the kitchen when he came in. The scattered peas, now thawed, had been swept into a soggy green heap, but she hadn't been able to get them off the floor. Her throat hurt when she swallowed, she was saying, opening her gaze to the room and speaking in a thickened, muted voice as if he might, or might not be, present. And all her joints hurt, and her shoulder. Howard studied her as she limped from table to sink with last night's plates in her hands. She looked lost and tremulous, feverish.

"Ankle?" he asked.

She lifted her straggling hair with her good arm.

"Not so bad. A sprain." She sighed and turned to the sink.

"Sit down," he said.

The table was still littered with his medicines. She sat down and began collecting them together; she popped the ones he was due to take out of their foil packets and set them in a line. Howard stood in the middle of the kitchen and thought. Tea, breakfast. He filled the kettle, switched it on, and paused. They'd made him practice all this stuff at Jocelyn Lodge. What else? He went slowly to and fro, fetching what was needed. When tea was made and their two cups were sitting on the table, he saw that she was too ill to notice what he'd achieved. She was too ill to be out of bed.

She drank less than half of her tea, then let him lead her back to his bedroom. There was a pile of clean laundry on the chest of drawers, from which he drew a pair of his pajamas. When she saw them in his hands she said nothing, simply sat down on the edge of the bed and raised her arms like a child. He pulled off her sweater, taking care not to catch her hair, then helped her out of the other clothes. It was years since he had seen her even partly naked, and the heavy, soft, downward-sloping roundness of her amazed him; a visceral, involuntary memory of being inside her brought a spring of life to his groin. She got the pajamas on by herself, with her eyes closed. When her head was on the pillow, Howard drew the covers up and left the room quietly.

Five days went by when he watched over her, doing what he could, bringing glasses of water to the bedside when her temperature soared, changing the pillowcases (he couldn't manage the sheets), finding her more clean pajamas. He worked out which analgesics she had taken and kept her supplied; he inspected the ankle as it turned a vivid plum and laid cold cloths on it until the swelling began to go down. He tried stirring honey into hot water (he couldn't find a lemon) for her to sip when her sore throat developed into a cough. He managed more than once to make porridge, of which they both ate a surprising amount. Most days she got herself in and out of the shower but she had no strength left to help him, so he set about doing it for himself. The first few times he flooded the floor and the effort of it left him helpless with fatigue for half the day, and he never mastered the washing of his feet, but he was pleased to be getting by, more or less. There were things he couldn't manage: he stopped trying to answer the ringing telephone because he never could get to it in time. He had to feed the Rayburn with handfuls of coal all day long because he could not lift the hod to stoke it right up, but at least it didn't go out. Once a day he mustered what scraps he thought could be spared and made his laborious way on the walking frame, with the bucket swinging from the handle, down to the end of the vegetable garden to feed the hens. He did not dare venture alone on to the moor.

Deborah slept for much of the time. He would leave the bedroom door slightly ajar so that from where he sat in front of the television (kept at low volume so as not to wake her) he could see her rounded bulk and the spread of her hair on the pillow. He could not explain to himself the pleasure he took in seeing her at rest.

Snow fell on the high ground above Stoneyridge. Around the house the ground froze hard and frost landed on frost, making his journeys across the yard even more perilous. He worried constantly that the next task, or the one after that, would be the one to go horribly wrong and leave him flat on his face with bones broken, or stranded or scalded or poisoned in some other undignified, self-made trap from which there would be no escape. His fear was not for himself. For what would happen to her if he had an accident, now that she was relying on him for everything?

One day Digger appeared with a brace of pheasants, which he held out to Howard from the back door. "Enjoy them last ones, did you?" he said. "Thought you could use two more. Left to rot, otherwise. Missus about, is she? I want a word about that flock of hers."

Howard remembered nothing about being given any other pheasants, and was not sure he could take the weight of these in his arms. Nor did he have a clue where to put them. He shook his head, took a breath, and got his mouth working.

"She's . . . resting," he said. "Bed. Not well."

"Oh, right you are. Here you go, then." Digger pushed past him over the threshold and dumped the pheasants on the draining board. Howard tried to follow with his eyes and focus on the birds, exotic and richly colored as they were, but as far as he could see they covered the draining board like two raggedy lumps of Turkish carpet.

"Poorly, is she?" Digger went on. "Well, you better tell her from me—"

Deborah's voice came from the door to the sitting room. "You can tell me yourself," she said. "I'm fine."

She stood in the doorway, wrapped squaw-fashion in a checked blanket, leaning on the doorpost. Only her head and bare feet were visible. Her eyes looked bright and naked and bewildered, as if the force of the influenza had given her a terrible shock.

Digger said, "I been out to your flock this morning. Seen to mine, then I went over and took a look at yours. They need feeding this weather. Can't get enough grass through the snow, see? You ought to know that. I left a couple of hay bales up there, in the old ring feeder."

"Thank you," Deborah said. "I'll get up there and take a look later."

"Ring feeder's broken," Digger said. "Lose half the hay, you will, if you don't get that fixed."

"*Fixed,*" Howard said, a little explosively, anxious to be part of the conversation. "Thank you. Pay you. For the hay," he said.

Digger grunted. "Few quid's neither here nor there," he said. "Point is, that flock's not fit. Way too thin. Couple of 'em's lame, could be foot rot. Ain't right."

"I'll see to them," Deborah said. Her voice was rising. "They're thinner because they're old, they can't graze like young sheep. They've got teeth missing."

Digger shook his head. "They ain't getting looked after. You want me to, I'll go up there for you, get 'em in the holding pen and see 'em on their way. One shot and none the wiser. Do it as a favor. I don't like to see 'em suffer."

Howard clenched and released his fists, fighting to find words.

"It's all right, Howard," Deborah said, in the old, tired, pacifying voice she hadn't used for days.

"I'll even bury 'em for you," Digger said. "'Cause you won't be wanting the meat. Beasts that age, the meat's rank."

"Of course we don't want you to kill them. Was there anything else?"

"Up to you. Just have to say the word, I'll see to 'em. Kindest thing to do." Digger moved to the door. " 'Cause you wouldn't want to go getting reported for cruelty, now, would you?"

Howard let out a bellow. As he stepped outside, Digger nodded at the hens' bucket on the floor. "They getting any grain on top of that? You got to give hens grain, come winter." He laughed. "I'll slit their throats an' all for you, if you like. No charge."

Deborah had turned away. Howard closed the door behind Digger and followed her out of the kitchen, and sat on the edge of the bed while she got in and settled back. She closed her eyes.

"At least now they've got some hay to be going on with," she said, "and maybe there'll be a thaw. Anyway, I'm much better. When I've had a little sleep I'll get up and go and see they're all right."

"All right," Howard echoed, referring to the sheep, not her plan to get up. She wasn't nearly well enough to do that. She mustn't go out on the moor alone again, ever. He would have to stop her, or go with her, if necessary.

But it wasn't necessary. Her fever grew worse again and it was another four days before it broke. She refused to call the doctor. On the second day Howard sneaked out to the hall to do it himself, but couldn't read the numbers well enough to dial. He tried to keep her face cool with flannels, and he made her sip water and sugar. He fed her rice pudding from a tin when she could be persuaded to eat, and he sat with her while she slept. When the fever was at its worst he crooned sounds of comfort and held on to her hand. Once he was woken in the night by an urgent, whispered stream of babble coming from her lips and he leaned in close to catch the words, in case she was telling him something important; she sounded angry. But she quieted before he could understand what she was saying, and besides, he realized, she hadn't been talking to him. At least, he thought, she couldn't be worrying about the sheep, for she didn't mention them again.

To: deborahstoneyridge@yahoo.com
Sent on fri 9 dec 2011 at 11.05 EST

Hi mum Managed to speak to Dad the other day, not sure how much he took in but he managed to say you've got flu. Will keep ringing – thought I'd leave you an email as well just in case you're up and about and in the village next week.

I rang the clinic and they said to tell you to ring them if you get worse or if fever persists. They said they'll try to find somebody to drop in but house visits very difficult because of state of roads, some of the staff can't even get in.

They also said Dad's had a flu jab so he won't get it, that's good to know.

Poor you – I hope you're feeling better.

My flights again:

Thurs 22 Dec   Arr Heathrow   08.35

Tues 3 Jan   Dep Heathrow   19.20

Still up to eyes here but light at end of tunnel. Take care!

I'll keep ringing – you must have the phone on some default where it disconnects after about ten rings – can you take the default off because D usually doesn't make it in time! (you need to go into settings, then it'll be under answer time or something like that – I'll check it out when I'm there). Then when I ring straight back there's usually no answer because I suppose he's wandered off again, very frustrating for both of us!

Please look after yourselves

lots of love A xxxx

I am more ill than I have been for years, since long before Howard's stroke. I'm robbed of any choice in what to do about it because I can't do anything except lie and wonder how bad I might get, in a way that reminds me of being young and small and powerless against most things that happen. For a number of days I move only from bed to bathroom and back again. It's banal, yet absorbing: I'm entirely in the grip of it, the fever and aching joints and headache and cough and breathlessness. On top of that, I take a curatorial interest in the progress of the bruising on my ankle. When I'm awake I lie and think of nothing, or only of myself. Then I feel guilty for being so selfish, and I rouse my thoughts and fret that nobody is looking after Howard. I worry that he's missing Stroke Club and I'm sure the emails from Adam will be piling up at the library. Adam is another worry. I must try to have a few words with him but it's too cold to stand in the hall for long. I must try to get Howard to say I'll ring him when I'm a little better. I think of Theo, of course, but he's away. Just when I need him the most, he's nowhere to be seen.

It's Howard who is a constant presence. If I open my eyes there he will be, and when I close them I sense him still, watching me and never going far. Now he lets me out of bed for a while each day. He places me tenderly in what has until now been his special chair and arranges a stool with a cushion on it for my ankle. I've been watching television again. Some of the programs are quite marvelous.

Sometimes Howard will take the other chair and sit with me, at other times he's up seeing to this or that, but he's always around. It was some time before I understood that he doesn't hover because *he* needs *me*—to give him food or tablets or explain something or staunch one of his weeping fits. No, it is for my sake that he stands in waiting. He is looking after me. I lie and ponder the words *looking after me,* and decide—though this may be just my fey and fevered mind—there is hidden poetry in them. It's strange that the phrase—*looking after me*—should evoke Howard's now dim and unreliable eyes, those same, once piercing eyes in whose sight a part of myself has been invisible since the day Adam was born. It may hint also at the idea that I am detaching from Howard and drifting away, leaving him to watch the distance between us grow until he loses sight of me altogether. But where and to what would I go?

I think these things looking out from the kitchen window as flurries of snow borne on the wind from the moor top swirl around the yard and collect as an icy silt in the corners. I'm watching for Howard—in fact, I'm *looking after* him. I was dozing in his big chair and heard the back door close almost half an hour ago, and the walking frame and the bucket aren't here so he must have gone to feed the hens. I wait. From upstairs I hear a dull scrape and click as the latch of the landing window frets its metal pin on the sill; it's been loose for years. I know the sounds of all the outstanding jobs in the house; the cold tap drips with a somber *tonk* into the deep iron bath, the door from the kitchen to the hall squeals. When a winter wind like this one blows, the whole house twitches. Little gasps of sound escape as if they've been hiding upstairs; they stray out from faraway rooms through doors, along corridors. To my ears there's a note of reproach in it; this place is too big and drafty, these sighs and echoes say, too many rooms meander one into another, and stairs and landings and half-landings lead off at confusing angles to more bedrooms than anyone needs. Someone must be up here, for the simple reason that so much emptiness couldn't be borne.

If Howard's not back within the next five minutes I shall put on warm clothes, take an umbrella or something I can use as a walking stick, and go and look for him.

I voice this intention aloud, and to my surprise it's Theo who answers. Where has he sprung from all of a sudden?

"Yes, go. But are you really ready for what you might find? Maybe he's fallen and hurt himself." His words swarm around my head and I try to bat them away, and nearly lose my balance. I move away from the window. "Maybe he's had another stroke. What then?"

I have to shut him up. Shouting at him won't work, but if I can get myself back to the chair and switch the television on, I might be able to ignore him. I'll concentrate on some loud, pointless noise until he goes back upstairs. And if I do that, by and by Howard will return and everything will be all right. But there is no let-up.

"Suppose Howard died out there. Just laid himself down and died, the way animals do. It would be very sad, of course. But wouldn't it be a kind of relief, in the end? For him, too. You could leave this place. Come on, Deborah. You know you've thought about it."

I try to picture again the shy, sad, sweet young fellow who came here at the end of last summer with that horrible patronizing man who left without paying. From the front bedroom window, very early in the morning, I watched the silver car drive away down the track. Adam should have been here, and he wasn't. I didn't want to be left alone again. I could not allow it. I didn't choose that Theo would stay, but now I can't choose that he should go.

I make it back to the chair, but he follows. I needed a companion around the place, that was all. "My name's Theo." What have I allowed him to become? "What have you turned me into?"

I must have noise, other people's voices, I must drown him out. The remote control for the television is not where it should be. I get up again and hobble around; I lift cushions, push my hand into a heap of newspapers on the low table, scan the floor. I look everywhere but can't find it. I collapse back in the chair, gritting my teeth against Theo's voice. "All this is your own doing." I sink both hands into the slit between the seat and the side cushions and rummage deep. "Are you afraid of what's inside your own head? I didn't put the thought there. Don't blame me."

There's no remote control lost down between the cushions. Instead I pull out a rolled-up wad of cloth. It unfurls. It's stained with faint, brownish marks, like an old bandage. But it's a T-shirt with "Love Life" printed on it—Howard's. Out of its folds fall other things: a scrunched-up cloth hat and a hospital identity band. I pick them up and study them, scarcely able to believe that they can be what they seem: the relics of a disaster that, no matter that so much time has passed, opens up like a wound newly cut. Fresh sorrow lunges at me; it stops my throat. I haven't the breath to weep. Several minutes pass, while the hat and bracelet, turned over and over in my hands, grow as familiar as the room around me, and my hands grow strange. They're old now, more grandmotherly than motherly. I have lived longer on this side of the tragedy—since that single day of de-marcation that sliced my life in two—as I lived on the other, impos-sibly carefree side I inhabited before that day. How have I survived so long, with the grief of it lodged in my bones?

That can't be answered. Prosaically, I prefer to wonder what the things are doing here, shoved down the side of Howard's chair. Only he could have put them there, of course, but why? When? We only got the chair after he'd come home after the stroke. Why has he kept them at all? No answer comes. A bandage is what his stained T-shirt became that day, and a winding sheet. The cap and name bracelet are coffin clothes. But my mind is quiet, full of a stillness that's deep and absolute, like sudden nightfall.

Theo has gone.

To: deborahstoneyridge@yahoo.com
Sent on wed 14 dec 2011 at 23.43 EST

Dear Mum, It was a relief to hear your voice on Saturday but you didn't sound well at all, so am writing this not really expecting you'll be at the library today.

I spoke to the clinic again and they said Nurse Jenny made it up the track last Friday and looked in, thought you were both coping pretty well – she said you were asleep so didn't wake you, and Dad seemed OK.

Third time lucky, here are the flights:

Thurs 22 Dec   Arr Heathrow   08.35

Tues 3 Jan   Dep Heathrow   19.20

And as I said I'll rent a car at the airport. Less than a week to go! lots of love A xxxx

ADAM'S BIRTHDAY 1983

Howard is angry again. The day is steely bright and a warm rushing wind is stirring the trees on the ridge and banging doors shut in
the yard. It puts him on edge. It'll be pulling over our bean canes and
clanking our field gates, which are only held with twine. He's always
mending our gates. And now he is angry with a couple who ventured
up the track to look at the pottery, because they want to see how his
teapots pour before they buy one. He's got five on the shelves at the
moment (because he likes doing spouts). I hear all this from the
kitchen where I'm working—or rather, trying to work in between
long pauses to press both hands into my aching back—with the door
propped open by a wheelbarrow full of rocks that we lifted from a
patch of ground we're trying to clear for winter cabbages. It's hard
work making bread in this weather; the wind drives down the Rayburn flue and fills the kitchen with a sharp, sooty heat that smells of
coal. Once or twice I've almost heaved and not been quite able to get
my breath.

So Howard carries all the teapots out to the yard tap and fills
them up, and the woman takes them one at a time and has a go at
pouring the water out, then hands each one to her husband to try. I
can see Howard thinking the man's a fool, tipping out water and
splashing his sandaled feet; he doesn't like men who laugh along
with their wives. She cannot abide a dribblesome teapot, she says,
and the husband giggles as if she's said something witty. She's right!

he says, and is it too much to ask that somebody should've come up with a no-dribble-guaranteed teapot by now? She turns serious: really and truly, it is so annoying because *the main thing* you want from a teapot is that it doesn't dribble. She's disappointed with just about every teapot she's got, and she has ever so many.

But not one of Howard's. They don't buy. Howard draws their attention to some small wood carvings he's done—hobgoblin figures and grinning faces—says they're old pagan household deities, for hanging up at the door. Or they make good Christmas tree decorations. The couple make phoney interested noises but are edging away. I wipe my hands and go outside to let them know we also do afternoon teas, but they're already walking back to their car. I go to help Howard carry all the teapots back, and I drop one of the lids and it smashes. I try to pick up the pieces but bending over requires a monumental effort now my belly's so big. Howard kicks the pieces out of the way and says something unkind and I burst into tears. He believes tears are manipulative, so now it's me he's angry with.

Just the sight of me sets him on edge, if truth be told, swelling up by the day as I am doing. He "accepts" my pregnancy, but he doesn't like it. It isn't the right time. The fact is it's more than a little inconvenient. Or rather it would be, if it were going to change anything very much, which he is determined it shouldn't because pregnancy's natural and women are designed to take it, and childbirth, in their stride. In fact it would be patronizing of him to treat me as if I were ill or incapacitated in some way; a pregnant woman living, as I am, with an awareness of her fundamental connection to the earth will naturally tap into her own primal, maternal wisdom and discover her own strength. It doesn't exempt me from doing my bit; I'm still a functioning human being! And after the birth he'll still regard me as his equal and we'll still halve the tasks, he assures me. Still, I wonder how am I going to do all the food and bedrooms for the spiritual retreat guests, and the afternoon teas, and keep up my weaving and see to the hens, as well as do my share with the vegetables and animals, *and* be a mother. I'm due to give birth at the very end of September and another winter is coming. I worry. He worries. The subject is difficult and neither of us raises it unless necessary; in fact there is more he should know that I haven't dared tell him yet.

Nor do we talk much of the fact that Stoneyridge isn't paying and the money's all but run out. Last winter was colder than our first and the spring was dry and late, so the garden this year is slow to produce, never mind that we have slugs and tomato blight and greenfly. We're behind with clearing the land and working on the sheds—it's so slow when there's just the two of us—and there hasn't been time to find partners for the bartering scheme Howard wants to set up. Apart from Digger and the shopkeepers in the village we've only really gotten to know Callum and Fee, who are doing much the same as us—hens, sheep, vegetables, bees—so there isn't much to swap. They had a pig but it tasted awful. They don't need any more pottery and Fee does some weaving herself. And her parents gave them their land and Callum also makes clogs and they sell lots of them at music festivals, so it's not really the same at all.

We're going to convert our old pig shed for yoga, but until we can afford it the people coming on Howard's spiritual retreats have to do theirs in the hall on the old red carpet, which smells when you're down close to it. He thinks that must be why bookings are so down this year. Another reason may be that last year it was mainly Howard's old London friends, who came for free, as guinea pigs, and we've lost touch with a lot of them since. Only two came at Easter, again for free, in exchange for doing a bit of painting in the house, which they didn't finish.

It feels too late now to ask why, with his devotion to doing everything naturally and tapping into the earth's natural life rhythms, Howard doesn't disapprove of the Pill. But he doesn't; in fact he made sure I went on it right from our first weeks together in London. When we came to Stoneyridge there was no reason to change that or even talk about it; there was so much to do it was obvious a baby couldn't be thought of, and it wasn't. Nor even the possibility of one; I paid no more heed to the notion of my fertility than I did, being young and healthy, to the workings of my gut or the beating of my heart. So I didn't think it would matter that I couldn't get to the village in late November because the roads were icebound and I'd be a few days late getting my prescription renewed. Then snow came and the few days turned out to be ten, but still I didn't worry about it much. It's absurd, but I don't think I made a proper connection between the taking of a tiny daily pill and Howard's thrusting between my legs which concluded, always, with a kind of throaty mumbling that told me he was nearly finished and made me feel, oddly, not wholly present; they didn't seem to be about the same thing at all. That was why I didn't think of trying to stop him reaching for me under the covers on a snowy night in December when we were barely warm enough in bed, which makes the pregnancy my fault, not his. That doesn't mean he won't shoulder the responsibility, but it doesn't mean he's going to pretend to like it, either.

I do get tired these days. On top of everything else, his anger tires me. Not that he shouts or goes storming around the place. No, he carries his anger about with him very quietly, like a grenade in a secret pocket, and just occasionally he'll bring it out and threaten to pull the pin; his rage flares up over nothing and he'll say one savage thing and go quiet again. For the rest of the day I'll walk around in shock and he'll give off a certain satisfaction as if, now I've been reminded he's still got the grenade and could explode it at any time, all is as it should be. So when he comes into the kitchen an hour after the incident with the teapot lid and suggests we go up on the moor together to check the sheep, of course I say yes, even though my belly feels so tight it's making me a little breathless and I could still burst into tears at any moment. Nevertheless, I remind myself, I am not ill. Howard even has his pipe and his knife and latest bit of carving with him—a good sign, suggesting we are going to spend some time sitting in the sun together—so once the bread is out of the oven I make a flask of tea, pack a rug to sit on, and we set off.

I can't go as fast as Howard. Your legs are so much longer, I tell him, off you go, and I'll catch you up. He frowns and says he'll head on and see to the sheep and I can meet him just over the ridge at the place where there's that slanting white rock, the one that's like an altar. I know the spot; I've always thought the rock more like an ironing board at a funny angle, but I don't say so. There are other big boulders in a loose group around it and the gorse grows thickly there, making a natural windbreak. It's almost always windy up there.

Soon Howard is a long way ahead. As he walks on up the moor his swaying figure in the distance loses color, blends against the green and steel-dark furze until it's part of the land- and cloudscape shifting under the wind, the sun and shadow on the move. I struggle on after him and because he's too far away to hear me I allow myself to give in to the need to cry, which has followed me up the hill. I'm absurdly sensitive today, I realize. It's the sight of him striding away, the regular swing of his body made blurry by the heat haze and now by tears, that makes me feel so alone and stupid. I stop and press my hands into my back. It might break with tiredness. And now that tightening, grabbing feeling comes again, more intense than before. I'm already huge; I think Howard's appalled at the size of me. If he knew anything about pregnancy he'd be even more appalled, because the reason I'm so big is I am carrying twins. Howard hasn't come with me to any of the prenatal checks (another thing he's angry about is that I'm putting my trust in conventional medicine rather than nature, even though I tell him about my breathing exercises and how natural they are) so he doesn't know, and I haven't dared tell him yet. I know his opinions on hospitals and I've been strongly advised against—in fact the midwife won't hear of it—the home birth he's been insisting on, so that will be another battle. I've only told Fee, and Auntie Joan in Edinburgh. They both say he has to be told. And he will be, but I have to wait for the right moment.

By the time I get to the slanting white stone I have a stitch in my side that's really sore, and I'm worn out. No sign of Howard down on the other side but I can hear the faint bleating of the sheep. He'll be wandering after them with his crook, to count and check; since we got the flock of twenty Jacobs, he's ever the watchful shepherd. The sun's gone behind clouds and it's cool in the breeze. I'm glad I brought the tea. I decide not to wait for Howard, and pour myself a cup from the flask, and drink. To my surprise I vomit it up almost immediately, and even when my stomach is empty I feel wretchedly nauseous. The gorse emits an astringent, purgative stink I've never noticed before. I lie back on the slanting rock, which holds some of the sun's warmth, and try to take deep breaths, but the nausea remains. I break out in a sweat and the stitch in my side seizes me again, and spreads around my body. It grips me hard: not painfully but very tightly, like a malevolent hug. Then it lets me go, and as I'm getting my breath back I wonder for the first time if what I'm feeling isn't a stitch at all, but a contraction. But it's far too early. I stand up and walk around. It's much too early; they told me there would probably be these false alarms. I'm incapable of deciding what to do, so I just wait. The likelihood is it will all just go away. But after some minutes it comes again, another squeezing crush. Now I can make out Howard tramping up toward me through the long grass, his shepherd's crook in his hand, beard and hair flying out in the wind. I have never been so frightened or so delighted to see him. As soon as I judge him within earshot, I let out a great shout that turns into a scream. He looks up, and starts to run.

The strange thing is that by the time he reaches me, I am calm. I tell him I think my labor is starting and we should hurry down to the house. But he looks at me and shakes his head, then makes great circles with both arms. Look, he says, look, Deborah, behold! The moor, the sky, the wind!

I don't understand.

He takes hold of both my hands. Listen, when I asked you to come up here with me today, he says, it was a sudden impulse. I don't know why I did. I didn't really want your company. Now I see I was—he pauses—I must have been responding to something. We're here for a reason. It's your time. Something's brought you here, for you to give birth here. You're going to give birth in the most natural place, in the most natural way you could. Look, you're on safe high ground. You're under the sky. I shall not leave your side. It could not be more beautiful. *You* could not be more beautiful. Don't you see?

I can't do it up here! I tell him. Of course I can't! My teeth are chattering now, and my legs are trembling. I'm cold. I have to get back down—you don't understand. Just then, another contraction seizes me, tighter than before, and for the first time it's really painful. I groan through it, and just as it's easing I feel a gush of warm fluid coursing down my legs. I cry to him, Howard, help me! I've got to get back to the house, you've got to call an ambulance! You don't understand—Howard, listen. I should have told you. I thought there'd be more time but listen, I have to tell you now. There's two babies. I'm having twins—I was going to tell you. I've got to get back to the house, you've got to help me.

Howard gasps, then lets out a great shout and a laugh. Twins? Twins, are you sure? He's grabbing me now and hugging me. Are you sure? Oh, my God, twins! He's practically dancing. I don't understand. He didn't want one baby, why is he delighted there are two?

But Howard, listen, I say. I can't stay up here. I've got to get to hospital.

Twins, I can't believe it! Hospital? Don't be silly! What d'you need a hospital for? Women have been having babies forever—long before there were *hospitals*! Your body knows what to do, you just need to trust it! Besides, you couldn't get down the hill now anyway—you're much safer up here.

Howard, listen—of course I have to be in hospital! It's twins!

But there's a look on his face that I know of old; it's full of ecstatic faith. He's filled with the spirit, charged with prophecy, unreachable. Another wave of nausea sweeps over me and I double over and vomit up a thin, burning string of bile. Behind me, Howard says cheerfully, Don't fight it! Don't be afraid—let it happen. I tell you, your body knows what to do! I'll look after you.

I can't stop shivering. Howard sits me down on the rug against a boulder and dashes off to the line of trees on the ridge, assuring me he'll be back in moments. He reappears with an armful of fallen wood. Excitedly, he scrapes out from the sheep-cropped heath a rough circle, exposing the peaty earth below. He places the dug-out divots around it and surrounds those with a ring of small stones. Then he goes off again and comes back with pocketfuls of torn-up, ripe moor grass, yellow and dry. All this takes some time, during which two more contractions come. I submit to them, and try to remember my breathing. I'm calm again. I must talk to him quietly, and explain that he's got to help me down off the moor before it's too late. His hands shake as he stuffs the straw into a crisscross of sticks in the fire pit and, after several attempts, gets it to light. Flame hisses upward and a plume of smoke blows at me horizontally. He lets out a whoop and feeds more wood on to the fire. I call out to him to be careful—surely you shouldn't light a fire up here? Howard shakes his head and says it's fine, and comes to crouch beside me.

I begin to cry. I want—what do I want? I want women, even though the ones I know wouldn't be much use. I want my mother, incapable of mentioning bodily functions and crippled with arthritis in her rainy town in the north, I want childless Auntie Joan who wears white gloves to meet her friends for lunch and plays bridge three times a week. I even want Fee, who believes in the power of crystals to ease labor pains. I try to get to my feet but Howard pushes me gently back. You couldn't get down the hill now, he says. You're much better staying here. It's going to be fine.

Time passes. Howard is wonderfully kind and encouraging, and I get myself into the rhythm of breathing between the contractions, which become ever more intense. From time to time the wind eases and I hear birdsong and the bleating of sheep, and I watch the clouds pass. Part of me remains incredulous that this is happening at all, never mind like this. Part of me continues to plead with Howard to get me home before the babies come. But he ignores this, and keeps the fire fed. He peels some strips of bark off a birch tree, which he also burns. They make a dry, aromatic smoke that he says is traditionally used for purification during labor. It becomes almost exciting; perhaps for a short burst of time, I even feel glad it's happening this way.

But then the pain gets vicious. I roar through the contractions, each one of which feels like another turn of a rack. I've become a tunnel, stopped with an immovable, swelling obstacle; there will be no outcome that does not involve breaking. Howard is white and drawn, and glances anxiously away to the distance, as if gauging how far I might make it if we set off down the hill now. I arch and push, and with every push I tear. With the fourth push, the last I will be able to stand, I scream, and the thing bursts from me. Howard, sobbing, tugs it out. The baby is small, but he wriggles and cries.

Howard places him on my chest and wraps the rug around us; he leans over and embraces us both, stroking the baby's head again and again. I cannot speak. The contractions stop. Howard takes his knife and I give him instructions on how to cut the baby's cord—I've seen it all on a video at antenatal class—and he ties it off with some twine from his pocket. When the contractions start again it takes only two pushes before the second baby slithers easily into Howard's hands. It's a boy, another boy! Howard cries. This baby is so very small, and he's quiet. When he is first laid on my chest I think he raises a hand and flexes it once. Howard takes him from me to cut the cord, and when he is returned to my arms I brush my lips over the top of his head. His scalp is much cooler than his brother's. I wrap him up closer, but his skin is changing color and his eyes are stuck shut. I manage to get myself almost to a sitting position and I call out for Howard, who is cleaning his knife on the grass.

There's something wrong! He's not right. Feel him, he's cold! Take him, take him! Take him down and get an ambulance! You've got to get him to hospital! Oh, God, he's not moving! Hurry up, Howard, hurry!

I'm hysterical. Howard doesn't hesitate. He strips off his T-shirt and wraps the baby up. After running everything his way, suddenly he's helpless and asking me what to do. What? What am I . . . what about . . . what will . . . what should I . . . ?

My mind's working much faster than his. This time I scream. Hurry, Howard! Take him and *get an ambulance.* Go! Go! I'll be all right, leave me here. Come back for me later. Just take him, hurry! Go!

I hold the first baby close in my arms against my bare skin while Howard stumbles away down the hill, carrying the sick one. I watch him go. Shaking with sobs, I pull at my clothes and offer my breast to the baby, who's squirming and yelling and warm. After some trouble he latches on to the nipple and sucks.

I have no idea how much time passes. The baby sucks and sleeps, and I go on lying there with my mind flowing with a mixture of rapture and dread, a mess of dark and light—after what's happened today, perhaps there never will again be single, explicable feelings for anything. The sun slips low and I manage to get to my feet and put more wood on the fire. I'm shaking with cold and also with fear; by and by I'll venture down the hill on my own, but I have to gather my strength first. I've recovered, I think, from the shock of the afterbirth sliding out of me but I think I'm still bleeding, and I'm split and sore and parched with thirst, and I'm afraid of starting out and not being able to make it all the way, and if I get stuck on the moor somewhere, there will be no fire and I will not be able to keep the baby warm enough. And it would get dark and Howard wouldn't be able to find us. I shiver, and face the fact. It has all come down to fire and warmth, and I do not have the courage to move.

I settle to wait for Howard, and my mind drifts; an insistent dream of the other baby's face, his curled hand and the feel of his damp, downy head, pushes against the sensation of this one filling my arms. Thoughts of the absent baby tear at my mind while the one present absorbs it; it's like being split in two by terror and delight, but it's one single, compulsive fascination that already they exert: strange yet familiar, indivisible, unarguable. I know myself enslaved, to both of them, without condition. Today I am learning, all in a rush, that becoming a mother exposes me to fear and love of a magnitude I did not know existed.

Dusk is coming. The firelight glows bright against the receding land and illuminates the edge of the rug around the baby's head and the contours of his closed eyes. I hear the dog before I see anything. I try to call out, but my voice is too feeble. I haven't the strength to get up and look farther across the hill. My eyes are sore and bleary from crying and from wood smoke, and the hillside has darkened, but soon from where I lie I can make out a walking figure. The dog runs at his heels, barking; the man is shouting and angry. It's Digger. I call back softly; I do not want to raise my voice, even if I could, because it would wake the baby.

He's still shouting as he reaches me. Get that fire out! Get it out *now*—are you out of your bloody mind? You'll have the whole of bloody Exmoor alight!

He strides into the circle of light and starts kicking earth into the fire. He's concentrating so hard that he doesn't look at me until it's almost stamped out.

Digger, I try to say, Howard built the fire. It was quite safe. It was to keep us warm. But my voice is shaking. Digger, the baby . . . look, my baby. My baby's born. He came early. Look!

Digger peers at me through the gloom but can't make sense of the bundle in my arms. Then the baby stirs and utters a small cry.

What the—? Digger comes forward and drops to his knees. I draw the rug away from the baby's face and show him; I'm smiling so hard I can't speak. Digger gasps, and to my astonishment, tears fill his eyes and start to roll down his face. My God, the babby! His voice drops to a whisper. My God, so he's come, you've got your babby now, oh, would you look at him? My God, look at him, isn't he fine, that's fine work you've done there. Up here all on your own? My God.

He laughs and wipes his eyes fiercely, but he doesn't stop smiling, either. For the first time I believe everything will be all right.

Howard was with me. He went down to get an ambulance, I tell him. Please, I've got to get down to the house.

Digger's working out what to do. I've given myself up to whatever he decides that is to be; I'm ready to be told. Aye, aye right enough, aye now, let's see. Can't have you lying there. Getting dark now.

There are few words said after that. He holds out his arms for the baby with such perfect, natural tenderness that I barely hesitate to hand him over. Digger places him inside his jacket and then helps me to my feet, averting his eyes from my body. It's almost too dark to see the bloodstains on my clothes, anyway. He hands me back my baby, still wrapped up, then rearranges the rug to give both of us some cover. Then he removes his jacket and places that around my shoulders, too. My face is burning hot but I'm beginning to shiver, and I cannot stand upright; a weighty, empty ache in my belly makes me stoop and bend.

Rightoh, m'lady, he says, drawing his arm over my shoulder. Steady now. Let's be getting the both of you safe down. Take it gentle.

I'm aware—and it's both funny and comforting—that this will be exactly the voice and language he uses to a newly delivered cow.

And he takes me, with infinite care and gentleness, across the darkening moor, holding me up when I stumble, never once letting go, keeping his arm around me even when I have to stop to rest. If he could carry us both, he would. My legs will hardly hold me up, but I don't complain about the pain or exhaustion; I don't need to. He understands it all. I'm a clumsy, bewildered, tender-fleshed, torn animal, and he leads me softly and kindly all the way, as he would a beast from one of his flocks or herds. Sometimes, silently, he takes the baby from me and cradles him himself, and also silently, when I have rested my arms, he hands him back.

We're within half an hour of the house when I see torchlight dancing on the ground a couple of fields below us. Digger shouts and sends his dog ahead, and soon three paramedics, carrying a stretcher, find us in the dark. Their urgency makes me suddenly feel shocked and frightened, and it's only then I collapse. The baby is taken from me; I'm strapped on to the stretcher and we are borne away down the hill to an ambulance before I have time to notice that Digger has melted away.

All the way to the hospital my questions go unanswered. I am told only that Howard and the second baby went ahead and are being looked after there already; they sidetrack me by asking about this baby and have I thought of a name, and I tell them, without really thinking, that he's going to be called Adam. It's only after we arrive and I've been medically stabilized and soothed and he is warm, fed, and asleep in a cot at my bedside that they—different people—come to tell me what Howard already knows, that Adam's twin brother is dead. They are incredibly kind. They think I should hold the dead baby and name him, that this will make it easier to bear. They leave us alone.

Howard begins to plead. It was not meant to be. He was so tiny. It couldn't be helped. He didn't suffer. It's Nature's way.

He's struggling to speak with certainty. All that Pentecostal, transformative faith—it's vanished. His voice trembles as he tells me that at least we have one child, a son, a beautiful son.

So I see now that Howard thinks death comes in different sizes, and the death of this baby—only a very little baby, after all—is to be regarded as one of the smaller ones. The baby's gone, but he was

never really with us, was he? Without quite saying so, Howard re-
veals his determination that grief for a child no sooner born than lost
will not cut as deep as that for a child I might have had time to know.
Especially as I've got another one. I'm overwhelmed by the impossibility of explaining—and by dismay that I should have to explain—
that it's not like that at all.

For a long time I cannot speak a word, and I can see that frightens
him. It frightens me, too; I do not know where this boulder of silence
about my dead son comes from, only that it is unutterably heavy and
at the same time hollow, that it rolled in and crushed flat all the
words inside me and lodged somehow, and is in me now, and is immovable.

Howard starts on again, in the same vein; it's unbearable. Howard, stop, I say. Shut up. Stop talking. He looks at me stricken, await-
ing judgment. Am I going to strip away his version of the truth, and
destroy his suddenly frail charisma? Am I about to say what we both
know: that if he'd helped me get to the hospital this baby would not
be dead? Will I allow our life together to continue, or will I throw
away all my belief in it, and denounce him? As I look at him I wonder if it matters either way. Everything is changed forever, anyway.

In my head I shall name the lost child. Alone in my head I'll open
his closed eyes, I'll study his face and wonder whose smile he has. I'll
talk to him; I'll explain the world as if he were in it and must heed its
dangers, even as my own world is turning inward. Maybe I'll hear
his voice, and learn what he feels, what delights and what frightens
him. That way, I'll keep him by me while his brother, no less adored,
grows, and grows eventually, as he will, away. Howard takes my
hand and draws in a long, careful breath. One look from me pre-
vents him from saying whatever he was about to say.

We will never, ever speak of this again, I tell him.

To: deborahstoneyridge@yahoo.com
Sent on tues 20 dec 2011 at 12.45 EST

Mum – WHAT IS GOING ON?? Is everything all right? I've been trying to get you on the phone all day, I want to speak to you urgently!!

I just got a Christmas card from Pat today – she put a note in with
it and says she saw you a few weeks back – she said she thought
you looked tired but were "so brave." And she also says it's great that
you've **got Theo to help you now** and since Stoneyridge is so isolated it must really help having someone else LIVING THERE. What
is she talking about? Who's Theo?

Mum, is she off her head? Has she got it all wrong because she
sounded very definite. Is there somebody there with you? WHO THE
HELL IS THEO??!!

You haven't said a word about anybody being there helping you
– I rang the clinic and they don't know anything either, so if you're
getting any help it hasn't come through them. Assuming Pat's not off
her head, who is this guy and where did he come from and why
haven't you said anything? When I get there on Thursday evening I
suppose he'll be there, will he?

If he's really a help that's great. I think maybe things have got
harder for you than you let on. Plus I should've been there this summer, I still feel bad about that. But you've never even mentioned him.
Plus, how are you paying him? I could help with the money, I WANT
to help. Anyway we can talk about it all when I'm there. I really, really
wish you'd told me though.

Thurs 22 Dec   Arr Heathrow   08.35

Tues 3 Jan   Dep Heathrow   19.20

If flight's on time I reckon I'll be with you between three and four. But I'll be keeping you posted anyway. You can call me any time, remember, my phone's always on, ditto email, lots of love A xxxx

The reason Howard is out so long is that he found all the hens dead. He comes back with his face stricken and raw with cold, tears running from his eyes. He is so upset I wonder he didn't fall over, hurrying back to tell me that a fox has been in. He explains it clearly enough—"Fox! Hens dead, all over blood, terrible, mess"—but I put on clothes and go out to see for myself. The corpses are already freezing under a dusting of sleet so they've been lying there for some hours, which means the fox was hungry enough to attack in daylight. Indeed, I count only four dead birds so two are missing; he probably ate one fresh killed and carried the other in his jaws back to his lair. We heard nothing; the wind's been in a contrary direction today and must have borne the noise of slaughter away from the house and across the moor. I find the broken wire in the mesh where he got in, and stare at it for a while. There is no way I can fool myself into thinking there's any point in mending it. I limp back up to the house, where I left Howard negotiating the making of a cup of tea: he takes such pride in his mastery of this task I would not dream of not drinking his sometimes lukewarm, overstrong, or watery brews.

When I return, I lock the back door. Tea is waiting on the table, and together Howard and I sit down as if we were once more setting about a task we have undertaken at this table a thousand times: the offering and accepting of consolation for one or another of our disasters, the mustering of resolve to carry on. It's been our currency of exchange for as long as I care to remember. We're good at it.

But there can't be any more of that. When I even think of opening my mouth on the subject of the hens, I can't find enough air to breathe. Their slaughter is sickening, of course, as are the deaths of all their predecessors killed the same way, or by viruses or for reasons we never did fathom, as are the deaths of the goats, sheep, and bees, as are the failures of every one of our enterprises with vegetables, pottery, weaving, and paying guests. But none of those things labored over and lost was ever the important one.

Until today I thought it was only I who knew this. I thought it was only I who walked around feigning optimism with a part of my heart dead in my chest, with the loneliness of that. I get up and go next door to Howard's chair, delve in the cushions, and bring back the T-shirt, hat, and identity bracelet. I place them on the table and sit down again. When he sees them Howard lets out a cry.

"It's all right, Howard. It's all right. You kept them. I understand."

He nods, still frightened. In fact I don't understand, entirely, but what changes everything is the possibility that all this while Howard's silence on the matter of our dead baby has been clamoring in his head as loudly as my own does in mine. It's possible that through the twenty-eight years we have walked side by side, all unbeknownst, in grief. Howard looks at the things on the table and touches them sadly, and for a long time we say nothing.

Adam's brother. He is our only true loss, the one too great to acknowledge. He determined the future, binding us to this place when otherwise, at some point before it was too late, we would have given up and left. For it was his lost life, our bungled waste of it, that made it imperative we stay. Shame of that magnitude being too great to walk away from, we tried to make it monumental; we turned it upon ourselves and persevered in the error of Howard's beliefs and my faith in them, we redoubled our efforts because we needed our crass visions for Stoneyridge, once realized, to disprove the futility of our baby's death. All the while, of course, we brought up Adam ignorant of his brother, but no less in his shadow for that.

Howard reaches over and pats my hand. I imagine the man our dead son would now be looking across at us, and I wonder what he makes of his parents, one deluded and frail, the other always weak-minded and suggestible, and both possibly worse than foolish. There is little enough to admire, God knows, but yet I do not believe he would hate us. Nor is he vengeful; as we age, more and more he will let us be. As we dismantle what remains of our lives here and depart, as we surely must, he may even, watching us go, wish us peace. A calm has already descended, and suddenly I am so tired—tired in my bones—and I know I will sleep soundly.

Over the next few days my strength returns. I see off another visit from Nurse Jenny, but leave the telephone unanswered. When I'm up and about again there's some return to routine, but no question of going down to the library to attend to emails. Howard and I are resigned and reminiscent, and little by little we go all through the house, usually hand in hand. It's not since the very first time we came to look at Stoneyridge that we've stood in rooms together like this, but there's no need to explain to each other why we do it now, reflecting sometimes aloud (but more often in silence, as if we were listening to hear the walls speak for themselves) on how we managed to stay here so long. The rooms somehow draw attention to their emptiness, and there's a reproach in it, as if they're still crying out for something definitive to be enacted within each one that will settle once and for all its proper purpose. We recall how excited we were that first visit, immune to the threat implicit in all the house's "potential." I remind Howard we used the expression *putting our own mark on the place.*

We didn't, though. After Adam was born the configuration of the rooms remained unstable, provisional upon the result of one or other new, always inconclusive experiment in our living habits. Amid talk of color energies and light direction we were always changing our minds about which bedrooms to sleep in, which rooms to use as sitting room or dining room; innumerable times we moved ourselves half-in or half-out of this or that one, unsure where to settle. It was not chaotic, exactly—there wasn't enough energy in our state of flux for that—but at the heart of it was a creeping lack of conviction about how to live. I used to tell myself it was creative, but it was only irresolute.

And it's the same now. It's as if year upon year we moved things all around this house without ever quite moving *in,* and now the contents of rooms seem to do it by themselves; we stumble across objects in odd corners as if catching them out in little secret escape bids to other places. As rubbish goes, it's strangely active. Roaming the house, half-trying to put it back to rights, we find doors forever open through which old echoes stray, as if the place has just been vacated by another who leaves behind shuffling currents of air and a bitter wake of sighs.

From the clutter I unearth the old albums again and we go through the photographs, speaking kindly of the people in them. We took grinning pictures of everybody: the woman who delivered the bee-hives, the men who installed the septic tank, the London crowd who came on the retreats for the couple of years, but we've forgotten their names and spend a silly amount of time trying to bring them to mind.

When we're not doing this or that upstairs, which we call "sorting things out," we rest together. Both of us tire easily. Side by side on Howard's bed, or at the table or in the sitting room, we hold hands in silence. I don't tell Howard this, but I'm reminded of couples waiting in stations for a train that only one of them will board.

One of the biggest tasks I take on, and that requires all my strength, is the removal of the antlers in the hall. Dragging the sideboard away from the wall is hard enough, but once that's done I climb the stepladder with a chisel in my hand and I gouge out the plaster around the wooden mounts that hold the antlers. The plaster is quite rotten and gives easily; great chunks of it cascade off the wall and land on the tattered carpet. So these mounts have in effect been holding the wall up, and some of them are very loose, anyway; God knows how long we have passed to and fro in the hall in danger of being speared by falling antlers. I keep Howard well out of the way (and am careful of my own head) while I yank them off the crumbling wall. This sets off an aerial bombardment of multi-spiked missiles, falling and tumbling, stabbing the floor as they roll. Some of them break, raising a yellowish dust very like the old fallen plaster and revealing a filigree interior of rotted bone. I chuck them all into a pile by the front door. They're useless for burning so will have to be taken out and dumped.

Despite all the sorting-out, I am perfectly aware of what time of year this is. We dig out the boxes of Christmas decorations from under the beds in the spare rooms. This time Howard doesn't try to call it Yule instead of Christmas, and we unwrap all the funny unpainted things he carved for the tree and we smile over them, even though there is no tree and neither of us has anything like enough strength to fell one and bring it in. Even if we had, proper snow is falling now; the pine wood where we might have got one will soon be invisible under it. We watch like children from the windows as the snow comes whirling down. It's beautiful and exciting. I picture the moor and the poor sheep and how they will look with snow accumulating on their backs. I cannot put off the thought of the sheep much longer.

The next day I manage to pluck and draw the pheasants Digger brought and I roast them with what vegetables we have left. The decanters in the dining room hold quantities of ancient brandy and port and sherry, and I tip it all in together and bubble it up into a syrupy liquor that tastes surprisingly good. Howard's not really allowed alcohol but I open a bottle of wine, too. It's a strange feast but we eat until we're sated. Adam's hamper, which arrived some days ago, is untouched. It doesn't seem right to open it now; it will be useful when he gets here.

The evening wears on into night. I persuade Howard to go to bed before me because tomorrow will be a big day. When he's settled I go back out to the hall, following the path of powdery pale footprints we left yesterday as we trod through the fallen plaster and scattered bone dust. The antlers still lie in a heap by the door, casting jagged shadows up the wall. It's too cold to linger but I sit for a while, listening. There will be no word from Theo now, of course, but I want to pause and offer a nod of thanks in his direction. But for him, this decision would not have been made. He was necessary. For a while longer I sit, thinking of all the things I must say when I pick up the telephone.

In the morning Howard wakes with a headache and a growling stomach. When he tests his mouth with the word *hello* it feels full of some sour mulch, rather like damp pheasant feathers, he thinks, remembering the sight of them yesterday, piling up in the sink. Deborah's awake, and they both get up slowly, and then Deborah makes him eat porridge, which makes him feel better. Afterward he sits, feeling full and dreamy, watching the floating currents of stray feathers cross the floor as Deborah moves to and fro, opening and closing doors. All morning she is restless. She puts on boots and coat and goes outside several times, even, he thinks, going as far as the henhouse though there's no point in doing that now; no hens to come clucking round her legs, no eggs to collect. He goes to the sink to wash up their breakfast things, as best he can with the bag of pheasant feathers in the way, and from the window watches her return and stand stock still in the yard, her head tilting upward as if listening for messages from the sky. More snow has fallen overnight and all the buildings are plumped and rounded in whiteness, transformed from dereliction into a kind of tumbledown picturesque; Deborah turns in slow circles as if studying every cleansed and beautified plane and angle. When she comes back inside she stands and strokes her hand across his shoulder and down his arm, which he takes as a little tactile thank-you for washing up. This close to her, he sees there is a bright, settled look in her eyes.

Later, when she brings him his jacket, he thinks she just wants him to go out with her to look at the snow, to make a slow circuit of the yard arm in arm or perhaps venture a little way along the track.

But she dresses him as if they're departing on an expedition—hat, scarf, gloves, extra socks, extra sweater, and snow boots—and she brings his walking frame to the door. When she tucks the T-shirt, muslin hat, and identity band into the pockets of her coat, he knows where they are going.

But he never could have guessed how difficult it is. On her command, he plants the walking frame carefully and deep into the snow in front of him, and brings each foot forward without trying to lift it. This makes progress possible, but once they're off the track and on to the lower reach of the moor, the snow collects in heavy suds on his boots and clings in frozen dags to his trousers, and he can take steps of no more than a few inches. Deborah's earlier restlessness has vanished and she coaxes him along patiently. Again it sweeps over him, an absurd (given the circumstances) yet pressing sensation of delight and completeness. He is who he is. Here, now. With her. It is so difficult. But he has all day.

There is no wind, not even higher up. The sky is opaque and massive with ice, the air bright and muffled and frozen; the only sounds are the faint trickle of a tree branch shifting under its ballast of snow, a brittle, high crow call, and the secretive crump of their boots. His body is warm from the exertion of walking but his cheeks are numb; now and then Deborah stamps her feet and blows into her cupped hands. For a little while a milky sun gleams down on them, and then it fades, trailing ghostly pink streamers of cloud. They walk on. The snow in the shaded distant slopes of the moor is deepening to an icy, absorbent blue. Howard can't distinguish anymore which parts of him are merely numb from the parts of him that are feeling pain. He tries to tell Deborah about this but she, now cheerfully heartless, pushes him on. There will be no end to it: to the cold, his freezing feet, the pain in his lungs, the breathlessness, all this weightless, stony, silent air, the expanse of white land. They really should not still be moving farther from the house this late on a winter day, but he knows better than to try to stop and turn back. They have not yet reached the place.

It's much farther than I remember. Under the contour-softening snow, can I even be sure of finding the slanting stone at all? And it's so cold. Howard is suffering; his face is mottled and his eyes are rimmed red, he grunts with every step and stoops lower over his frame. Nonetheless we press on. It's always the last part of anything that's hardest to do, I tell myself, and the most necessary.

It's after three o'clock when we get there, but it's not difficult in the end to make out the group of boulders amid the gorse; snow lies differently on stone than on thorns, smoothing over the one as if it were misshapen flesh, blunting the others' spikes into innocuous-seeming bumps. I scrape away the snow from the slanting stone and ease Howard down to rest. I feed him a handful of snow to slake his thirst, then leave him to walk over the ridge. He'll need several minutes to get his breath back. Now it's the sound of my own breathing I'm aware of, how shallow and excited it's become, mingling with the creak of snow underfoot which has also surely risen in pitch, though this could be fanciful.

When I get to the ridge I turn and search for Howard, a dark shape against the white, and I wave. I want him to know I'm slipping out of sight over the ridge and he is not to worry, but how can a wave convey all that, and is he even able to see me? Large flakes of new snow are beginning to fall. I keep my hand raised and wait, but there is only stillness around the slanting stone. I walk on over the ridge and stop again. The land makes a dip downward into the combe over to my left. I must be almost on the very spot where I fell and hurt my ankle.

As I'd hoped, there is no movement, no sound from the dip in the land. Very carefully I walk on, slanting away from the combe and continuing down, going lower on this side of the ridge than I have been for years, until I'm standing at the top of the copse of beech trees. It's only half a mile beyond and farther down to Digger's farm. I pause, feeling furtive, although there is not the slightest chance I'll be seen. I walk on a while until I hear, and then I see.

The calls of the ravens and crows are coming not from the wood but from beyond it, on a gentler slope of the moor not far from our old ring feeder. Through the trees and the falling snow I can make out the black smudges of birds moving low above the land, rising and dropping, flapping and quarreling. I draw nearer thinking I'm prepared for what I'll find, but I am not.

"I'll do it tomorrow first light," Digger told me on the telephone yesterday evening. "Put 'em out of their misery, wanted doing long ago."

Our eight sheep, or what's left of them, lie among tufts of their own scattered wool. At least they were dead—one clean shot through the head—when the carrion eaters came for their eyes and tongues and split their bellies open. Digger will leave the bodies until the ground thaws enough for him to bury them, he says, and meanwhile the foxes and badgers will leave him less to do. They'll be along to tidy up—a glut of meat this time of year, they don't get that often.

The new snow is landing like fragments of tissue paper on the torn bodies; I step among them, going from one to the next, pulling a lock of wool from the back of each one and folding them into an inside pocket.

The climb back up and over the ridge takes four times as long as coming down, and the snow is falling faster. When I reach Howard he's dozing under a dusting of snowflakes and I wake him by shaking him and brushing the snow off his shoulders. I explain about the sheep. His mouth opens and closes, he shakes his head. I go on to explain that it's all over. Where we will go now I am not sure, but Digger's entitled to put us out, now we're not keeping stock anymore. Howard raises his fists. He's always believed Digger cruel; I know better, but I also know he feels not a scrap of sentimentality for any living creature and he'll want us out by the end of February to get the place done up for the summer. He'll get us off his hands the way he sends his livestock for slaughter, with not a backward glance.

I tell Howard that we've come here for one last look, and because we have one last thing to do. I pull out from my jacket his old T-shirt and the baby's hat and identity band. We have to bring these back here.

Howard reaches for them and begins to mumble and cry. I wipe his tears away with the T-shirt. If tears dry on your face in this weather your skin will get very sore, I explain. He pushes himself forward with surprising strength and struggles to his feet, then points away back to the ridge in the direction we came from. His legs are shaking.

"Go . . . go back!" he says, shaking his arm. "Now, please, back now. Going back home . . ." He searches my face for a sign I understand what he wants. Of course I do, and it isn't revenge that makes me tell him I'm not taking him back down the hill. We're here for a reason, I say. Come on, get comfortable.

He moans and sinks, lets his legs collapse under him, and arranges himself back in his place against the rock. I snuggle in close to him and take his hand. I feel the rock press into my back. I reach for another handful of snow and share it with Howard; it's oddly toothsome and I find myself comparing it with the excitement of eating ice-cream as a child, and search for some way to describe the taste.

I'm sorry it's not much of a picnic this time, Howard, I say. This strikes me as funny but either Howard doesn't think so or he doesn't hear.

He's gone very quiet, and his face is colder. I wipe the snow from his mouth and rouse him again. Though his cheeks are cold he's not shivering at all; in fact he seems very relaxed. We can't bury the baby's things, I explain to him quietly. The ground's much too hard. So I'm going to find somewhere else they'll be safe. I get up and roam around, never going out of Howard's sight. Everywhere's under snow, but I kick it up in thick clumps under the gorse and find a patch of flat stones that in the spring are probably part of a streambed taking meltwater down the hill. I scrabble with my hands and place the baby's things as deep as I can in the shingle, and cover them over. It'll have to do. I return to Howard and he takes my hand and gives me a questioning smile. "Why?" he asks. "Why . . . them . . . you buried up here?"

Why do I want them buried up here? Such a simple question, but I have to think to find the answer. Because he was here. And they are all there is, I say.

Howard accepts this, or I think he does, because he shuts his eyes and soon his breathing slows. He stirs just to remove his glove, and I do the same, so that when he takes my hand again flesh touches flesh. But I feel him recede from me; I have the idea that my thoughts henceforward will not be shared. Perhaps when he wakes up we'll talk about where we could, in theory, go after Stoneyridge. There must be places for people like us; I imagine a very small flat with handrails everywhere and windows too high to see out of. But I can't worry about it now, and perhaps there's no need to consider alternatives. I'm not cold anymore, and not in the slightest afraid; the stiffness that's spreading all through my body is insulating and kindly. This absence of fear feels like a gift, or a late reprieve. If we are to get hypothermia and die, if someone months from now is to find our torn clothes half-hidden under a rock, spilling their odd collection of bones, if a stranger is to turn up in the stream the shreds of a soaked little hat and an illegible name bracelet wrapped in an old T-shirt, all washed clean, so be it. The years of failure will be only ours, and the means of bringing those years to a conclusion ours also. And Adam will survive.

The thought of Adam makes me cry, suddenly, and Howard squeezes my hand tight. Still, my yearning to see Adam must be fought down, as I've fought down every day of his life my yearning for his brother, whose name, unknown to everyone but me, was Theo. The snow goes on falling and gathers warmly around us. Howard's hand relaxes, and then he doesn't move.

It's a little later when I peer through blurry eyes and try to make out the hill against the sky, but huge snowflakes loom at me and I'm drowsy, and unsure of what my eyes are telling me. I half-remember some old fairy tale about a figure appearing—or was it disappearing—in a blizzard, although I don't need any such story, not now. So it is not from any desire or striving on my part that I begin to sense that someone may be near at hand, and I sit up, suddenly alert, and strain to see in the distance a movement that some instinct tells me will be slow and faint behind the veil of snowflakes. And then, from the comfort of my nest in the snow, I see him. It is the walking figure again, in the last of the light. He is unchanged, colorless. He seems hardly to touch the ground or sky but shimmers, caught in the tug of a gentle tide between the two; he advances and recedes and with each step I long for him to draw me to him, yet he does not; even as he approaches, his remoteness deepens. He is earth and sky, he is the snow's luminescence, and the twilight air. He is Adam come back to Stoneyridge at last and following our footprints across the snow to find us, or he is Theo, my Theo, conjured from my mind's own wanderings. It doesn't matter. Because whether Howard and I are now trapped or freed, out of our long habit of love for each other, inarticulate and disappointed as it may be, is born a love for both our sons that's infinite and equal.

I hold fast to Howard's hand. If I were able now to find the breath, to shout out once would bring Adam running toward us and set in train all the hurry and bustle of rescue and explanations, the return to Stoneyridge. Or the sound might merely pinch the surface of the air, disturbing it for a moment, and then vanish into the winter quiet as if there were no one here at all, not a soul to return an answering cry or even hear the echo of my voice across the moor.

Professor Louise Newman, a child psychiatrist and Director of the Monash University Centre for Developmental Psychiatry & Psychology, Victoria, Australia, says, "Most children grow out of imaginary friends. But in some cases an imaginary friend can emerge in adulthood, usually in response to trauma, inability to cope with stress and sometimes psychotic illness . . .

"Other people believe in angels and guardian angels, and they don't think there's anything out of the ordinary about that," she says.

—ABC (Australian Broadcasting Corporation) *News in Science,* May 2006

ACKNOWLEDGMENTS

My sincere thanks to Kate Miciak at Random House, New York, for her dedicated care and wise editorship of this novel, the latest of many she and I have worked on together happily and, for me, always rewardingly. I am relieved that when, on first reading this one, she found herself forgetting to breathe, it was in a good way.

I also thank my two brilliant agents, Jean Naggar of the Jean Naggar Literary Agency in New York and Maggie Phillips at Ed Victor Ltd in London, for all their guidance, advocacy, and kindly support.

I dare not list by name, for fear of gushing uncontrollably, the friends, family, and colleagues whose company, advice, good humor, love, and encouragement helped sustain me during the writing of this novel, but I thank them all from my heart.

Our Picnics in the Sun

Morag Joss

A Reader's Guide

A CONVERSATION BETWEEN
FRANK DELANEY AND MORAG JOSS

Frank Delaney: There are tides in this book always running against each other. Howard is the one whose body has failed but whose love hasn't. His beloved wife, Deborah, cares less and less for him emotionally as she has to care more and more for him physically. Their son, Adam, is always farthest away when they want him most, nearest when his mother wants him least. That sounds like a novelist's life statement—is it, in your case? The more one wants the less one gets?

Morag Joss: Not so much "the more one wants the less one gets" than "whatever one has, one wants something different," perhaps— the paradox and circularity of that. I like your "tides" metaphor— I do think of the action of my novels rather like that, a story emerging as the characters work with and against forces of various kinds, not all of which they understand or are even conscious of. And they're not just emotional forces within and between themselves, but also the tides of circumstance, obligation, accident. There are opposing tides in your novels, too, aren't there? The tides of history and politics and myth in your novels of Ireland, for example.

FD: I find it fascinating that you choose to write about people of educated values and previously manageable positions in life being reduced almost to shreds. Why did you go in that direction?

MJ: There's a theory (not mine) that writers write about that of which they are most afraid. While I haven't consciously done that, I think there may be something in it. Perhaps because of a precarious childhood I have never felt very safe or taken such safety as I have for granted, and my response to adverse reversals in the lives of others is always to think that it might be me next. (The trick, of course, is to accept the possibility of such reversals, yet not live cautiously.) My characters are pretty unlucky, now I come to think of it. But the world *is* unlucky for so many, even (or especially?) for confused, high-minded people, and I think my novels reflect that. By definition, luck, good or bad, is undeserved and usually unexpected, and has nothing to do with justice, which makes it rather frightening, wouldn't you say?

FD: Nothing in the novel is what it seems at first glance—everything fails and disappoints. And yet—outside the front door is a glorious landscape. Is there a sense in which you're saying that Nature is the ultimate, maybe even the only, redemptive force?

MJ: No, I think I'm saying that Nature is at best an indifferent force, and morally neutral. The landscape is glorious but the moor is heartless; it inspires but also injures. Nature enthralls but it also disgusts (the dead sheep), under beautiful sunny skies there is predation, and birth is quickly followed by death. In other words Nature is bound to fail and disappoint Howard and Deborah, because they want to believe in it as a benign force that they can trust in; they want to harness it, befriend and even worship it. The only redemptive force, which although on its last legs dictates how the novel ends, is the power of love.

FD: On that same point—in a previous novel, *The Night Following*, you also take your characters up to "high ground"—up onto the moors. This follows a classical English novelist tradition, the landscape as metaphor for the emotional condition. How does that drive your narrative?

MJ: Ah—the pathetic fallacy. At the conception stage of a novel I often begin with setting; I love its possibilities, the depths of its effects on people's sensibilities and behavior. Before I'd written a word of this novel I spent some time on Exmoor, one day walking alone for twelve miles over the moor (slightly foolish, in retrospect).

The setting of a novel—in this case an imposing natural landscape—is as you say a "metaphor for the emotional condition," that is, a mirror held up to the internal life of the characters. That's why it's so variable. At times the moor embraces, at other times it threatens, because the landscape described through a character's eyes is a two-way viewfinder: to the world the character experiences, but also to the state of the character's soul.

Setting, and weather (seldom irrelevant in the English novel), can be catalysts for action, too, both direct and metaphorical. For instance, when Deborah responds to the arrival of September, her desperate stopping-up of leaky windows and silencing of rattling doors express a fear of encroachment and invasion on a much more sinister level than the rain and wind.

And then there's setting as character (the masterly example of this is Hardy's personification of Egdon Heath, which opens *The Return of the Native*). I do seem to return to this; as you say, it's there in *The Night Following* as well as in this novel, and also in *Half Broken Things* and the river setting of *Among the Missing*. Then there's the mighty river in your novel *Shannon*. It's a classical tradition, all right.

FD: There's always menace in your novels, and it always seems to come from sources that are supposed to be helpful. Digger, for instance, in this novel, settles somewhere between creepy and frightening. The young man, Theo, may be extremely dangerous for all we know. What does this force of contrasts allow you to do?

MJ: It allows me to add another layer of instability and precariousness to Howard and Deborah's world. Their relationship, health, livelihood, family bonds, and home all hang by a thread, and Digger and Theo can't be relied upon as lifelines. Nothing is certain, nobody can be wholly trusted (perhaps not even to exist?). I hope the sense of doubt about Digger and Theo makes a reader feel anxious about what's going on and curious to find out, and vigilant on behalf of Howard and/or Deborah, who most often seem unaware of the menace. I hope to create an expectation that nearly every character in the novel will turn out to be complex, and most motivations impure. But as well as that, Digger and Theo's ambiguity drives much of the plot insofar as the plot hinges on Deborah and Howard's inability to see clearly—literally and metaphorically—what is going on around them.

FD: You call down a number of classical tropes: the head of the household shearing off his own hair; the generous caller who turns out to be the opposite. If you had to describe a tradition which you think your novels observe—what would it be?

MJ: That's a question that requires me to stop stirring, step back from the stove and try to remember the recipe I'd forgotten I was supposed to be following. . . .

I invariably think up a story and can't see what it's "about" (I mean in terms of theme) or what it "means" until afterward, sometimes long after it's written. It's possibly odd to write this way: the tug of a story idea and the impulse to write it coming before the point of it, and apparently (but never in fact) independent of a tradition or thread leading back to hidden influences. For example, I didn't see, until it was nearly finished, that the central character in *The Night Following* is a sort of *Ancient Mariner* figure and her story a similar tale of transgression and attempted expiation. I wasn't aware until I was some way into writing it that *Our Picnics in the Sun* may owe something to Henry James's *The Turn of the Screw*.

You suggest a Samson-like figure with the shearing off of hair, and the wolf in sheep's clothing in the duplicitous caller at the door. Perhaps my novels—yours too, perhaps all novels—keep returning to some of the fundamentals of story: the fall from power, danger masked and unmasked, love lost and restored, the return of the prodigal. These are the fundamentals of myth and fairy tale from the Greeks onward, aren't they?

FD: One of the rivers running through this book is that of failed optimism. Adam hopes to be in more contact and visit soon. Howard hopes for a return of Deborah's old loving. Deborah still hopes for a life that she glimpsed but never achieved. Many people might read this novel as a metaphor for much of current society: is it?

MJ: There is, certainly, a lot of failed optimism in the novel. Moreover, Deborah and Howard fail to recognize or understand each other's failed optimism, and it's in the microcosm of the silence—of the inertia, rather—of their shared disappointment that there may be a metaphor not so much of society in the collective sense, but of all of us individually.

The power of disappointment is, I think, strangely underobserved in this society, which seems often minutely obsessed with every other nuance of every emotional reaction to every possible life event. But disappointment: it's a slightly underground, privately endured little emotion, isn't it? It holds a note of resignation. But I don't think it's always like that. I'm interested in a kind of disappointment that isn't resigned at all but is full of anger and, if not acknowledged, can be dangerously corrosive of spirit, love, and of life itself. By the end of the novel the power of that disappointment has found expression and is spent. There's a closing peace, a reconciliation with failed optimism.

FD: There's a most powerful—let's call it "birth device"—at the end of the book that seems to unify, even justify, all the failed hopes. How do you work? Did you always have that idea in mind and worked toward it, or was it organic—did the book reveal it to you?

MJ: It came organically. With each book I'm learning more and more to trust the book to show me what it needs (and I have listened to wise advice on this matter). I still plan quite meticulously but am braver about deviating from the plan if it seems right. This is partly a question of trusting the book but also of trusting myself, that is, trusting the act of writing—and, of course, *re-* and *re-* and *re-* and *re*-writing—to reveal what exactly the story is to be and how it should be told: why this happens and not that, why a character feels this way and not otherwise.

FD: I have to ask—it seems right! Who is your favorite character?

MJ: I honestly don't have one. I look upon all the characters with feelings of great kindness because I understand them completely, and they are all, in their various ways, vulnerable. I like Adam at all the stages of his growing up—I enjoyed writing through the eyes of a seven-, then fourteen-, then twenty-one-year-old lad. I came to love even Howard.

FD: You've now established yourself as a significant contemporary English novelist. I know that comparisons are odious—but of whom, if anyone, do you remind yourself?

MJ: That's another difficult question, as well as an extravagant compliment, for which I give grateful and incredulous thanks! While I'm actually writing the answer is nobody at all, because I'm writing from inside the world of the novel, so to speak, and the task is a solitary, single-handed and unique-to-me battle to close the shortfall between my intentions and my abilities. Though I bring to it all my enthusiasms for other writers and no doubt some influences, it still feels like me vs. the task, and a very unequal battle it is.

The morning after battle, looking at my work dispassionately, if I knew a way to be influenced a great deal more by the writers I admire, I'd grab it. I wish my writing *did* remind me of, for example, William Trevor, Alice Munro, Carol Shields, E. L. Doctorow.

FD: In many of your novels there's a deferred apocalypse, it feels, just around the corner, or the characters go through a series of mini-apocalypses. Is Life, after all, in your artistic view, a matter of Thoreau's quiet desperation and/or Edna St. Vincent Millay's "just one damn thing over and over"?

MJ: I've been thinking quite a lot about this lately. Does a novel have to present a view of life as leading somewhere, or can it reflect Thoreau's or Millay's view of it as repetitive and unavailing—put another way, if the obstacles to happiness or fulfillment for the characters in a novel are not, by the end, wholly overcome, does at least the failure to overcome them have to be meaningful in some way? I think it does, even if the twenty-first-century novel can't rely for its bearings on a coherent, universal moral order without being either nostalgic or conservative.

So I come down on the side of neither Thoreau nor Millay—the struggles my characters undergo aren't meaningless, though I do see that the resolution of those struggles—which sometimes is the putting aside of anguish and the "good" death—may seem less than comforting.

I like the rest of the Thoreau quotation: "Most men lead lives of quiet desperation and go to the grave with the song still in them."

The song—whatever it is in us that strives to dispel the "quiet desperation"—that's the important thing.

He also wrote, "In human intercourse the tragedy begins, not when there is misunderstanding about words, but when silence is not understood."

From the moment Theo appears, Deborah's and Howard's lives become a slow and sometimes painful progression, after years of misunderstood silence, toward giving voice to their songs. So if there's a unifying artistic view in my work, maybe it's that the song does not go unsung.

For his BBC radio and television shows FRANK DELANEY has interviewed more than 3,500 of the world's most important writers, and judged many literary prizes, including the Booker. Born and raised in Ireland, Delaney spent more than twenty-five years in England before moving to the United States in 2002. Author of more than two dozen works of fiction and nonfiction, his first "American" book was the *New York Times* bestselling novel *Ireland*.

QUESTIONS AND TOPICS FOR DISCUSSION

1. Have you ever considered picking up and moving to the country? What about that appeals to you? What do you think the biggest challenge would be?

2. How does grief influence the life choices Howard and Deborah make?

3. What do you see as Howard and Deborah's relationship to technology? Are they truly off the grid? Does their outsiders-to-society status provide more help or detriment in the end?

4. What do you see as being the significance of the title *Our Picnics in the Sun*? What do you think it means?

5. What would be different, in your opinion, if Howard had his power of speech back? How do you think that would change his character? Or alter his dilemma?

6. How much of Howard and Deborah's marriage, from its inception, do you think has been based on attraction? Do you think there's anything else mutually important to them? Where do you see these two characters connecting? Where do you see the disconnect?

7. Why do you think it is so important to Deborah that her son visit? Do you think Adam is a good son? Why or why not?

8. How would you describe Adam's relationship to his parents? How does it differ from Theo's relationship to Deborah and Howard?

9. What is more important than money? For Deborah and Howard, who cling to the notion that there are many things better than money, and that Adam's quest for it is soulless, what do they have that is better than financial stability?

10. What is the effect, for you as the reader, of the author's use of multiple narrative voices?

11. Who do you think is the most dangerous character in this novel? How is that person dangerous, and why?

12. Compare and contrast Nicholas's [the companion with whom Theo arrived at Deborah's B & B] role to Theo in comparison to Howard's role to Adam.

13. Could a story like *Our Picnics in the Sun* occur in a city, do you think? How would it be different?

14. How would you handle a situation like Deborah's, running a B & B in the middle of nowhere with a disabled partner? How would you handle the monotony of the chores, or being constantly subjected to the elements?

About the Author

Morag Joss is the author of several novels, including *Among the Missing* and the CWA Silver Dagger winner *Half Broken Things,* which was also adapted as a film for U.K. national television. In 2008 she was a recipient of a Heinrich Boll Fellowship, and in 2009 she was nominated for an Edgar Award for her sixth novel, *The Night Following.*

www.moragjoss.com

ABOUT THE TYPE

This book was set in Sabon, a typeface designed by the well-known German typographer Jan Tschichold (1902–74). Sabon's design is based upon the original letter forms of Claude Garamond and was created specifically to be used for three sources: foundry type for hand composition, Linotype, and Monotype. Tschichold named his typeface for the famous Frankfurt typefounder Jacques Sabon, who died in 1580.